A

YEAR

OF

RAVENS

A
YEAR
OF
RAVENS

A Novel of Boudica's Rebellion

Kate Quinn, Ruth Downie,
Stephanie Dray, Eliza Knight,
Vicky Alvear, SJA Turney,
and Russell Whitfield

With an Introduction by Ben Kane

WILLIAM MORROW
wm *An Imprint of HarperCollinsPublishers*

A YEAR OF RAVENS. "Introduction" copyright © 2014 by Ben Kane. "The Queen" and "Epilogue" copyright © 2014 by Stephanie Dray. "The Slave" copyright © 2014 by Ruth Downie. "The Tribune" copyright © 2014 by Russell Whitfield. "The Druid" copyright © 2014 by Victoria Alvear. "The Son" copyright © 2014 by Simon Turney. "The Warrior" copyright © 2014 by Kate Quinn. "The Daughters" copyright © by E. Knight. All rights reserved. Printed in the United States of America. No part of this book may be used or reproduced in any manner whatsoever without written permission except in the case of brief quotations embodied in critical articles and reviews. For information, address HarperCollins Publishers, 195 Broadway, New York, NY 10007.

HarperCollins books may be purchased for educational, business, or sales promotional use. For information, please email the Special Markets Department at SPsales@harpercollins.com.

Previously published as *A Year of Ravens* in the USA in 2023.

Interior text design by Diahann Sturge-Campbell

Library of Congress Cataloging-in-Publication Data has been applied for.

ISBN 978-0-06-331060-5

24 25 26 27 28 LBC 5 4 3 2 1

CONTENTS

BRITANNIA

60AD

Dotted line indicates course
of Roman road later known
as Watling Street

VENICONES

Lvgvvalivm

CARVETII

Fortress of the
Brigantes

BRIGANTES

Mona

DECEANGLI · Deva

CORNOVII

CORITANI

ICENI

ORDOVICES

Viroconivm

Dvrobrivae

Venta
Icenorvm

TRINOVANTES

Camvlodvnvm

Sabrina R.

Glevvm

CATUVELLAUNI

SILURES

Vervlamivm

ATREBATES

Tamesis R.

Aquae
Svlis

Calleva

Londinivm

CANTIACI

REGINI

Isca
Dvmnoniorvm

CHARACTER LIST

ICENI TRIBE

Boudica, Queen of the Iceni
Eisu, an Iceni horse trader
Vanus, an Iceni warrior

OTHER TRIBES

Cartimandua, Queen of the Brigantes, Friend and Ally of Rome
Caratacus, leader of the Catuvellauni, legendary rebel against Rome
Yorath, young Druid in training on sacred island of Mona

ROMANS

Claudius, Emperor of Rome
Nero, Claudius's stepson and successor
Seneca, a powerful senator in Rome
Paulinus, Governor of Britannia, commander over its legions
Decianus, Procurator, the emperor's personal agent in Britannia
Agricola, Tribune of the Second Augusta

Calvus, Centurion of the Second Augusta, Tenth century of the Tenth Cohort

Naso, Optio of the Second Augusta, Tenth century of the Tenth Cohort

Magnusanus, Batavian cavalry Decurion of the Twentieth Valeria Victrix

Flacca, Centurion of the Twentieth Valeria Victrix

Stator, garrison commander at Londinium

INTRODUCTION

Ben Kane

THE warrior queen Boudica is for many one of the standout characters from the ancient world. A woman violated, the leader of a people wronged by Rome—their erstwhile ally—she ignited a rebellion in first century AD Britain that saw panic sown the length and breadth of the land, London burned and tens of thousands of citizens killed. The uprising failed, but its effects reverberated through the empire. Ancient sources tell us that the cataclysmic events almost persuaded the emperor Nero to abandon Britain, and that punitive operations conducted in the months afterwards were stopped, for fear of causing another tribal backlash.

After the fall of the Roman Empire, Boudica's name was lost to history until the late fifteenth century. Since that time, she has been romanticized somewhat, and identified as a symbol of the small who take on the large, of the wronged who fight evildoers, and as a doomed hero who did what she thought was right, regardless of the consequences. As with the gladiator Spartacus, another historical character who almost brought Rome to its knees, it's likely that Boudica herself had no great guiding ideals, no sense of the divine guiding her actions. She may have been, plain and simple, a strong, charismatic character who wanted revenge for the violent and unjust wrongs done not just to her and her family, but to her people as well.

In the past, historians have been known to describe Boudica's rebellion as a war for national independence, with the 'good' British tribes lined up against the 'bad' imperialist Romans. This couldn't be further from the truth. Like their fellow peoples throughout Europe and beyond, the ancient tribes did not think of themselves as a nation; in fact, we don't even know what word they would have used to describe themselves or the island of Britain. Boudica brought together an alliance of peoples who disliked their new masters, the Romans, and together they did their utmost to defeat them.

As with all conflicts, past and present, the war between Boudica and the Romans was marked by savagery on both sides. It's impossible for a responsible historical author to write about these events without showing the brutal atrocities committed by the Romans, and also by Boudica's army. Inter-tribal warfare—a common feature of life in ancient Britain—also had to be mentioned.

In *A Year of Ravens*, seven talented authors have conjured up a powerful and vibrant representation of Boudica. She is seen through the eyes of a fascinating cast of characters, a number of whom are historical, and some who are fictional. Each of the novel's seven parts has been written by a different author and comprises a complete tale. This makes it possible for the reader to move on within the book should one story not take their fancy. Note that the plot spans from the novel's beginning to its end, weaving together each story, so there's far more enjoyment to be had by reading the entire book!

Writers of historical fiction always have to make decisions that will impact on the reader's experience. These decisions bear explanation, and follow hereafter. For the sake of accessibility, and where practical, English words and conventions have been adopted over the Latin. While the Romans did not use weeks to measure time, the authors did so. The rebellion's timeline is not recorded; ancient sources tell us that it lasted about a year, and so its battles and annexations were fitted into the warmer times of year, when armies were more likely to march. Timelines for the rebellion vary between experts; the authors have made some educated guesses based on the weather. The timeline for Cartimandua's story mirrors that set out in Nicki Howarth's biography of the queen.

Given the previously mentioned lack of historical clarity on the cultural identity of the people of ancient Britain, the authors opted to call them Britons, Celts and Cambrians. They also used Romanized place names such as Mona for the island known today as Anglesey, or previously as *Ynys Môn*. The names might be modern, but the legends are eternal. Any errors contained within these pages are the authors', for which they apologize in advance.

A Year of Ravens is the compelling story of one of history's bravest women, and of her fight against injustice. Visceral, tragic, gripping, it propels the reader straight into the harsh and unforgiving world of first century AD Britain, and holds them there until the final, emotional page. I was lucky enough to work with four of the authors on a previous collaboration, *A Day of Fire*, so I knew this novel would be a great read. I wasn't mistaken, and the addition of three new fabulous writers has merely added fuel to the fire, making *A Year of Ravens* a true "must-read."

I hope you enjoy it!

PART ONE

THE QUEEN

Stephanie Dray

A miserable peace is better than war.
—Tacitus

PROLOGUE

WE were both queens. We both wore crowns of fiery red hair. We both stood so tall that we towered over the Romans who came to subdue our lands. We both tried to protect our people.

But she is a hero to the Britons while I am despised.

Boudica.

You've heard her name. Of course you have. Everyone has. And when you've heard it spoken, you've heard the hushed awe of her admirers or the grudging respect of her enemies. You've heard her legend. And you may think you know the story of the proud rebel queen who humbled the Romans, burning and slashing her way to eternal glory. But you cannot know her story without knowing mine.

And mine begins as it will likely end, with ravens.

For ravens made me a queen.

Or so it seemed to me during my twentieth winter, when they circled the air over a dozen fresh graves, their harsh avian cries an eerie echo of those who had died of fever, including my royal family. In my grief, I felt the ravens' dark eyes upon me like the expectant gaze of the gods. Felt it again during the festival of *Imbolc*, celebrated in honor of our high goddess, for ravens are the first birds to nest when the lambing season has begun.

They flapped above us from their perches on the rocky outcroppings—the bridestones—while we brandished torches to banish the dread crone of winter and summon forth the maiden of springtime. Then we flung garlands into the river, where a woven boat filled with winter flowers awaited me. And I prepared to take the oath that would bind me to my people.

Descended of great kings, I was young and radiant and beloved by everyone—a thing I took much for granted. But then it is easy to be loved when you're a young and beautiful queen, for the people make you a vessel into which they pour all their hopes . . . and you have not yet had the chance to bitterly disappoint them.

So while I swore my oath, I did not worry about keeping the love of my people, for I had never been without it. What I worried about was whether I would be a *good* queen. I was no warrior, even if I was long and lean of limb, and the mystery of how to become the earthly incarnation of our high goddess still eluded me. *Brigantia*. She was the maiden, the mother, and the crone. She was the patroness of poetry, craft, and healing. In kinship with her, I would take a white snake as my companion animal.

But her omens that year I did not understand.

It had been a strange and devastating winter that made me fear for the survival of my people; now the thaw had come, and the river ran swiftly, more treacherous in its depths than we could have anticipated when I stepped into that woven boat.

To this day, I cannot say how it overturned. I only remember plunging into the frigid depths, grasping wildly to pull myself out. One of my servants slipped under the water and disappeared. The others I could not see as I was swept away. It was far down the river, as I gasped for air and my limbs grew heavy with fatigue, that I felt the seductive pull of death.

There would be pain as the water filled my lungs, but it would not last long. Then it would be done and my sorrow at an end, reunited with my family. But what of my people? Without a Druid to make of me a sacrifice, my death would not bring them prosperity. What they needed was the embodiment of their high goddess. What they needed was their living queen. I could not leave them. So I flailed desperately against the implacable force of the river until at last my fingers caught hold of a thick branch of a tree. I grasped tight. Though the bark cut my palms, I held that branch with all my strength, knowing that if I let go, I would drown. But if I held fast, my people would rescue me. They would be searching, even now. I was sure of it.

I found strength in their love for me and mine for them. But how long until the branch began to crack under my weight? I didn't know. While I struggled in the churning water, half-in and half-out of the river and unable to pull myself farther, I thought only to stay alive for them. I endured the torment of the cold. I endured the agony in my hands as they melded with that branch. I endured the ever-present temptation to heave one last ragged breath and give myself to the rush and the ravens.

But I held fast even when I could feel nothing *but* the cold— the cold and the challenge in the eyes of the ravens who watched me from the trees above the river. Did I have the will to survive, no matter the forces conspiring to pull me under?

I did.

My tribesmen found me before darkness fell, so rigid that they thought they might have to cut the branch from my grasp. "The queen lives!" they called to one another in celebration. And as I was warmed with blankets and love and gratitude, I knew that, though I might never heft a warrior's sword, there was a strength in me that would serve.

For my people, I could endure. I could withstand the very forces of nature.

I was no longer afraid that I would not be a good ruler. And so, on that day, I, Cartimandua, became Queen of the Brigantes.

But not as the Romans count it, of course. *They* mark my reign from the year they invaded. That is how the Romans measure things. It all starts and ends with them. Yet there was, for me, a life and a kingdom before the Romans. *Without* the Romans. Julius Caesar had already come and gone by the time I was born, driven from our shores with the fig leaf of a promised tribute that we never paid. So as a princess coming of age so far north amongst the craggy bridestones of the high moors, I had never laid eyes upon a

Roman. Oh, I'd heard tales of their soldiers, wearing brush-topped helmets and skirts of decorative leather strips. About how they swarmed like mindless ants, advancing behind shield walls, without even paint upon their face to distinguish them.

And yet never did I suspect that they would stomp their tiny booted feet in unison to shake the very earth beneath me. That they would come to our shores, wave upon wave, forcing upon tribal queens like me—and like Boudica—only two choices.

Either seize hold of any branch of peace, or surrender to the relentless rush of war.

DECIANUS

On the Road to Durobrivae
Winter, 60 AD

"ARE you sure it's quite proper that you should personally ride out to meet a barbarian woman?" sniffed the wife of Catus Decianus with an impressively imperial arch of her brow. "You're the procurator, after all. You report directly to the emperor. Surely an underling would be better suited to the task."

"The task of telling a queen to return to her kingdom?" Decianus asked as their *carpentum* jostled its way up the road to the Roman fortress near Durobrivae.

"A *barbarian* queen," his wife muttered.

Barbarian, yes. But Cartimandua of the Brigantes was also a Friend and Ally of Rome. Decianus would prefer to keep it that way. As he understood it, the barbarian queen had been wintering in the Roman fort by the bridge, buying up pottery and recruiting extra protection for her stronghold in Brigantia. But now it was time for her to go home, and Decianus intended to tell her so.

Meanwhile, his wife was plainly irritated by their uncomfortable winter journey, but she was too stiff-necked—too Roman—to whine. Instead, as was her habit, she confined her remarks to pointing out the irregularity of her husband's mission. So Decianus confined himself to counting the days until he might visit his little villa in Gaul, where juicy blue-black grapes grew in fat clusters over the tranquil pool into which he dipped his feet while studying the geometry of Euclid and the paradox of infinity.

The thought of his villa soothed him. And he needed a great deal of soothing whenever his wife decided to be displeased. She was right to say that as the chief financial officer in Britannia, he did indeed report directly to Emperor Nero. But as procurator, he felt like little more than a glorified tax collector in this gods-forsaken western outpost—from which he hoped soon to retire.

Which he should have done *before* the governor marched off west, leaving Decianus to deal with the brewing mess of tribal unrest.

"I am attempting to be politic, my dear," Decianus said, straightening his toga over one arm and sucking in a gut that had become a bit soft with middle age. "That is what you're always advising, is it not?"

"I'm sure you know best," she said.

You're a moronic milksop, she meant.

Given her noble pedigree, she wouldn't stoop to speaking undignified insults aloud. No. Valeria simply let him know with a variety of sighs and side-glances that after fifteen years of marriage, he had proved to be a colossal disappointment.

"What sort of woman is she?" his wife asked.

Decianus' attention snapped back with an accompanying pang of confusion. "Who?"

"This Cartimandua woman, of course," she said, with the unspoken question: *Or is there some other barbarian you've dragged me out into the cold to see?*

Decianus jolted as the wheel dipped into one of the ruts in the ill-made road. "Ah. Well. I haven't met her, but she's terribly unpopular. The local tribesmen call her the Betrayer of the Britons and the legionaries call her the Cleopatra of the Celts. Given recent tensions within the tribes, and *between* the tribes, it would be better for her to go home."

Valeria's brow arched higher. "You're not worried just because of the complaints of a few ruffians, are you? These tribesmen are prone to complain about anything."

Decianus felt his jaw tighten. "Well, the Iceni, in particular, have much to complain about thanks to Seneca and some of the emperor's other friends."

"Seneca has become a great man in Rome," Valeria said.

"Yes, well, this isn't Rome. And Seneca's calling in loans with little notice and sending private collectors to rough up the natives . . . well, it's not a friendly way to do business, is it?"

Valeria glanced out the curtain at the countryside, all covered in snow. "I do hope the emperor's friends don't get the wrong impression of you. Just because you grew so fond of that Iceni boy that we fostered doesn't mean that you'll be too soft on *all* barbarians when duty calls."

By which she meant, *You're too soft on all barbarians.*

And truthfully, she might be right. Decianus thought he might be exactly the wrong man for this job. Since he was a small child, he'd been able to memorize tables of numbers and spit out quick calculations. That's how he knew precisely who owed what to the emperor down to the smallest copper. He liked that part of his job. But he found the *collection* of imperial debts to be profoundly unpleasant business. "It isn't a matter of softness. It's that trying to explain the concept of accrued interest to giant tattooed tribesmen who are deep in their cups is a harrowing experience, even with battle-hardened centurions and soldiers at my side."

A concern his wife dismissed with a wave of her hand. "True Romans never show fear."

Easy for her to say when she wasn't the one pressed to squeeze the tribesmen. The cost of occupying Britannia was enormous, and the locals were expected to pay their share, not that *they* seemed to view it that way. Money was tight and getting tighter. Meanwhile, the natives were angry and getting angrier, so Decianus had every reason to dread the coming confrontation.

Still, he needed to say something to counteract his wife's apparent belief that he was a damnable coward. "Not to worry, my dear. I have fearlessly levied a land tax. A property tax, too. Customs duties. And a grain levy to feed our legions. The governor will get all the glory, of course, for subduing those trouble-making Druids in the west—but our soldiers would be marching on empty bellies if I wasn't snatching every last kernel of wheat from the mouths of small tattooed babes."

That came out rather more sarcastically than Decianus intended. And his brand of sarcasm was one of the many things for which his wife had little patience. "Do these savages tattoo their babies that young?"

Decianus' jaw hitched tighter because babies—with or without tattoos—were not one of the subjects upon which he and his wife could converse without resentment. Childlessness was one of the many ways his marriage was lacking—though perhaps the only insurmountable obstacle to marital accord. "The point—" Surely he had a point, though he had forgotten it now. "The point is that the Iceni king has died, the Iceni tribesmen are in an uproar, and the last thing I need is the controversial Queen of the Brigantes anywhere in the vicinity."

He had hoped to impress his wife with his forward thinking

on the matter. Stomping out problems before they happened. It *should* have impressed her. But Valeria seemed entirely unimpressed. "I should think the death of the Iceni king a rather fortunate circumstance for us. Client kings have proved to be nothing but trouble for Rome, and now there is one less. We should keep it that—" His wife cut herself off, as if only now remembering that a woman ought not have political opinions. And in the awkward silence that followed, Valeria absently adjusted a ring upon her finger. It was their betrothal ring, and it was perhaps as irritating to her as the marriage it represented. Or the role she felt that marriage demanded of her.

A role to which she was as ill suited as he sometimes felt to his own.

Between the two of them, it was Valeria who had all the ambition. Decianus had little doubt that had his wife been born a man, she'd have conquered a province in the same orderly and efficient manner she marshaled his household.

But that wasn't the way of the world, or at least not the way of Rome.

SHE'S taller than me, Decianus thought, peevishly. But then, the barbarians were giants. Even their women, and this one was no exception. He had perhaps expected to find Queen Cartimandua—the so-called Cleopatra of the Celts—luxuriating upon some imported silk couch while servants warmed a bath for her of goat's milk and honey. Instead, he came upon the impressively tall and red-haired Queen of the Brigantes with a ghostly white snake twined between her fingers.

Which was worse. Infinitely worse.

Decianus hated snakes. And he gave a shudder.

Inside the Roman enclosure at Durobrivae, where she'd sought respite for the winter, the queen stood giving directions to servants who were dashing about bare-armed in the cold as they packed her belongings into a wagon. Of course, the Brigantes were northerners, better prepared for the cold than poor Decianus, who was shivering as he fantasized about the warm atrium of his little villa in Gaul overlooking the sun-drenched coastline of Narbo.

Meanwhile, wearing a marvelous white fur cloak over a garment dyed in striking green-blue checks, Queen Cartimandua did not seem to notice the snow gathering upon her red tresses. From rings upon each finger to earrings and girdle and shoulder brooches, she was adorned in gold. That was to say nothing of the golden torc she wore upon her neck, intricately carved with scenes of battle—more suited to a warrior than a woman, but the Britons did not discriminate between genders when it came to leadership *or* spear wielders. Which is how Decianus came to the uncomfortable situation of facing a woman who had the full sovereign authority of a client king.

But of course, Decianus had the authority of the emperor, or nearly so. That should help matters. Decianus announced himself while extending an arm to get the full effect of power conveyed by the folds of his snowy white toga. "Greetings, Madam. I am Catus Decianus, procurator. Personal agent of the emperor."

"Procurator," Cartimandua said with a surprisingly charming smile. "How pleased I am to make the acquaintance of the man who oversees the treasury. It is said that he who holds the key to a strongbox filled with gold holds the keys to the world."

Decianus was accustomed to the eloquence of the Celts, who seemed, as a people, even more prone to poetry than to drink. But he hadn't expected Cartimandua to flatter him in perfect Latin. "I like to think of myself as merely an accountant," he said in self-effacing reply while blowing warmth into his hands. "And I see we shall not need an interpreter. Shall we go in?"

She agreed, following him inside. Decianus cleared his throat before presenting his wife.

Queen Cartimandua set her white snake into a basket on the floor, and then, in greeting, warmly clasped Valeria, who all but recoiled. His wife would, no doubt, insist upon a delousing later, but if Cartimandua noticed Valeria's dismay, she did not mention it. Instead, the queen said, "Would that I could introduce my own consort to you."

"Oh?" Valeria asked, trying desperately to withdraw from the queen's embrace without looking as if she was doing exactly that. "Is he away on some business?"

Ordinarily, Valeria managed astute chitchat with barbarians as easily as she did anyone else, but in this case, she was so appalled by the serpent and the savage that she seemed to have quite forgotten who she was speaking to.

Otherwise, she'd have never asked about Cartimandua's husband.

Cartimandua gave a rueful shake of her head. "No, my husband is off brooding in some tent in the snowy hills, still sulking because I crushed his last rebellion against me." She nodded in acknowledgment. "I must thank you Romans for your assistance there."

Valeria paled as if the impropriety of discussing such marital woes in mixed company made her blood run cold. "Well!" Valeria managed to say.

How uncouth, she meant.

"Queen Cartimandua, it looks as if you are packing up to return to your kingdom," Decianus began, not liking the thread of anxious hope in his own voice. His wife was right. This should be a simple matter of commanding the barbarian woman to go home. And yet he feared it would not be a simple matter. It never was with women. "Is that the case?"

"No," was the reply of Cartimandua, who sobered and stared off into the fire. "I've had word that King Prasutagus of the Iceni has died, and I intend to pay respects at his funeral."

That was exactly what Decianus had feared.

But before he could say as much, the queen called for wine and refreshments, to which she was entitled by the local rules of hospitality, if not by way of her status. After that, Cartimandua insisted on treating them to the poetry of her bard and introducing everyone in her party. Including the armor bearer. Decianus did not find an opportunity to raise the subject again until his own wife retired to bed and he was left alone with the controversial queen. Decianus had intended to lure the woman slowly into the subject, but instead he blurted, "You're not well loved by the Iceni."

"Am I not?" Cartimandua asked, as if it were a great surprise to her, but her weary blue eyes told a different tale. "The Brigantes and the Iceni are both loyal allies of Rome. Why should I not be welcome?"

How to phrase it delicately? "Because . . ." Decianus scratched at the back of his neck and cleared his throat. "Because of your conduct in the matter of . . . because of what is said about . . ."

The fire crackled, and a spark lit behind her eyes. She gave him a charming smile, leaning in conspiratorially. "Procurator, it is kind of you to try to spare my feelings, but I prefer candor. There is very little you could tell me about my reputation that I don't already know. Collaborator. Betrayer. Roman whore. I've heard it all."

Decianus was surprised she could say it so calmly. Weren't women supposed to care for their reputation above all else? His wife certainly did. And he felt the tips of his ears burn at the word *whore*. Especially given that Cartimandua was a remarkably attractive woman for her age. At least in firelight.

The procurator had always been drawn to petite women like Valeria, but given the cool state of his marriage bed, he supposed that he had the wrong priorities when it came to such things. "Well then. In complete candor . . . yes, in complete candor." He cleared his throat again, aware this was becoming a nervous habit. "The Iceni are in an agitated state since the death of their king, and we cannot guarantee your safety should you attend the funeral."

Cartimandua gave a deep, throaty laugh that was somehow both unfeminine and alluring. "Do you mean to say that the legions you have on this island won't be enough to defend a single woman against some aggrieved and unarmed Iceni tribesmen? Goodness, how can you hope to hold your province of Britannia if that's the case? I never thought to see the day Roman honor would withstand a plea of impotence, even to achieve a convenient end."

Decianus stiffened on the word *impotence*. He would not discuss the subject of Roman honor with the likes of Cartimandua. Nor did he want to discuss the fact that the bulk of the soldiery was in the west with Governor Paulinus, which she surely knew. Moreover, he did not wish to explain that he had a reason for wanting her far away from Iceni lands—a very good reason that had nothing to do with her personal safety.

To be exact, ever since he'd had word of the Iceni king's death, Decianus had been making a grim little game of counting the days it would take before an order arrived from the emperor commanding the annexation of Iceni territory. Client kingship was a temporary arrangement. King Prasutagus had enjoyed a lifetime stewardship over Iceni lands, but now that he was dead, that arrangement was at an end. If he had died with a male heir, perhaps the emperor would allow the family to continue their rule, but since Prasutagus had only daughters—

"Procurator, your warning is very much appreciated," Cartimandua said, breaking into his thoughts. "But I'll simply have to muster the pride of my ancestry, and the courage for which my people are known, and risk attending the funeral anyway."

This was not how this conversation was supposed to go. A woman should be more pliable. Even Valeria, for all her sighs and arched brows and sidelong glances would still, in the end, always obey a direct order. So Decianus said bluntly, "Go back to Brigantia."

"I cannot."

He stared. "Why not?"

"Because I made a promise."

"I don't see what promise should so obligate you."

Cartimandua's smile became wistful. Touching a fingertip to the torc at her neck, she said very softly, "No, I don't suppose you would. But the fact remains that I must go. I must go with Roman protection or without it. In truth, I would go even if I were stripped of my crown, lost my servants, and was forced to walk barefoot upon icy roads."

That seemed a rather extravagant statement, but the barbarians were tremendously dramatic. Decianus had had years of close observation to form such an opinion, after all—a few years back, he and Valeria had fostered an Iceni youth. A hostage, in truth, but Decianus had come to care for the boy. A wild boy, romantic and energetic and verbal like all the Celts—if Decianus instilled anything in that young Briton, he hoped it was a measure of . . . well, measured judgment. Which Queen Cartimandua apparently lacked. "Madam, I should very much like to know why you insist on attending this funeral. Despite my request," he forced himself to add with squared shoulders, "as the emperor's agent."

Cartimandua tilted back her head, stretching her elegant limbs as her white snake twined around her ankle for warmth. "Would you like to know, Catus Decianus? Would you really? You seem to me the sort of man who likes the tangible. Roads. Coins. Lists. That sort of thing. Am I right?"

She *was* right. But Decianus felt small in admitting it, so although he nodded, he added, "As I said, I am an accountant. I'm here to ensure that the emperor's financial interests are seen to. So if there is some money you hope to reclaim, some outstanding debt of the Iceni to the Brigantes—"

"A debt?" She snorted. Like a man might snort, no self-consciousness at all. "Oh yes, a debt is involved. But not the kind that goes in a ledger." The woman turned onto her side on her dining couch, fixing her gaze on his. "I never thought to tell anyone this story. But you might be exactly the man to tell. Because you're an accountant, Catus Decianus. And I am going to the funeral of King Prasutagus to make an accounting . . ."

CARTIMANDUA

Twenty Years Earlier

THREE is a very important number in the lore of Brigantia. We worship the high goddess who has sovereignty over our land by burning three fires upon her altar. We acknowledge her three faces: the maiden, the mother, and the crone. We honor her three cherished vocations of healing, blacksmithing, and poetry. And so it was that in the first year of my rule, when all the most prominent princes of the land flocked to my kingdom to make merry and mischief under the auspices of seeking my hand, I narrowed my choice to *three*.

The first suitor, my kinsman, Venutius of the Carvetii. The second, Prasutagus, an older nobleman of the Iceni. And the third,

Caratacus, the boastful and brash youngest son of the King of the Catuvellauni.

Venutius. Prasutagus. Caratacus.

Familiar names now. All famed kings. But that summer, I was the only one with a crown. And only one of these three seemed worthy in my young eyes to be my consort.

It is a bard's trick to say that someone who rises to legend was recognized by all at the start as special, remarkable, destined for greatness. But in the case of Caratacus, it was true. From the moment he appeared in my Great Hall, I saw in him a burning ambition as bright as any star. Decked out in ostentatious finery, he sparkled from the gold torc at his neck to the gold thread in the checkered length of his trousers to the gold laces of his shoes. He leaned so insolently upon his painted tribal shield that I knew he must be royal. Who else would dare to slouch like a peasant while awaiting a private audience with a queen? The brash young prince with his lime-washed hair and still-sparse mustache could not smother his smile when my herald announced me. Indeed, he laughed. He laughed so long that I began to take offense.

Only then did he hold up his hands in apology. "When my older brother told me to seek your hand in marriage, we decided that I must say that you were beautiful, even if you should have a beak and beady eyes. But you are so lovely in truth, that I now know the gods smile upon me and upon our alliance."

Though I was still young enough to be flattered by praise of my beauty, I only smirked. "The gods smile upon *you*, perhaps, Prince Caratacus. But as for our alliance, that remains to be seen."

"Oh, come now," Prince Caratacus said. "Have a look at the fine steeds I have brought you as a gift. And the silver faceplates you may adorn them with when you ride in your war cart, to say nothing of the portion of wealth I will add to our marriage settlement. You will find no suitor from a tribe greater than the Catuvellauni. And the son of a king at that."

"The *youngest* son of a king," I replied, not willing to let him get too above himself.

Now it was his turn to smirk. "You shouldn't hold that against me. I'll be a king in my own right one day, that I promise."

I believed him. That was the problem. "By displacing your older brothers, one by one?"

Set back on his heels for the first time, he let his mouth fall open, then snapped it shut again. "I don't know what you've heard—"

"I've heard that you have taken advantage of your father in his dotage and convinced him to banish your older brother. That's one prince down and one to go."

"My eldest brother was not fit to rule the Catuvellauni. He would sell our tribe to the Romans across the narrow sea. He is too enamored of their ways, never realizing the true price of the trade we do with them."

His vehemence startled me. "Was not your father acknowledged by Rome as the so-called King of Britannia? What could you have against the Romans?"

As I would come to learn, I had unwittingly drawn him out on a subject upon which he was delighted to opine, and he drew me close in conversation. "There is no glory in them. Not *one* of these small-statured Romans is so glorious a warrior in his own right as to instill terror."

"Yet, banding together, they have somehow humbled the world beyond our shores. There is a lesson in that, don't you think?"

For we Brigantes were a federation of tribes—the most numerous, powerful, and peaceful of the Britons, not as given to cattle wars and border squabbling like the Iceni or the Coritani or the Catuvellauni. I could not help but think it was because we, unlike our southern kin, came together to enjoy pastoral pleasures instead of stealing one another's sheep and raiding each other's villages for glory. Perhaps that was a romantic view of my people, but it was one I held earnestly.

Meanwhile, Caratacus seemed to be enjoying the debate, even as it pricked at his temper. "My beautiful Queen Cartimandua, here you are too far north, too far away to understand the danger of the Romans. Trust me when I say that every glass bottle and amphora of wine we buy from the Romans gives them a new temptation to return to our shores."

He might be right, I thought. I was not yet so enamored of luxury goods from Rome that I could not give them up. But I saw in Caratacus a man who was willing to turn on his own brother for ambition or principle. And if the prince would do that to his own flesh and blood, what might he do if he coveted his wife's power? "I must think upon your offer."

Caratacus smiled brightly, with a great show of teeth, as if the warrior in him appreciated the challenge of my reluctance. "Perhaps you would like to do your thinking while riding upon this beautiful snowy white pony—my gift to you, whether you accept my hand or no."

With equal parts charm and hubris, he seized my hand in his rough one as ardently as a lover, even though we both knew he pursued me as a matter of strategy. Yet I could not claim to be a Brigante if the sight of a fine horse did not send my heart racing, and the snowy white pony waiting outside my Great Hall was the finest I ever saw. White was an unlucky color, some said. But others believed it was a sacred color. Brigantia's serpent was white. White was the color of the Druid's mistletoe berries and the symbol of the wintry crone. In any case, white looked very good upon this pony, and I could not resist hiking up my tunic to mount her, delighted by her nicker.

Starting her off toward the meadows, I was surprised when Caratacus launched himself onto the back of another horse and forced it to a trot beside me. "What are you doing?" I asked.

"Riding beside my future wife," the bold prince replied.

"I said that I would think on your offer."

He grinned. "I heard you. But surely you don't need to do all your thinking alone . . ."

After that, he was at my side almost every moment. Waiting upon my answer. Pressing to know the reasons for my hesitation. "Is it your kinsman, Venutius? I am told that he presented you with a wonderfully ornamented sword with patterned metalwork. But I could get you one twice as fine if—"

"He *made* that sword," I protested, remembering its fine craftsmanship and the earnestness of the man who forged it. "What's more, Venutius knows how to use it."

We were returning from the stables, and Caratacus stopped in his steps, cornering me beside one of the lodges. "Do you fear that I could not defend you, Cartimandua? I am skilled at war—"

"I have heard," I said, not daring to glance at his strong, battle-hardened arms and the blue tattoos on his biceps. I already feared my attraction to him would be my undoing. "But perhaps you like war too much. You have been making war on smaller tribes. When I see the glint in your smile as you speak of war, I think you do it because you enjoy it."

The prince came close enough that I felt the heat of him through my clothes. "Do I deny the thrill of battle, Cartimandua? No. The glory, I want. The lands, I need. But for a greater purpose. We can unite all the tribes. You and I can do that. The Brigantes and the Catuvellauni are too powerful to resist. If we join together, every tribe between us must fall into an alliance with us. Can you not see that?"

My mouth ran dry at the magnitude of his suggestion. At the

audaciousness of it. At the way my own blood heated at his ambition, and a yearning echo of it resounded in my bones. I had never known a time when the southern tribes were not fighting one another or making war upon us. But if we could *all* unite in common purpose . . .

The idea shook me. It shook me to my foundations. Which is why I made certain to absent myself from the prince's company in the days that followed. Because I sensed in him the magic of a poet, a storyteller who can bind you with tales of things that had never been and could never be. And I felt myself so bound. Pulled under. At a loss for breath in his presence, just as I once was in a river, clinging to life.

Under siege by my ardent and determined suitor, the only place I felt the air fill my lungs again was on my long walks on the moor. There it was that an Iceni nobleman, Prasutagus, found me. He did not bring me intricate swords or swift ponies. He did not talk to me about great ideas, nor promise me that he would one day be a king and worthy of my hand. But he walked quietly with me and let me think.

He let me be. He let me breathe again. He made me feel better.

His company was a balm.

OH, wily Brigantia, I thought upon a startle. You have given me the choice between a bard, a blacksmith, and a healer.

As I spent more time with Prasutagus on our quiet walks, whispers began amongst my people that Caratacus had lost my favor. But this did not discourage the Prince of the Catuvellauni. At my table one night, Caratacus raised a cup of wine in toast and laughingly suggested, "Call a fight! Let us compete for the hand of Queen Cartimandua with a test of arms."

His rival Venutius, who had warmed in friendship to the charismatic young prince, readily agreed. My brawny-armed kinsman, who spent as much time fighting as at the forge, thought he could win. My people thought Venutius could win, too, and cheered for what they said would be an easy victory. But I knew better. Ambition and cleverness burned in Prince Caratacus' breast, and in my estimation, such counts much more than strength when it comes to a fight.

Besides, I was not going to turn the matter of my nuptials over to chance. As with everything in my life, it would be a choice. *My* choice. So though both the two younger suitors strutting about my Great Hall were handsome, virile men yearning for a show of arms, I refused to call combat. My eyes kept drifting past them to the quietly dignified Iceni nobleman. *Prasutagus.* He had neither their youth, wealth, nor status, but there was a calm intelligence in his dark eyes. He did not heat my blood, but I enjoyed his company.

One might not think this would be the start of any sort of romance. And clearly Prasutagus did not see our courtship in those terms because, walking beside me one foggy day amongst the stone outcroppings, he said, "I should soon return to my Iceni lands."

"You're giving up your suit already?"

He smiled wryly. "Queen Cartimandua, you're not going to choose me for your husband."

"You can't know that," I said coquettishly.

"You prefer Prince Caratacus. And your people prefer Venutius," he pointed out reasonably.

"They both come with trouble," I replied, pressing my back against a bridestone. "If I was to marry Venutius, favoring one tribe in the Brigante federation over all the others, there might be jealousy."

"Then you will choose Caratacus."

Hope threaded itself through my voice. "They say an alliance between such powerful tribes as the Brigantes and the Catuvellauni would unite all the people."

"Or cause a war such as we have never seen before," Prasutagus replied, crushing that hope. "Drawing the Romans to our shore besides."

I had not considered that, and the mention dispirited me. Still, I appreciated that Prasutagus did not tell me what he thought I wanted to hear. What I had wanted to hear was that I was *right* to like Caratacus. Because I did like him. I liked him very much. I sensed even then that a man like Caratacus comes along only once in a generation. I admired him, though warily. Like a boar must admire the cunning and deadly skill of a wolf without falling prey to it.

Prasutagus seemed less dangerous by far.

I felt at ease with him. Comfortable as I had not been since before I was queen. "You are a strange suitor to help me decide between two other men without feeling jealousy."

"Oh, make no mistake, Cartimandua. I burn with jealousy for every gaze you cast upon another," Prasutagus quietly remarked. "But a man of my years learns to smolder rather than blaze."

My mouth parted in surprise. "It would seem a man of your years, who smolders, ought to have a wife."

He chuckled. "Which is why I came here."

Prasutagus seemed to me a quite remarkably mature man— and that brought out mature thoughts of my own. I did not wish my choice in a husband to be the cause of bloodshed. And if the tribes would not unite peacefully, I would not marry Prince Caratacus only so that he could slaughter his way to becoming the King of Britannia.

Just like that, the fog in my mind he had roused with a bard's poetry cleared away. No matter the order of his birth or the worthiness of his dream, Prince Caratacus meant to rule. He would do it by conquest or connubial means, or both. If I took Carata-cus for my consort, soon *he* would be the King, and *I* would be the consort.

Which is why I could not marry him, and I said as much. "So you see, Prasutagus, you are the only choice without serious disadvantage."

The Iceni smiled, reaching for my hands with his big, scarred palms. "But still, you will not choose me. Because I bring you no advantage, either, except for the fact that you enjoy these walks of ours together. I flatter myself to think we have become friends."

I laughed uneasily. Friends, yes. But more than that. They say opposites attract, but like meets like, too. In Prasutagus, I'd found a kindred spirit.

As queen, I drove my own war cart; my limbs were lithe and hard—but I would never have the bodily strength of a king. To survive in a world of men, I would always have to rely upon my people's love instead of their fear. Upon stratagems rather than bluster. And even though Prasutagus was so strong that his neck bulged with power underneath his golden torc, I recognized in him a fellow tactician. To be sure, he was employing some persua-sion upon my heart even as we spoke together in the shadow of the bridestones.

I felt as if he knew me in a way no one else knew me.

Which is why I gave myself to him, there, on the moor, while I was still free to give myself.

When it was done, we panted in mutual satisfaction, and he tangled his hands in my red hair with delight. "Now I shall never be happy again unless I am running my fingers through flame."

It ached to hear him say it, ached right beneath my breast. "Then I wish for you to take a beautiful red-haired bride who will love you and cherish you and—"

"Ah," Prasutagus said with a resigned sigh. "This was good-bye, then."

How glad I was he did not make me explain myself.

In the end, I did not marry the Catuvellauni prince whose boldness called to my blood and whose vision shook me to my bones. Nor did I marry the Iceni nobleman who so quietly stole my heart. I put aside my feelings, and in faith to my first marriage—as a bride of the Brigantes—I made the sensible, inoffensive choice that would please my people and leave me unentangled by foreign alliances. I chose for my consort my uncontroversial kinsman, Venutius: handsome, rock-strong, uncomplicated, and loyal.

It may be difficult to believe it now, but we got on well, Venutius and I. Given his battle prowess, I did not fear the tribes at our borders. And when Venutius was not busy fighting, he was content to spend his days hammering things near a forge and his evenings hammering, well . . . as I said, we got on well.

So I never doubted the wisdom in turning away Prince Caratacus, not even when he took a wife and began amassing real power in the south. But neither did I forget Prasutagus, whose child I lost before my wedding day.

To my great sorrow, it was the only time I have ever carried a child inside me. The only time I have ever known such a bitter loss. It was a loss I could not share with my new husband. Nor with Prasutagus, who never knew.

And who I never thought to see again.

But two years later, a rider thundered up to the ramparts of my new stronghold with urgent news. Roused from bed, I hurried out into the night with my husband to greet the messenger and was struck dumb when the moonlight revealed his weathered face. It was Prasutagus, sweat dripping in rivulets down his cheeks and his expression grim. "Queen Cartimandua," he said with the utmost formality as he dismounted his horse.

"What brings you to my kingdom?" I asked, noticing the froth on the animal's lips and wondering how hard he had ridden.

"Prince Caratacus has conquered the Atrebates and taken their lands."

"I have heard," I said, puzzled by the urgency of this news and more puzzled by the messenger. For in the time since we had parted, Prasutagus had risen to become one of the chieftains of the Iceni tribes. He was of such prominence now that he might have sent someone else to carry word to me. Instead, he had come himself.

Prasutagus gave a curt nod. "Did you also hear that the dispossessed chieftain of the Atrebates fled to Rome to plead for help in reclaiming his territory?"

A pit opened in my stomach. "That I did not know." For almost a hundred years, the Romans had kept away from our shores. Now they had an excuse to return. Had Caratacus' loathing of them actually *drawn* the foreign enemy back?

"It is only bluster," my husband said. "The Romans have threatened to come before. They will not risk a humiliating defeat. If Julius Caesar could not humble us, it cannot be done."

That seemed to be the consensus of my councilors as well. But Prasutagus, my former lover, met my eyes and said, "The Romans have already come. They were met by the army of the Catuvellauni."

Well then. Good. The strongest army but mine was in the field to repel them. "Who leads the army?" It would be Caratacus, surely.

Prasutagus shook his head. "There is no more army."

A collective gasp went up from the Brigantes, and my husband's eyes bulged. "How can that be?"

"The Romans are fast and formidable."

I pressed my hands to my face in dread of the invaders. "This is a disaster."

"It's not possible," my husband half shouted. "Not possible that such a battle would be fought without our having heard of it sooner!"

Prasutagus shook his shaggy head with a helpless shrug. It was not his fault that the kingdom of the Brigantes was so far north that we were almost the last to know anything. "Caratacus has managed to escape capture."

"We must get word to him," I said. "Offer him shelter."

I was grateful when my husband nodded his ready agreement. "Our Brigante warriors will march south, ask every tribe to join us, and beat back these puny Romans from our shores."

A battle cry went up from my warriors. Because we are a proud people, there was excited talk of glory. If the Romans had defeated the Catuvellauni, perhaps the army of Caratacus was not as fearsome as we had always supposed. Perhaps they had been badly led. The Brigantes would now lead the way, everyone agreed.

But Prasutagus said nothing, and his silence weighed on me such that I slept not at all that night. Neither did he; I found Prasutagus staring out at the rising dawn while the rest of my encampment still slumbered.

Clutching my checkered cloak tighter around my shoulders, I said, "It now falls to me to unite the tribes against the foreign invader." Caratacus and I both dreamed of it, but he had failed. "Do you think I can succeed?"

It inspired me to think so, and I hoped to inspire Prasutagus, too.

Alas, he gave another shake of his shaggy head. "If anyone could, it would be you. But you will be met by treachery from every tribe along the way if you try. Every tribe, including my own."

I startled. "Why should you say such a thing? What have I done to make the Iceni my enemy?"

"It's *over*, Cartimandua," he said, daring the familiarity of my name. "We have seen the most powerful tribal army assemble and be cut down. The Romans are here to stay. All that's left now is to surrender to Rome and the Roman way or face utter annihilation."

I could scarcely believe him. How was it that my life, that our very *way* of life, was to be lost without my ever having set eyes on the Romans who meant to take it from us? "I would face death rather than slavery," I flung back with all the pride of my ancestry.

"Fortunately, the Romans offer a third option," Prasutagus replied. "Their emperor has made landfall to await the tribal leaders who will surrender to him. I know of ten chieftains, including myself, who will go to meet the Roman emperor. I have come here to Brigantia to plead with you to be the eleventh."

Had this suggestion come from any other man, I'd have spit in his face. But the suggestion *had* come from this man, and though I disagreed with him, I knew I must hear what he had to say. "You will have to persuade me, Prasutagus. Shall we walk together, as we used to?"

"If it would not provoke your husband."

Heat stung my cheeks at what I took for a rebuke. "I am the Queen of the Brigantes. I do not answer to a husband about where I stroll and with whom."

That should have chastened him, but it did not.

Instead, he gazed upon me with naked longing. "I have not yet married, Cartimandua."

"But I have," I replied upon a swallow, deciding that I could not stroll with him amongst the bridestones, after all.

I went to meet the victorious Roman emperor under a banner of peace, but upon seeing Roman legionaries—their modest stature, their short but well-muscled bare legs—I began to reconsider the wisdom of it. These men did not seem so formidable. The plumed helmets of their officers did not frighten or impress me.

How were *these* the soldiers that had smashed the army of Caratacus? Why, my own husband was a bear of a man who could have crushed the skulls of any of these Romans with one swing of his mighty fist. Shame blushed my cheeks for meeting the Romans in peace instead of leading my Brigantes into battle. I wondered, was it the wisdom of Prasutagus that had persuaded me, or was it something far less admirable? The pleasure of his company, the desire to be near him again, was strong. I did not like to think it was strong enough to lure me to folly. "You're certain of this course?"

"Yes." Prasutagus offered me a hand down from my mount amidst the Roman soldiers who had come to greet us.

"Why?" I asked, eyeing the invaders around me. They were clean-shaven men, their armor well ordered, with little to distinguish one from another. They spoke a language with hard sounds and moved with crisp efficiency. As I would come to learn, the Romans were an orderly people. Orderly in their architecture, in their ambitions, and in their thinking.

That last bit, at least, the Romans and I had in common.

Prasutagus' hand warmed the small of my back when I dismounted, and he quietly said, "When the Romans last came to our shores, they did not stay. They left us to ourselves. Should we give them our pledge of tribute, perhaps they will leave again."

It was a thin hope, and it did not go down easily with me. Perhaps I had the orderly mind of a Roman, but I still had the passionate heart of a Brigante. Every step toward the elaborate tent in which the emperor awaited us, seated upon his strange, backless *curule* chair, was an agony of the spirit. That agony doubled when I saw that the ruler of the Romans was a balding man lacking in all obvious majesty despite the trumpets blaring in his honor and the herald announcing his impressive list of titles. He wore white with a sash of purple, and atop his head of thinning hair rested a wreath of laurel.

"I greet w-warmly this delegation of k-kings," said Emperor Claudius, with a slight stammer, before his curious eye turned to me. "And a queen?"

Amidst the humiliated chieftains, I felt more acutely my shame and our devastation. Perhaps that drove me to the folly of saying, "Surely you know of queens, even in Rome. We have heard stories of one named Cleopatra."

It was a testament to my nerves that I was careless enough to mention one of Rome's greatest foes. But the emperor's eyes brightened with amusement rather than offense. "You've heard of her?" I nodded because everyone who had heard of Julius Caesar had heard of his paramour, the queen who was rumored to have been the cause of his assassination. "How splendid. I usually make a point not to mention it, but I am descended of Cleopatra's f-famous paramour, Marcus Antonius."

The emperor had apparently taken a liking to the subject . . . and to me. Sweeping his arm in welcome, the emperor said, "Tell me, Queen Cartimandua, are you to be my Cleopatra of the Celts?"

He was the first to call me that. And if I felt shame before, now it seared my insides; for it seemed as if his question carried a hint of salaciousness. Beside me, Prasutagus clenched his jaw. But both of us quite misunderstood Emperor Claudius, who was a different sort than the emperors before or after him. He liked women. He appreciated them without seduction. And he swiftly charmed me by setting out terms that were startlingly generous.

"You are not to be s-slaves, but honored Friends and Allies," he said, explaining that we were each to be given a gold crown, an ivory scepter, a purple robe, and a *curule* chair like the one upon which he sat. We would be granted Roman citizenship as well, to which various rights and privileges were attached.

The Roman concept of alliance was not easily broken. This alliance would require mutual responsibilities and shows of loyalty. Tribute, yes. Grain, yes. We would have to honor Claudius with shrines, as if he were a god. That stuttering little man, a god!

But there were benefits for us as well.

Roads to facilitate trade. Loans to bring about new settlements. Advisors to teach us of warfare and architecture. All things that would mean a better future for my people. And that was a vision that shook me anew.

That night, Prasutagus and I climbed a hill to overlook the Roman tents and all the stunning weaponry they'd brought with them, including siege engines that could be used to defend our lands or to subdue them.

Sitting next to me in the tall grass, Prasutagus whispered my name as if he loved the sound of it. "*Cartimandua*. Sleek pony. That is the meaning of your name, is it not?"

I nodded. "It is as if my parents knew that even though I was born to be queen, I would strain against the reins of that responsibility every day of my life. I am straining still."

He nodded. "Will you make an alliance with Rome?"

Knowing that he had been elected by one of the Iceni tribes to lead them in this, I asked, "Will *you*?"

"Yes. And my fellow Iceni chieftains, too. Though we will all be hated for it. You will be, too."

No, I thought. My people loved me. I could make them understand this was the only way. They had loved me in the bloom of my maidenhood, and now I was more like a mother to them, making difficult choices for their protection. They would love me still.

But Prasutagus went on grimly. "Be prepared. The pride of the tribesmen will make them hate us until the day we die, alone and unmourned. And even if the dictates of our gods insist that we be given funerals, no one will come except for the children who want to spit upon our graves."

I thought he needed to have more faith in our people. Nevertheless, the torment on his face was such that I humored him. "If you should die before me, I will come to your funeral, Prasutagus. You have my word in that."

He barked a bitter laugh. "Well, that *does* console me. I return the vow."

Drawing my chin to my knees, I reached my decision. "I will make the treaty with Rome. There is no other choice; my people will understand that. And even if they don't, and children of the Brigantes one day spit upon my grave, I will rejoice that they are free to spit upon me instead of perishing in some faraway slave ship."

How lightly I said it . . .

Prasutagus sighed bitterly. "Now *that's* certainly something to celebrate."

I knew we would cry if we did not laugh, so I teased, "Yes! If we had wine, we could toast to attending one another's funerals and all the little children who will live to spit on our graves for making peace with the Romans."

"I would rather celebrate that we have finally made a promise to one another," he replied.

He was wrong, of course. Our bodies had already made a promise—a promise I couldn't keep. A child I couldn't keep. And so I was silent.

"My heart breaks to surrender to the Romans," he finally admitted, looking up at me with both sadness and longing in his expression. "But then . . . my heart is already broken. As I said, I have not yet married."

I did not ask why. I had seen the heated looks exchanged between him and a spirited Iceni girl in the camp. Boudica was her name, and she was only a few years younger than me. Tall like me, too. Hair of flame, like mine, and cunning in the sparkle of her eyes. *A girl he could marry*, I thought. A girl he could love . . . unless I gave him reason not to.

With the world as we knew it at an end, it would have been easy to lie down in the grass and find comfort in one another. But I have rarely done the easy thing, the thing I wanted, the thing that would please me. So I did not play my husband false. Not even for Prasutagus. For whatever else may be said of me, I am no one's whore.

I have been married three times. Once by sacred rite to my people. Once by vow to my husband. Once by treaty to the Romans. And in spite of what is said about me, I have been a faithful wife to all.

DECIANUS

Roman Fortress Near Durobrivae
Winter, 60 AD

"I thought you commanded Queen Cartimandua back to Brigantia?" Valeria sputtered.

"I *asked* her to return to Brigantia," Decianus replied evenly. "I did not *command* it. Not precisely, anyway." He could have commanded it, of course. But something in the queen's story had touched him. It was not her brazen confession that she had taken a lover before marriage with the same freedom a man might. Nor was it any sentimentality for the fact that she had once lain with the dead king. Their love affair was long ago. Nearly twenty years by his reckoning, and when it came to such calculations, he was invariably correct.

No, it was not her shameful lust that moved him.

It was the grief in her voice as she spoke of the child that died in her womb. A child that—were she a Roman matron—would have been cause for her family, or her husband, to kill her.

Or to demand that she kill herself for honor.

Yet Queen Cartimandua had expressed no relief at the loss of the child that could have been her shame and ruin. Only grief. Grief for the man who gave that child life, grief for the death of that child, and grief for her childlessness . . . a grief Decianus knew all too well. So he had, in the end, agreed to accompany Queen Cartimandua to the funeral of Prasutagus in spite of the risks.

But of course, he told his wife none of this.

In the quarters given over to him in the fortress, Valeria reached for her hair as if to let it down for the evening, but she was too steeped in propriety, even in her husband's presence, to relax in such a way. "Still. For this Cartimandua woman to refuse even a *request* from the emperor's own agent—I do hope an unfortunate precedent has not been set."

Decianus knew what his wife was thinking. That he was too soft on the tribesmen. That he was supposed to enforce the might and majesty of Rome and preserve the honor of the empire in all his dealings.

But frankly, he was not very good at that.

He was meant to be closeted away with scrolls and ink, tabulating. Numbers made sense to him. They were predictable. But people? People were mercurial and puzzling. Like Queen Cartimandua. And his wife. His wife, who, given her movements upon the bed, seemed to be trying to discern how to share a blanket without actually touching beneath it, skin to skin. It was not their custom to sleep together at night. They kept to their own chambers, as was only fitting and proper.

BUT when in Britannia . . .

Decianus girded himself to climb under the blanket with her, and for the briefest moment, wondered if there had ever been another man in Valeria's bed. Her family's pedigree vouched for her purity, but there had been no blood on their wedding night. That meant nothing, he knew. And given Valeria's rather chilly conjugal embrace, he never imagined she might give herself to any man except for duty, much less one who was not her husband.

But Cartimandua's tale made him wonder . . .

. . . until his wife caught him staring and laid back in surrender. She had mistaken his intention but remembered her duty. That was Valeria, whose delicate bones, tiny fingers, and girlish body comprised the most unlikely vessel for the iron-willed creature he knew dwelled within it. And that body had been, thus far, unable to provide either of them with the comfort of a child they both so desperately wanted. He assumed that was her fault, of course. But a tiny voice worried at the back of his mind that the weakness was in him.

"Take the blanket," he said at last, tucking it up under her chin tenderly, a gesture so little practiced that it must have felt as awkward to her as it seemed to him.

"Won't you be cold?" she asked, obviously confused.

But he saw, too, a bit of hopefulness in his wife's eyes that he would do something terribly manly, like claim that he was too tough of a Roman to need a blanket on this icy winter night. *She would like that*, he thought. He knew that now. Too bad that his younger self had not known it when he was still capable of suffering to impress a woman. "I have my cloak, and I'll send the servants to fetch another blanket."

Her sigh of disappointment was scarcely audible, but she shifted away from him, onto her side, so that he was left only with the sight of her back. Which of course, prompted him, in a huff, to do the same so that they would sleep with the blades of their shoulders pressed together in silent battle.

"It will be much warmer in Gaul," Decianus muttered, thinking again of his villa in Narbo, where he imagined he would roam the hills with a flock of sheep, a crook in one hand, a loaf of flat bread in the other. "I should like to retire there this summer, if possible."

"*This* summer?" Valeria asked in the tone that always presaged that imperial arch of her brow.

To which Decianus replied, "I can't imagine that you'd want to stay. Haven't we toiled long enough in this accursed place?"

Her silence told him that she was struggling against her temper, and he almost wished that, just once, she would let it fly. Instead, she sweetly said, "Of course. But after more than ten years here . . . to return empty-handed? To spend more than a decade of our lives here and achieve neither honor, nor glory, nor even the wealth my family—"

"You may put aside your worries on the matter of wealth at least," he snapped. He was a careful manager of money. They would never go hungry. But he could not make her a great lady in Rome—could not make her the wife of a great man. He had not advanced himself. He had not served very long in the military before retiring to civilian life. He had not politicked in Rome, nor even here, having declined to stroke the ego of Governor Paulinus. He would never lead an army, and no one would ever erect an arch to him.

But money he had, even though he had never skimmed so much

as a copper from the emperor's share; he took some foolish pride in that. He'd never administered any grand enterprise that would enrich him before, but that was about to change, whether he wanted it or not. "There is a very good chance that our financial situation may improve quite markedly after the funeral of King Prasutagus."

He had told no one of his anxieties regarding the emperor's inevitable command that the dead king's lands be seized and added to the empire. He had not meant to tell Valeria, either, but she was too shrewd to miss the implication.

"So the Iceni kingdom is to be dissolved," she deduced at once, sitting up in the dark. "And you're to oversee their annexation to the province of Britannia?"

Decianus sat up, too, holding out his hands to fend off her excitement. "I have received no official word from the emperor as to the fate of the Iceni yet. Or his judgment on the king's last will."

Valeria was now animated, eyes bright even in the shadows. "What is there to judge? The king left his kingdom to the emperor, as is customary, did he not?"

She was curious about something Decianus had to say for once, so he found himself confiding in her. "The Iceni king left his kingdom and his property to the emperor and his young daughters, as joint heirs."

Valeria's eyes widened. "How irregular."

"The Britons do not distinguish between the sexes in choosing their leaders."

Queen Cartimandua was living proof of that.

Valeria gave a disgusted shake of her head. "Savages."

Decianus was inclined to agree. But the king's will was, he thought, the desperate gambit of a dying man who hoped to build a dynasty. Ultimately, a doomed gambit. Even if Rome were to approve the plan, it had been Iceni custom to *elect* their leaders. More importantly, Rome would *not* approve the plan.

Even under the best circumstances, Emperor Nero was prickly about prominent men who died without leaving him the better portion of their fortunes. He would never settle for half. Especially when the other half was to go to two unmarried girls.

"Surely the Iceni suspect what is coming," Valeria said. "Will you need more soldiers?"

BY which she meant, You will need more soldiers.

"With the governor on campaign, there aren't any more soldiers to be had. I hope the emperor's order does not come until after Governor Paulinus returns to execute the matter himself."

Valeria actually touched her hand to his arm. "But there's an opportunity for *you* if the order comes sooner. If you orchestrate this effectively, you will not only get a share of the wealth but commendation for it in Rome."

His wife was touching him. Willingly. She was staring at him with more interest than she had since the day they married, and it was more intoxicating than he remembered. Valeria giving her full fierce attention was a head-spinning thing. And he began to think that perhaps she was right. Perhaps he could settle this matter with Roman *gravitas*. Perhaps he could do this better than the governor could and be the great man of Rome that his wife wanted him to be.

But he doubted it.

CARTIMANDUA

I keep my promises, I thought, staring down at the husk of a body that was once my beloved friend.

Men and women are so different in life. We are locked in battle from birth but cannot create life without each other. So we must forge a treaty and join together for one ecstatic moment in which we become one. Then, when we unravel after, it is only a kind of magic that lets us keep the promises we made in the first flush of joining.

Yes, men and women seem such different creatures in life, but in death we are all the same. Withered husks in a grave with nothing but our legend when we are gone. And I wondered what the legend of Prasutagus would be. For myself, I feared I knew already the reputation that would follow me to my death. But would the Iceni honor the memory of Prasutagus and his practical wisdom?

At least he would not go unmourned. He'd been washed with sacred waters, his mustache combed neatly, and his body wrapped in a death shirt. Now he was upon a bier in the Great Hall, surrounded by as many torches as notable people—Britons and Romans—come to bid farewell to the dead.

Perhaps it was in this spirit of respect that I was welcomed as a guest of the Iceni, greeted properly—but briefly—by Prasutagus' grieving queen, Boudica. The girl with the red hair like mine was now a dignified mother of two. "He's to be cremated," a child said from the shadows of the fire, and I looked down to see a girl not quite flowered into a woman. The king's daughter, she was—the younger of the two. The elder princess took after her mother in red hair and height, but I saw Prasutagus in the features of the younger princess. To know that he was still alive—in *her*—made me smile in spite of my grief.

"Surely not cremated," I told her, for that was more the Roman way than ours. It was bad enough with the Roman persecution of the Druids that there would be no one to pass the dread fey rod over the king's body and whisper instructions to the spirit on how to navigate the next life.

"Yes. Cremated," repeated the young princess. "Like the old Romans. That was the king's last wish."

I sighed. With this final wish, Prasutagus would remind the Romans that he was a loyal client king, steeped in their traditions, and whose family—and people—must be honored for his sake. The last of his stratagems. Yet I worried that this gesture on behalf of the people he ruled would risk his place in the next world.

That is what rulers do, of course. Risk ourselves for our people. The good rulers, anyway. And Prasutagus was good.

The world would be colder now without Prasutagus in it. He was my lover, my advisor, my friend, my comrade and—I was quite sure—the only person in the world who ever understood me or the things that I have done. And while I hoped he came to accept the resentment of the people for our submission to Rome, I was still struggling.

CARTIMANDUA

Seventeen Years Earlier

"YOU shouldn't have allied us to Rome," my husband said. We were standing atop the round tower being built in my stronghold—a feat of engineering that would now be made much easier with Roman gold. A fact that seemed quite lost upon my Brigantes.

Prasutagus had warned that we would be hated for surrendering to the invaders, but I had not believed him. I had been truly shocked at their dismay, grieved by the cold, resentful looks where I had only ever seen love before. I could not bear to have Venutius turn upon me, too.

"It's done," I said, tucking tendrils of red hair behind my ears to keep them—and my temper—from flying away in the fierce wind. If I was grieving, I was also frustrated.

"It can be undone," Venutius said, reaching for my hand.

I took it and held tight.

It's important to understand that I loved my husband. People assume that when something breaks, the crack—the flaw in it—was always visible. But there was a time my marriage was as strong and solid as a stone tower.

"I gave my oath," I whispered. "With ten other kings, I stood before the Emperor of Rome and swore. To turn and make war upon the Romans now would not only be foolhardy but unworthy. Dishonorable. We must make our peace with it."

And so we tried.

But my onetime suitor, Caratacus of the Catuvellauni, did not make it easy. He was out there, always, in the mists, in the hills, raising the tribes of the west not far from my kingdom. Year after year, he would emerge from the shadows to attack the Romans.

And his legend grew.

So, too, did the frustration of the Romans. They had humiliated the Catuvellauni, confiscating their weapons so that they could be of no help to their rebel king. But the Romans came to believe that he had sympathizers in every tribe. And perhaps he did.

Even the Iceni were forced to prove their loyalty by surrendering their weapons. Weapons that had been passed down in their warrior class from generation to generation: swords, shields, and spears. All the tokens of strength and manhood, gone. The Iceni were left degraded, with little more than farming implements and hunting weapons.

But no such demands were made of my Brigantes. Perhaps because we were so much larger a federation. Perhaps because we were far north of the skirmishes and minor rebellions. Or perhaps because I administered my kingdom with the good order of which the Romans so approved. Whatever the reason, my kingdom grew in wealth and prospered. My fortress was made stronger, stone by stone. My court grew in prominence and prestige, such that even Roman nobles fostered their sons with me to help learn our ways.

But the love of my people I felt slipping away. And oh, how it pained me.

I had once been their maiden of spring, loved by all, but as time marched on, I had become the harsh mother of glaring summer who was not appreciated for making the difficult decisions that ensured her children survived and thrived . . . my people being the only children I seemed capable of having—and I wondered if that was the cause of losing my husband's love, too.

Seven childless years of marriage passed before he finally announced to me in our bedchamber, "We have been living together in dishonor."

Thinking that he knew—that he had somehow divined that I once gave myself to another man—I rose up from the bed to stare. But my husband's thoughts were not of Prasutagus or our marriage bed. Venutius was thinking of Caratacus, whose name was increasingly spoken only in hushed whispers amongst my tribesmen.

Caratacus, the man who would unite us against the Romans.

Caratacus, the savior from the mists.

Caratacus, the Hero of the Britons.

"You made the wrong choice all those years ago," my husband said. "It is a stain on our honor to prosper in servility to Rome while other tribes are crushed beneath Roman boots. Cartimandua, if we'd raised an army instead of surrendering—"

"We'd all be dead or in chains," I snapped. But my husband had opened up inside me a near-fatal doubt. What if I had supported the fugitive Caratacus when he began his rebellion? Would it have made a difference?

"You are so stubborn," Venutius said with unnecessary hostility. He had never before challenged me this way. "When you latch on to a thing, you never let go of it. The strongest metal bends. I learned that at the forge. But maybe it isn't stubbornness in you. Maybe it is *fear* that has carved you out so hollow that you cannot give birth to a child, much less an act of courage."

It was as if he had struck me. I wanted to lash out at him, too, but I did not wish to hurt him, even as he was hurting me. "I want to survive, Venutius. I want our people to survive. Our traditions. Our gods. I want all of it, everything, to survive. If that is fear—"

"Yes, it is fear!" he shouted, launching himself up from the bed. And I realized it was the first time he had *ever* shouted at me. "Better that we take our traditions and our gods and our ways into the next life with glory than to live at the mercy of Rome. We should be helping Caratacus fight the invaders. Instead, your fear has unmanned the Brigantes. You are not their darling anymore, Cartimandua. You are losing the respect of your own people."

Having this thrown in my face like cold water made me furious, but still I clung to hope. "Perhaps in a few more years, they will come to understand—"

"No, they will not! And neither will I. We look to Caratacus and—"

"Caratacus!" At long last, my temper burst free. "You think Caratacus the very epitome of a man, do you? It is a wonder you did not offer to become *his* husband instead of mine."

With a sweep of his huge arm, Venutius overturned a small table, sending my fine Roman glassware crashing to the ground, where it shattered. "At least as the husband of Caratacus, I wouldn't have to live in shame and servitude to the Romans. Better to be buggered in the cause of a hero who fights for our people."

I narrowed my eyes at him. "Is that what he fights for? How many tribesmen have died fighting Rome? Caratacus is engaging in a pointless exercise that inflames the populace, undermines our rule, and lures young tribesmen to a lost cause."

"We would *win* this cause if you would command our warriors to his side!"

I gave a frustrated shake of my head. "He will not have our warriors *at his side*. Caratacus will only have them bent at the knee."

"As you bent for the Romans?" my husband asked with a sneer, implying with his tone that I had done less bending than *bending over*. "They look all the same, stinking of olive oil and fish sauce. Wanting to make us just like them. And you'll let them do it because they own you."

A surge of outrage made my eyes spring wide. "You would merely have me trade one master for another. And if I must have a master, I prefer one who will not bring war to my doorstep."

"Of course. Easier to cower behind your stone walls like a nursemaid instead of a queen." He knew full well that I'd heard whispers that Brigantia would be better off with a warlord *king*. For the first time, I began to wonder if he was stoking those whispers.

We slept that night in separate beds.

The next morning, a group of young legionaries led by one Numerius Gratius Helva arrived at our stronghold. I took an instant dislike to Helva when he insisted on speaking to my husband instead of me. The Romans did not like to acknowledge the authority of women, even women given authority by their own emperor. The irony being, of course, that the power and authority I held as queen was the only thing keeping my husband from slitting Helva's throat.

The soldiers had come to exact tribute for the Roman emperor. Taxes. Donations for the temples being built in his honor. Nothing out of the ordinary.

But Helva also had bad news. "There has been a rebellion of the Iceni. We have rounded up the troublemakers and sought reprisals. The governor believes it's important for the Brigantes to know that it will be considered a breach of our treaty should you offer shelter to any of them."

"What of Prasutagus?" I asked, my heart in my throat.

Helva unstrapped his helmet to stare at me, dumbfounded, as if he found it quite impossible that a woman should demand answers of him. But one of the other soldiers whispered into Helva's ear, and then Helva directed his answer to my husband—as if I had not been the one to ask it. "That Iceni chieftain remains loyal to Rome. The others were killed in the fighting."

My legs nearly swept out from beneath me in simultaneous horror and relief. So it had not been a rebellion of *all* the Iceni. It had perhaps been a rebellion *amongst* the Iceni. Something I could never allow to happen in my own kingdom. But if Prasutagus was the only chieftain left, and the only one loyal to Rome, he was likely now the high king, facing the same opposition I was facing within my own kingdom . . . and within my marriage bed.

DECIANUS

Venta Icenorum, Kingdom of the Iceni
Winter, 60 AD

ONE thousand denarii, Decianus thought. That's how much value he put on the dead king's well-bred and very rare royal steed.

Though, with inflation what it was . . .

Drinking deeply where he sat in the dark and rounded Iceni Great Hall, he searched fruitlessly for the Iceni boy he'd once fostered. But as much as he would have liked to see a friendly face in the crowd, given the recent tensions between the Romans and the Iceni, Decianus supposed the young man would not like to remind his kinsmen of their once-fond connection.

Meanwhile, Decianus observed that Celtic funerals were quite a bit more raucous than their counterparts in Rome. No death masks or hired mourners to stand about the impressive bier atop the rushes. There was quite a bit of keening over the body of the dead king, though. And many of the mourners stood in praise of Prasutagus, drinking wine and telling very loud stories of their happiest remembrances.

To die in battle would have been more honorable than to die of old age; in that, both the Britons and the Romans agreed. But King Prasutagus had lived a long and full life, with many battles in his youth and vast wealth in his old age. Unfortunately, he had no sons, leaving behind only two daughters and an impressive widow with flowing red hair. Though her eyes were swollen with grief, Boudica had a proud bearing and made plain that she would preside over the games and feast held in the king's honor.

Six hundred denarii, Decianus thought. That's the value he put on the queen's slave girl who filled his cup with more wine. Though perhaps she was worth much more—after all, she bore a resemblance to the dead king. Drinking deep and nearly knocking his cup over when he set it back down, Decianus consoled himself that even though *he* had no children at all, it seemed as if the virile King of the Iceni had only spawned daughters, in and out of his marriage bed.

Not that Decianus would have minded a daughter or two. A gaggle of girls to make Valeria laugh . . .

Prasutagus' daughters looked as though they'd never laugh again. Come morning, they faced a burial and more games and feasting and more visits to the grave. Decianus supposed that only twenty years before, the savages would have been hunting heads and dropping them into sacred springs to propitiate the gods in the dead king's favor. Thankfully, the Iceni had been at least *somewhat* civilized and were content to celebrate mostly with a few fistfights and an abundance of wine. An abundance in which Decianus was happy to share.

Two denarii per sextarius, he thought, eyeing the king's extraordinarily fine wine in its decanter. And he would have to drink more of it—much more of it—to find his courage. For the emperor's order had come to him as soon as he arrived with the Queen of the Brigantes in his entourage.

The Iceni kingdom was to be annexed immediately, all debts collected and scores settled. Decianus could not wait for the governor. But he feared that the moment the ruling was announced, violence would erupt. These hulking tribesmen, their gullets filled with wine and their hearts filled with grief for their dead king, would surely mount a resistance even if only with their bare fists.

So how could he meet it? He must be very covert about taking his inventory. He would pretend that the emperor meant to honor the wishes of King Prasutagus, and that in accordance with the will, he was only making a valuation of everything so that he could take the emperor's half-share.

That would delay the confrontation as long as possible. That seemed like a clever idea. At least in his inebriated state.

Two copper pieces, Decianus thought hazily, staring at the very shiny young tribune sitting near his wife. Agricola was the name of the handsome tribune whose rippling muscles could only have taken on such sheen after being bathed and carefully scraped by a bath attendant who would charge two copper.

A bit much, really, but so far from the civilized world . . .

His wife's laugh cut through the dingy interior of the feasting hall. Decianus had so seldom heard his wife laugh that it startled him. And when he looked up, he saw she was laughing for that smarmy tribune. Valeria was *laughing* while Tribune Agricola nattered on about Greek philosophy and flexed those strong soldier's biceps for her.

What nerve! To openly make a play for another man's wife . . .

Decianus snatched the platter of roasted goat from the tribune when he reached for it. Which made the handsome tribune grin. "There's plenty to go around, Procurator," Agricola said with a glance at Decianus' wife. "No need to be greedy."

Greedy, was he? Decianus would see to it that this no-account tribune's career suffered! He would ruin him. Ruin him utterly. Yes. If he remembered any of this by morning.

Or if he could get past the anguish of knowing that here was a man—young and virile and battle-ready—that his wife might prefer. Tribune Agricola would not be sitting with his stomach in knots at the thought of dispossessing some barbarian tribe. Tribune Agricola would have no fear of these savages. Any man bold enough to flirt with Valeria—why, that man would show no hesitation at doing his duty.

Later, stumbling away from the Iceni Great Hall into the inhospitable little hut that had been given over to him for the night, Decianus thrust a cup of unwatered wine at his wife. "Drink."

"Pardon me?" Valeria asked, and not just because she considered strong wine to be inappropriate for a respectable matron of Rome. She was already on edge, seemingly afraid to touch the wolf pelts on the bed that had been made ready for them lest she rise with mites.

He pushed the goblet into her hand with a force that made her eyes widen. Her shock deepened when a note of true command crept into his voice. "*Drink*, I said."

Valeria stared into the depths of the cup, then back up at him, her bemused expression giving way to a frown. But she drank because he commanded it. There might have been poison in it, and yet still she drank. Because she was an honorable Roman wife, or so she wanted him to believe. "May I ask the purpose of this, husband?"

"Because I am drunk," Decianus announced. "And so should you be, for any conversation about the state of our union."

Valeria arched that infernal brow.

Decianus cleared his throat. "It is a conversation long in coming, and you won't open yourself in free words unless Bacchus pries your tongue loose. Yes, only a god can do it. Certainly, *I've* never been able to break through your walls with mere mortal powers."

His wife's lips thinned. "I cannot imagine what you mean."

"You laugh at me, don't you?" Decianus poured more wine for her into the empty cup. It was the only way he could think of to reach her. "From behind that mask of cool reserve, you're laughing at me. Not with me. Not for me. Not as you did with Agricola, that pretty tribune."

"Oh, *Decianus*," she said without raising her voice, but he still heard her disdain.

"Did you let him touch you?"

Decianus hadn't known he was going to ask that question, but when he did, Valeria's ears went from pink to red, and she clenched her teeth so tightly that her beauty turned grim. At last—at long last—Bacchus did his work, and the mask fell away. She flew at him in fury, jabbing his chest with a finger. "You dare to accuse *me* of infidelity! After all these years of lying under you whenever you wish it, managing your household exactly as you like it, and picking up after you when your mind gets lost in numbers, this is my repayment?"

Decianus pointed at her accusingly, sloshing wine from his cup. "That is not an answer!"

His wife recoiled as if he had run her through with a sword.

"You know the answer. If you did not know it already, you would have killed me or demanded that I kill myself. Even asking the *question* is such a stain on my honor that I shall be forced to find a dagger!"

With that, she lunged for the chest at the foot of the bed, and he grabbed his wife's arm. "Don't," he whispered hoarsely, unnamed dread coursing through him. "Never say that. I would never want that, Valeria. Never."

"You believe I am an adulteress!"

"No," he said, feeling the pressure of tears stinging behind his eyes. Tears he could not shed lest she loathe him for a weakling. Loathe him even more than she already did. "No. I am sorry. I should not have said it."

"But you did say it." Valeria made a soft sound that was nearly a sob. "And now you have stained me."

"Stop," he said, though whether he meant it for her or for himself he could not say. "Stop. Enough. It does not matter. It did not happen. I am sorry. I am foolish. A foolish man. I am sorry. Forgive me."

She stood there, her chest rising and falling as she struggled to get her own emotions under control. And at the sight of that pale, delicate bosom rising and falling, he could not bear the thought of a dagger pricking so much as a drop of blood there.

"I knew a woman once," he whispered, thinking to console her. "A woman who took her own life for honor. I was only a boy then. I came upon her in my father's kitchen, where she lay sprawled upon the floor. One pale arm cupped around a slightly rounded belly that may have been her shame. Her hot red blood still flowing in a line from her heart to where it pooled beneath her body."

Valeria's hand flew to her own heart and pressed there. "Oh, dear gods, how ghastly."

Ghastly. Yes. Decianus nodded. That was all he was capable of doing in his drunken state, the god of revelry having turned his inebriation into jagged memories that tore at the very center of his being. So he just kept nodding. "Ghastly."

"Who was she?" Valeria asked softly. "Did you know her?"

"In a way," Decianus allowed, his gaze falling away. "She was my mother."

"*Oh.*" Valeria gasped, then stroked his arm in what felt like true sympathy. "Oh, Decianus. Your mother. How terrible."

"Yes, terrible," he agreed, realizing he had never told anyone this before. Half wishing he was not telling anyone now. "I never knew why. Perhaps she was violated. Perhaps she was an adulteress. Perhaps she would not have done it if a child had not come of it. As I said, I never knew why. It was merely agreed by everyone that she had done the right thing to restore honor. And then no one ever said her name again."

It was all very noble, or so he had been told. But as a motherless boy, he had thought it an abomination. Some part of him still did.

Valeria touched him more tenderly than she had ever touched him before, bringing her lips softly to his cheek, stroking his hair. "Oh, Decianus, of course she did the right thing. For a woman's honor. Family honor. Roman honor. What a sacrifice she made so that her son could become a great man of Rome. You see that, don't you?"

He did not see that, but he was lost in the nearness of his wife and the softness of her kiss. At least until she whispered, "Every moment of your life has led you to this opportunity to impress the emperor and make your name. Here and now, in subduing the Iceni, you can give meaning to your mother's life by making something of the family name that she died for."

You're too soft with these savages, she meant. It reflects badly upon the emperor. And if you are a real man, you will do what needs to be done.

CARTIMANDUA

"CARATACUS killer," someone hissed at me from the darkness.

And though it was my practice never to reply to indecorous hecklers—not even when they awakened me at knifepoint—I managed to snarl, "He isn't dead, you imbecile."

A hand slapped down over my mouth then, pressing me back into the bed furs, and I realized that this was one situation I was unlikely to negotiate my way out of. Even if one *could* negotiate with a shadowy fanatic who clearly wanted revenge against Cartimandua, *Betrayer of the Britons.*

Thus, while the drunken Iceni tribesmen and other notables slept beyond the wicker partition that divided my chambers from the Great Hall, I began the fight for my life. Venutius had taught me to defend myself when we were first married. We made a game of it, wrestling in our marriage bed as a prelude to a more pleasant kind of wrestling. So I knew how to bring my knee up sharply into my attacker's side, and it made him lose hold of the knife.

It *was* a man trying to kill me, wasn't it? I couldn't know, but as I cried out for help, I thought I caught the scent of a mistletoe potion and burned bread. *Druids*, I thought. So that's why I was not simply stabbed to death in my sleep. Sacrificial killings are complicated and rare. Not a simple slit throat in the darkness. Perhaps something more than murder was intended here.

These were the nearly incoherent thoughts that flew through my mind as I pushed against the weight of my attacker, groping for my own blade in the dark. That's when the fiend wrapped his hands around my neck. I couldn't call out again for help. I hadn't the breath for it. As the blackness closed in on me, my fingers caught the edge of a hilt, and I held on. I had survived before, after all, by holding on. Maybe I could survive again. Or at least draw the villain into death with me.

What happened next was a blur. I remember thrusting blindly with the blade. The man atop me howled in pain, then crashed backward into a support beam holding up the thatch roof and sent the pots tied to the beam above his head clattering to the floor. My limbs, which were going cold as they had once done in the river, were suddenly warmed by a rush of hot blood. I was gasping sweet breaths of air when Romans burst in with swords drawn. And as the space filled with the torches of people roused from their slumber by the commotion, I saw that I was covered in blood. Was it my blood? I couldn't tell.

"Assassin," I choked out, my throat raw.

"He's dead, Queen Cartimandua," said the irritating Centurion Helva, who had moved up in the ranks since he paid call upon my kingdom all those years ago to tell me that the Iceni had rebelled against Rome. He looked baleful, as if he thought I should have more properly let myself be strangled than do something so unfeminine as to stab my own attacker.

The corpse was on the floor, and the Iceni Great Hall was in an uproar. Dogs barked madly. Warriors rushed in and out. Even the grieving widow of the king we had come to mourn was drawn from her quarters to demand answers as to who would dare to violate the protection given to a guest under her roof. Sweeping in with an ageing warrior at her elbow, Boudica said, "Find who is behind this. Question every Iceni nobleman." Then to a slave girl, she snapped, "Fetch Queen Cartimandua some water for washing and clean garments."

I was impressed with Boudica's sense of command at a time

when her heart must have been broken and her anxieties keen. Impressed enough that I couldn't allow her—or anyone—to see that my hands were shaking, so I tucked them behind my back as she made apologies that such a thing should ever befall a guest of the Iceni royal family.

"There is no need for apologies." I glanced down again at the dead man, and then forced myself to speak over the lingering pain in my throat. "I know him. He is not Iceni. He is a kinsman of my husband. Which makes it no great mystery who is to blame."

My husband was to blame. He was trying to kill me.

And not for the first time.

CARTIMANDUA

Twelve Years Earlier

THE motley band of rebels was brought before me, tied at the hand and foot. Some of them had wiped the dirt from their faces and made themselves neat and presentable.

Others were still smudged with blood and dirt.

They were Brigantes. My people. My children.

One of them, a chieftain of my own council, spat at my feet. "I will not be judged by you, Cartimandua. But you will do as you will. That is your way."

"Because I am queen," I said, reassured by the sensation of Brigantia's white snake twining between my fingers. I didn't need anyone's permission to punish the rebels for leading an uprising in my kingdom. The uprising had so alarmed the Romans that they felt forced to turn back from their campaign against Caratacus to ensure that mine wouldn't be a hostile kingdom at their flank. That was, I guessed, the real reason for the disturbance. The security of my kingdom was threatened to buy some breathing room for the Hero of the Britons.

But still, I had to know. "Tell me why you've risen up in defiance of your queen."

None of the rebels answered, but I saw the eyes of the ringleader flicker toward my husband, then away again. Chilled to the bone, I asked, "Have I abused you in some way? Cheated the craftsmen building this stronghold? Have I brought our kingdom low, or are we more powerful now than ever before?"

They remained silent . . . and insolent.

But later, once I'd had the rebels dragged away, my husband spoke for them in the quiet of our bedchamber. "We *are* more powerful, Cartimandua. You're right. And we still have our weapons. Which means we can still join the fight against Rome and win."

"Not this again," I said, turning to pace. "I have emphasized to every chieftain in our federation the benefits of our treaty with Rome. Have we suffered for it? No. We are left to our own governance. We are left to our own ways. We are not only surviving but thriving."

My husband took me by the arms and made me look into his fierce warrior's eyes. "There will come a time, Cartimandua, when you must choose."

"I made my choice years ago. It is still the best one for our people. Not just the warriors with their pride. I understand that I will never again have the love of *all* the people," I said, though it hurt to say it. "I will content myself with the love of *most* of them. I will not be undermined in this. I will not tolerate opposition in this. Not from those men I arrested, and not from you."

Venutius touched my cheek tenderly, as if it might be the last time he ever would. "If you execute those men, you will be hated by *most* of the people. And I will leave you. I will not be tarnished by your doings. That is the choice you face. I will leave you."

I could not fathom what he meant. We had spoken sacred vows. Oaths that could never be broken lest we *truly* live in dishonor. "We are married," I said, stunned.

To which he replied, "What is done can be undone."

He should never have said that to me. He should never have put that thought into my mind, where it would fester. He should never have provoked me so. "Leave, then," I said, for it felt to me as if his heart was already gone. "I am the queen, Venutius. You are the consort. We will see if anyone even notices that you are gone!"

I executed the rebels.

Not all of them, of course. My heart was not hard enough for that. But the man who spat at my feet I killed with a knife to the heart. I did it myself. My blade thrust deep beneath his ribs. He collapsed forward, and we danced a final farewell, surprisingly intimate as I breathed in the last breath he took. As his warm blood stained my clothes, my hands, my very self.

He was the first man I ever killed. But I did it to remind my resentful audience that if I would not be universally loved, I must still be feared. And I was not sorry for it, though I would make an offering to Brigantia that she might spare me from making such a dreadful choice again.

It was, of course, a hopelessly naive prayer.

Two years after my husband left me, another prisoner was brought before me.

One whose visage was weathered from hard fighting, but whose gleaming grin was still familiar to me. "Caratacus?"

He held up his fettered wrists with a shrug of apology. "I would offer an embrace to greet you properly, my old friend, but . . ." Every spare ounce of flesh had been burned away during his years of harrying the Romans from the mists. But still, he wore that cocksure smile in spite of his peril. "This is not the reunion between us that I envisioned, Queen Cartimandua."

"Cut him loose," I said to my bodyguards because it was painful to see the man in fetters. But I did not send the bodyguards away, for I knew Caratacus to be desperate and dangerous. "You envisioned a reunion between us?"

The moment he was set free, Caratacus took a step toward me while rubbing his sore wrists. "Why else would I be here, my beautiful red-haired queen of the mists? I have come again to offer an alliance between us. Years ago, I promised that we could unite all the tribes. You asked time to think on it. I think I have given you enough time."

"You have come to court me again?" I jested, charmed by his hubris in spite of myself. He still had the bearing of a bard and the theatrical voice of a singer. I could not help wanting to hear what song he would sing, even though I knew it would be *only* a song.

"Yes, I have come to court you and ask for your hand in marriage once again," he said quite seriously. "But this time without gifts to offer. Except for freedom, the most precious gift of all. It would make a fine dowry for our marriage."

Freedom for who, exactly? I wondered, for though the nobles chafed under Roman taxes, and the warrior class resented our client status, my people were freer in some senses than they had ever been. "I am already married, Caratacus. And so are you."

"Your husband has abandoned you," he replied evenly. "Divorce him. As for me, my wife and children have been taken captive by the Romans and are lost to me forever."

It was then that I was no longer charmed by his hubris. This was his pattern—had been his pattern all along. Lead an army against the Romans, then escape to leave his followers to the consequences. I understood it as a matter of survival. I admired it as a matter of strategy. But I had been castigated for building alliances and stone walls to protect my people, whereas he was celebrated for leading other men to stand and die while he ran free. First from the Catuvellauni. Then from the tribes of the west. Now from his own family—and he was already speaking of them as if they were dead.

My heart hardened, and I no longer wished to play this game. "You did not come to my kingdom to propose an alliance, Caratacus."

He chuckled ruefully. "Why else would I venture into this wintry north? I have nowhere else that is safe for me to hide."

"If you wanted to hide, you'd have adopted a new name and taken up farming. So large is my kingdom that I would never have known you were here." I stood up to say the next part, for indignation drove me to my feet. "You did not come here to hide, and you did not come here because it was safe. And you did not come to see *me* at all, or you would not have been caught miles north of my stronghold."

"Even a man of my experience can get lost in the mists—"

"Let's not lie to one another," I said, closing my eyes upon a sigh, then opening them again. "We both know you're here to start a rebellion in my kingdom, to take my people, if you can, and make them your own. Anything in the service of fighting the Romans."

He opened his mouth as if to deny it. As if to say something clever. But our eyes met in flame and fury until the fire dimmed in his. His bright smile fell away, and weariness finally showed itself in the slump of his shoulders. Seven years was a long time to fight from the mists.

To live as a legend and not a man.

"Who was it that betrayed me?" asked the Hero of the Britons.

"You were only betrayed by the predictability of my enemies.

The men I pardoned in the recent disturbance—I had them watched. Like will always seek out like, and so your attempt to meet with disgruntled Brigantes came to my notice. I am only surprised that my husband was not amongst them."

Caratacus said nothing to that.

A lump lodged itself in my throat. So then, my husband was behind this, too. Twice now, I had survived attempts to remove me from power. Attempts that would have meant my death.

My husband wanted me dead.

Perhaps Venutius had been right to say that strong things bend because inside me, I felt my heart shatter and I sank down into a chair.

Caratacus motioned to the seat beside me. "May I?"

He did not wait for permission and settled down into it. We were quiet for a long moment. "Bring wine and refreshments," I finally said to a servant, for I realized how tired and thirsty he must be. Or perhaps it was only my own mouth that had run dry. When the wine was poured, Caratacus drank sparingly. But I emptied my cup.

"This is a fine stronghold," he said, breaking off a piece of bread. "All this stone. Very Roman. Strong but inflexible. Our roundhouses are made so that we can up and move whenever we like."

I narrowed my eyes. "Oh, I intend to stay awhile."

Caratacus smirked. "It must be quite an expensive undertaking, even with Roman gold. You know . . . the Druids would ransom me. You have few friends left amongst them in Mona. Freeing me would restore your reputation, the love of those who—"

"Please." As I set my wine down, my voice was quiet but firm. "My reputation is nothing when weighed against the good of my people . . ." I trailed off there because I said it more to convince myself than him, and it had opened the wound wider to speak aloud something I could not seem to make myself believe. "I did not capture you for a ransom, Caratacus."

"Didn't you? Surely you are anticipating some manner of reward for turning me over to the Romans."

"By the terms of the treaty—"

"The *treaty*," Caratacus said with utter contempt.

My throat tightened. "You were their enemy before you were mine. Trust me when I say that it is a profound act of friendship to give you over to Rome. I speak not of my friendship with Rome, but with you. For all the affection I bear you, I will turn you over to Rome to parade about as an exhibit. Because they can afford to let you live. Whereas I . . ."

I did not say it. I did not have to say it. We both knew the truth of it. As long as he was alive, he would be a threat to me and my kingdom. I could not spare him. I would not spare him. As much as I wanted to.

Caratacus drank the rest of his wine, savoring it as if he thought it the last he would ever drink. "I suppose I am pleased in one thing. All the might of Rome could not capture me. It took a clever Brigante to do it, and a woman at that."

"Why say it that way?" I challenged. "Men will fight and die for a woman. Who do they worship here but the high goddess Brigantia? Not a god, but a sovereign goddess."

"So they do." He smiled. "Perhaps, someday, when I am gone, the mantle I have dropped will be carried by a red-haired lady of iron will."

Perhaps, I thought.

But not by me.

I still remember that the Romans took Caratacus away in fetters, and it was with unnecessary roughness that they shoved him into an iron cage, like a giant bear to be baited. I told myself that I would remember their names, those young Roman soldiers who gloried in the capture of their formidable foe. But I was mistaken. For of the Romans there, I can now only remember that Helva fellow.

I stood alone that day, watching with a broken heart as Caratacus was carted away. Glad that my husband was not there to heap abuse upon me. Glad to be so far up on that hilltop that I could not hear the jeers or curses of those Brigantes who would condemn me. For if they had not hated me before, they would now. I had been a much-loved maiden and a stern but respected mother to my people, and now I wondered if the blame I would take for giving Caratacus to the Romans would make me a bitter, twisted, old crone.

But the crone is a wise woman, I told myself. She sees what others do not.

Alas, that was cold comfort.

Especially since the Romans didn't appreciate what I'd done, either. If I expected thanks for capturing and delivering the Hero of the Britons into the hands of Rome, I was to be disappointed. For though they delivered to me several chests of coins—as if I sold Caratacus to them for gold pieces—I heard the whispers of the legionaries, who spoke of how they despised a woman who would trick a proud warrior like Caratacus into chains.

I had stripped them of their glory in capturing him, too, it seemed.

But what would have happened if I had not given Caratacus over to Rome? They would have taken my gold crown and my ivory scepter, my purple mantle and my *curule* chair. They would have dismantled my tribe, disarmed them, and shamed them, as they had done to all the others that resisted.

Sometimes there was no winning with Rome.

No winning with the people.

No winning at all.

Except for Caratacus, of course. When I told him that the Romans could afford to let him live, I did not dare to dream that they *would* let him live. But the silver-tongued bard delivered such a stirring speech in Rome that he was actually pardoned by the same emperor who had called me the Cleopatra of the Celts.

Caratacus, who had meant the death of so many Romans—to say nothing of Britons—was set free to roam the forums and admire the basilicas of the Eternal City, admired by the people who lived there.

He, the rebel, pardoned and celebrated.

Me, the loyal queen, despised and insulted.

CARTIMANDUA

Venta Icenorum, Kingdom of the Iceni
Winter, 60 AD

"DRINK this." Boudica pressed a cup of warm liquid into my hands, and I finally tore my eyes away from the corpse upon the floor. The assassin I had killed. "It's a potion that will help ease the pain in your throat."

So she was a healer, as her husband had been. Though I was keenly aware of the lingering crowd, I accepted this gesture of kindness from Boudica. Perhaps she sensed my discomfort, for she sent a baleful look in the direction of the gawkers. "Leave us."

When we were alone and I was pressing my fingertips to the sore spots on my neck in some awe that I was still alive, she said, "You're sure it is your husband behind this?"

"Yes. You have my apologies for dragging my marital strife into your kingdom in a time of such sadness and distress. I am very sorry for your loss."

"As I am sorry for yours," she said, confusing me. "Better to lose a husband to the next life than to lose one to differences that cannot be reconciled."

"What a tactful way of phrasing it." It was too delicate by far. Since I turned over Caratacus to the Romans, my husband had raised arms against me, laid siege to my stronghold, and tried to murder me in my bed. This latest attempt was particularly well timed. I was too far away from my kingdom to order immediate retaliation against his family, who I had been forced to hold hostage for his good behavior. If he had succeeded in this attempt . . .

"I shouldn't have come," I admitted, and it went down hard with me. Because I had been warned by the procurator, and I hadn't wanted to listen. I had been wrong. And when a queen is wrong about one thing, she begins to worry that she has been wrong about everything. "I must go back to my kingdom before Venutius makes another move."

"Marriage is a hard thing, is it not?" Boudica asked. In spite of the fact that I was covered in the blood of a dead man, I found myself gripped by the most intense curiosity. I was fairly certain the bitter acrimony in my own marriage was entirely unique. "Was it so hard for you and Prasutagus?"

She gave me a sidelong glance that made me wonder what she knew. "Oh, we agreed on very little."

Like me, Prasutagus had remained loyal to Rome. Had he, too, been challenged for it in his marriage? "But you had children together. Surely that made it easier."

"It made it harder, actually. I bore love and respect for him as a husband and a king, so I could accept that he was making the wrong choices for me. As a mother, however, it was harder to accept the choices he was making for my children and their future."

Children. A life together. Love and respect.

Even if their opinions differed greatly, it seemed like an idyll.

"But I console myself in one thing," Boudica said. "As a widow, I will now be like you—free to make my own choices without having to bow to a husband whose decisions do not sit well with me."

It was good that she was finding ways to console herself because the days ahead for her were likely dark ones. The treaty between the Iceni and the Romans expired with King Prasutagus' last breath. With it, Boudica's wealth and status were likely to be swept away. "What will you do now?"

Boudica's chin jerked up, and she snared me with an intense gaze, strangely reminiscent of a prince who once came to court me. "A better question is . . . what will you do?"

I felt a light-headedness that I did not think came from having been so nearly strangled. I had the sense that something very unexpected was afoot. And I said her name rather more sharply than I intended. "Boudica. I do not wish to be the bearer of such bad tidings, but you must prepare yourself. In coming here, I was nearly turned back by Procurator Catus Decianus. He said he could not guarantee my safety—and given the events of this night, that is abundantly clear. But Romans seldom inconvenience themselves out of unselfish concern for the Cleopatra of the Celts. No. The Romans expect trouble here, and not on my account, but on yours. The most likely reason is that they intend to seize the lands of the Iceni."

This should've been shattering news, but it didn't seem to surprise her in the least. "They may *intend* to seize the Iceni lands, but that doesn't mean they will keep them." She reached to wet a cloth in a basin of wash water for me. "If the Romans are wise, they will honor the last wishes of my husband. If they are wise, they will allow my daughters to inherit, and I will serve as regent over them until they come of age."

A shocked breath puffed from my lips. If she was to be believed, Prasutagus left his kingdom jointly to his daughters—not to his wife, which might have been more palatable. Romans had grudgingly acknowledged widowed queens before. Prasutagus must have had some reason for *not* naming his wife, and I came to realize it might be those very differences of opinion she had spoken of.

"The Romans will never honor your husband's last wishes," I said, reaching for her hand to make her see sense.

"Because I am a woman, and I have only daughters?"

"Yes," I sighed. "Emperor Claudius acknowledged me as a queen. But that is because I already *was* a queen before he ever limped onto our shores. You're dealing with Emperor Nero now. He will not give crowns and *curule* chairs and purple mantles to two young, untried girls, neither of whom have seen more than sixteen summers. Besides, Romans don't like dividing kingdoms between siblings. It has not gone well for them before. I hope, for your sake, that I am wrong, and that your husband's scheme will win the emperor's approval. But I don't think it can happen. It is against Roman convention. It is not even in keeping with Iceni tradition."

She gently withdrew from me. "Well, if the Romans want to leave us to return to the old ways of voting for our chieftains, I have no objection."

How strange to hear her speak of what she would or would not object to given her vulnerable position. I told myself that perhaps, in her grief, she didn't understand what was happening. That she couldn't accept that her life, as she knew it, was gone. "My dear lady, you must swallow your pride and be ready to cooperate lest—"

"Cooperate?" Her eyes flashed even as her voice remained calm. "As we cooperated in giving up our weapons? As we cooperated in taking gifts from Romans that they later claimed were loans? As we cooperated in fastening a chain upon our own necks?" A pause. "Or upon the necks of our own heroes?"

Caratacus, she meant. I turned, shamed by the mention. Angry, too, that it should be held against me. "That chain would have been on my neck if not his."

"Yes," Boudica agreed, sponging the blood off my arms. "The Iceni were loyal to Rome, and yet our weapons were taken from us, and we have been left to the mercy of rapacious tax men. After years of outrage piled upon outrage by soldiers, the rough treatment of our people by private agents from Seneca and his ilk upset my husband so much that I believe it hastened his demise. Prasutagus was loyal to Rome, and yet now you tell me they will take his lands, his wealth—leaving nothing for his family. What would you do if Rome were to repay your loyalty with such abuse?"

"They have always honored their treaty with me," I said stiffly.

"So far," she said. "The Romans devour and devour, and their hunger never ends. It is only that you are so far north that you will be one of the last morsels to be swallowed up."

I wanted to say that she was wrong, but it wasn't easy to argue with her calmly reasoned grievances. She wasn't like my husband, ranting about how we must fight only for the sake of fighting. Nor did I sense in her the unbridled ambition of Caratacus.

But she did remind me of him.

Indeed, maybe she was not only a healer but also a bard because even I was stirred when she said, "We are not sheep. We are Britons. Someone must remind us of it. And when the time comes that my tribesmen remember there are some transgressions against honor that cannot be tolerated, what will you do, Cartimandua?"

"What will I do?" I met her eyes, seeing in her a mirror of

myself. She was the queen I might have been if I had chosen a different path. A different outlook—one that doubtless made her much loved by her people. I liked her. I respected her. In another life, I might have allied myself with her. Even in *this* life, some part of me hoped she might triumph. But the rest of me hardened in terrible resolve. "I will do what I have always done. I will be a faithful queen, wife, and ally."

To the Romans.

I would not start a war, not even for the sake of Prasutagus' beloved memory. Not for the love of my people. No, not even for that.

DECIANUS

TEN denarii, thought Decianus. That's about how much silver's worth of wine, meat, and bread he vomited up into the pail. He'd spent the night in such a deep and drunken slumber that he had not learned about the attempt on Queen Cartimandua's life until sunrise.

Now it was going to take all his willpower not to remind the foolish woman that this was precisely what he had warned her against. It was a lucky thing she had survived. The kingdom of the Brigantes was too big and too strategic an outpost to be lost. And the timing was terrible. With the legions in the west, an unfriendly north would leave the governor's flank exposed at the very moment the entire southeast of Britannia was undefended. Good thing the barbarians weren't noted for their strategic thinking, or Decianus might have suspected a conspiracy.

In any case, Decianus made it his business to call upon the Queen of the Brigantes, who—in clean garments but gaunt expression—he found in the stables at dawn, stroking the coat of her horse. A white pony—the descendant of a fine line that she'd once been gifted by a man she nearly married, she said.

Decianus cleared his throat. "On behalf of the emperor, may I extend to you our gratitude that the assassin is dead and that no lasting harm has come to you, Madam?"

"Thank you," she said. "Now there is the matter of bringing my husband to justice or at least ensuring that he makes no more mischief."

His belly burning with acid and his tongue just as sour, he joked. "I begin to think I prefer open warfare in marriage as opposed to tepid battles of emotional attrition."

The queen didn't laugh. Which annoyed Decianus since he only meant to bring a smile to her face. But then, there was just no pleasing women, was there?

"Is that the way of it in your marriage, Procurator?"

He wished he had not brought it up. Only this throbbing headache could have made him so candid with a stranger about something so very personal. (And of course Valeria had no headache whatsoever—she had sailed out this morning with immaculately pinned hair and an energetic stride as he was still vomiting into the pail.) "My wife and I, well—" It was then that he noticed that the queen's satchels and traveling trunks were stacked in the corner. "Madam, after all the fuss you made about coming, you're now leaving before the burial rites are performed?"

"It's Queen Cartimandua."

"I beg your pardon?"

The tall woman lifted her regal head and pulled a curtain of red hair over her shoulder. "I am a client queen of Rome, duly vested with the emblems of that office, and in keeping with our treaty, I am to be addressed in a manner fitting my station. I am not *Madam*. I am Cartimandua, Queen of the Brigantes."

Decianus supposed that knowing her own husband wanted her

dead was bound to make her prickly. But he was still fighting a hangover, not just of wine but of painful memories. His patience was thin.

"Why don't you just divorce him?" he heard himself asking bluntly.

This seemed to startle Cartimandua, as if attempted murder wasn't cause enough to end a marriage. Instead of being grateful for his good advice, she snapped, "Why don't you divorce *her*?"

It was his turn to gawp. *Divorce Valeria?* What grounds would he have for it? She had never disobeyed him in word or deed. Given her pedigree, his honor might more likely be besmirched by a divorce than hers. No. Divorce was unthinkable. Why was he talking about this at all, much less with a barbarian?

Cartimandua gave him one last fearsome glare. "I am returning to my kingdom to manage my own affairs, but you must be careful in managing yours here, Procurator."

His head fogged over with belligerence. "What is it you think you know of my affairs here?"

She pressed her cheek against the horse's mane before dragging her eyes to him again. "If the Iceni are to lose their independence, you must tread carefully. You must show respect to the nobles. You must give them reason to see the opportunities in this change—"

"I daresay there is nothing I *must* do on your say-so," Decianus replied, startled at the brazen authority with which she spoke.

"You are known as a mild-tempered man, Procurator," she continued as if he had not just shown his displeasure. "That will serve you well. But do not discount Iceni pride, and do not discount Queen Boudica."

He wondered what on earth the woman could be getting at. "What possible threat could be posed by a grieving, middle-aged widow without any sons?"

Cartimandua gave an exasperated shake of her head. "Women are not always what we seem to be. What our reputations would tell you. Nor do we only exist in reference to our fathers, husbands, and sons."

Bewildered, Decianus asked, "Do you know of some plot to make trouble?"

Cartimandua eyed him levelly. "What I know is that you must guard against being provoked to any precipitous action. Do not be goaded to something you will regret."

Why would anyone try to goad him? With his head still throbbing and his mouth dry, he could hear nothing of her words that made sense. All he knew was that he was facing another nattering woman telling him what he must do. And she kept going. "Roman strength is shown in restraint. The order, reason, and lawfulness your people employ, the true source of your honor. *Restraint.* In the matter of the Iceni, you must reflect that most manly of virtues and show yourself to be a true Roman, honorable and just."

Was he to now take instruction on how to be a true Roman from a barbarian trollop? His head was already ringing with Valeria's declarations of how a Roman conducted himself; now he had to listen to another version on the same theme from an uncouth queen of the icy north? How was it that women could simultaneously give a litany of specific instructions as though admonishing a simple-minded child and then imply that only by obeying them completely could one live up to the standard of masculinity they had just eviscerated?

The acid in his belly now boiled like a cauldron set over a fire. In spite of the winter cold, he felt a river of sweat running down the back of his neck. Maybe Valeria was right that he had been too soft on the barbarians if he was letting himself be lectured by an uppity savage who likely still lived in an uncivilized hut.

"Good day, Madam," Decianus said stiffly. "Safe travels north."

Towering over him, her eyes blazed. "Procurator, have you heard even a word—"

"I said good day!" Decianus shouted, turning on his heel.

DECIANUS was still sweating that morning long after the dead king was burned to ash and interred in his burial chamber with a magnificent sleeping couch, amphorae of wine, and baskets of bread to help ease his way into the next life. Prasutagus was buried shortly after dawn, with a magnificent sword that he had been allowed to keep in spite of the disarmament of the tribe. Decianus saw Valeria's brow arch at the sight of it. As if she feared a less friendly barbarian might dig up the tomb and use that sword against Rome.

Decianus was not about to object. Nor did he protest the burying of this hoard of wealth without counting it as part of the emperor's estate.

But this was all the accommodation he was prepared to give.

He had a reputation as a *mild-tempered* man, did he? That was another way of saying that he was weak. Lacking the character necessary to maintain the honor of the empire and the esteem of his wife. Midday passed, and though the Iceni lingered at the burial mound to pay last tribute to their fallen king, Decianus left early to pack up Valeria and send her back to Londinium. As she was driven away, he thought, in the back of his mind, that perhaps he should wait a few days more to get about the emperor's business, when the heat of grief might have cooled. But of course, it was winter. Everything was already so cold, and he did not wish to return here until spring, if ever at all.

By the time the weather turned, he hoped to be in his villa in Gaul, swimming in the warmth of the blue sea, sucking sweet rosemary-flavored honey from combs the bees left in his orchards.

But first, he had his orders.

He commanded his servants to assemble in the Iceni Great Hall, where he would establish his center of operations. "Either bring more torches in, or we will have to drag everything else out into the sun to examine it properly. Bring me every item you find of possible value. Nothing is too small." It was now early afternoon; with luck, he could be done by nightfall.

He was taking note of the extraordinary metalwork of a silver platter when the king's widow and daughters returned from the king's burial mound to find the procurator's slaves dragging all manner of gold items into wagons in the clearing. Standing by the table upon which Decianus was making a ledger, Boudica put both of her indelicate hands upon her indelicate hips. "Procurator, what is the meaning of this?"

"I am making a valuation of the late king's property so as to take payment of outstanding debts and settle your affairs."

This did not seem to upset her as much as he feared it would, but her eyes were riveted upon the roundhouse. "You are allowing lowly *slaves* to ransack my house and paw through the king's belongings."

Ah, these proud Celts. "I am just as happy to have Roman soldiers do it if that will please you better." Decianus called to the nearest centurion. "Numerius Gratius Helva! Please relieve my slaves of their duties."

Boudica's color rose, and several of the royal family crowded around her as she said, "In these past days, you have feasted in my hall, Procurator. Slept beneath my roof. Drunk my wine. But now you do me the disrespect of taking my—"

"I am taking inventory," Decianus protested, in no mood to be challenged again by a woman. "I remind you that these belongings are not yours, but the late king's at the sufferance of Rome.

You have no legal standing upon which to object. Now if you will let us be about our business . . ."

Boudica pressed her palms flat to the scroll Decianus had been trying to write upon and glowered. "Would that be the business of thievery? I have lived enough winters to know how it is that you Roman magistrates enrich yourself. You will take this silver platter for your governor, this one for your wife, that one for your emperor and tell him that there was only one."

Helva snorted from beneath his centurion's helm, and Decianus felt the acid boil up to the back of his throat. This woman was accusing him of dishonor and theft. Accusing him in front of all her royal kin. Accusing him in front of the soldiery, most of who had no loyalty to him and would be more than happy to report such a thing to Emperor Nero if they thought it would advance their careers.

Catus Decianus might never have been an ambitious man, a brilliant man, a man to light the world on fire—a man like Valeria wanted. But he had *always* been an honest man. To be accused of corruption was too much to bear. One offense too many. Honor demanded outrage. For once, his own temper and the strictures of Roman honor were entirely in agreement.

His stomach went from boiling acid to ice. "Madam," he said in a voice so cold he scarcely recognized it as his own. "Understand that your kingdom is to be annexed by order of the emperor."

The gasps and angry shouts that went up from the tribesmen made a cacophony as Decianus had never before heard. The sound of it crumbled the walls within him—that inner fortress that defined the parameters of who he was and who he had been. In this moment, he only knew how to imitate the Roman he should be. Standing, he called to the soldiers. "Search all the houses in the enclosure for valuables. Debts must be settled."

Hulking Iceni men clenched their fists while their women shouted in that grating way of the Britons, but the soldiers went about their business, grabbing armfuls of glassware and bolts of cloth and—

"This is an insult," Boudica said again, quite calmly. It was eerie how calm she was in the center of the storm. He did not understand it. Yet she continued. "Recognize that you do an insult to the memory of a loyal king. A Friend and Ally of Rome. My husband left a will, yet his wishes are dismissed, and you are abusing his people."

Her voice rose in volume only toward the end, and it was not for his benefit. This damnable woman was playing to an audience. He realized that now. What could she possibly hope to accomplish except for infuriating him?

She must have seen in him some weakness. The same weakness his wife saw. The same weakness that had always existed in a motherless boy who learned to count things to drive the bad memories away.

Well, he could not be that boy any longer.

"Seize the cattle and the horses!" he shouted. "And if anyone should interfere, we will seize the grain as well."

Boudica stared hard at him, as if bracing herself for something. "Know that it will be a hard winter for both the Iceni and the Romans if you should *dare* to seize our grain."

Was she threatening him? Yes. She was threatening him. Even Centurion Helva realized it and snarled, rushing forward as if to backhand the insolent woman. The other soldiers also seemed ready for a fight. Keen for it, even. But they all waited on Decianus for orders.

No Roman magistrate should tolerate a threat from subjugated peoples. Decianus did not even need Valeria to tell him that. It was a matter of honor.

"Seize the king's wife," Decianus commanded.

Helva shoved aside a grizzled Iceni warrior and grabbed hold of Boudica's arms. "Should we flog her?"

Gods, no, Decianus thought. He had never considered such a thing. He was opening his mouth to countermand the idea just as one of the Roman soldiers shouted, "A sword! I found it half buried under the furs."

A *sword*. The Iceni were forbidden weapons. This should not be. "Whose sword is this?" Decianus asked, his eyes turning to the royal kin of the king—all of whom looked either outraged or terrified.

"It was the king's," Boudica finally said. "As I was his queen, it is now mine."

She was lying. He could see that plainly. The king was permitted his ceremonial weapons, but he would not hide them. "The king is dead, Madam, and the treaty has expired. You are not a queen. Not anymore."

"If the treaty between the Romans and the Iceni has expired, then we are not bound by it, either," Boudica replied. "If we are not Friends and Allies, what does that leave? Neither you, nor Rome, has any rights over me or my people—"

"Continue to argue, and I *will* have you flogged."

Boudica managed to fling herself free of Helva's grasp long enough to confront Decianus, and this time she was not calm. "Would you *dare* show such a lack of decency, you sad little man?"

The words came out. "Flog her."

Decianus waited for her to beg his mercy. She *should* beg for it, and that would help even the scales. She was a woman with honor to defend. She need only beg his pardon, and he would give it. But the damnable woman merely lifted her chin. And he stared at that chin, haughty as his wife's brows, until he knew it to be the one challenge to his Roman mettle he could not back down from. "Strip her."

It seemed as if the whole of the Iceni tribe gathered around in shock, some blubbering, others screaming insults at him. Though they had no weapons, some of the Iceni rushed forward and were clubbed to the ground with gladius hilts. One of them might have been the boy Decianus once fostered, grown into a warrior. The procurator felt a twinge of horror to know *that* relationship must be severed now, for the boy would never forgive him this.

And Decianus could afford no softness anyway.

Not even for the queen's young daughters, struggling to get to their mother while being held back by retainers. Decianus stood rigidly as Helva and his men tore the queen's garments from her body, but he did not hear Boudica scream or cry out.

He only heard the jeers of the Roman soldiers as her pale naked flesh was exposed to the cold air, her nipples hardening and the auburn thatch of hair between her legs shamefully on display. He wanted to avert his eyes, but Boudica seemed to feel no shame. She said nothing. She did not cry for help as they tied her to a pole.

She did not cry out at all.

Only her body told the tale of her mortification as it trembled under the gaze of the crowd. "Harlot queen," Centurion Helva said with a snicker.

But Decianus thought not of harlots, nor even of the wife whose body, by all the laws of Rome, was at his mercy, if never her heart and mind. No, he thought of his mother.

Was my mother bared this way when she was dishonored? Decianus wondered. Was she stripped of her dignity while she struggled against an attacker, or did she quietly submit to some act that a man wished to force upon her? Did she—unlike Boudica—ask for mercy? Or was she never forced to her shame at all? Perhaps she willingly, even eagerly, removed her own clothes for a man . . .

He didn't know. He couldn't know. He would never know. But he couldn't shake the questions in his mind. He couldn't even count them. And all those questions disappeared the moment Boudica turned and locked her eyes with his.

In them, he saw such unexpected resolve that it shook him to his core.

He broke eye contact and moved several steps behind her so that he could not see her face. But still, when the first stripe was laid upon the queen's back, Decianus shuddered from the impact. Then they struck her again, and this time she did cry out—for the vicious blow left upon her back a line of blood.

Decianus stood transfixed by that line of blood. Taken out of time and place. Taken back to his childhood and another line of blood.

His mother's blood.

Blood for honor. That was the price then, as it was the price now. It was always the price of honor. Always blood. Always pain. And as the queen was scourged, he wondered if such a thing as honor really existed at all. For what was honor if it could not strip the pride from a barbarian woman even as she was beaten before her people? What was honor if he could only defend his own by doing this to her?

Honor, Decianus thought, was just an excuse for war and mayhem. An excuse for taking. Whether the taking of a woman or the taking of one tribe against another, one empire over another, one emperor over the world. An emperor like the one he served . . .

If this was *honor*, he wanted no part in it.

Shaken, Decianus quite suddenly lost his footing. Catching himself on the edge of the table, he stared at his feet. And watched them start walking.

Centurion Helva called after him, "Where are you going, Procurator?"

Decianus kept walking. He had to find his horse. He had to leave this place. He had to leave these accursed lands. He was not the man for this job. In truth, he was exactly the wrong man for it and had always been. He wanted no share in the plunder. No part in the so-called glory. No measure of his wife's approval if this was the cost.

What he wanted was his little villa in Gaul, where juicy blue-black grapes grew in fat clusters over the tranquil pool into which he dipped his feet while studying the geometry of Euclid and the paradox of infinity.

"Procurator!" the centurion barked. "What are your orders?"

"My orders," Decianus murmured, the sounds of the flogging—leather upon flesh—scourging his own sense of himself in the world. It took him a moment to realize he was clutching the emperor's missive in his hand. "My orders are for you to do your duty by Rome, if you feel bound to it."

Which Decianus did not.

Decianus read from the emperor's letter, giving the words a bitter twist. "Seize it all and treat any interference, of course, as an act of war."

With that, Decianus let the letter with the emperor's seal fall to the icy mud.

Then he mounted his horse and rode away.

CARTIMANDUA

"YOU'VE come back to reconcile, then?" I asked my husband, shoving his legs from where they rested upon the table in my fortress. He came awake with a shocked snort from what appeared to be a drunken slumber.

The entire hall stank of wine, which confirmed there had been a celebration in my absence. A premature one, though.

While Venutius struggled to catch up, I said, "I cannot think of another reason you might return here to my stronghold unless, of course, you thought me dead."

Venutius let his eyes drink me in, as if he couldn't decide whether or not he was disappointed at my survival or impressed by it. "Did the Romans save you again?"

"I saved us all with the nearest implement at hand," I replied. "Which is what I have always done, incidentally."

Venutius tensed for battle, but he must've understood that if I returned by stealth, so did my soldiers. "You don't wield the sword of Rome, Cartimandua. If that's what you tell yourself, then you have not yet realized that Rome is a blade always at your throat."

Talk of blades at my throat—from him, no less—did not put me in any better mood.

And he was decidedly somber, realizing his peril. "What happens now? Will you have me beheaded with the sword *I* made for you?"

That was a very good question. "Unfortunately, I am too weary from my journey to arrest and execute you today."

Venutius smirked. "Liar. You fear that the people would turn against you completely if any harm came to me. And you should fear it."

"Perhaps," I admitted. "But I'm not afraid to execute your brothers and the rest of your kin."

Venutius reddened from cheek to jowl. "You are a she-bitch."

I patted his arm because I had nothing handy to stab him with. "And you are a pale imitation of the man you want to be, so perhaps we might work out a truce between us since we apparently deserve one another."

But no sooner had the words left my lips than I knew they were not true. I had clung with the greatest tenacity to our marriage, to my vain hope that his love for me was stronger than his pride. Just as I still hoped my people's love for me was greater than their resentment. But the desire to be loved was not a branch to reach for when I was drowning.

It was, in fact, the water rushing to tug me under.

Venutius was a man bound by what people would think of him—he was, for the sake of pride and accolades, forming an image of himself as the perfect warrior against the usurper. And he could not be that unless he made me his enemy. But I realized that I no longer cared for his good opinion or the opinions of those who concocted lies against my character to the detriment of my kingdom.

No. I had been the *true* protectress of the Brigantes, whether they knew it or not.

I would no longer cling to a husband who wished me dead—a husband who was, in fact, the only choice I made in utter deference to the wishes of my people. And look how that had turned out.

Venutius was right about one thing. What could be done could be undone. And Boudica was right to think that there was no wisdom in honoring a treaty with a faithless partner. I was finished with Venutius and would be rid of him as soon as it was practicable, because it was his survival or mine. And I needed to stay alive, if only to steer my kingdom from the coming troubles.

With a strange relief and a moment's silent thought, it was decided. Not only the matter of my marriage but of my reputation, too. Taking up my newest white snake where it slithered on the floor, I let it coil for warmth within my lap while remembering a long ago conversation with the man I should have married.

Let them all hate me, I thought. And this time I meant it. Though children of the Brigantes would one day spit upon my grave, I would rejoice that they were alive to spit upon me instead of perishing on some battlefield or rotting away in the belly of some faraway slave ship.

Because I was not what they said of me. No collaborator, betrayer, or Roman whore. I was not even the Cleopatra of the Celts. No. I was exactly, and *gladly*, what I had promised to be. The embodiment of Brigantia. First the maiden. Then the mother. Now the wise crone, whom people fear and despise, but who sees beyond seeing . . .

Unaware of this epiphany, this fundamental change in me, Venutius puffed up with effrontery. "A pale imitation of the man I want to be? And just what man do you think I want to be?"

I smiled a false smile at him, and it felt strange upon my lips, but I would have to endure it. For my people, I could endure anything. "There is only one Caratacus, my dear. Only one Hero of the Britons. There will never be another."

But in that, of course, I was wrong.

Far to the south, a weeping Roman procurator had galloped away from a whipping post as his centurions stormed through roundhouses full of screaming girls, and the ravens were beginning to circle. Far to the south, a queen's back was laid bare, those bloody stripes the first lines to be sung in her legend. The mantle of Caratacus lay on the ravaged ground and, as he hoped, it was about to be taken up by a red-haired lady of iron will.

But what happened after Catus Decianus rode away on that cold wintry day is now, of course, all part of Boudica's legend.

Not mine.

PART TWO

THE SLAVE

Ruth Downie

This is a woman's determination; as for men,
they may remain alive but enslaved.
—Tacitus

BLOOD has to be washed out straightaway in cold water or it stains. That is one of the few things I know that is still safe to say aloud.

The hundred paces beyond the gates to the river might as well have been a hundred thousand because if the Romans came back, I was not going to let them catch me down there in the reeds on my own. So I smashed the thin ice on the horse trough in the yard instead and dunked the mass of soiled clothing in there. When I saw the pink streaks of the princesses' blood starting to drift across the floating ice, I began to scrub.

I scrubbed till my knuckles were raw with the coarseness of the wet linen. While the older women hurried in and out of the Great Hall with salves and washcloths, I scrubbed till I lost the feeling in my hands. Perhaps if I scrubbed long enough, I would lose the feeling everywhere else: the aching head, the jarred limbs, and the shame.

"Ria?"

The boy from the cooking-house smelled as if he had run into the cowshed to hide from the Romans, and his pale face was streaked with tears. We had all seen things this afternoon that no one should ever see: I could not imagine how they might seem to a motherless child of seven winters.

"I don't know what to do, Ria."

Did he think I did? What are you supposed to do when Roman soldiers—soldiers of the people who said we were Friends and Allies—smash your warriors aside, rampage through your houses, steal or trample all that's precious? When a king's funeral ends with his widow tied to a post, stripped naked for everyone to see, and flogged raw? When the grieving daughters who should rule half his kingdom are dragged away and violated?

I stared down at the linen floating in the cold water. I didn't know what to do any more than the boy did.

"Ria?"

Useless to send him to his father; the man was slave to a leather-worker miles away and had never shown much interest in him. I tried, "Go and find the cook."

Luci sniffed. "Cook's boiling up a poultice for the princesses. The healer says the queen might die."

I leaned on the trough and willed him to go away. I could not help him. I could not help anybody. My legs weren't holding me up properly.

My mind kept running back to the same moment. Not the terrible thing that had happened to Queen Boudica. Not the blow when the soldier knocked me to the floor of the storehouse. The moment when, instead of getting back up to fight, I crawled behind the wicker partition and lay like an animal playing dead. From just a few paces away—and inside my head, still—I could hear the younger princess crying out for help that wasn't going to come because the Romans had put guards on the door to keep our warriors out. There was no sound from her sister.

"Don't scream!" I wanted to call out.

Don't scream. It only makes things worse. Close your eyes and leave your body limp and hide away inside yourself until it's over. It feels like it will never end, but it does. I had found that out for myself not many days before.

I should have helped the princesses. I should have done *something*. I was the only one of our people inside the storehouse with them, the only one who could possibly offer them any comfort or support. But I did . . . nothing. All the time it was happening, I lay pressed against the cold mud floor with my eyes shut. Praying that the brute who hit me had forgotten about me. Praying that none of the other soldiers waiting for their turn with the princesses would notice there was a third girl.

"Ria? Did you hear me?" Little Luci lifted both skinny arms, showing elbows covered in the same muck that was all down his tunic. "I fell over."

"Go and wash," I told him.

"My clothes are all smelly."

I tried very hard to think what to do about this one problem. "Go into the slave-house," I told him. "Look in the chest behind the door. There might be a clean tunic." Unless that had been stolen, too.

"Then what shall I do?"

I looked around. Afternoon was becoming twilight, but I could still see thick columns of black smoke on the horizon and smell the stink of burning in the air. Inside the royal enclosure, people were moving slowly between the roundhouses, clustering together, staring and pointing, talking in low voices. Where the horses should have stood, there was nothing but a few strands of twine and a half-eaten hay net. A couple of old women were on their knees where the queen had suffered, scrubbing the stones. Someone was trying to restack the logs against the wall of the Great Hall. "I don't know," I snapped. "Tidy something up."

I was not used to giving orders. I was a slave and the daughter of a slave, and the things I was used to were doing laundry and being invisible.

I was—I am—also the daughter of a king.

Those princesses, the daughters of Boudica, were my half sisters. We grew up in the same royal household, but they wore the fancy linens and delicate wools that I had to wash, and if I was lucky, they might pass something on to me once it needed patching. I cannot say we were fond of each other, but the little mousy one was kind to me sometimes and gentle in a way that reminded me of my father. Even the bossy one—who was older than me, but not much, and a great deal taller and more beautiful—had shown me understanding when I wished to pay my respects to my father's body. All these things added to my shame.

I took a slice of willow bark and began to chew on it, silently willing the gods to make it dull not only the ache in my head but the screams echoing through my memory. It was as if my mind kept dragging me back to that moment in the false hope that *this* time I could make a different choice. That *this* time I would behave as the person I had believed myself to be: a person who would fight to save someone in need. It was not only my duty as a slave and a sister; it had also been my vow.

"What are you doing, girl?" I jumped as the slave-master's hand reached into the trough beside me. He pulled out something sodden and dripping. "Nobody's going to want these again."

I held up the underskirt I was washing. He was right: I could have scrubbed it until the end of time, but it would still be ripped and stained and ruined.

I was still wondering what to do with it when I saw Duro walking down from the warriors' house with some of the other men. His limp was worse than usual, and his graying hair was wild and smeared with blood. He ordered little Luci to call everyone to the yard, and the boy hurried off full of his new importance. I had good reason not to be grateful to Duro, but it was a comfort to see him take charge. He was an elder and a warrior, the queen's right-hand man, and this was not the first time he had suffered at the hands of the Romans. Duro would tell us what to do.

When we were gathered in the cold, he glanced around at the crowd of the disheveled and the battered and the confused: Iceni farm boys and warriors and elders and slaves, old people leaning on sticks and children clinging to their mothers' skirts. "Is anyone missing?"

Only the royal family we were all here to serve and those who were tending them.

When nobody answered, he called, "Take heart, everyone! The queen will live!"

Someone called out, "Thank the gods!" A couple of people took each other by the arm. It was as much celebration as any of us could manage.

I knew what my mother would have said if she were still alive, although not loud enough for anyone but me to hear. *Of course she'll live. That Woman won't die until she's good and ready.* And for once, I was glad that my mother was safely in the next world because this day was bitter enough. Losing the queen would have been too much for any of us to bear.

"Our princesses . . ." Duro paused, as if he was trying to find a way of saying it that would not cause everyone further pain. "Princess Sorcha and Princess Keena have been cruelly dishonored. The birthing-women and the healers are with them now." He went on to say that anyone else who was injured should ask for help. Chewing willow bark had not soothed my throbbing head, and I wondered if I should tell someone about the pain. Then I thought, *What if they ask what happened and where I was?* So I kept silent.

While Duro was talking, the slave-master had been counting. Now he spoke aloud. "Twenty-two, twenty-three"—that was me—"twenty-four. All here."

Duro nodded. He counted the dogs, and everyone called and whistled for the missing ones, but none came. The horse-boys were sent to see if they could round up any animals that had escaped from the Romans. The farm workers had already penned and counted what remained of the stock.

"The rest of you can best serve the queen by going back to your usual duties." As he spoke, a gust of wind sent soft feathers drifting across the cobbles. All that was left of the fowls that had been plucked for tonight's funeral feast. If the day had gone as it should, the feast would just be beginning. Now all the food had been stolen.

"Ria?" It was the slave-master. For a moment, I thought he was going to ask if I had been hurt. "Go and get the poultice mix from the cook and take it over to the Great Hall. Give it to the healers."

And that was it. I was number twenty-three, somewhere just above the dogs. Which was no worse than I deserved.

IT did not take long for the news of the desecration to spread beyond our settlement. By the following afternoon, riders were coming in over the trackways. Elders, healers, messengers. People from miles away bringing words of support and more stories of theft and outrage at Roman hands, not only against wealthy Iceni nobles but against poorer families on ordinary farmsteads. The other houses used by the king had been raided, too. There were small consolations: a horse trader came in with a string of three escaped ponies he had managed to round up and three more as gifts. Windblown strangers delved inside their layers of traveling clothes and pulled out little pots of salve and healing charms to offer the princesses and their mother. Some of the potions went into the Great Hall; the healers used the rest on the bandaged heads and battered bodies of the fighters who had tried to defend us.

They had no chance. Our warriors had not been allowed proper weapons since I was a baby, when the Romans decided we weren't to be trusted to bear arms. It was an insult that our people were quick to avenge in rebellion, but the gods did not grant us victory. My mother said there were injured Iceni fighters laid out in all the houses for weeks afterward, and I am almost sure I remember pale figures lying in the beds around our own. Not content with dispatching many of our greatest warriors to the next world, the Romans took Duro's only son and sent him as a hostage to Londinium. Then they sent extra troops to finish stealing our weapons and to build roads and forts across our territory, and my father, the king, had to find a way to make peace in a land filled with enemy soldiers.

There are people who say that King Prasutagus wasted his life. That nobody can ride two horses at once. They say—and they said it then, too—that he handed over his dignity and betrayed his people just so he could enjoy the riches that Rome could offer. But as my mother said, many of them hadn't seen the aftermath of that battle: the sufferings of the wounded and the grief of bereaved Iceni families across the land. *If you cannot defeat Rome,* he told the elders, *for the sake of our people, do not provoke her.* Instead, he tried to calm her with soft whispers.

Agreements were made, and we were Friends and Allies of Rome once more. So whenever a gang of their soldiers beat up some of our traders or set light to somebody's hayrick or stole our livestock, the governor always told my father how shocked he was. It seemed some men had disobeyed orders and would be disciplined, and usually we never saw them again. If you ask me, I think the soldiers were just moved away or even promoted, but that was the story, and my mother said that my father pretended to believe it because there was no point in picking a fight. Then later on, when some mysterious fire destroyed a Roman staging post on the road, he was all surprise and sympathy, offering condolences, asking if there was anything his people could do to help rebuild.

It was a pretense that suited both sides, or so it seemed, and my father worked hard at it.

I used to run to watch when the royal family arrived back from their visits to the Roman governor at Camulodunum. The sisters were usually asleep under furs in the carriage by the time it rolled into the yard, but the queen never slept. She never seemed tired, either. My father always looked gray and exhausted and glad to be home from the endless parades and sacrifices to the emperor.

Once, two summers ago, I was in the cooking-house when they came back from some Roman festival or other. I was cleaning a pan by tipping ash into the hot fat when I heard the rumble of wheels, so I went to the door with the pan still in my hand. The cook looked out over my shoulder and said, "You know, the king's looking older."

Some man who had no right to speak at all—he was only there to deliver cabbages—said, "It's all that lolling about in the governor's bathhouse. Makes the lazy old fart's skin go crinkly."

I felt my fists tighten, but the daughter of a peacemaker should not lower herself to punch a cabbage man in the eye. "He goes to Camulodunum to keep the Romans off our backs," I told him. "Would you rather they came to us?"

He said, "Who asked you?"

The cook laughed. "Don't mind her. She thinks the king is her father."

I aimed for royal dignity, but I could not prevent my voice from rising. "He *is* my father!"

The deliveryman said, "Then why are you here washing pots?"

So I tipped the fat and ash over his bald patch. It didn't shut him up, but I like to think he learned something.

After that, the slave-master put Luci to work in the cooking-house instead of me, which was a shame because it was always warm in there no matter what the season. To be fair, the cook did tell the slave-master that I attacked the man because he had insulted the king. So I just got a not-very-serious beating and a never-ending supply of dirty clothes and blankets to wash. I had hoped my father might thank me for defending him, but I suppose nobody told him.

Anyway, even after all my father's efforts to keep the peace as a

Friend and Ally of Rome, our warriors were still allowed no weapons. They looked the part, with the scowls and the muscles and the striding about with helmets on, but when you looked closely, you saw only wooden clubs and sharpened sticks and the soft leather bundles of slingshots. They might frighten a few Trinovante sheep-stealers, and they frightened me, but they were never going to strike terror into the hearts of the men in the fort only half a day's march from us: men who came with bright swords in their hands, metal plates strapped around their chests, and orders from Rome.

The men with clubs and sticks were back at the gates now, letting in visitors and patrolling the raised banks of the royal enclosure, stamping their feet and blowing on their fingers to keep warm and trying to act as if they had some dignity left.

I gathered up a couple of sheepskins and hung them on the rack outside the cooking-house to beat the dust out of them because I needed to hit something.

Smack.

A jolt of pain shot through my head. The fleece jumped out of the way and then swung back for more.

Smack.

One or two slaves who'd arrived with their owners wandered across to ask for news about the queen. I told them she probably wasn't going to die after all and was glad my mother was not here to hear how relieved I sounded.

Smack.

My mother had good reason to resent That Woman. It was not my mother's fault that my father sometimes sought respite from the royal bed in the arms of a house slave. His flame-haired queen was passionate and beautiful, but—like her eldest daughter—she was full of opinions, and people with opinions can be very tiring. When That Woman found out my mother was pregnant, and whose child it was, it was her opinion that my mother should be sold with me still unborn inside her. The slave-master had already been given the order when my father put a stop to it.

Somehow his soft whispers persuaded the queen that instead of being sold, my mother should be moved from the job of personal slave in the Great Hall to grinding wheat and scraping vegetables in the house just across the courtyard. That was where most of the royal food was prepared because nobody wanted the Great Hall to smell of boiled cabbage.

My mother said we should be grateful to him that we were in the royal household at all instead of huddled in rags in a field somewhere digging parsnips. But it didn't help me understand why, if my father had the powers of a king, two of his daughters were princesses while the other was expected to be invisible.

Smack.

"And the princesses?" someone asked.

I felt my face grow hot. "As well as can be expected," I said, feeling bad about all the times I had hated them for being what I could never be. They hadn't deserved what was done to them. No one could ever deserve that.

Smack.

Just as I didn't deserve Verico.

Smack.

There he was now, swaggering around with the visitors who were gathering outside the Great Hall, showing off the blood-stained bandage tied around his head. Verico, the big blond bear that women said was good looking and that everybody said was a great warrior, and who should have been drowned at birth.

Smack.

I had never liked the way Verico looked at me. Then, on the day of my father's death, he took it into his head that I might want what he called "comforting." "You're all alone in the world now, little Ria!" When he slid his hand around my waist, I dared not make a fuss in front of all the guests who had come to show respect to my father.

The rest of his "comforting" came later, when all the mourners had gone to bed. Somebody must have heard me cry out, but nobody got up. Perhaps they all thought somebody else would deal with it. Perhaps they didn't care enough to leave their warm beds. But I vowed afterward—some time afterward, when I was able to think—that if ever I heard a cry in the night, I would get up and see what it was. I wouldn't leave it to everybody else. No man should be allowed to do that to a woman if there was someone else around to plunge a knife into his back.

Except, when it came to the test, I was too scared to do the brave things I had told myself I would do. And now everyone was clamoring for justice for my sisters, and I was silent.

Verico thought I wouldn't dare complain about him. He was wrong. But then I was wrong, too, because it did no good. People said our men were more honorable than the Romans, but I know the truth. Duro might be a famous warrior and an advisor to the queen, but he was also Verico's foster father. He'd trained Verico to fight, just as he had trained my older sister, although much good it did her against those soldiers. Duro seemed to think that the sun shone out of Verico's backside, and I should be grateful to be chosen. But I had seen Verico's backside and everything else he had, too. There was nothing shiny down there. No matter how often he hid under the blankets to polish it.

Smack. Smack. Smack.

Another pause to answer, "Is there any news of the queen?"

What everyone was really asking was, *What now?* What will happen now that the king's will has been thrown aside, his women have been trampled upon, and Rome's men think they have free rein to rob us? What is to stop them claiming everything for the emperor and leaving us to starve? What will we do?

The fleeces were the cleanest they had ever been by the time I was called into the Great Hall. They told me to find the green-and-gray plaid shawls and the thick skirts and the plain belt-braids. All the things that the princesses hardly ever wore in public because the older one said dressing like that—like everyone else, she meant—made them look like goatherds.

I couldn't see why clothes were needed. Both the sisters were safely burrowed down under warm furs by the hearth. Princess Sorcha glared at me through a tangle of red hair as I knelt to place the clothes beside her. The lucky princess, the tribe all called her, because her birth had been blessed by some good omen or other—but all her good luck had been stripped away now. I stepped back and crouched by her sister instead.

Princess Keena was thirteen winters old, two winters less than me, and the few people who dared to mention it said we both took after our father: narrow-faced and dark-haired. But huddled in the furs and staring into the flames with those big dark eyes, she reminded me more than ever of a little mouse. As I knelt to place the clothes beside her, I saw she had a shiny red bruise on one cheek and a split lip. I wondered what sort of fighting hero had done that to her and whether he was proud of his day's work. "I am so sorry, mistress."

She looked at me as if I were a stranger. "I will be all right," she mumbled, her words misshapen by the swollen lip. "I will feel better soon."

"Of course you will," I told her. What else could I say? Until that day, she could have had no idea what men were capable of. Nor had I. Those monsters had made even the hateful Verico seem restrained. I said, "They told me to bring you some clothes, mistress," but she did not seem to hear me.

Neither of my sisters looked as though she wanted to get up and pull her boots on. The queen, though, had other ideas. Whatever her faults, she never lacked courage.

I was standing to one side of the yard. I saw the surprise on the faces of the crowd as the queen came out under the thatched porch of the Great Hall. She stumbled a couple of times, held up on one side by Duro and on the other by one of her women, but she *was* on her feet. As she came into the fading daylight, her head lifted. Hair that was still caked with blood fell in a red tangle around her shoulders, tumbling down over a linen wrap. Her neck was bare of the golden torc that usually encircled it, and her pale arms were gooseflesh in the cold. Instead of her usual tunic, a fine green woolen wrap skirted her hips. Her companions helped her up onto the back of a heavy cart that had been pulled up close to the porch. Someone had draped a red cloth over the side to smarten it up.

For a moment, there was an anxious silence. Then came the shouting.

"The queen! The queen! Bou-di-ca! Bou-di-ca!" Cheering, whooping, stamping, as if they could lift her up on the sound.

She looked out across a yard filled with Iceni who had traveled here to offer her the kind of honor her husband had never been given. And then she turned her back on us all.

I was one of the few who could see the agony on her face as Duro stepped forward and lifted the bloodstained wrap. The cheering died. People gasped. I had endured the sight of the flogging, but even I was not prepared for the torn and bloodied mess that was revealed. It was as if her flesh had been mauled by a wild beast. Someone wailed, "No!" and a child started to cry.

Very gently, Duro replaced the linen. Finally, on his nod, I passed up the thick woolen mantle, and it was draped around the queen's shoulders and fastened with a pin. When it was done, she turned to face her outraged audience. Still, she did not speak. Instead, there were shouts of "Make way!" from the warriors, and moments later the girls stumbled out of the Great Hall. They were both in simple Iceni dress with their hair loosely braided around their pale faces. The little mouse moved awkwardly, clinging to her sister's arm, head down. Her sister, tall and slender and beautiful, looked like a ghost bent on vengeance.

After they were helped up to join their mother on the back of the cart, I saw why she had chosen such a humble vehicle: there were high sides for them to hold on to. And that cloth, the color of blood . . . People said later that Boudica was driven by blind fury, but they were wrong. She never did anything without thinking it through first.

"My friends." Her voice had lost its usual force, and the hush that fell as she spoke seemed to be willing her to save her strength. The sight of her wounds and her violated girls—dressed just like anybody else's daughters—was enough. "My friends," she said, "I am told mine is not the only family to suffer at Roman hands."

There were murmurs of agreement. One or two names were called out. "My house burned, my sons taken as slaves!" cried a voice. Boudica lifted her head toward the sound. "I grieve for them, Mato, and for you," she said, "and for every sorrowing family amongst our people."

Someone was pushing his way through the crowd. I saw the lithe form and sleek dark hair of Duro's son: not disgusting Verico, but the real son, Andecarus, the one who had been brought up as a hostage by the Romans. His gaze was fixed on Princess Sorcha. There were people who didn't trust him because of his Roman education and his fancy cavalry horse and his years in their army, but my elder sister wasn't one of them, and I thought they would make a good match.

Andecarus gripped the back of the cart as if he wished he could haul himself up to embrace his princess. She turned her face away from him.

Above them, the queen was thanking all the true friends who had come here; some had traveled a very long way, and tonight there would be food and beds for all. My sister was still refusing to meet Andecarus' gaze. He leaned in close to me and murmured, "Will she be all right?" I nodded. I dared not speak over the queen to say that I did not know what *all right* meant anymore.

"It was a betrayal of promises . . ." For a moment, the queen seemed to be lost for words. I held my breath, willing her to carry on. Duro leaned forward and whispered something in her ear.

"A breaking of oaths," she continued. "An outrage against all of nature and the will of the gods!"

There were cries of "Shame!"

"But listen well, my friends. Listen and remember. There will be a record of the many wrongs committed against us. The gods see everything. Andraste will not be mocked. Our wounds will heal, and we will grow strong again. And all the time we are healing, we will prepare. And then, when the gods give the sign . . ." She tugged one arm free of Duro and raised her fist in the air. "We will have vengeance!"

"Vengeance!" They were screaming for her now, waving fists and sticks and chanting "Vengeance! Vengeance! An-dras-te!" And then "An-dras-te!" turned into "Bou-di-ca! Bou-di-ca!" because with those few words their queen had turned their minds from, *what now?* And, *what will we do?* To, *when will we do it?*

I was one of the few who saw the agony on her face as they helped her down from the cart. She paused to steady herself, then put one arm around each daughter and led them back inside the house. Only those of us who followed her in saw her collapse and heard her cry out as they dragged her across to fall facedown on the bed.

She was a brave woman, and the people loved her for it. Was I the only one who was still afraid? The only one who was thinking, *Oh, what have you begun?*

I rolled over in the bed, willing the headache to ease and the memory of what had happened to my sisters in the storehouse to fade.

If only my mother were alive and lying next to me. She would have found some way to make me feel better. She would have been glad I was safe.

"But I did nothing," I wanted to whisper to her. "After that vow I made about answering cries for help—"

"You had a bang on the head. You were dazed."

"The queen was flogged, and she still got up and made a speech. I should have—"

"What was the use of you throwing yourself away?"

"But—"

"Child, the Romans only came to take *things*. She could have let them pile all the things they could find into their carts and go. None of it was hers; the king left half to the emperor and half to the princesses. But That Woman chose to pick a fight."

The truth is the queen was not the only one with opinions. Even I could not pretend that my mother was always right, but I know now that right and wrong are never as important as everyone thinks. Sometimes what you need is not to be right, but to have a warm body to curl up with and a sigh of friendly breath in your ear. And always, you need sleep. That was another thing my mother would have said. "Things are never as bad after a good night's sleep."

When I finally slept, I dreamed of my father. He was calling me by name. He had a gift for me, and he needed my help. I followed his voice, stumbling and bumping into things in the dark, groping along a twisted path, calling to him to wait for me. But every time I was close, there was something else in the way, and my father, the man I wanted to please more than anyone else in the world, was growing angry with me.

"Ria!" he called as my feet tangled in another tree root and he drifted farther out of reach. "Ria!"

Then he turned into the slave-master, kicking my feet to wake me into a frosty world where my father was as dead as my mother, I was a shameful coward, and nothing was as it should be.

The sun did his best to cheer us, making the ice retreat into the shadows and almost warming the bench outside the cooking-house. I tucked a thick shawl around my shoulders and began to pick the dirt out of a pile of clothes that had been clean yesterday morning. I wondered about the dream and whether my father really had been calling to me from the next world. It had seemed very real at the time, and besides, although I had forgotten all about it in the horror of yesterday, there really had been a gift.

My father's will never brought my sisters anything but grief. It led directly to the Roman raid because handing over half the kingdom to the emperor was not enough; Nero wanted all of it. Yet there was another part of his will that nobody remembers. A part that brought joy and comfort to me: the part where a pair of brooches was promised to "my daughter Ria." Me, the invisible laundry girl, mentioned by name! I was to have two bronze clasps that had once belonged to my father's mother.

In all the confusion immediately after his death, nobody seemed to know anything about them. I dared not ask the queen or my sisters, so I had spoken to the slave-master. He said it would be dealt with. Two days later, with no brooches, I asked him again.

"It was the will of the king, my father, that I should have them," I reminded him.

"And it's the will of the queen and the princesses that we organize a decent funeral," he pointed out. "First things first, eh? We'll get to you. They're probably put away somewhere over at the king's family house."

The house he meant was a grand farmstead beyond the bend in the river. The people who lived there were, I suppose, my aunt and my cousins, but if you had asked them to name their family, the word "Ria" would never have passed their lips. So there was no point in me going there to ask for myself.

I was still waiting for news when the Romans came to rip away my sisters' inheritance and leave them battered and misused on the mud floor of the storehouse. So now, as they lay recovering in the Great Hall and I sat on the bench outside the cooking-house trying to pick mud out of the queen's underthings, we were equal. Three violated nobodies, with no chance of receiving anything our father had wanted us to have.

And then came hope. It came and sat next to me in the shape of a frightened little shepherd girl who had hidden in a ditch until she was more scared of starving and freezing than she was of the soldiers, or of being beaten for running away from my aunt's burning house after the Romans had marched the family away in slave chains. Glad that my father was not alive to hear such news, I put one of the princesses' wraps around the girl and called to Luci to bring her some broth.

The girl knew nothing of the brooches, but she thought they might be with the things in the east paddock.

"In the paddock?" Perhaps her mind was wandering.

"They buried a lot of things before the funeral," she explained. "I don't know why, but everyone knows the soldiers take away money chests and dig up the floor, so some of the things were buried in the paddock. And I think some in the woods."

She did not know exactly what was buried, nor where, but it was a start. Nothing I could do for my sisters would be of much help, but if I had those brooches, I could offer them a gift each from our father's will. That must be the meaning of the dream. That was what my father wanted me to do, and maybe it would quieten the memory of the storehouse.

There is never as much laundry in the dead days of winter, with the household bundled in thick wool and heavy boots, hunched over against the east wind and more interested in keeping warm than in smelling fresh. That afternoon, with the clothes chests refilled and everyone's gaze fixed on the queen and the princesses, I carried a bundle of clothes out toward the river just like I had done hundreds of times before.

"You be careful out there, little Ria."

I jumped. I hadn't noticed the blond hulk of Verico lurking by the gates.

"Down there by the water, all on your own," Duro's foster son went on, reaching out to swat my hip. "You never know who's hanging around. I might come down later and make sure you're all right."

I stalked out without answering him, hoping he could not see that I was shaking.

When I was out of sight, I hid the bundle in the reeds, then cut back across to the path, hitched up my skirts, and ran all the way to the house where my father's family had met such a dreadful fate.

The place was deserted. There was only a black stinking mess where the buildings had been. I skirted around it, pinching my nose and stepping over the fallen hurdles to pick my way around the back of what had been the cowshed. There was no sign of the animals. The emperor must have decided he owned them, too. Either that or the neighbors had helped themselves. Even the hens were gone: stolen or fluttered away to hide in the woods.

The east paddock must be the one with its gate flung down into the churned mud and the turf cropped close by animals that would never graze here again.

Ahead, black feathered shapes rose from something in the grass and flapped lazily skyward. I swallowed, then took a step forward, craning to see. There was a new stink as I approached: not burning, but something worse.

It was one of the dogs. She must have been trying to defend the house, with no more chance against the soldiers than her owners had, and without the understanding to surrender. I stood over her and spoke a curse on the men who had killed her, praying to Andraste that the birds would carry her safely to wherever brave dogs go after death. Then I began to search.

The girl had said the paddock, but nobody was going to hide anything in the middle of an open field. The disturbance would be too obvious.

On the far side, opposite the gate, someone had been working on the hedge and clearing out the ditches. Shovelfuls of ditch muck had been slapped against the bottoms of the hedges, and branches that had been lopped had been piled up and left ready for sorting and burning.

It is not easy work moving a pile of branches because when you pull one, all the others want to come with it. I was hot and breathless by the time I found what I was looking for under the third pile: a raised patch where the turf had been chopped into chunks that could be lifted aside. The girl had been right. There was something hidden here, and if someone had taken the trouble to bury it, it must be valuable. Like a family heirloom that had belonged to the king's mother and would now be a comfort to his daughters.

The turf was heavier than I expected. I flung my winter wraps aside and gave up all hope of keeping anything else clean. Once I had the turf lifted off, there was a patch of freshly dug soil about the width of a man's arm. In one place, I could even see a boot print where someone had stamped the loose filling down.

The carrion birds had settled again on the dog. I turned my back on them and kept working. I had to find those brooches.

I have learned since that the first rule of doing something you shouldn't be doing is to post somebody else on lookout. At the time, I was more bothered that I hadn't had the sense to bring something to dig with. I had supposed there might be tools here, but the fire had destroyed everything. With only bare hands, it would take far too long to dig out a pit this size. I stepped across to the pile and disentangled a hawthorn cutting that was almost straight. Then I stripped off the spikes with my little eating knife and plunged the stick into the middle of the boot-print.

It came to a stop no more than a hand-span down. I tried again a little farther away, twisting the stick to ease its way through the heavy soil. Again, a stop in the same place. Whoever had buried this thing had been in too much of a hurry to dig deep.

More stabs found what might be the edge of whatever it was. I loosened the earth over it with a stouter stick, then knelt and began to scoop with cupped hands. I stopped to lift a surprised worm to safety, and when I turned back, there was a pair of heavy winter boots standing on the far side of the hole.

The boots might have belonged to anybody. The bare legs above them, the calves roughly wrapped in sheepskin against the cold, could mean only one thing.

I did not breathe. I did not even blink. My heart thudded in my chest. Above me, a man cleared his throat.

For a moment, the sound of familiar words gave me courage to look up. The man standing with the three soldiers was one of us. Then I heard his southern accent, and the hope faded. He was from another tribe, there to help his Roman friends deal with the troublesome Iceni.

"What is your name?" he said again, speaking for them. Romans never bothered to learn any tongue but their own.

I had a name. I knew I had a name. Now, of all times, it had chosen to hide from me.

One of the soldiers said something, and they all laughed.

You be careful out there.

"Ria!" I remembered.

"Ria," he said, as if he were testing it to see if it were a lie.

One of the soldiers spoke again, and the southerner said, "The officer wants to know if you have lost something."

Everything.

I tried to think what I might have lost in the ground in someone else's paddock. Nothing came to mind. Every part of me was trembling, and my legs burned from the strain of kneeling at this angle.

"This land is imperial property. Looting on imperial property is a serious offense."

I said, "I came to find news of my aunt."

"And what did the worms tell you?" The southerner was enjoying himself.

The soldier in charge said something to him. My Latin is only good for the marketplace, but it sounded as though the southerner was being scolded for speaking his own thoughts.

The officer's thoughts were that if this was my aunt's land, and there was something buried here, then perhaps my family was guilty of withholding assets from the imperial authorities.

"Hiding the goodies," the southerner added, in case I was too stupid to understand how much trouble I was in. "Or are you hiding illegal weapons?"

I hadn't thought of that.

"The officer says you can keep digging."

Praying there were no weapons here, I scraped and scooped the cold earth with my bare hands while the four men watched. At least it was a chance to move. The pain in my legs eased. The fear did not.

My fingertips stubbed against a smooth surface. I cleared more of the mud away and saw oiled wood. The officer gave an order to his men, and the southerner told me to get out of the way.

They hauled the box out. When I said I had no key, one of them broke the lock open with his knife. I caught a glint of silver inside, but they snapped it shut before I could get a proper look. Whatever it was, they seemed pleased with it.

They were making me carry it to the gate when a new voice called across from the track by the ruined house, "Ho! Optio!"

The gray-headed figure on the horse was Eisu, the Iceni trader from near the fort who had come to the Great Hall yesterday with a gift of three ponies. He used to visit the Great Hall whenever my father had Roman guests who might pay well for horses, and he spoke Latin with ease. Listening to him now, I understood, "What have you found?" but after that, the words ran by too fast.

The officer seemed to know him. From the way they were looking at me as they spoke, I wondered if they wanted to trade me, too. Then Eisu said, "Give them the box, girl."

I was glad to hand it over.

He said, "The officer thanks you for finding the money this treacherous family tried to hide, but he wants you to know that from now on his men will do their own searching."

He was *thanking* me? I looked from one to the other of them and tried to make sense of it.

"Clear off," said the southerner.

Still covered in mud, I raced for the Great Hall before they could change their minds.

I had not gone far when I heard the thud of hoof beats growing louder behind me. There was open grazing on one side of the path and the river on the other: nowhere to hide. I turned. Eisu drew his horse to a halt and looked down at me.

"Whatever you know," he said, "or you think you know, you will keep all of it to yourself. Is that clear?"

I nodded.

"Swear before Andraste."

Swearing was not difficult. I did not know why he had stepped in to save me, but I never wanted to speak of this afternoon ever again. It was not until he was riding away that I remembered to shout, "Thank you!" but I don't think he heard.

I washed off the mud as best I could, but I forgot the laundry. As I stumbled in past the gates, Verico grabbed me by the arm. "What happened to you?"

"Soldiers," I gasped, breathless from the running.

His yell of "Soldiers!" was so loud it made me jump. There were echoes of "Soldiers!" all around us, and then the high wail of the alarm horn.

He said, "Where?"

I shook my head. "Gone now."

Verico swore and yelled, "Too late!" and someone shouted, "What?" and Verico shouted back, "False alarm!"

The horn gave the three blasts that told of safety, and all the people who had run out of the houses inside the enclosure turned to go back inside, and all the people outside who were rushing for the shelter of the gates stopped and gathered to talk instead. I prayed the horse trader would keep silent about saving me. I did not want to guess what would happen if word got out that the laundry slave had revealed hidden Iceni money to the Romans.

Verico turned to me. "Weren't you doing some laundry?"

"I dropped it in the river, running from the soldiers."

He dragged me to one side and reached behind the open gate. Then he brought out the bundle I had hidden in the reeds and held it up in front of me. "Something you want to tell me, Ria?"

I shook my head.

"I'll find out," he promised. "Remember that next time you think about running to Duro to complain about me."

I was afraid of more questions about the soldiers, but back in the courtyard, the slave-master just looked me up and down and said, "Go and wash." I did my best to become invisible again and prayed that was the end of it.

WINTER is always hard: first for the weak and the sick and then, as the stores run low, for the rest. Some of the tribe were poor now for the first time in their lives, and the bite of hunger and cold was sharpened for everyone by knowing that the fort half a day's walk away held enough stolen Iceni grain to feed five hundred men for a year. Andecarus, the sleek-plaited son of Duro's who had been fostered by the Romans, was sent back and forth on his smart horse to plead with the commander, but he never came back with anything more than words, and there were those who said he only went there to get himself a good meal. I thought they were unfair but said nothing. I was doing my best to be invisible.

I was avoiding Verico because I was afraid of him, and the Romans because we all knew they were vicious and dangerous, and my older sister because there were days when she would snap at the smallest fault. Andecarus must have noticed the difference in her, too: she had a grim set of the mouth that had not been there before, and although I saw her watching as he came and went, the warmth of her welcome was gone. She trained harder than before with Duro and the other fighters, and everyone pretended not to hear the clash of forbidden swords coming from the warriors' house.

The little mouse was paler and quieter than ever and vomiting every day. She must have understood why, and I grieved for her, but the slave-master told us we were all to mind our own business. So I cleaned up after her and pretended not to hear the worried conversations between her mother and the birthing-women, and I thanked the gods—and the charm I had bought from one of those women—that I wasn't in the same state after Verico's "comforting." He was still bothering me, his horrible hands grabbing and fondling whenever I sidled past, and I dreamed of killing him before he could go any further—but the truth is that I dared not even complain. All I could do was duck into the shadows whenever I saw his big swaggering shape and never be caught alone.

I kept my eyes open for Eisu, hoping to offer him the thanks I still owed him for saving me from the Romans—and to beg him not to mention my failed treasure hunt to any of our people. But whenever he came on business with his ponies, Duro and Verico always greeted him like an old friend and went about everywhere with him, and I dared not approach him in their presence. So I had to hope he knew I was grateful without me saying so.

I gave up all hope of ever seeing the brooches. It was sad to have nothing from my father, but my present troubles were eclipsing the shame of what had happened in the storehouse, and I saw now that no amount of jewelry would ever be a comfort to my sisters.

Meanwhile, the queen was more and more in control. That would not have surprised my mother, who always said she behaved as if she had been chosen queen in her own right instead of just being the wife of a king. First, she ruled from her bed, with Duro and the other elders gathered in council around her, deciding how the remaining food and firewood and blankets should be guarded and shared. Later, she hauled herself into the carved chair where my father used to sit—not the backless Roman chair given to client kings; they had snatched that one back from us— and made the speech about how thieves and secret hoarders were our enemies and should be reported and punished.

That was what she wanted the emperor's spies to report: a woman organizing food. Did they not see how she was placing herself as protector of the people? Did they never wonder why so many traders came and went through the worst of the weather that winter to do business in a Great Hall where nobody had money to spend anymore? Did it not strike them that if you can organize food, you can organize anything? But Romans do not think like we do. I know for a fact that there are Romans who think every beehive is under the control of a King Bee. They would rather believe a male can lay eggs than accept that a female can be in charge.

Besides, they never had the benefit of growing up with my mother, who had learned even before I was born how unwise it was to cross That Woman.

The truth of that became clear to everyone just after the first lambs had been born to shiver through the tail end of winter. A hungry boy and his father were caught stealing a very small sack of oats. The queen had them brought before the elders in the Great Hall and then had both father and son marched into the woods and beheaded there amongst the white anemones. I heard she wept at their deaths, but the heads were still put on poles outside the gates.

There were not many reports of theft after that.

I had sworn before the gods not to reveal whatever I knew or thought I knew, and I tried not to wonder exactly what the secrets were that Eisu thought I might betray. About him? About hidden hoards of treasure? But trying not to think about something just makes it sing louder in your ear, and as the days went by, there were more and more things I began to think I knew.

Perhaps because I was always on the alert for Verico, I noticed how many new warriors seemed to appear and disappear. The rasp of saws seemed especially loud on the east wind, and the clang of the smiths began at dawn and carried on past the ends of the short days. They must have had a ferocious number of broken carts and tools to fix.

I would not reveal what I thought I knew, but I feared that now that my father was gone, his people were being led into exactly the kind of conflict he had tried to avoid. The queen's revenge was going to be beyond anything any of us had imagined.

Andecarus still rode his smart cavalry mare back and forth to the fort, bringing orders from the prefect, but I could not imagine what he was telling them in return. It was obvious they were not expecting trouble. Their vehicles traveled lightly guarded and unhindered. Their road patrols still barged everybody else aside, and I heard that their foraging parties wandered out from the fort collecting firewood as if they were taking a stroll. Every few days, their centurions took groups of legionaries out on what they called "routine training runs" that gave them the chance to snoop around the countryside.

They still sent soldiers to watch what used to be the market, although it was now more of a sharing-out of food stores. One damp morning after the worst of the frosts were over, I had just come out of the weaver's with a length of wool for my younger sister's new tunic when one of them stepped up far too close and looked to see what was in my basket. "Very nice, love," he said in Latin slow enough for me to understand, and blocked my path. "I like a girl in blue."

The thought of a man like this going anywhere near the little mouse made me want to vomit just like she did. I pretended not to understand, and he said it again more clearly, pointing at the cloth and then at me with a broad smile over his stinky breath. Then he glanced at his comrades, who were watching from across the street, before he pointed to himself and then to me and said, "Friend? What is 'friend' in Iceni?"

I told him. He repeated it. Then he reached under his cloak and held out an apple. It sat in his callused palm looking shriveled and yellowish and bruised and wonderful. I had not eaten since the night before.

"No, thank you." I pushed it away, looking around for someone to help, but the weaver had gone back into his workshop, and nobody else seemed to be watching.

The soldier shoved the apple back in front of me. "For you."

"No!" Since I could not move forward, I stepped back and then around him. To my relief, he did not try and stop me, although he called out something, and all his comrades laughed. Perhaps he really was trying to be friends. But I knew better than to trust a man, and besides, we Iceni were past friendship. We were what they called "pacified."

I had no trouble believing the stories of Romans waving loaves of bread at hungry children so they could watch them beg. Nor those of women who offered themselves to soldiers to get extra food for their families. Perhaps their officers did not know. Perhaps they thought our women did not mind. More likely, though, the official line from the Great Hall—*no reprisals*—suited them so nicely that it never occurred to them to wonder at the strength of will that held us back. The will, mostly, of one woman.

IT was a few days later and very early in the morning when the queen shooed everyone out of the Great Hall and told to us stay out. In case we had other ideas, she had two warriors stationed outside. Even my older sister was not allowed in, although the younger one remained. We all understood why when one of the birthing-women hurried past the guards carrying a covered basket, and we heard the door-bar drop behind her.

I watched Princess Sorcha go out with Duro and some of the other elders, two of them moving gracefully beneath the antler headdresses they wore when they made special offerings. I too spoke prayers for my little mouse sister while I was smoothing the linens. There was no way to do what the birthing-women were trying to do that was not dangerous.

The sound of chanting drifted in from the woods for a long time, but when it was over, the door was of the Great Hall was still barred.

It was still barred at midday when Andecarus arrived. I was sitting on a bench by what was left of the woodpile, scraping dried mud off a pair of trousers in the hope of brushing them clean. My older sister was doing what the cook used to tell me off for— standing in the opening of the cooking-house door so she got the warm air from the hearth behind her and a good view of the courtyard in front while everyone else inside had to put up with the cold draught. She was pretending to be busy sharpening her knife, but every few moments she paused to put one hand on the little bronze figure of a boar strung around her neck, and I knew she was thinking of the hidden battle being waged behind the doors of the Great Hall.

We both stopped what we were doing to watch as Andecarus leaped down from his big chestnut mare and threw the reins to one of the boys. The horse's coat was dark with sweat, and there were flecks of foam around its mouth.

Andecarus ran to the doors of the Great Hall. When the guards blocked his way, he hurried over to the warriors' quarters instead.

Within moments, the yelling started. People paused to listen as it got louder. Andecarus and Verico. Some of the onlookers shouted encouragement, mostly for Verico.

The warriors were always having fights. By the next day, they'd usually sobered up and forgotten what they were arguing about. But this was broad daylight, and Andecarus could have fitted twice into his foster brother. Besides, he was steady and quiet by nature, not a brawling bully like Verico. My sister rushed across the yard as if she expected to drag them apart herself, and I ran after her.

The two men were circling each other like fighting dogs, each one gauging who would make the first move.

Duro had to yell both their names more than once before they took any notice of him. When they were finally listening, he said, "Our Princess Keena is sick and in need of rest, and I will not have her disturbed!"

He ordered both sons indoors as if they were ten winters old and then seized Princess Sorcha by the arm and walked her back across the yard with me beside her. She did not look very pleased about it.

"Your mother asked me to protect you," he told her, ignoring the muffled shouts from inside the warriors' quarters.

"I don't need protecting from our own men!"

I thought, Then you are lucky.

Duro should have known better than to cross That Woman's daughter, though, because as soon as he hurried back to deal with the argument, she said, "Ria. You bed that Verico, no?"

Who had told her that? "Not willingly, mistress."

She looked surprised, as if it had not struck her before that a slave might not have the choices a free woman enjoyed. "Well, anyway, they're used to seeing you around. Go and find out what's happening. Mother needs good warriors. We can't have them killing each other."

That sounded like something else I wasn't supposed to know. Because why does the queen of a tribe that has been *pacified* have such dire need of good warriors? I shoved the thought out of my head because it just meant more trouble for me and went obediently to be Sorcha's eyes and ears.

I never liked going into the warriors' house even when Verico wasn't there: the skulls of old enemies nailed up over the door made me shiver. But my sister was right about everyone being used to seeing me; when I wandered in with a couple of blankets to put on the shelf, nobody took any notice at all. I slipped behind a wicker partition and sat on the end of someone's bed in the dark, trembling at the thought of what would happen if Verico caught me in here. At the moment, he was too busy shouting at his foster brother, "What's wrong with them drowning in a bog?"

"Why would they be in a bog if they were looking for firewood?"

"They weren't looking for bloody firewood!"

"Boys!" Duro cried. "Boys! Enough!"

There was a moment's silence, and I decided that whoever slept in this bed needed to wash his feet more often.

"We know they weren't looking for firewood." Andecarus' voice was lower now. "And the prefect must know that we know. But that's the official line he's given me." He paused. "If I'd been told about this as soon as it happened, and if this fool and his pals had had the sense to make it look like an accident—"

"We're past that now," put in Duro.

"Yes," Andecarus agreed. "Now I have to give the prefect a story that explains how two of his men disappeared while they were out foraging. Even though we all know they were snooping around for weapons. It has to make so much sense that the prefect doesn't ask any more questions. Like, *Where are they now?* And, *Which of your people did it?*"

"No." Duro again. "You don't. There is nothing to explain if they don't find the bodies."

"They won't." Verico sounded proud of it.

Andecarus said, "Then it doesn't matter what I tell him. They'll keep searching."

"The question they're looking to answer," said Duro, "is how two men went out of the fort yesterday afternoon and never came back. And the only answer you can give them is, *we don't know.*"

"Never saw them," said Verico. "Tell them we'll help them to look if they want."

"I can tell you what they'll want," said Andecarus. "They'll want hostages. And then they'll set the questioners to work on them. Have you *seen* Roman questioners in action?"

"My lads are staunch," Verico said. "They won't talk."

Andecarus sighed and said, "You tell him," and it was left to Duro to explain that when the soldiers came, they would arrest anyone they fancied. Not just Verico's lads.

"It's a mess," said Andecarus.

"Oh, right," Verico said. "So tell us what you'd have done when they stopped a cart full of weapons, then? You with the fancy training and the—"

"Enough!" Even Duro was tiring of Verico now.

Andecarus said, "Does the queen know what's happened?"

Duro said, "The queen's busy."

"For how long?"

"As long as it takes the birthing-women to get rid of that Roman bastard inside the princess," Verico told him.

Andecarus swore quietly. Then he muttered something else I couldn't catch. Duro said, "What?"

"Deserters," Andecarus repeated. "We make the prefect think his men have deserted."

Verico snorted. "You think he'll believe that, coming from us?"

"Roman soldiers run off just like anybody else's," Andecarus assured them. "Eisu can go to the fort and complain that he's had two horses stolen."

Verico said, "*Eisu?*" as if he were the last person who should be asked. "One of us'll have to go with him."

Duro said, "If they think he's lying . . ."

"They won't." Andecarus was sounding happier now. "They know him; he's traded horses with them for years. Anyway, he'll be telling the truth. We can slip across and take a couple of ponies ourselves. It'll look as if the men hid out overnight and took off today."

They were still talking, but I was not listening. I was thinking about the way Verico had said, *Eisu?* I was remembering a wet afternoon and seeing Eisu's horse splashing away through the puddles on the track. Duro and Verico had been standing side by side in the gateway, watching the figure huddled in the winter cloak until he was out of sight.

At the time, I had thought they must be sorry to see their friend leave. But now I thought again about the way he was never left to wander about the royal enclosure alone, and I knew I had been wrong. What they felt for Eisu was not friendship. And I knew, hiding away on the smelly bed behind the wicker partition, that I had found out something I really, really did not want to know. That Duro and Verico didn't trust the horse trader, but they didn't want to say so in front of Andecarus.

The meaning of *whatever you know, or you think you know, you will keep all of it to yourself,* was shifting in ways that I did not understand. I only knew that the gloom of the warriors' house suddenly seemed much darker than before.

The men must have reached some sort of agreement. The talk had ended, and I heard the soft tread of boots on the mud floor. I kept very still as they passed on the other side of the wicker, then the door rattled and crashed shut, and whoever it was had gone.

Beyond the partition, there was a creak and a sigh as if someone was settling into a chair. Duro said, "From now on, we don't move weapons in daylight."

"The stuff had to be shifted fast," Verico told him. "The prefect's men have been sniffing around like they know where to look. Someone's talking."

"I still can't believe it's Eisu."

"There's nobody else it can be," Verico said. "We know he's still doing business with the Romans."

I had seen Eisu doing business with the Romans. He had done it to save me. It was exactly the sort of thing my father had done for years, and it had kept men like these safe so they could plot and practice and brag about what they would do if only they had the chance.

Duro sighed again. "We used to go fishing together when we were boys."

I sat very still. The slightest movement would tell them they were not alone.

Duro said, "Andecarus will make sure he says what he's supposed to say and no more."

"After that, let me deal with him."

Duro said, "It's not so bad. He can't have told them much."

Verico said, "Yet."

The silence lasted for several breaths. Finally, I heard that *oof* noise that old people make when they get up out of a chair, and Duro said, "You're right, it has to be done. Make it quick. And make it tidy."

"Don't worry," Verico told him. "It'll be a tragic accident."

They both went outside. I watched through a crack in the door for a very long time until it was safe to slip out after them. I had heard things I should not have heard, and I was very much afraid that I had understood them.

PRINCESS Sorcha must have been waiting for me because she hurried across to meet me in the middle of the yard where nobody could hear us but a couple of pack ponies.

"No news," she said before I could ask, glancing over to where another of the birthing-women was hurrying toward the Great Hall. "Well?"

I had no idea how much was safe to tell her. "Two Roman soldiers went missing yesterday, mistress. The prefect wants them back, but we don't know anything about them."

"Of course not. Mother's told everyone to leave the soldiers alone. No reprisals. So what were they arguing about?"

"Verico says he doesn't know anything, and Andecarus doesn't believe him."

"Why not?"

"Because Verico is a filthy lying bastard and nobody should listen to a word he says, mistress."

The expression on her face reminded me of her mother. I hoped she would say something like *I shall ask Duro to make him leave you alone,* but she didn't. It was as I deserved. I had not tried to rescue her; she did not try to rescue me.

I was saved from further questions by a cry from the Great Hall. A young girl, in pain.

The princess leaned against the nearest pony and curled her fingers into its mane. She said, "I have prayed so hard that my sister will live."

"And I have prayed that the men who hurt her will die very slowly," I told her.

"Yes." She bowed her head until it was resting on the pony's neck. "I would rather it had been me who had to endure this."

I would rather it had been her as well because she was much tougher than her sister, but I could not say so, so I said that I wished it had been me, too. For a moment, as we stood together beside the ponies, I wondered if this was what it felt like to be proper sisters. Then she lifted her head and said, "Do you not have work to do, Ria?" and the moment was gone.

I must have brushed the same pair of trousers a hundred times, trying to tell myself that I had misunderstood what was said between Duro and Verico in the warriors' house. And that even if I had not, the fate of the horse trader was none of my business. No matter how mad and dangerous That Woman's plans might be, anyone who betrayed our people to the soldiers was even worse. And had I not sworn before Andraste that I would not reveal anything I knew?

But . . . surely that vow did not include anything I had found out later? And besides, Eisu, a man I barely knew and who had no reason to show me kindness, had saved me from the soldiers when nobody at the Great Hall had ever offered to help me, even though they knew I had been wronged. There were many good reasons to do nothing, but that one act weighed heavier in the balance. Whatever else he had done, the horse trader had saved me.

So I watched Andecarus and a couple of the other warriors ride out, and I waited because I supposed they were going to sneak across the fields and steal Eisu's horses, and then it would take awhile for him to ride to the fort and report them stolen, and I knew Verico would not harm him before he had done that. There was time.

I walked out of the gates carrying a basket filled with hanks of spun wool to deliver to the weaver, but Verico was not around to care. At first, I walked calmly along beside the river, basket in hand. Not looking suspicious at all. Then I began to worry that I would be too late. In the end, I ran as if a troop of Roman cavalry were chasing me, and by the time I got there, I was only fit to hang on to the gate and gasp and thank the gods that Eisu was there in front of me, alive and well and busy working.

He was training a gray pony to the long rein, standing in the middle of the paddock with it running in a circle around him. "Trot! And whoa, and canter! And whoa. Good boy!"

With the animal and the man working so calmly together, it seemed unthinkable for a slave to interrupt. And then I remembered how Duro had said, "Make it quick," and I got my breath back and shouted, "Eisu! Sir!" until both pony and man were so distracted that he had to give up and bring it to a halt.

"Eisu! Sir! It's Ria, the laundry slave from the Great Hall!"

"Ria?"

I glanced around to make sure there was nobody listening, glad that the paddock was set well away from the house. "Did you go fishing with Duro when you were a boy?"

"What?"

"I need to know, sir!" I needed to hear the word "no," and then I could decide I had made a mistake and run all the way back again, leaving him thinking I was just a mad washerwoman who had escaped from her keepers.

The word I heard was, "Sometimes."

"Verico and his men are coming to kill you," I told him. "They think you are a spy."

His face turned gray. Then he started to gabble. All the sorts of questions people ask when they want something not to be true, silly questions like, *Why should I believe you?* And, *Who told you? Are you sure? How can I leave the horses?*

"I was there when they said it! If you don't believe me, you will be leaving the horses whether you wish it or no."

He strode toward the pony, gathering up the reins in his gloved hands and tying them in a big bunch above the withers.

"You must go!" I urged him.

"So must you." He asked if I had run all the way, and when I said yes, he called over one of his men to take me back to the Great Hall on his pony cart.

I didn't look to see whether Eisu fled. To be truthful, I was past caring. I had repaid the favor I owed him, and now I just wanted to get back to doing the laundry and being invisible and not knowing anything I wasn't supposed to know.

We were halfway back to the Great Hall when Andecarus rode up behind us and drew alongside to chat to the driver about Eisu's missing horses. Seeing me, he leaned across and said, "Is there news of Princess Keena?"

To my shame, I had almost forgotten about her. I forgot about her again as we heard horses thundering along in our wake and Verico yelling, "Hey! Where is he?"

There were five of them. They spread out around us so that Andecarus was hemmed in against the cart.

"Where is he?" Verico leaned over and shoved his brother sideways. "What did you say to him?"

Andecarus straightened up and said coldly, "Where's who?"

"Fucking Eisu, who else? What did you say to him?"

I said, "He didn't—" but Andecarus spoke over me.

"Nothing. We reported the horses stolen, he went home, I stayed on to talk to the prefect."

I said, "He didn't—"

"Don't lie to me! You warned that fucking spy!" Verico made a grab for Andecarus' reins. The other hand went for his knife.

Andecarus kicked the chestnut mare forward, barging the other horses out of the way. I hung on to the bench as the cart lurched and the driver swore, and we nearly went into the ditch.

Ahead of us, Andecarus was galloping for the safety of the Great Hall. Verico and his men went after him in a blur of hooves and tails

I said, "We must go after them!" I knew Andecarus' horse was not fresh; she had already been ridden hard this morning.

"You're joking, love. You'll not catch them in this."

"If they catch him," I said, "they'll kill him."

We jolted and banged along through the puddles at a speed that the driver said would have the cart in bits and the animal lame, and what did I think this was, a bloody war chariot? But it was as well that we did. Andecarus had not made it to the Great Hall. He was curled up in a ball on the road by the time we got near, hands over his head, trying to fend off the boots and clubs of men who should have been ashamed of themselves. Perhaps they were, because as soon as Verico noticed the cart, he shouted, "Enough!"

They hauled him up. He hung between them like a dead man, his dark hair fallen over his face and blood dripping down between the stones. I stared in horror. *Andecarus.* Son of Duro and once the intended of the Princess Sorcha. Holy Andraste, what had I done now? I was the one who had warned Eisu, and Andecarus had been punished for it.

Verico took a couple of steps toward the cart, club raised. I had pulled my winter wrap over my head; now I lowered my gaze as if I was frightened. Which I was.

Verico said, "Stay out of this. He's being taken in for questioning."

"He's not looking too well," said the driver, as if this sort of thing happened every day. "I'm on the way to the Great Hall. Why don't you drop him in the back? Easier than carrying him."

Verico still hadn't recognized me. I dared not look up, but I could picture him with his mouth open, wondering what to do next now that he had been stupid enough to beat somebody up in the middle of the road—and not just anybody, but his foster father's real son. The son of the queen's trusted advisor. Perhaps now people would see what Verico was really like.

"He's a traitor," Verico spat.

"Best to put him under these," the driver offered, shifting on the bench, and I suppose showing him the jumble of empty sacks in the back of the cart. "In case we run into a road patrol."

Andecarus was still breathing when we set off, but we could not tend to him with Verico watching. When nobody else was looking, I managed to jump down with a mumbled excuse to the driver and run across the fields to the Great Hall, calling out that someone had to fetch the healers because there was a badly injured man arriving at any moment. When the cart pulled in, Andecarus was carried into the warriors' house. Nobody was allowed to follow except Duro and the healers.

One good thing happened that day: although the little mouse looked paler than ever when I saw her lying beside the fire, she had survived whatever potion they tipped into her. The invader growing inside her had not.

Andecarus, too, survived. But his foster brother was not exposed as a vicious brute. Instead, morning brought the news that Andecarus was to be taken before the queen and the elders and tried for treason.

IT was always gloomy in the Great Hall, even when the doors were open, and this morning they were shut and guarded. I only got in by telling the guards I was wanted as a witness in Andecarus' trial. Inside, by the light of a thin fire—it was good that the days would soon be warming into spring because there was almost no wood left—I saw the queen sitting tall in the carved chair, surrounded by the soft shapes of furs, and on her neck the golden torc I had thought was stolen by the Romans, and which must have been safely hidden, after all. Around her, the elders' faces were pale and serious. Duro looked as if he had been carved out of ice. Verico and his pals were standing to one side in front of the wall hangings. At first, I could not make out Andecarus. Then I realized he was the shape on the floor. They were going to kill him if I did not speak.

They were going to kill me if I did.

Knowing that you will be in the next world very soon makes you surprisingly bold, even if you dread the pain of the journey. I had never known what it was to be free, but I felt it as I stepped over Andecarus' body and stood facing the queen across the fire. I was not afraid now. Not of Verico, not even of the—well, perhaps of the Romans. But I was no longer afraid of That Woman. She had punished my mother for my father's lust, she had kept me in slavery to my sisters, and she had brought us to the brink of starvation and the point where we were killing each other instead of the Romans. I would no longer do her bidding. She saw it in my eyes as I stood before her and declared, "Andecarus is innocent. The one who warned the spy was me."

BOLDNESS does not thrive in the cold and dark. That night, I shivered in the empty storehouse, feeling for the first time the hated weight of a slave collar around my neck. I tried not to think about what had happened to my sisters the last time I lay cowering on this floor, nor about how the queen was going to have me killed. I would be an example to everyone, like the food thieves executed in the woods, but I could not expect the mercy of a swift sword. Betrayal was much worse than theft.

Even my little flash of courage was nothing to boast of. I would have been found out anyway. My elder sister would have told her mother that I had been eavesdropping in the warriors' house. If they asked Eisu's driver, he would say I had been to visit his master. Duro, doing his best to save his son, would say that Andecarus had not been there when the spy was discussed. Confessing was not a brave act. It was just walking forward into the approaching storm.

When faint gray began to show around the outline of the door, I felt the insides of my empty belly shrivel even smaller. I closed my eyes tight shut, but I could still hear the birds singing in the new day. Then came the rattle of the latch and rough hands dragging me up from the straw.

SHE was sitting in the carved chair again, but the elders were gone. The space where Andecarus had been lying was empty. I stood before her, my head bowed, my neck clamped in the iron collar that was a mocking echo of her golden torc.

"Daughter of Prasutagus."

My head jerked up. She had never called me that that before.

"I knew from before you were born that you would cause trouble."

Her eyes glittered in the firelight. I did not lower my gaze. I had not asked to be born.

"I tried to have your mother sent away, but my husband the king did not like to make harsh decisions."

My father had insisted I should be brought up at the Great Hall. He could not have known how much easier life would have been for all three of his daughters if we had been ordinary people rather than the children of a king.

"And now one of our best young men lies injured. Because of you."

I told her I was sorry for what had happened to Andecarus. It was true.

"What shall I do with you?"

I swallowed. There was no good answer to that question.

"I have spent much time thinking about what sort of punishment you deserve."

So had I. I doubted I had enjoyed it as much as she had. Hide away inside yourself until it's over. It feels like it will never end, but it does.

"So," she said, shifting in the chair as if she were tired and stiff, "you have a choice."

What will it be like in the next world? Will I—"What?"

"A choice," she repeated. "You can swear loyalty to me in front of the gods and make it your task to tend the man who was falsely accused of your treachery. If he dies, you die. If he lives, you will have your freedom when he returns to the ranks of our warriors."

Freedom? Had she really said—

"Or you can die this morning and join your mother in the next world. Out of respect for your father, and for no other reason, I will tell my men to make it swift." She sat back in the chair. "It makes no difference to me which you choose."

Freedom?

"One breath of betrayal and you will be dead either way."

I swallowed. I was having trouble standing upright.

"So, Ria, daughter of Prasutagus. Make your choice."

I hated the slave collar, and I hated the laundry, and I hated having to sit spooning broth into the unshaven and understandably not-very-grateful Andecarus, but it was better than being dead with my head on a pole.

Nobody was speaking to me. Apart from Andecarus, who babbled in his sleep, and to my surprise, my younger sister. She came in one sunny morning carrying a bowl of broth from the kitchen and announced, "My sister says I'm not allowed to talk to you, Ria."

"Thank you, mistress." I took the bowl of broth and blew on it. "I am glad to see you looking better." In truth, she did not look a great deal better. She might be up and about again, but she still had her mouse-like scuttle, and her eyes were shadowed and unsmiling. She jumped at the smallest noises and avoided almost everyone she met.

Except me, it seemed. She seemed to be worried about me. "People are saying neither you nor Andecarus can be trusted."

"I have sworn to follow the queen, mistress."

She peered at Andecarus. "Poor man. Is he very ill?" Keena was more interested in the healer's arts than the warrior's, and I was glad to see a flare of her old self as she looked over Andecarus' injuries.

"The healers say he was lucky nothing was broken, but he was hit on the head and bruised all over, and his knee is badly wrenched."

"Luci from the cooking-house told me that the cook says you and Andecarus are two traitors who deserve each other."

I smiled. "The cook will never have any secrets while Luci is around."

Keena put a hand on my arm. "Was it really all your fault, Ria?"

"Yes, mistress."

"You must feel very bad when you see him like that."

"Yes. I am trying to make amends by nursing him."

Andecarus stirred. Even a little motion like that made Keena jump to her feet. "I have to go now."

I said, "I'll tell him you were here."

"I told my sister she should come and see him, but she won't." Keena shook her head. "She doesn't trust anyone who deals with the Romans."

It seemed unfair, but I never did understand my older sister.

I was looking at my patient and wondering whether to wake

him while the food was hot and whether I could steal some by dipping one finger in to test the warmth when Andecarus said,

"Why does the cook think I'm a traitor?"

I noticed he did not mention Princess Sorcha. "You were awake?"

"Answer the question."

"You're an Iceni who speaks Latin in your sleep," I told him. "That's enough."

His hand went to the swollen side of his jaw. "So it would seem."

I said, "I am truly sorry. I did not know Verico would blame you."

He winced, trying to ease himself up in the bed. I lifted his head and moved the pillow.

When he was settled, he said, "What did I say I in my sleep?"

"I don't know." And then, without thinking, "Was Eisu really a spy?"

"Probably," he said and opened his mouth for the spoon.

Probably.

I spent a long time wondering whether *probably* made it better or worse. The gray pony I had last seen on the long reins was in amongst the new horses grazing in the paddock. I wondered where Eisu was now, and whether, if he was still alive, his life had been worth what had happened to Andecarus.

You do a lot of wondering when hardly anybody will talk to you. I wondered if I would ever get my freedom, and if I did, where I would go and whether anybody would want me. I wondered why the queen had shown me mercy. Wondered if perhaps I had been wrong about her. Wondered whether she was right when she said that my father *did not like to make harsh decisions*. He had tried to pacify the Romans, putting up with their arrogance and their interference, and look how it had ended. He would never have had that hungry boy and his father put to death for stealing oats. And perhaps the stealing would have carried on until some people were fat and a whole lot more were dead from starvation. Maybe, if you looked through the eyes of our queen, the world was a very different place from the one you thought you understood.

WITHIN a couple of weeks, quite a few people had started talking to me again, if only to get the right clothes back from the washing. If they suspected me of muddling them on purpose, they couldn't prove it. In any case, most of them had more important things on their minds. I was surely not the only one who dreamed of food and woke hungry and disappointed. As we tightened our belts and dreamed of the sweet fruit that would one day come from the early spring blossoms, the regular sight of well-fed Roman soldiers stung like an insult.

The princesses were both looking stronger now, and although the queen was still pale, I was sure that was more from her travels after dark than from the wounds of the flogging.

No one ever talked about where she went at night with Duro and her other advisors or what they did when they got there. I guessed they took paths through thick woods and across the wetlands, where a horse and rider who strayed off the path could sink without trace, and where the Romans only dared venture in daylight. The queen was never gone for long, but Duro and some of the other elders disappeared for days. Then suddenly they would be back, as if they had never been away.

Every sunrise, the sounds of chanting rose louder from the woods, and every day more merchants and messengers came to the Great Hall. Even the Romans couldn't fail to notice.

They spoke about it to Andecarus when the queen sent him to ask whether we would be allowed to hold the spring gatherings this year. He told the Romans we were chanting prayers for the food to last out and that travel was easier for the traders now that the weather had improved. Besides, he said, if you will keep building roads, you must expect people to use them.

I know this because not long after he got back, he came and stood in the steamy air around the linen tub and told me. I wasn't sure why. At first, I thought it was because he was proud of his reply. Then I wondered whether he was not sure he had given the right answer, and he was waiting for me to say that he had done well. Then I saw how silly that was: a warrior asking the opinion of a slave. If he wanted an opinion, he would have gone to his father or maybe to the queen. I decided it was because he was worried, and he needed to tell somebody who didn't matter and wouldn't pass it on.

So I spoke of things slaves are allowed to talk about and said, "How is your knee?" I was sure he no longer needed the support of the stick, and it was just a good excuse to keep away from the other warriors.

He said, "Painful."

"Really?" I carried on swishing the linens around with a long wooden spoon. "Did the queen tell you that when it is healed and you join the warriors again, I will have my freedom?"

He looked at me as if I had promised him a honeycomb and handed him a wasp's nest.

"Don't worry," I told him. "I shan't tell them."

"Tell them what?"

"That your knee is fine."

"No, it isn't—"

"Really?" I raised my eyebrows. "Then you need to limp all the time, not just when you think people are looking."

He grinned. "It's not entirely true that you can't be trusted, is it?"

I banged the spoon on the side of the cauldron. "It is mostly," I admitted. "But I'm trying to improve. Why don't you want to go back to the warriors?" I wished he would. I wanted my freedom, even though I was not sure what I would do with it. Not laundry, for certain. Perhaps I would learn to weave or grow vegetables or find a husband—or all three. Perhaps Verico would finally get the message to go away.

"The warriors all want vengeance against Rome," Andecarus said. "They don't understand what it will mean. Nobody bloody listens. I keep telling them the Romans aren't fools. They're mounting extra patrols. This game can't go on much longer."

"No," I said, thinking of the queen's night travels and the hidden weapons and all the unexplained visitors. "It can't."

Andecarus studied me. "At least somebody around here has their feet on the ground."

I much preferred his company to that of his foster brother, but now I wished he would either go away or talk about something else. You never knew who might be listening, and the queen was a woman who kept her word. She had offered me freedom. She had threatened me with execution for the least breath of betrayal.

She had also promised her people the vengeance Andecarus dreaded.

SOME mornings, I watched the Romans tramp past on their patrols, and I marveled at their confidence—they seemed to have no idea how much danger they were in. Then another day, I would catch one of our warriors picking his nose, and I felt a jolt of terror about what was going to happen to all of us when we were caught.

With ten days to go, the Roman prefect decided that groups of no more than thirty might be allowed to meet for the spring gathering as long as things remained peaceful beforehand. How they ever imagined they could control the numbers, I don't know. They never had the chance to try.

I dreamed I heard chariots in the night: the creak of harness and the stamp and shuffle of impatient ponies. The rumble of iron wheel rims on cobble gradually fading into—

A sudden rush of cold as the blanket was whipped away, and a voice cried, "Up!" and then groans of complaint and someone saying, "It's still dark."

"Up!" The slap of a hand on flesh. "Work to do!"

There was always work to do, but not like this. As I groped about for my boots, I heard the scrape and swish of bedding being dragged across the floor. People were moving beds and making space as if we were expecting to be overwhelmed with guests, but the ripping of old linen into bandages told a different story. So did the position of a heavy table near the light of the door and the sight of the healer sitting on it, sharpening his surgical knives.

Someone had built up the fire from the embers, and my younger sister was sitting beside it, rolling bandages along her knee. There was a bowl of what looked like porridge uneaten beside her, but when I urged her to try it, she said she wasn't hungry. Princess Sorcha and the queen were nowhere to be seen.

After all the activity in the house, the yard was strangely silent. The only men of the tribe I could see were two sentries standing lookout on the bank above the gates, their oval shields stark against the dawn sky. I squinted into the gray light, but no matter how hard I looked and listened, there were no men clumping about the yard as they usually did. The ponies really were gone, just as I had heard in my sleep, and as I looked again at the two men above the gates, I saw the lines of forbidden swords at their sides.

I felt oddly calm. Maybe others felt the same; we barely spoke as we cleared space to lay out the wounded warriors who were clearly expected. Whatever fate awaited us, we were powerless to do anything about it.

Well, almost.

"Buckets," said the slave-master, grabbing my wrist and beckoning two more slaves as he led us outside. I gazed up into what was turning into a bright and clear morning.

"Every bucket you can find," he said, and I guessed he had only just remembered this part of his instructions. "Tip out whatever's in them unless it's water." He indicated the porch of the Great Hall. "I want this barrel filled and at least eight full buckets of water along here, but not where somebody's going to fall over them. Then four outside each of the smaller houses. Quickly."

We hurried across the courtyard from the cooking-house, empty buckets swinging in each hand. Usually at this hour the gates were open, but today one of the lookouts on the bank above had to signal to the two below to lift the bar.

As one gate swung open, I gazed up into cloudless blue. Somewhere under that sky, our people were killing or being killed. Our queen. My older sister, too—the thought of a sword piercing that perfect pale skin made me shudder. Duro and Verico and—no, there was Andecarus, still supposedly only fit to drag the gate open—but so many of our people were out there somewhere, fighting for their lives. Fighting for us. And if things went as they had the last time our warriors took on the Romans . . .

My calm did not last. As the families from the houses outside the royal enclosure began to flock in for protection, I wanted to tell the slave-master that it was useless to fetch water. What was the point of sluicing the thatch if we couldn't defend the banks around us? We would all be trapped inside the houses, choking on the smoke and—

"Get a move on, girl!"

Don't think. Plunge the buckets in the river, stagger breathless back through the gates, splash the water into the barrel. Then run again, the three of us sticking close together without speaking, hoping that if the Romans came, Andecarus would hold the gate for us. Knowing that if we were too slow, he would have to slam it shut and leave us outside.

I was gasping and muddy and wet from trying to run with full buckets when there was a shout from one of the lookouts. They were both straining to see something to the north. Then cries of "Yes, yes!" and the first fighters came thundering back in, whooping and yelling, waving swords and spears and Roman helmets in the air. There were things bouncing against the side of the chariots that looked like—that were—human heads.

Everyone was out of the houses now. Running for the gates. Screaming and shouting, dragging our men down from their horses, embracing and kissing them. I said, "Where's the queen?" but nobody heard. I had never seen such joy on the faces of our people, and when the cook grabbed me and kissed me and whirled me around in a circle, I laughed and hugged her back. Above us, the guards up on the gates were stamping and chanting and lifting their arms up to the sky gods, and then everyone was joining in, and some of the riders fought their way free of the crowd and ran up to the top of the bank carrying the captured heads and making them dance, too.

Below them, the lone figure of Andecarus, the only man who understood how the Romans thought and planned and fought, had planted both hands flat against one of the gates and was straining to push it shut.

But his caution was not needed. Soon he had to open the gates again to the sounds of more triumph as Verico roared in with his men, battle-stained and jubilant. In the end, the gates stayed wide open, with a row of Roman heads on each side of them, looking out over the land they had thought they controlled.

There was no news of the queen. Verico and some of his men grabbed food and drink and rode out again, going north. The celebrations went a little quiet as the afternoon passed with no message. Then suddenly there were shouts of, "The queen! The queen!" and Boudica was cheered back in at the head of a great group of warriors, her hair wild and her chariot ponies dark with sweat. There was blood on her hands and on her clothes, but it was not her own. She, too, raised a sword in the air, and suddenly there was an eerie bellowing sound I had never heard before. For a moment, the people were hushed. Then the cheering started, even louder now, with the strange noise filling the air all around us.

I saw the red flash of my sister's hair below a helmet. There was rich crimson spattered on her clothes, and her smile was broader than I had ever seen it. Behind her, Duro's clothing was torn and stained, his eyes glistening with tears. I knew then that we were hearing a sound that had been silent for thirteen long years: the cry of the warriors' battle horn ringing out across the lands of the Iceni.

PEOPLE spoke later of other triumphs, but this was the one to be proud of. No one could say for sure if every Roman in Iceni territory was dead. Certainly, most were; few could have escaped when our warriors rose as one great army across the land. The soldiers had been outnumbered and caught completely unawares. There had been no chance to call for help; all the roads and likely escape routes had been blocked before dawn.

Less than half the spaces that had been cleared in the Great Hall for our wounded were needed, and while their dead were left as carrion, ours were brought home and honored beside the river on a great pyre made from the palisade of the fort many of them had helped to overrun. It was not our usual way to bid farewell to the dead, but the queen said these men would fly to the next world safely on the waft of smoke from the destroyed Roman fort.

Verico led the mourning for two of his men, and my cries of

anguish sounded no different from the others, although partly I was sorry Verico was not among those being sent to the next world in the flames.

Andecarus was standing alone on the other side of the pyre. When he saw me, he looked away. I wondered if he was glad that the men he visited at the fort were all dead now, possibly some of them at the hands of Princess Sorcha. And I wondered whether he feared that an Iceni who spoke Latin in his sleep, and who had not taken part in the fighting, might soon be sent to join them.

More people were streaming in to join us now. The queen must have been exhausted after battle, but she was still about after dark, going around to every camp fire and every new arrival, welcoming, questioning, and marveling at glory so great that already the singers were composing new verses to honor the names of the fighters. From what I managed to overhear, it seemed she knew people in every group that arrived.

"Sleep now," she urged them. "I shall begin the day with more good news, and you will want to tell your grandchildren you were there to hear it."

The slave-master was of the same mind: he went around trying to gather us up, ordering us to go back indoors and rest. But how could any of us rest with the Great Hall and the fields and tracks around it alive with campfires and music and dancing, and yet more people arriving throughout the night? Even if I had gone to lie down, how could I have slept?

It had been a great day. Tonight we were celebrating our just revenge with a lightness of spirit I had never seen among my people before. Yet only a fool could fail to see that the Romans would soon come looking for vengeance of their own.

A lot of nonsense has been passed on about the queen's words, much of it by Romans who were not there to hear them. I can remember little of what she said, but I can remember how I felt when she said it. As if the sun had suddenly burst into a house where we had all sat for too long huddled in the dark.

This much I do remember. Our queen said it as she stood on the earth mound of the ramparts around the Great Hall. My sisters were proud on each side of her, looking very different than the way they had looked a few months ago, huddled beside their stricken mother. I suppose she welcomed everybody and praised them and made us all feel proud of whatever we had done. She was good at that. And then she went on to remind us of the outrages we had suffered and to tell us we were not alone. And if these are not her exact words, they are something like them.

"Everyone has seen how we Iceni have chased the monster off our land. But we will not stop at our borders! We will not allow the Romans and their feeble emperor anywhere near us! My friends, the Trinovantes are allied with us, and others are following behind! Together, we have a mighty band of warriors who will chase the Roman monster all the way down its own road to its own lair, and when we get there . . ." We all strained to hear, eager not to miss her next words as she raised her spear toward the god of the skies. "We will take its head!"

The roar of approval was so loud I could not hear my own part in it, and then it settled into a chant of "Camulo-dunum! Camulo-dunum!" that must surely have been heard in the Temple of Claudius itself, four or five days' march away.

Up on the ramparts, the queen put down her spear and raised both hands for silence. "I have sought counsel from the elders," she declared. "I have visited the High Druid of all the tribes, and he has read the omens! This morning as I made sacrifice, the great Andraste gave me a sign to show you all."

We all fell silent, waiting. Suddenly, the fabric of her skirts shifted. Something leaped out from beneath them.

"A hare!"

"It's a hare!"

"Look at it run!"

"Look!"

The hare bounded along the ramparts as far as the gate, then ran down through the grass, and I lost sight of it.

"Where did it go?"

"Down that way, look!"

The queen turned to my older sister and asked her to tell the people what she had seen.

Princess Sorcha stood tall and shouted, "Andraste has sent a hare!" and the people at the front cheered.

She turned to the younger one. "Daughter, tell our people which way it ran."

Mouse-like Keena looked stunned, as if she had been caught daydreaming.

She looked at her mother, but her mother gave no guidance. She looked at me. I nodded, wishing her courage. She took a deep breath, lifted her left hand, and pointed down the road toward Camulodunum.

The roar of "Camulo-dunum!" erupted again. The mouse looked surprised and pleased at the effect she had had.

"Camulo-dunum!"

And so we set off.

I cannot imagine what it was like down in the Roman colony of Camulodunum over the next few days. I know that for us, those days were like a giant traveling celebration that grew bigger with every mile we marched.

Our army had no food supplies beyond the little that had lasted the winter, but as I said, our queen never did anything without thinking about it first. After they stormed the fort, they had raided the granary. All along the way, people flocked to the road to bring food and to march alongside us. Many of them stayed. Already whole families had come to support their fighters so that the numbers swelled beyond counting—thousands and then tens of thousands, they said. Winter was dead at last, the cold retreating more each day from the fickle warmth of spring— but this was a spring like no other. There had been few crops planted in Iceni lands this year—almost the entire tribe, or so it seemed to me, was pledged to sow vengeance rather than seed, to reap Roman lives rather than grain.

Wherever we stopped, any families who hadn't fled at the sight of us gave what shelter they could for the night, with grazing for the horses and the stock that were being driven along with us for meat and milk. There was singing and dancing all along the road that the Roman soldiers had built, and after dark, our warriors would brag around the campfires about what they were going to do to the Romans when they caught them. Of course our men were already heroes, which was good news for me: Verico now had his pick of girls eager for his repulsive embrace, and most of the time he kept his hands off me.

Beyond boasting, nobody seemed to be giving much thought to what would happen when we got to Camulodunum. I found out why when I fell into conversation with a Trinovante girl in the queue for water. According to her, the Roman veterans who had retired to Camulodunum had not only not bothered to put up defenses, they had even knocked down most of the old fort and built houses over it. This was hard to believe, but she assured me it was true.

"Ask anybody," she said. They had built themselves a massive temple and a thing called a theater, and they had a great big statue of the dead Emperor Claudius on a horse. "I don't care about any of that," she said. "When we take over, I'm going straight to the forum. There's a bronze plaque in there with names of all the soldiers who think they own our land. I'm going to rip it right off the wall and dance on it."

The queue shuffled forward. Luci arrived to join me, and the women behind me tutted but said nothing. Water was a problem with so many people and animals in one place at one time. So was waste. It was just as well we broke camp each morning.

As we came to a halt again, the girl seemed to have been thinking. "When I've finished dancing," she said, "I'll have that plaque melted down. I'll have a little bronze horse statue made for Epona as thanks for victory and getting our fields back."

Luci was clearly impressed. "Will there be a big battle like before I was born?"

She laughed, put down her bucket, and grabbed him, lifting him above her head and turning him in a circle so he could see the size of the crowd. "When the people in Camulodunum hear this lot coming," she told him, "you'll see how fast they can run."

THAT night, rolled in a blanket under the kitchen cart and listening to the cook snoring, I thought about all those royal visits my father and his queen had made to celebrate Roman festivals and dine with the governor. Our queen must know exactly what defenses Camulodunum did or didn't have. Had she been planning something like this even then? I could not believe that. But I could believe that she had looked over the town with the eye of a warrior sizing up an enemy, and now, with an army that had grown to tens of thousands, we all knew she was going to take it.

Looking back, it was a party for us, but not for the leaders. I was working for the cook again, trying to keep the royal household fed. I knew how long the queen and the elders spent going about the camp after dark, chatting and encouraging, checking on the sentries, and making sure the warriors from the different tribes weren't using their sharpened weapons on each other or getting too drunk to fight.

The day before we marched on Camulodunum, the news came that our warriors had routed a strong force of Roman soldiers who had been hurrying to defend it. That evening while others celebrated, I found Andecarus wandering alone—or as alone as you can be among tens of thousands of people—just outside the area that was kept clear around the queen's tent. He had lived as a hostage with the Romans and served with their troops. Whatever his blood, there must be some part of his heart that was with them and would grieve for their dead.

I paused with the bread I was supposed to be delivering. I dared not mention the killing of the soldiers. Instead, I said, "It may not be as bad as you think tomorrow."

He looked up and scowled. "I'm not afraid."

"I don't mean that," I said, wishing I had put it better. "I mean, not as bad for your old friends in the town. Everyone says they'll run before they fight."

He stared at me, the brown-and-green eyes clear in the dark of his unshaven face. "You have no idea," he said. Then he turned away, picking his way awkwardly over the tent ropes and fading into the dusk with his walking stick on one side and his sword on the other.

I felt suddenly cold. I needed to get the food delivered and myself wrapped inside a blanket and asleep.

The guard motioned me forward, and I paused just outside the entrance of the tent, waiting for the right moment to interrupt and announce food.

That was when I heard Duro say, "They haven't left? You're certain?"

"Nobody's moved," said a voice with a Trinovante lilt. "They know there's no legion coming, but they've been told the procurator's sending men from Londinium."

"The place is indefensible, and he's sending a couple hundred flabby office-boys! Didn't you tell them that?"

"Nobody believed me."

Duro grunted. "This wasn't supposed to happen. What about the statue?"

"Tipped over like we agreed. The priests all said it was a bad omen. The mad women danced around prophesying doom like good'uns, but the buggers still wouldn't budge. Said they've got the land and they're not moving off it."

"Is it a trap?" The queen's voice took me by surprise.

The Trinovante said, "If it is, I can't see it."

Duro said, "Perhaps they'll surrender," although he sounded as though he would be disappointed if they did. "What do your people want to do?"

The Trinovante snorted. "Some of them remember seeing their fathers' and brothers' heads on poles outside the fort gates. What do you think they want to do?"

I do not know what was said next. I was seized from behind and held tight. I dropped the bread. Something sharp and cold pressed against my throat. "Traitor!" hissed my elder sister. Then louder, "Guards! This slave is listening outside the tent!"

"Ria." I could barely make out the queen's face from the shadows of her hair in the lamplight, but I could hear the disappointment in her voice.

One breath of betrayal. And oh, I had been so close to freedom. I said, "I was bringing bread."

"What did you hear?"

I opened my mouth to say, "Nothing." What came out was, "The veterans and their families are still in Camulodunum, even though we have tried to frighten them off. They think the procurator's men are going to save them, but they are not. And now we cannot hold the Trinovantes back even if we wanted to."

My sister said, "You see? She was listening!"

The queen clasped her hands together and closed her eyes as if she was thinking, and it struck me how much responsibility rested upon her.

"I always said she would betray us!"

Her mother looked up. "And who will she betray us to, here, tonight?"

My sister glared at her. "She will report to someone who will take messages to the governor—"

I said, "I wouldn't—" but she was still talking.

"They will try to use it against us! What if they try to separate us from the Trinovantes?"

I said, "It's too late. Our warriors will never let the Trinovantes have all the glory tomorrow."

"You see? She's thought about it! She was spying, Mother. You have no choice. You said you would have her executed at the least breath of—"

"There is always a choice," her mother declared. "Leave us, Sorcha."

"But—"

"Tomorrow there will be another great battle. Tonight you need to rest and prepare."

"But—"

"I will be obeyed!"

My sister stalked out of the tent, still glaring at me, and I was left alone with the queen for the second time in as many months.

When she spoke, it was more gently than I had ever heard her. "Is it your wish to betray us, Ria?"

I said, "Never."

She took a long breath. "We both know that what will happen tomorrow is not what your father would have wanted."

I said, "Perhaps if we chase the Romans out—"

"My children were violated," she said. "Keena still wakes crying in the night."

My mouth went dry. I would never forget the sound of her screams in the storehouse.

"Tomorrow I shall do what has to be done. But no amount of killing will make them whole again."

I bowed my head and said what I ought to have said long ago. "I should have done more to save them. I was there, in the storehouse."

That was the real treason. Not accidentally handing silver to the Romans, nor warning the spy, Eisu, nor Andecarus' suffering, nor overhearing battle plans, but the failure to do everything in my power to defend my sisters. Princess Sorcha was right: I did not deserve to live.

It was a moment before I felt the queen's hands on either side of my face, lifting it so she could look into my eyes. "We might all have done things differently," she said.

Do not cry, I told myself. *Do not . . .*

After a moment, she let go of me and delved into a wooden box beside her. "I was going to grant your freedom when Andecarus was whole, but the gods alone know where we will be by then." She was placing things into my hands, things that were heavy and metallic and cold.

"Your father wanted you to have these," she said as I stared at my brooches. "You are a free woman, Ria. You may leave in the morning if you wish."

I am still sorry for what I said to her. It sounded grudging and ungracious. What I should have said was, There are thousands of people wanting your attention tonight, and the whole future of our people is resting with you, and still you take the time to think of a slave. That is why I will not—cannot—leave you now, even though I am afraid of the terrible things that lie ahead. You are my queen, and the allegiance I swore before on pain of death I would willingly swear again now. Or I could simply have said, Thank you. Instead, I said stupidly, "Where else could I go?"

She pressed her hand on my shoulder, and I stepped out into the moonlight a free woman, clutching the gift from my father that I had never expected to receive. I picked my way through the jumble of tents and vehicles and makeshift shelters, catching the odd murmur of conversation from around a dying fire and hearing the swish of a weapon being sharpened and a baby crying out and its mother trying to shush it. Back at the cart, I pinned the brooches to my tunic for safekeeping, folded myself in my blanket, and lay down next to the sleeping Luci. Then I wrapped my arms around him and held him tight and tried to think beyond tomorrow. To the freedom our queen had the power to bring: not just for me, but for all of us.

PART THREE

THE TRIBUNE

Russell Whitfield

*The Druids lined up, with hands raised, invoking
the gods and shouting horrible curses.
The strangeness of the sight struck the Romans with awe and terror.*
—Tacitus

SWEAT burst out on Agricola's brow as he tensed for the final push. His shoulders were on fire, arms trembling with fatigue. The freckled face of his friend, Roscius, blotted out the sun for a moment.

"Come on." He grinned, showing the cavernous and—to Agricola's eye—unsightly gap in his front teeth. "You can do it."

Agricola gritted his teeth, breath hissing out as he pushed; the *halteres* weights rose slowly, wobbling as he struggled to lock out his arms. Midway through the repetition, he knew he would fail. "No," he heard himself say. Roscius hopped away as Agricola released the weights, their dull thud on the earth a statement of his capitulation. "Shit," he said as he sat up, rotating and stretching his right arm. The *palaestra*—the exercise ground—was all but deserted save for a few new recruits enduring the punishment of extra sword drills: endless hours of striking wooden posts armed with a heavy oak sword and an overweight shield. The making of a legionary was all in the training.

"I don't know why you do this to yourself," Roscius observed.

Agricola eyed him. "You could do with more training," he noted, jerking his chin at Roscius' thick middle, "and less gorging."

"I'm built like a fucking gladiator," Roscius shot back. "But I'll admit: being off duty in Gaul for four months hasn't helped."

"I'm sorry about your uncle," Agricola offered. "He was a good man."

"He was that," Roscius agreed.

"How was my mother?" Agricola brought her face to mind, stern-eyed and gray-haired.

"Upset. You know they were . . . close."

Agricola shrugged. His mother had been widowed when he was only a boy, and he had grown up knowing of her "friendship" with Roscius' uncle. In later life, he realized they were more than friends. But rather than be outraged or offended, he was pleased—more than pleased, in fact—that she had found some happiness. "I'm saddened that another man she loved has passed before her."

"I would be if I were you." Roscius shook off his grim expression like a man discarding a rain-soaked cloak. "All she spoke about was you. And by the gods, she can talk—so even though I've been away, I've hardly missed you. She has plans for you, man. Kept telling me she's made sure you're going places."

"She and I agree that politics is the best path for me, Roscius. I'm inspired by Athens, the great men—"

"If I didn't know you better," Roscius cut him off, "I'd say you were turning Greek. Philosophy, poetry, and you even look like one of their statues." He gestured at the hard ridges of Agricola's stomach. "That isn't natural."

Agricola shrugged. "Girls like it," he said, rising to his feet.

"And Greeks."

Agricola ignored the jibe. "I'm for the baths," he said. "I'll let you rub me down like I know you secretly want to."

"Fuck you, Tribune." Roscius made an obscene gesture.

"In your dreams, Tribune."

Roscius laughed, big and booming like the man himself. "Come on, Blondie," he said and ambled off, leaving Agricola scowling in his wake. His sand-colored hair was a constant reminder that he was of Gaulish—and not Roman—stock. Even if his family could boast governors and procurators in its history, his heritage was one of those things that irked him because he could do nothing about it. "Even a god cannot change the past," he muttered.

Roscius stopped and turned around. "What?"

"I was quoting Agathon." Agricola trotted to catch up. "A Greek philosopher."

"To annoy me? I know who fucking Agathon is. We had the same pedagogue, didn't we?"

"We did, but no one would know it." It was true; like himself, Roscius had Gaulish roots, and their families were close. Roscius had seven more years on him than Agricola's twenty, and his mother had ensured that he had been posted to the same legion as the older man—the Second Augusta—for his military service. *To keep an eye on you,* as she had said. "I just don't know why you insist on speaking like someone from Subura when you had the finest education money can buy."

"The ideal man bears the accidents of life with dignity and grace, making the best of circumstances," Roscius replied in flawless Greek.

"Aristotle?" Agricola arched an eyebrow. "I don't see the relevance." This was good, he thought. Perhaps Roscius would engage in a proper debate for once—because argument and educated discourse were in short supply at Isca Dumnoniorum's fortress.

The two moved from the *palaestra* toward the newly constructed bathhouse. It was a building of which Agricola was truly proud; it had been constructed at his suggestion, its design influenced by the Hellenic style of which he was so enamored—more graceful and stylish than the modern Roman bent.

Like all forts, Isca was constructed in exactly the same way—a man in the legions could find his way around a base whether it was in Britannia, Bithynia, or Belgica; but as far as Agricola was concerned, if the placement of the buildings had to have uniformity, it did not mean that they had to lack panache. Even if panache was wasted on most of its inhabitants, Agricola thought ruefully as an eight-man *contubernium* marched past singing a song about a whore with a bad case of piles.

The cold water of the bathhouse *frigidarium* did much to ease the pain in Agricola's muscles; he worked hard on his physique and took pride in the results, but it was a constant effort to maintain the sculpted look he wanted. The two stayed in as long as they could bear it, Agricola exiting first as he knew that Roscius would rather die than admit to any hardship. "You were quoting Aristotle," he prompted as they moved into the *tepidarium*, Agricola taking time to nod and greet the straw-haired female slaves in attendance before entering the *caldarium*—the hot room—that was the heart of the bathhouse. Steam rose from the braziers, obscuring the statuary therein, giving the place a mythic quality—or so Agricola fancied. Britannia was a mythic sort of place—it turned even the most prosaic Roman mind fanciful.

"You're a Gaul, I'm a Gaul," Roscius said. "It's an undeniable fact—look at your hair. Mine, too, for that matter. Sand and rust—we don't look like we're swarthy farm boys from rural Campagna, do we?"

"I rather think you speak as though you are." Agricola sniffed.

"That's because I have no political ambition." Roscius was sober for a moment. "I love the army. I want to remain a soldier for as long as I live. The lads relate to someone on their level more than they will to some career officer who's only here to serve a bit of time before moving on to political office." He looked pointedly at Agricola from under red brows.

"My duty is to serve in politics despite my heritage." Agricola added more coals to the brazier. "We cannot shape the destiny of the empire from the army, Roscius. You're an educated man—you know this."

"We cannot manifest the destiny of the empire without the army, you dozy twat."

"Elegantly framed."

"But on the nose," Roscius said. "Look. The only person who thinks coming from Gaul is some kind of hindrance is you.

You're a fucking tribune in the best legion in the empire—your old man—a Gaul—was a praetor and a senator . . ."

"And was unjustly executed by Caligula." Agricola said it quickly. "Which is why politics must be served," he went on, "lest tyranny take root once again." The thought was a bitter one: Agricola's father had been a great man—his writings and thoughts on Hellenic philosophy and temperance had inspired Agricola since boyhood.

"Caligula was a cunt." Roscius stated the vulgarly obvious and unarguable.

Agricola got up and walked back toward the *tepidarium,* where the slaves awaited to oil and massage them. The prettier of the two blond Britons made a beeline for him, making Roscius shake his head as he, too, entered the warm room.

"Make sure you oil his bollocks well, love," he advised. "No doubt they'll be resting on your chin the moment I'm out the door. As for you, Chunky," he turned his attention to the other woman, "I'm all yours."

"Forgive my friend," Agricola said as the girl troweled the oil onto his chest and abdomen with abandon. "It is an affectation of his that he believes is endearing."

Roscius got a laugh out of that. "Look, Agricola," he said after a moment, lowering himself onto a massage bench with a groan. "Life is short, Hades is long. As Agathon says, *you can't change the past*, and as Aristotle says—paraphrasing—*things are as they are, it's how we deal with them that counts.*" He grunted as "Chunky" worked his back muscles probably harder than he wanted. "Life—or the Gods, if you like—has a way of throwing shit at you that you least expect. On the other hand," he rolled over onto his front, "there's always an upside. Isn't that right, Chunky?"

"As you say, sir," the woman replied with practiced neutrality.

"She's a bath slave," Agricola said pointedly as Roscius' hand crept around the woman's hip. "Not a whore. There are women in the town for that sort of thing, Roscius."

Roscius scowled. "You've been reading Seneca again, haven't you? Chunky here has got me right in the mood—my ball sack is ripe to burst."

"Then empty it into someone who provides that service," Agricola snapped. "That they are slaves is bad enough for them. It is ungentlemanly to impress their servitude upon them by forcing them to bed you."

Chunky stepped away from Roscius, which clearly irritated him—more so as both women gave Agricola a thankful and, he fancied, appreciative glance.

"This from the man who has cuckolded more husbands than I can count," Roscius observed.

"Ah yes, but young wives are willing, Roscius. Married to fat old windbags, they find my 'unnatural' physique appealing. Slaves are under duress to perform."

"Don't get lofty, Agricola. You'll knob anything that gives you the go-ahead to do so. Trying to take the moral high ground when you're ruled by your dick is—in military terms—an untenable position." Roscius grinned over at him.

He was, of course, right. Agricola believed that slaves should not be treated harshly—as Seneca advocated, he lived by the tenet of treating others as he would wish to be treated himself. However, the lure of new flesh—and especially forbidden flesh—was a vice that he could not seem to break. A part of him suspected that when he was an older man, it would be he who would be the cuckold, and the irony of his youthful behavior would be impressed upon him. And, he realized, the ministrations of the straw-haired slave had started to arouse him. "I think," he said, "a few cups of wine in the town would go down well."

"Do you, now," Roscius mocked. "Come on, then." He winked at Chunky. "Another time, love. We're off to pay a couple of whores so the paragon of virtue here can maintain his elegant disposition." He began to thrust his hips, grunting like a sow. "That's what he looks like when he's doing the business," he explained.

The sun had turned into a livid orange disc, massive and somehow ominous as the two men made their way to the camp gates. The end of another perfect early spring day. Agricola felt good—training and massage had made his skin sing, and he was eager for a whore. Native women were a strange lot, he thought. Most of them were as tall as a Roman soldier, fair-haired and large-breasted; nearly always drunk on mead. They were enthusiastic professionals, which made the transaction even more appealing.

"How was that funeral at the end of last winter?" Roscius asked as they made their way through the encampment. "Your first political mission went well, I assume?"

Agricola gave him a sidelong glance. "It was interesting," he offered. "With no male heir, the Iceni king has left his kingdom to his wife—Boadicea, or Boudica as the Britons call her. She has red hair like you. Taller than us both. Full of gristle. And what a voice." Agricola shook his head. "She sounds like an early morning *buccina* on a hangover," he referenced the harsh braying of the Roman military trumpet.

"You tried to bed her, didn't you?"

"No," Agricola lied, remembering the disdain with which she had rejected his halfhearted advances. "I was more interested in the procurator's wife, Valeria. Catus Decianus is a spineless little pen-pusher," he added. "I felt sorry for the poor woman." Though she hadn't been any more interested in his advances than the Iceni queen—Valeria had given him a few smiles, but the moment he brushed a hand against her hip in invitation, she looked at the physique that melted most women like ice in the summer and just raised a pair of terrifyingly imperious eyebrows. Two rejections in a row; that trip to Iceni territory at the end of last year hadn't been his luckiest when it came to bed-sport.

"You're a whore, Agricola." Roscius laughed. "I look forward to your wedding day—for you, it will be the march of the condemned gladiator, won't it?"

"That day will never come," Agricola said with real feeling. "But I'll tell you, Roscius . . . that Boudica. There's something about her—she's not the mug her husband was, that's for sure. She has more balls than Catus Decianus. I see concessions—lots of them."

Roscius grunted. "You want to be a political man? What do you read from the situation?"

"Decianus is a bean-counter," Agricola said. "He'll roll over as long as there's profit in it for him and it keeps the Iceni quiet. This Boudica's a proud one, though. Her husband not even on the pyre yet, and already the tribesmen were looking to her as if to a queen. Decianus will have to eat some shit and kiss her arse to keep her quiet—and then everyone's a winner. Which seems to be how it's played out given that the annexation must have gone ahead by now." He'd ended up leaving Iceni territory before the funeral was over, certainly before the procurator carried out his orders. "And I can tell you this, Roscius—if there's anyone who knows how to eat shit and kiss arse, it's Decianus. His wife is wasted on him. She was one of those cool ones—you know, fire underneath for the right man, a real challenge—"

"Sir!" They were interrupted as a young legionary trotted over to them, his segmented armor clattering on his skinny frame.

"Felix, isn't it?" Roscius identified at once.

Felix grinned, showing his teeth. He looked to Agricola to

be about sixteen years old—skinny, enthusiastic, with a mop of white-blond hair. Probably another Gaul. "Yes, sir. Sallustius Secundus Felix—"

"Tenth of the Tenth," Roscius finished. The tenth century in the tenth cohort of the Augusta was the least regarded of the entire legion—indeed, as it was in any legion, manned largely by new and untried men. Like himself, Agricola realized. "What is it, legionary?" Roscius asked with the correct military severity, letting the boy know that the greeting was over.

"Begging to report, sir, that the camp prefect requests your presence in his quarters."

"At this time?" Agricola glanced at the sun.

"He said at once, sir." Felix was earnest. "I've been looking for you two for a while now. I went to the *palaestra* and all—the lads say you're always there, sir. Working on your muscles."

Roscius chuckled. "Looks like the town will have to wait," he said to Agricola. "All right, Felix. Run along." Felix saluted and did as he was told—a new recruit, clearly eager to be away from the ancient stare of his superiors.

"I wonder what this is all about," Agricola said, miffed that the pleasure trip had been curtailed.

"He's probably hammered," Roscius said. "He nearly always is these days. You wonder how his wife puts up with it." They turned back and headed toward the center of the fort where the praetorium—the commander's quarters—were located. "Mind you, that's one wife *I* wouldn't mind a ride on. She's Iberian, isn't she, his other half?" He eyed Agricola, who felt his cheeks reddening. "Big tits," he pressed. "Lovely, lush lips . . . You've bedded her, haven't you?"

"As you say, Poenius Postumus is always drunk. He invited me for dinner on my first night here. He passed out . . ." Agricola trailed off. "She was lonely."

Roscius shook his head. "You've shit on your own doorstep. And mine."

Agricola did not reply. The truth of it was that despite his hard-earned role as camp prefect, Postumus had now chosen to go to seed. A drunken bore, he treated his wife worse than a slave, upbraiding her constantly during their meal, making lascivious comments about her "barbarian skills in the sack." The man was an utter bastard and, even in Agricola's inexperienced view—a bad officer. Isca was a secure, pacified area, and the fact was that Postumus looked on this appointment as a grand opportunity to fleece money, get drunk, and shirk duty. He had, however, been correct about his wife's skills in bed—Lavinia Postumia was in her thirties, twenty years her husband's junior, and evidently sex-starved. She had drained Agricola dry whilst Postumus snored and farted in the adjacent room.

"Let me do the talking," Roscius advised as they approached the *praetorium*. "If he's pissed *and* pissed off about something, it's better I talk to him in his own language. Rank-and-file lifers like Postumus always hate you career tribunes."

The *praetorium* was large, dimly lit, and dominated by a desk of heroic proportions and, Agricola noticed at once, equally dominated by the flatulent reek of Postumus' belly gas. A wine jug was in evidence on the table and the prefect's white tunic was jeweled with purple spots, mute evidence that he'd been walking with Bacchus. Like Roscius, he was broad at the shoulders and must have been an imposing man in his prime. Now, however, his belly seemed to begin at his chest and carry on outward—it wasn't the corpulent flab of a senator, but seemed solid, as though he had a large boulder hidden under his clothing.

"You two pricks are late," Postumus growled, stabbing a stubby finger at them. His eyes were glazed, glinting with anger and something else that Agricola couldn't quite read.

"Apologies, sir," Roscius said as they drew to attention and saluted. "He was training—under my instruction. The boy needs toughening up."

Postumus turned his attention to Agricola, who kept his eyes front, not wanting to antagonize a drunkard. "He does," the prefect agreed with some malice. "He looks like a fucking catamite."

"As I keep telling him, sir." Roscius could evidently not resist the gift.

"I've got news for you." Postumus grasped a wax tablet on his desk. "Do you know what this is?"

"A wax tablet, sir?" Agricola offered and could feel Roscius willing him to stay quiet.

"You're a namby fucking cunt, Agricola," Postumus told him, fury etching its way across his weathered visage. "I hate everything about you. Your face, your high-and-mighty attitude, your fucking Greek ways. If it were up to me, I'd have you executed. You, boy, are a cocksucker of the lowest order."

It was all Agricola could do to keep from sneering at the man and advising him that his wife was a cocksucker of the *highest* order. But to say so *would* mean death, so he offered a neutral "yes, sir" that any put-upon legionary would have been proud of. What he had done to arouse such ire in the man was beyond him, however. Unless . . . Agricola felt himself pale as he wondered if Postumus had learned of his wife's infidelity. He swallowed. No, that couldn't be the case; she wouldn't have said anything, for the shame was hers. He had simply taken what had been offered, as any man should. But to admit she had offered it—no, that she would not do.

"Orders," Postumus hurled the wax tablet at their feet, "from Gaius Suetonius Paulinus."

"The governor?" The surprise in Roscius' voice was evident.

"Yes," Postumus said. "The governor. As you know, he's up

in Cambria, sorting out the natives," the prefect went on. "He's been contacted by Agricola's family." He turned a baleful eye onto Agricola himself. "As part of your *cursus honorum*—your path of honor, which by the way is a fucking contradiction in terms— you're to be seconded to his staff."

Agricola's eyes flicked to Roscius. Clearly, this is what his mother had been referring to when she'd told the big man that Agricola was "going places."

He looked back to Postumus; the prefect's fist was clenched tight on his cup. "You don't know how lucky you are." He tossed back some wine and winced before looking back to Roscius. "You're his keeper," he said. "You go with him. And I want reports, Roscius. Since you and the cocksucker here are educated types, I can think of none better to conduct the operation. I'm sure the correspondence will be fucking epic."

"The cocksucker is a fine writer, sir," Roscius agreed. "An assignment that we'll relish, I'm sure. I've always wanted to go to Cambria," he finished with an evident lie. No one in their right mind wanted to anywhere near Cambria, a mountainous land full of wild-haired savages, harpy-like women, and gods-cursed Druids.

Postumus grunted. "You won't be going alone. I want those dickheads in the Tenth of the Tenth blooded. They're just as useless as you two. Hopefully, the woad-skins will do me a favor and wipe the lot of you out. You know what they do to Roman prisoners, don't you, Agricola?"

"Offer them for ransom?"

"Torture." The prefect took a more-than-healthy draught of wine, draining the cup. He refilled it—and drained that, too. "Things you wouldn't believe, boy," he slurred. "I can't even make it up. Skin you alive, cut cock and balls off and shove them in your mouth, and slowly roast what's left alive. And they'll laugh at your screams. I've seen it happen before a battle with prisoners they've captured. They do it to shit the life out of you. It works."

Agricola felt himself paling once again because, despite the fact he wanted to come back with a witty retort, he knew that the drunken old bastard wasn't lying. He opted for keeping his mouth shut. Postumus continued to look at them, but it seemed to Agricola that he had drifted off into vile memory, his face slack and melancholy.

"You look tired, sir," Roscius said when it was clear a dismissal wasn't coming. "I could get some of the lads to escort you home to your lovely wife . . ."

Postumus squeezed his eyes shut for a moment. "My lovely wife," he repeated. When he opened them again, they were full of hate. "She's dead, boy."

Agricola was shocked to the core; Lavinia Postumia was a woman in the prime of her life, and because he held some small affection for all the women he bedded, he spoke before he could stop himself. "I—I'm so sorry to hear that, sir."

"I killed her myself. This morning, as it happens." Postumus' gaze bored into him. "As *paterfamilias,* it is my right."

"But why?" Agricola could not contain the words.

"A funny thing," Postumus said, tipping back yet another cup of wine. He was so drunk it was difficult at first to understand him. "We never had children—and I've fucked enough tail to know that that was my fault and not hers. So imagine when she told me that she had one in her belly. Four months gone," he added. "You've been here . . . what . . . four months now, Tribune? I remember I invited you into my fucking house for a dinner when you first arrived. It seems to me that you took more than just food from my table."

Agricola wanted to be sick, but it was lies and not bile that rushed to his throat. "Sir, I can assure you that—"

"Don't lie to me!" Postumus exploded to his feet, his chair smashing into the wooden wall behind him. "Don't!" he screamed. "I can see it in written on your face, read it in your eyes. You fucked her. Fucked her while I slept! In my own house, you bastard." Postumus lunged at Agricola, who leapt back in shock, but the prefect's foot caught on his desk, and he crashed to the floor. He tried to rise but, near paralytic as he was, he lost his balance, toppled backward, and hit the floor again. He rolled into a fetal position and started to weep, repeating his wife's name several times before passing out.

Agricola could only stare, aghast. He could tell that Roscius, too, was stunned, but the older man snapped out of it first, going to the prefect's desk. "What are you doing?" Agricola asked, appalled at the tremulousness in his voice.

Roscius looked up at him, anger in his gray eyes, but did not reply. Instead, he scratched out some words on a wax tablet and moved over the snoring form of Postumus; taking the man's hand, he pressed his signet ring into the wax.

"Wha-what are you doing?" Agricola stammered, his mind reeling.

"Postumus takes orders from the governor. We take orders from Postumus. And now we have them. And," he rose, glancing at Paulinus' missive, "we have the governor's location, too." He noted this on the tablet. "Let's get the fuck out of here," Roscius said, grasping his arm and propelling him toward the door. As they exited, slamming the door behind him, he looked to the sentries. "What did you hear?" he asked.

"Nothing, Tribune," the legionary replied. "Nothing at all."

"Come on." Roscius dragged Agricola away with force.

"What am I going to do?" Agricola wailed. He could hear the weakness in his own voice, and it disgusted him even as shame overwhelmed him. He pulled away and vomited onto the earth—much to the unknowing amusement of the soldiers passing by.

"You've done enough," Roscius snarled.

It was the first time Agricola had seen the big man genuinely angry. It was worse that the uncharacteristic rage was directed at him. He was sick again, dredging up whatever was left in his guts. He straightened and wiped his mouth on the back of his hand. "I'll turn myself in," he announced with all the earnestness of a martyr. He would do it and atone for his actions—death because of the dishonor he had caused.

"You're a fucking idiot," Roscius said. "Turn yourself in for what, exactly?"

"It was me. My fault . . . I . . ."

"And how is he going to prove that? We don't even know if she was up the duff—he could have killed her in a drunken rage for all anyone knows."

"No," Agricola was resolute. "I know what I did . . ."

"Maybe," Roscius cut him off. "But the fact is that no one will believe anything Postumus says. *Everyone* knows he's off his head on wine. And let's be honest—how do you know you're the only one that plowed that particular field?"

Agricola prided himself on his *virtus*—his honor. He could not allow this to stand. "If I confess . . ."

"Then we'll both be for it the next time he gets pissed, you stupid bastard." Roscius was dancing on the edge of fury. "He'll make sure I get the chop before you do."

"But why?"

"Because I'm your friend!" the big man shouted. He breathed in through his nose, almost shaking with rage, forcing his voice to calm. "He knows how you think—he'll have me offed, and you'll go to Hades knowing that you got me killed. You might think

that death is noble, Agricola, but the closest you've been to it is
in the arena. *Watching* people die. When someone's coming for
you, it's a little bit different. A man will do anything . . . *anything*
to survive."

Agricola's gaze fell to the ground, a guilty boy upbraided by his
elder. "I'm sorry, Roscius."

"So you fucking should be. Now. We have to get out of here
before he wakes up. Let's get kitted up."

"IT'S highly irregular, sir." Calvus, the Tenth of the Tenth's
centurion, eyed Roscius as Agricola lurked behind him. Calvus
was newly made to the rank, hence his position in the lowest
century of the legion. Tough, bald, and short, he was still in
his thirties and looked like a man no one wanted to get on the
wrong side of.

Roscius played hard. "Look, *centurion*," he said, impressing
who was higher in the pecking order. "I don't like it any more
than you do, but what do you want me to do about it? You can
read as well as I can." He indicated the wax tablet hanging loosely
in Calvus' hand. "The Tenth are to attach to Paulinus' Twentieth
Valeria Victrix. A training mission for your lads and an attach-
ment for my colleague, Tribune Gnaeus Julius Agricola."

"Training mission," Calvus repeated, clearly not believing a
word of it. He looked at the wax tablet. "This doesn't even look
like the prefect's handwriting."

"Let's just say that the prefect was tired and emotional when
those were issued," Agricola put in, rewarded by an appreciative
glance over the shoulder from Roscius.

Calvus grunted. "I see."

"The lads have eaten?" Roscius asked.

"Yes, sir."

"Excellent. Then round them up, get them kitted and ready to march. A night on the road will do them a world of good. It's all experience, Calvus."

"And of course, you'll countersign these orders, sir." Calvus didn't move. "I'm sure everything's in order, but you have to admit, it's a bit irregular. I want to make sure that my lads aren't in the shit because someone fucked up. If you take my meaning, sir."

Roscius looked as though he was about to erupt; before he could do so, Agricola interceded. "I'll countersign, Centurion," he said. "Now. Get your men ready." He could not, he decided, let Roscius take any blame for this. The responsibility for the predicament was his and his alone.

THE Tenth of the Tenth marched out with no fanfare, drawing only a few amused looks from men who were on their way back from duties and not about to embark on what looked like—given the cadence that Roscius was setting—a forced march. He led the eighty-man column on a bay mare while Agricola brought up the rear on a black gelding. The beast's flanks had the white, chalky marks of spear scars, and he had the air of a mount who would not be hurried.

The men were muttering at the prospect of a night march, and a fast one at that, but their complaints were silenced by a round of particularly vile cursing from Calvus and his *optio*, a weasel-faced sadist called Naso, who waded in with his *hastile*—his staff of office, which was both ceremonial badge and offensive weapon. Agricola couldn't blame the legionaries. Usually, each eight-man *contubernium* would have a mule and cart assigned to it to carry kit and non-military essentials; as it was, they'd be sleeping under the stars and humping their own gear. The *scutum*—the curved legionary's shield—was a heavy item and caused the most complaint. Each man had rigged a strap to the shield's inner handle and looped it over his right shoulder to take some of the weight. It was the only way it could be carried for any length of time on the march. Water, food, spare leather thonging (the most used item in any man's kit), and other essentials were carried on a *furca*—a yoke—resting on the right shoulder, gripped in the same hand as his javelin.

"Stop your complaining," Calvus bellowed as they pounded down the road. Agricola noted that he'd chosen a moment when no one was actually griping to say this. "It's just like training—you soft bastards need it."

"I need my bed and my right hand, Centurion," a wag from the ranks called out.

"Wanking yourself off is all your right hand is good for," Calvus observed. "It's useless with a sword in it, that's for sure." If the wag had a response, it was drowned out by a chorus of mockery from his mates.

Agricola envied their easy humor; on any other day, he would have smiled indulgently and thought himself above it all.

But not today.

As they marched on, the fast pace eating up the miles between the century and the fort, Agricola found himself wrapped in gloom as thick and as heavy as any spring fog. By his own actions, he had caused the death of a man's wife because he could not resist bedding her. Had she begged for her life? Pleaded with Postumus as he killed her? Begged him for mercy as the light faded from her eyes? The shame of what he had caused was all but unbearable and weighed upon him like the manacles of a quarry slave.

He glanced over his shoulder, wondering if Postumus had woken up and ordered the cavalry to pursue them in a fit of drunken vengeance, but there was nothing save for the smudge on the horizon that was the town of Isca. Agricola squeezed his eyes shut, a shiver going down his spine despite the temperate spring evening. Guilt, he realized. Guilt that nothing could assuage. He wanted to scream, imagining that by doing so he could absolve himself, shout out the shame, call on the goddess Clementia for forgiveness. But nothing he could do would change what he had done.

The march continued as the sun finally capitulated, giving the land over to semidarkness; the springtime days were lengthening—even at after sundown, it was never truly dark, the sky having a strange pinkish-orange glow that was far brighter than any moon.

The soldiers pressed on, and Agricola—like them all—allowed himself to become hypnotized by the sound of the march: the tramp of the soldiers' feet on the ground, the rhythmic *thunk-scratch* of armor on shields, the squeaking and clattering of the *lorica segmentata* they all wore, the labored breathing of the men as they did what Roman soldiers always did—march till they were told to quit.

The night was half-gone when Roscius called a halt; the century had made good progress, and they were now far from Isca in the heart of the countryside. By day, it was a beautiful land—now that winter was done, at least—all rolling hills, tilled farmland, and thick woods. By night, it had a mystical quality that, at any other time, would have spoken to the poet in Agricola's soul.

"We'll camp off the road," Roscius told Calvus. "Get the lads into the woods and bedded down. Double-watch, Calvus."

Calvus saluted and chivvied the men along; Felix, Agricola noted, was limping toward the trees, trying to look as though he was not. Agricola nudged his black gelding toward the lad. "Everything all right, Legionary Felix?"

Felix squared himself up. "Just a bit footsore, sir," he said. "It's once you stop walking that the blisters hurt—they numb up once you get going."

"Carry on," Agricola said, swinging himself out of the saddle as Optio Naso approached Felix.

"You namby cunt, Felix," he said. "If I ever hear you whining to an officer again, I'll ram this pole so far up your arse you'll be sneezing fucking woodchips."

"Yes, sir," Felix offered.

"You have to put a knife through the blisters," Naso advised with sadistic glee. "It'll hurt like a bastard when you do it and worse when you get moving again. But your feet'll leather up in no time, boy. See to it—and no, I'm not going to hold your hand and wipe away your tears. Go on." Felix made off, and Naso swung a kick at his rump, which sent Felix trotting forward a few paces. The lad looked over his shoulder with a grin and trotted into the woods.

Despite their lowly status in the legion, Agricola found the men of the Tenth to be professional in their work, setting a perimeter, posting guards, and getting down to the business of serious sleep with minimal fuss. He sat apart from the rest, spreading his scarlet cloak on the ground, hoping that sleep would come. As he did so, Roscius wandered over.

"You all right?" he asked.

Agricola looked up at him. "I . . ."

"I know you're sorry." Roscius squatted down. "But like I said, we don't—and never will—know the truth of it."

"I know the truth of one thing, Roscius," Agricola replied. "I'm a hypocrite. A liar. I read and I talk, I judge others because I'm educated. I espouse Seneca and the words of the Greeks that talk of living well and true. But what you said in jest is true—I'm ruled by my . . . passions."

"Your cock." Roscius was mild. "You're ruled by your cock. And most men your age are."

"Perhaps. But it's not just that, Roscius. There are any number of women I could have bedded. But for me, it was not about that. It was about bedding *other men's* women. That was the thrill. I am ashamed, Roscius."

"There's nothing you can do about what happened—or, in fact, what Postumus did or didn't do."

"Maybe not." Agricola was resolute. "But I can stop playing lip service and start living as I . . . espouse . . . a man should."

Roscius regarded him for long moments. Agricola expected to be chided, mocked, or for the big man to crack a joke at his words. But he did not. "It is a youthful failing to be unable to control one's impulses," he said.

Agricola arched an eyebrow. "Seneca?"

This time Roscius did laugh. "Yes," he said. "Here's another: one should count each day a separate life. All of us make mistakes, Agricola. That's what being an adult is all about. Being a man is bearing them, learning from them, and moving on. As you said you would. All right?"

Agricola's smile was wan. "I'll do better."

"You couldn't do much worse. Now—get your head down. Get some rest."

THEY pushed on, Roscius taking them on a detour to Glevum for a rest stop five days into the march. It was a new town, populated largely by veteran legionaries and their families. It was something that Agricola admired in his people, this willingness to tolerate another people's gods. It was no skin off a Roman nose to allow the local deity his ancient place of honor. Most of the men headed straight for the taverns, flexing muscles for the admiration of the local girls and the hostile glares of their fathers, who, not too many years before, had been doing the same thing.

Before Lavinia Postumia, Agricola knew well that he would have secured himself a tumble for tonight.

Before.

Instead, he found a tavern—run by an ex-legionary and crowded now with men of the Tenth, including Felix, who was getting smashed out of his mind, encouraged by his mates, who were telling him it was an "initiation." He nursed a cup of over-priced wine—clearly, the proprietor was not above fleecing his former brothers-in-arms, who had ready cash and raging thirsts after five days on the road. Roscius joined him, wincing at the taste of the stuff.

"He's got a fucking nerve," the big man observed. "My piss tastes better than this," he added, putting the cup down and re-filling it from Agricola's jug.

"But not enough to stop you from swilling mine down." He smiled.

"You're rich. You can afford it."

"So can you."

"I'm making sure you're on the straight and narrow." Roscius tipped it back. "Now then," he said. "We're at something of a crossroads. We can take boats up the River Sabrina right into Cambria. Or we can go the whole way on foot."

"I hate boats," Agricola said. "But that aside, it doesn't seem like much of a choice."

"Ordinarily, no," Roscius said. "But it's risky. If we happen on a pissed-off war band, they'll take potshots at us all the way downriver—we'll be for it, and we won't be able to hit back. They can track us until we're all dead or we're forced to come to shore. And then we're all dead anyway because fighting amphibious is a fool's errand."

"Caesar managed when he invaded this place."

"I'm not Caesar. And neither are you. Your thoughts, Tribune?"

Agricola looked up at the ceiling, calculating. "We've come about a hundred miles," he said, "with another two-twenty-five to go. Another ten days on the road? I say we take the boats—the likelihood is that Paulinus has the war bands on the run—they'll be going inland and not closer to our territory."

"Eager to start your new tenure," Roscius mocked.

"Eager to get my arse out of the saddle."

"You call it."

"You're senior tribune."

"I'm deferring to your book-learned generalship. Make the decision, Agricola."

Agricola knew that Roscius already had in mind what he wanted to do. And he knew that the older man was giving him the decision to make as a lesson in leadership. He frowned, drawing the map of Britannia in his head. "It'll be dangerous sooner or later," he said. "The land between Viroconium and Deva runs right along the border—unless we push east, which'll take us out of our way. So the river gets us there faster—same risk at the end of the day, Roscius."

"The Sabrina it is, then."

"What was your call?" Agricola had to know if he'd made the right choice.

"Doesn't matter," Roscius drained his cup and helped himself to another. "Decision's been made. That's the thing about commanding, Agricola—you need to make the call and go with it. If you're right—glory to your name. If you're wrong—you usually wind up dead."

"There's such a thing as changing your mind," Agricola muttered.

"When you have the luxury." Roscius nodded sagely. "Be flexible, my friend. Always flexible. But in this, we needed to make a choice, and it's been made. If we wind up dead at the bottom of the Sabrina, know that I'm holding you fully . . ."

He trailed off, realizing that his joke was a little close to the bone, but Agricola waved it away. As Roscius had just illustrated, men made choices. He had made bad ones in the past and had to live with the consequences. But that did not mean that Roscius or anyone else had to treat him as though he were made of glass. "If you wind up dead, I'll drink to the fattest shade in Hades," he said, toasting his friend.

"I'm not fat," Roscius huffed. "I'm built—"

"Like a fucking gladiator, I know. A fat gladiator."

"Oh, fuck you."

"In your dreams, Roscius. In your dreams."

Roscius laughed, and Agricola smiled in response, but even he knew that it did not reach his eyes. He would try, he decided, to be a better man.

THE Sabrina was slow flowing and brackish, a dirty slash on a beautiful backdrop. The Tenth had secured ten barges from an ex-patriot Greek whose eyes came alive with avarice when he realized he could claim his costs back from the army—with interest, of course. Agricola had been in charge of the negotiations and frankly could not be bothered to haggle—it wasn't his money, after all, though Roscius had taken a dim view when he'd seen the receipt.

The men rowed the barges north toward Cambria, giving Agricola as much time as he wanted to admire the countryside and brood on his own sins. Roscius was right—there was nothing he could do about it; but he could try to live the life he so espoused. That, he realized, would be easier thought than actioned. But others had done it—were doing it. Men like Seneca—men of principle.

"I've never seen grass like this," Felix observed to no one in particular. "It's really green."

"All grass is green, you dozy cunt." This from his optio, Naso.

"Yeah, but not this green," Felix pressed on. "It's proper lush."

"You a fucking poet now, Felix?"

"No, sir, I was just saying . . ."

"Well, don't. Just fucking row and keep your hole shut. If I want your views on things, I'll beat them out of you. Clear?"

"Clear, sir."

Agricola wanted to agree with the young legionary but knew he could not. To speak in the boy's defense would only cause the mockery of the others in his *contubernium* for being the officer's pet and worse, the ire of the optio, who would see the contradiction as a personal affront. Naso, like all optios, had that way about him; it seemed to Agricola that they all swapped their personalities for their *hastilae*. When they made the centurionate, they became altogether less bitter and twisted.

He scanned the riverbanks, looking for the war bands that Roscius worried were out there, but there was nothing save for the occasional farmstead and an innumerable amount of sheep. If there was one thing Britannia had in abundance, it was sheep, an animal most suited for the hostile winters of the "isle at the edge of the world." Still, in springtime, it was a beautiful place to be.

They made good progress, the steady work of the legionaries covering far more miles than they would have done on foot and with far less effort. Rowing was hard, true; but lugging armor and kit was much harder in the heat. Even riding for that length of time each day was not pleasant—so Agricola could only imagine what it was like being a foot slogger, and the image wasn't pleasant. He tried to convince himself that this was all for the lads and that he was a good, considerate offer—not that his arse was paining him after five days of bouncing up and down on the black gelding's broad back.

He looked forward and saw Roscius, too, was on the lookout for the enemy, but Agricola was sure it was as he had surmised—

whatever rebels there were would be either dead or literally running for the hills. Paulinus was an extremely competent general—everyone knew that. And everyone—even the tribesmen—knew that a Roman army could not be defeated.

But for all that, as the river turned west into the lands of the Ordovices, Agricola could not suppress a chill down his spine. It was as though he could feel the change in the air, that they had passed from a land that had been pacified into one that was wild and untamed. He referred to the wax tablet they had taken from Postumus' office. They were still a good few miles away from the governor's location by Agricola's reckoning.

Roscius' words in the tavern came back to him. If he was wrong, and they were caught in open water by a war band, then they would stand no chance. He cleared his throat. "Naso. Turn into shore—north bank. Let the others know."

"Sir," Naso nodded and took a deep breath, at which Agricola braced himself. "Century will row for the north bank to disembark!" His scream was high-pitched and echoed across the river, and Agricola would lay money that every man and sheep within a fifty-mile radius had heard him.

The barges made their ungainly way to shore and, to the amusement of everyone, Centurion Calvus fell into knee-deep water as he tried to leap from boat to land. Sputtering, he was pulled from the drink by one of the men, who was red-faced from trying not to laugh. "Very fucking funny," Calvus coughed. "You won't be laughing when you're polishing the rust from my *lorica*."

"Crest as well, Centurion?" the legionary asked. "It looks . . . what's the word, sir?" He eyed Agricola.

"Less than flamboyant," Agricola offered. It was true. The once-glorious cross-crest of the centurion's helmet was now bedraggled and dripping with dirty water. Much like the man himself.

"You'll see to it all later, then," Calvus glowered. "Naso?"

"Form the fuck up, you useless pricks!" the optio screamed. "Fucking now, I mean now! Into your *contubernia* and sharp. *Your contubernia*, Felix, you idiot! The fucking holiday is over. Now we march. I love marching now that I don't have to hump a shield and yoke. Just think, boys, one day you could be just like me . . ." He trailed off, daring someone to make a joke about it. They didn't, and he pressed on: "Yes. Soldier well, work hard, and you too could one day carry the *hastile*. That is if you don't get killed in this barbarian shithole."

"And on that cheery note," Agricola muttered under his breath.

Calvus eyed the disposition of the men and glanced at Roscius for his approval. The big man shrugged and flicked his eyes to Agricola.

"Sir?" Calvus asked.

"Carry on, Centurion."

Calvus nodded. "Century will march . . . by the right . . . forward . . . march!"

"What about the boats, sir!" Felix called out as they stamped off.

"Some Cambrian sheep-fucker is going to think he's won the big one," Naso said. "Now how many more times am I going to have to tell you, Felix? Shut. Your. Fucking. Hole. You. Dozy. Cunt."

As the men marched, Agricola approached Roscius. "He seems to use the word 'cunt' a lot," he observed.

"I think it's part of the oath they take as optios," Roscius quipped. He sobered then. "You're all right?" He looked at Agricola from under his brows.

"Yes," Agricola said. "Yes. I'm fine." He was not sure if he meant it or not.

"You better be." Roscius was serious. "We're on our own, and we're over the line. We need to stay calm. And alert."

"Got it."

"Good." There was no more time for talking. Roscius trotted after the men to take his place at the front of the order of march. For his part, Agricola brought up the rear.

As was his habit, Roscius set a fast pace and, after the relative comfort of the saddle and the boat, Agricola was feeling it. However, he kept his mind and his eyes focused on the surroundings, not on his protesting calves and feet. The scenery—so wonderful in Britannia—now took on a sinister aspect. The rolling hills, lush and green, could be concealing men who desperately wanted to kill them. He shivered again and pushed the thought aside: Paulinus had the Cambrians on the run. His report had said as much.

They traveled a good ten miles before the sun began to turn orange, and Agricola felt like he wanted to weep with weariness when Roscius called a welcome halt. The men pounded up the nearest hill to make camp, Roscius ordering a ditch and rampart to be constructed, an order that made him no friends amongst the rankers. As they set to work with their shovels, Agricola spied a billowing stain on the horizon.

"Smoke," he said to Roscius, nudging the bigger man.

Roscius peered into the distance. "Yes," he agreed. "We'll pass right by it tomorrow."

"Shouldn't we send a detachment to see what it's about?"

"No. I'm not sending men out into the field at night. Not here. Whatever it is, there's nothing we can do about it now."

AGRICOLA dreamed.

He dreamed of Lavinia Postumia and her muted sighs of passion. And her screams for mercy as, in the landscape of Morpheus, Postumus killed her in many varied ways. By the sword. By strangulation. By beating her to death. And all the while, he, Gnaeus

Julius Agricola, stood by and watched. Even in the dream, his own conscience screamed at him: *You don't even know how she died. And she died because of you. The fault is yours. The blame. Yours. Her death. Yours to bear.* He cried out against the judgment of his conscience, but nothing could stop the images . . .

If the scenes of his murder-by-proxy were different, the screams were always there. Loud. Incessant. Agonized. Guttural. The sound of iron on iron . . .

Agricola's eyes snapped open to the cries of dying men. "Shit!" he cried, his voice shrill in the rising chaos.

"They're over the ditch," someone called out. It was the last thing he would ever say as his words eddied off into a scream.

Agricola lurched to his feet, eyes casting around frantically for his sword—much like the vast majority of the Tenth. He looked to the defenses and saw bobbing torches as the huge wild-haired outlines of the Cambrians streamed into the camp like wine into a cup. He saw his weapon and grabbed it, hauling it from the scabbard and rushing toward where the fighting seemed to be thickest.

"Form up!" Calvus was shouting at the top of his lungs. "Two lines, back to back, one to five, six to ten!"

The men—well drilled—were doing as they were told. Some had elected to sleep in their gear, some—like himself—had not, and he guessed were sorely regretting it now. At least, he thought, they had shields.

There was nothing he could do to assist Calvus, so he rushed to the rampart, aiming to help out there. Men swarmed around him; in the dark it was hard to tell who was who.

A huge shape loomed up at him, wild hair and wide eyes, all teeth and stinking of beer. The tribesman swung an axe at his head, and it was only by instinct that Agricola managed to duck, feeling the wind on the back of his neck as the sharp iron whizzed by. Training took over then, and he plunged his gladius into the man's exposed side. He was unarmored, and the weapon went in with ease, sinking deep into the Cambrian's vitals. Hot, stinking blood burst free, soaking Agricola's arm from hand to elbow. He tried to drag the sword out, but he'd struck too hard, and it was stuck in the tribesman's body as he writhed and screamed. Agricola twisted his wrist, and the barbarian's legs went from under him. As he fell, the impetus forced the sword free.

The man lay on the ground, his blood coursing out onto the black grass as he wailed piteously, transformed in a moment from howling enemy to desperate victim. Agricola's first victim, there at his feet: the pain-racked body of the first man he had killed. The glory of battle, the honor of combat laid bare. No epic spoke of the stink of shit as the man's bowels went, the mewling and begging for life . . .

Agricola went to put him out of his misery, but another man came at him, cursing him in his barbarian tongue, sword raised and ready to strike.

Agricola kicked him hard in the balls, and he doubled over, clutching himself, his curses now strangled gasps. Agricola cut them short, smashing his sword blade into the tribesman's skull; dark lumps of hair, brain, and skull that he was grateful he could clearly not see spewed skyward as he made to strike again, but the enemy was already dead. He realized in that moment that killing the second man weighed on him far less than the first.

"Sir! Look out!" Agricola heard Felix's shrill voice as the lad ran toward him; he turned too late as a barbarian warrior slammed into his side, taking him to the ground. They rolled, fighting furiously on the blood-sodden earth, growling like beasts. Then, the ground beneath them vanished, and they rolled over the side of the rampart and tumbled into the ditch below. Agricola crashed onto his back, the breath driven from his body. He could feel his lungs trying to work and his throat trying to scream, but there was nothing in him. Then the barbarian was atop him, iron-hard fingers clamping around his neck. The man's teeth were gritted, his eyes white and huge in the dark. Above him, Agricola could hear the sound of battle, the clash of sword on sword, the bass thudding of iron on shield, the panicked shouts of men about to die and the triumphant yells of those who had bested them.

Agricola tried to fight back, but he had no strength left. Panic took him then, a desperate fear and the need to live. "Please," he gurgled. "Please . . ."

The barbarian must have understood because he laughed and squeezed harder. Agricola tried to claw at the man's face, but his attacker simply craned his neck back out of reach and left him flailing in the dark. White spots began to dance in front of his eyes, and then his vision tunneled into blackness, and he felt the cold hand of Hades tugging at his soul. As he gave up the ghost, he felt the barbarian's grip slacken and the heavy weight of him fall across his body.

And he heard Roscius. Calling for help.

"HE'S alive."

"Thank fuck for that."

"Come on, sir, come on . . ."

Agricola opened his eyes to see Felix looming above him. The young legionary helped him to a sitting position, and it seemed to Agricola that he had awoken in Tartarus. The bodies of dead men surrounded him—mostly barbarian, but here and there were the red tunics of dead Romans.

"You all right, sir?" Naso looked down at him, weasel face drawn and pale.

"I think so," Agricola croaked, rubbing his throat. "What happened?"

"Young Felix here saved your arse." Naso glanced at the boy with something like approval in his beady eyes. "In contravention to orders to form up, but I've decided not to put him on a charge."

"Good. Thank you, Felix."

"Just doing my duty, sir," Felix replied, looking as though he was going to burst with pride.

"All right, piss off," Naso told him. "Go and help your mates setting up a pyre for those we lost."

Felix rose, saluted, and did as he was ordered. "How many *did* we lose?" Agricola asked Naso.

"Twenty-two dead."

"Wounded?" Agricola got gingerly to his feet. Every part of him hurt.

"None serious."

"None? That's lucky."

"Not for some." Naso spat in the grass, still dark with drying blood. "The Cambrians took some of 'em. If I was those poor bastards, I'd rather have a foot of iron in my guts. No telling what the woad-skins will do to them—but asking for a ransom won't be on the list."

"Shit." Agricola shook his head, not wanting to imagine the fate of the unfortunates who had become prisoners and soon-to-be burned offerings to the Druidic gods. "We need to get out of here, then. We can't risk going after them, can we?" He shouldn't have framed it like a question, not talking to an optio, but he couldn't help it.

"I wouldn't," Naso offered. "No telling how many more of them could be out there."

Agricola nodded. "And they could be back, so we'll need to move fast. Forced pace. Where's Calvus? As soon as burial detail . . ."

"Calvus is there, sir." Naso jerked his head toward a headless corpse in the dirt.

"Roscius?"

"They took him, sir. I'm sorry; I know he was your mate."

Agricola gaped at the optio, the full weight of his words hitting him in the chest like a hammer blow. A sick sense of dread opened up inside him like the gaping maw of Tartarus, dark and bottomless. If not for him, Roscius would be safe at Isca, not being roasted alive at the hands of the Cambrians. If not for him, Calvus would not be lying on the filthy, bloodied ground. If not for him, twenty-two good men would still be drawing breath. If not for him—

"Sir!" Naso barked.

Agricola's hands were shaking uncontrollably, and bile rushed to his throat. Naso stepped in close as Agricola bent and puked, wet vomit dribbling down his chin.

"First fight, was it?" Naso stepped away, ignoring the puke on his boots. "I've seen it happen more than once," he said louder. "But you're alive, that's what counts. You're not the first to hurl after your first, and you won't be the last."

"Roscius . . ." Agricola said. "We have to . . ."

"Listen," Naso's voice was a harsh whisper. "The senior tribune is dead. The centurion is dead. We've lost men here, and we're at the arse-end of cunt-land with only a vague idea of where we're going. You're in command now, sir. You have to hold it together, or we're all dead. If the lads get an inkling that you've lost the fucking plot, they'll fall apart."

Agricola balled his fists to stop his hands from shaking. It barely worked, but the tension seemed to give him some measure of control. "All right," he said, wiping his chin. "All right."

Naso looked into his eyes, gauging him for a moment. Then: "Orders, sir?"

Agricola took a deep, trembling breath. "Get those men on a pyre. Leave the barbarians for the ravens. Put anyone not on burial detail on guard and keeping a sharp lookout. Full kit and shield—ditch everything else but water. I want us moving and moving fast. Get 'em fed, watered, and on the move."

"Very good, sir." Naso saluted, turned on his heel, and began haranguing the troops, leaving Agricola alone to survey the carnage. Then he looked out of the encampment and to the wilds of Cambria. Somewhere out there, Roscius was being tortured to death. And there was nothing he could do about it. Nothing but soldier on. "Naso!" he called.

"Sir?"

"You're acting centurion now. Choose your own optio—you know these men better than I."

Naso nodded and glanced at Calvus' body. "We used to joke that this was the only way I'd get a fucking promotion. It was funny at the time, I suppose."

"Carry on," was all Agricola had to say.

AGRICOLA led now, marching at the front of the column and, like Roscius, he set a fast pace. He referred only once to the tablet from Paulinus—they were not far away from his last given location. But, Agricola thought, not far was still far enough; the Cambrians were out there somewhere, probably still hungry for Roman blood, even though they'd left forty corpses in the marching camp.

Forty.

Almost two to one losses, he realized. Why, he wondered, would they attack a defended position? Admittedly, the assault had been a surprise, but still—the tribesmen had come off worse and must have known they would.

It made no sense. Why would men just throw their lives away like that? True, the best tactic any barbarian could employ against a Roman force was ambush and surprise: it was the *only* way a legion could be bested.

He focused on the question to keep from dwelling on Roscius' fate, and it continued to vex him until they drew close to the ruin that had once been a village. The smoke he had seen from the marching camp still drifted skyward from the blackened buildings, and the place stank of death. Roman cavalry patrolled the outskirts, but the village itself was alive with legionaries of the Valeria Victrix—the Twentieth Legion: two centuries of infantry and one *turma* of horsemen, a full thirty-man squadron. Such a force would be a hard target and one that answered his question as to why his men had been raided. They would have been easier pickings.

Shrill screams intermingled with the rhythmic sound of hammer on nail rent the air as the soldiers erected crucifixes—children writhing in agony on the wood, screaming for their mothers for succor. The women could provide none—those left in the village were being systematically raped and murdered by the men of the Twentieth.

Agricola drew to a halt, mouth agape, unable to comprehend the horror of the scene. The "work" must have been going on all night. He looked at Naso, whose weasel face was grim.

"They had it coming to them," he said, but the look in his eyes betrayed the harshness in his voice.

Fury burned through Agricola, coursing through his veins like white-hot lava. A cavalryman approached, munching on an apple. "Hey, boys," he said, his lispy accent betraying him as a Batavian.

"Who is in *command* here?" Agricola screamed at him—clearly taking him aback.

The Batavian shrugged—a big ruddy-faced man, his long brown hair streaming from the back of his helmet. "A couple of centurions—they in there," he added. He pronounced his *T*'s like a *D*, and his Latin was not the best. "They . . . how you say . . . getting into the swing of things."

Agricola stormed past him, leaving the men of the Tenth in his wake. He came up behind a legionary on top of a blond-haired woman; she had turned her head to one side and was staring vacantly into space as the soldier grunted and gasped over her. Agricola seized the back of his armor and hauled him off, throwing him to the ground. Furious, the man looked as though he was about to leap up and attack him, but he saw the crest on Agricola's helmet and recognized him as an officer. Agricola kicked him in the face, sending him sprawling. "You fucking animal!" Agricola's voice was strangled with fury. "Stop this. Stop this now! All of you!"

His voice cut through the chaos around him as men stopped to look. "You are Roman soldiers!" he shouted. "Not barbarians!"

"What the fuck is going on?" another man's voice—so strident it could only belong to a centurion—cut over his.

The centurion—a tall man with a livid scar down his face—shoved his men aside and made his way forward. As he saw Agricola, he shook his head. "Sir." He drew up and saluted. "Centurion Mamercus Mummius Flacca of the Second Century . . ."

"I don't give a fuck who you are!" Agricola cut him off. The man's face reddened with anger, but it was matched by Agricola's own. "Cut those children down. *Now!* And call your men off! I'll have you on a charge for this—"

"We're following orders, sir," Flacca interrupted. "From the governor himself."

It gave Agricola a moment of pause, but the smug smile of victory on Flacca's weather-beaten face burned it away. "The governor isn't here," Agricola said. "I am. And I am ordering you to cut those children down and call your men *off.*"

They glared at each other for long moments; Agricola could see righteous fury warring with army procedure within Flacca. Procedure won. "Cut 'em down!" he shouted. "And put your cocks away. The *tribune* here orders it."

"I'll have you broken to the ranks for this," Agricola spat.

"I expect you'll have to report it to the governor, sir," Flacca's tone was even, laced with the certainty that it would be Agricola who was going to be called to task. But at that moment, Agricola didn't give a damn.

He turned away from the man. "Naso!" he shouted as the men of the Tenth made their way cautiously forward. "Get Felix and some of the younger ones to round up the women. Have some men see to the children—get their wounds bound."

"Most will have broken legs, sir," Flacca put in from behind him. "Easier to nail them up that way, and they die quicker."

Agricola rounded on him. "Then that's tough shit for your men," he said. "Because they'll be bearing their stretchers. Get your people together," he added. "You—and your Batavians—will escort me to the Twentieth's encampment."

"We have orders, sir . . ."

"And so do I. While you bastards were engaged in all this mindless brutality, my century was attacked last night. We lost *men*."

"And so have we," Flacca said. "Your boys' shields—Second Augusta, down in Isca? Everybody knows the south is quieter than a houseful of Vestal Virgins—we've seen the sharp end here. We're soldiers, not guardsmen."

"Shut your mouth. And obey my orders, Centurion."

Flacca saluted and turned away, haranguing his men. Agricola watched him, the fury ebbing out of him like wine from a cup as Naso approached.

"If he's telling the truth about his orders, this could go hard on you, sir," he said. "Like as not, these people would do worse to ours if they had us. You know that. Your mate Roscius . . ."

"Like I said, Naso. We're not barbarians. We're Romans. We're better than they are."

THE march was cold and silent; Agricola had the Batavian cavalry decurion—Magnusanus—throw his *turma* out in a screen around the legionaries to keep a look out for the war band who had attacked them the previous evening.

War band.

It wasn't a war band, and Agricola knew it. Those men were poorly equipped and hardly warriors—they were men driven to desperation by the acts of Flacca and soldiers like him. And good men like Roscius were now paying the price. Somewhere out there, Roscius was screaming in his own hell as they were taking savage vengeance on him and the others. It made Agricola sick to his stomach. Sick because he could not help his friend, sick that his actions were the cause of Roscius' fate, and sick that this was the reality of what they now faced. Slaughter and vengeance, vengeance and slaughter. The seeds of generations of hatred had been sown here.

Hatred.

Agricola could feel it emanating from the men of the Twentieth as they marched north, their glares, their muttered comments, and the wads of phlegm spat on the grass as they tramped on. He had not won any friends here, and these were men who would—perhaps—have to follow his orders in the future.

As they marched on, he saw that the evidence of war was scored deeper on the landscape with each mile they traveled. Farms destroyed, villages burned, civilians killed. Each place they marched past seemed to Agricola to be more vile than the next. Crucifixes jutted from the ground in ever-increasing number, the rotting bodies that hung from them a feast for the ravens. It was more than simple detritus of battle, Agricola realized. This was deliberate and systematic—the most horrific tortures had been inflicted on these people. That the Cambrians inflicted barbarism on their captives was to be expected—but these tribesmen hardly presented a Hannibalistic threat to the empire, and he could not understand why a Roman governor would allow such savagery to be perpetrated in the name of Rome.

Or indeed, order it perpetrated, as it seemed.

The images were branded on Agricola's mind's eye by the time they drew close to the Twentieth Legion's marching camp.

"There we go." Magnusanus trotted up to him as the fortification came into view. "Home for a while at least." The decurion did not seem to hold him in the same contempt as his infantry counterparts. He leaned down in his saddle. "Me and my boys don't like it any more than you do, sir. But Flacca's right—those were his orders. As you saw on the way here, it isn't only his century and that lot. This is how the whole campaign has gone."

Agricola looked up at him. "It's wrong, Decurion."

"It's war, sir."

The encampment was truly vast, surrounded by a broad, deep ditch, well defended with a rampart and palisade. Agricola saw cavalrymen on the horizon in all directions, patrolling the vicinity, ready to gallop back with the news of any prospective assault.

As the Tenth and their escort plodded across the muddied plank that led into the marching camp, they were greeted by howls of derision by the men of the Twentieth, who instantly recognized the dual Capricorn blazon of the Second Augusta's shields. Agricola bore the insults with stoicism; the men of the Tenth, however, had no such compunction and hurled abuse back, insulting the mothers, fathers, and manhood of their counterparts. This went on for some time until they were met by the Twentieth's primus pilus—the leading centurion—a gladius-straight hard case with the face of a man who seemed to have been born old.

"I'll get your men billeted, Tribune," he said, nodding a greeting to Magnusanus. "I take it you're going to get drunk and fuck your horse."

Magnusanus sighed. "I wish I could," he said. "But ever since you've had your lips around my horse's cock, he doesn't want to know me anymore. It's breaking my heart. This, perhaps, is why I get drunk all the time." The Batavians got a laugh out of that, but Agricola was relieved that if his own men were amused, they kept their eyes front and their mouths shut. The primus refrained from response, deigning only to make an obscene gesture at the Batavian.

"Primus." Flacca shouldered his way forward. "A word."

"What is it, Flacca?" the primus asked. "Are you all right?"

Agricola glanced at the centurion. The man's face was pallid, and he was pouring with sweat, seeming to be in some pain. He rotated his shoulder a little.

"A touch of indigestion, sir," Flacca offered by way of explanation. It looked to Agricola to be far more than that, but if the bastard was in pain, that was only a good thing.

"This officer prohibited me and my men from carrying out our duties." Flacca mopped his face with a piece of cloth. "I want to raise it as a complaint—"

"You and your men were raping women and torturing children, Centurion," Agricola cut him off. "To your eternal shame."

The primus folded his arms. "I'll take your report," he said to Flacca, who—despite his evident discomfort—sneered at Agricola. "As for you, sir," he said to Agricola. "If you're a tribune from the Second Augusta, then you're Gnaeus Julius Agricola, am I right?"

"That's right."

"You're to report to the governor. I'll get your men sorted with beds and grub."

"There are wounded civilians with us," Agricola said. "I want them seen to. And I want them treated well, Primus."

"That ain't—"

"Put your report in to the governor if you have an issue with my orders, Primus. You'll obey me *now,* and we'll see who has the rights of it later."

"If you say so, sir."

"I do. Consider it a direct order," Agricola said.

"Very good, sir. I'll send word of your quarters." The primus rocked back and forth on his heels, clearly eager to get going to hear what "gossip" Flacca had.

"Carry on, Primus," Agricola said. He wasn't going to give the man the satisfaction of asking where Paulinus was, which seemed to disappoint him somewhat. Without another word, he made off, heading towards the marching camp's *praetorium.*

If it was true that all Roman encampments had the same specifications, the men of the Twentieth had a different look to his own in the Second Augusta. They were leaner and more drawn, and their kits—whilst in good condition—were not pristine. And many sported wounds; the difference between a garrison legion and one on campaign was all too apparent to Agricola. He located the *praetorium* with no difficulty and was announced by the guards on duty.

Governor Paulinus was sitting behind his desk but rose as Agricola entered. He was a tall man, and Agricola gauged him to be around sixty years old. Whip thin and hatchet-faced, he had straight, iron-gray hair and dark, perceptive eyes. Agricola snapped to attention and saluted, eyes front, looking through the older man, staring at a spot on the wall.

"At ease, boy, at ease," Paulinus said, offering his arm. They shook, and Agricola went to the seat offered to him, resisting the urge to groan like a forty-year-old as he sat down. He desperately wanted to be free of his armor and to wash the filth, blood, and stench of death from his body. "You look tired," Paulinus noted.

"It was a long march, sir," Agricola said. "We saw some action on the way."

Paulinus sat and poured wine for them both. He watched Agricola as he drank, tapping his fingertips together, not touching his own drink. "I can see that you did," he said at length. "You won, clearly."

The wine was excellent, the smooth Falernian taste warming Agricola. "We repelled an attack by a superior force. They attacked our marching camp," he extrapolated. "At night. We killed forty but lost twenty-two men in the assault with seven wounded—those were taken by the enemy." Agricola heard his own voice saying it in the correct military fashion. The entire, horrifying incident, the death of some sixty men, both Roman and barbarian, the pyres for his soldiers, the loss of his best friend—all summed up briefly enough to be noted on a wax tablet. The Roman way.

"I see." Paulinus finally took a drink. "You are aware of what they do to our prisoners, Agricola?"

"I have been told, sir."

"They're vermin," Paulinus said, his voice colder than his eyes. "And like vermin, they must be exterminated."

"Yes, sir." The images of the ruined villages flashed in his mind.

Paulinus gazed at him, his eyes cold and serpent-like. "You find it distasteful," he stated.

"Arms observe no bounds, nor can the wrath of the sword, once drawn, be easily checked or stayed; war delights in blood," Agricola offered.

Paulinus laughed, the sound of it brittle as frost on a winter morning. "Seneca?"

"A wise man, sir."

"A man whose wisdom is afforded by the sword. We fight out

here so the likes of Seneca can sit on his corpulent backside in Rome and wax lyrical on such things. Besides which, I've met the man—for all his talk, he has no objection to spilling blood if it means more coin in his purse. He has investments over here that he's called in, and he cares not how much unrest his debt collectors stir up. The blood of tribesmen and the hunger of their children, that's what feeds Seneca's letters, Agricola. But he's right on this: war is an unpleasant business at the best of times. This kind of war is the worst of all."

"So I have seen on my way here. Your men have been extremely efficient." He took a breath. "Your man, Centurion Flacca . . ."

"A first-rate officer," Paulinus said.

"I stopped him and his men in a craven assault on a village."

"He was following my orders." Paulinus' dark eyes flashed with cold anger. "Which you, in your wisdom, saw fit to countermand?"

"Was raping the women also in his remit, sir?" Agricola shot back, the cords holding his temper in place fraying. "Raping them whilst their children were strung up on crosses?"

Paulinus opened his mouth to speak and checked himself. Then: "As your Seneca says, soldiers, once let off the leash, can be brutes."

"I put a stop to it."

Paulinus regarded him. "Yes. Perhaps I would have done the same if I were in your position. As a younger man, at least," he added. "That said—you're aware that your captured men are now having their skins peeled off and the Gods know what else by these animals you've . . . protected."

"I have heard tell, sir. But should we condone a descent to their level?"

Paulinus sighed. "Condone? No. Accept? Yes, I am afraid that we must, Agricola."

"But why? Rome has faced far greater threats than this."

"No, it hasn't."

Agricola was taken aback by the assessment. "I don't understand."

"No, I expect that you don't," Paulinus murmured. "This is a rebellion, yes. We have faced those before—a punitive expedition, a few crucifixions to show the local populace that the risks far outweigh the gains of a precarious freedom. This, however, is a rebellion of a different sort. Do you know what a Druid is, Agricola?"

"Yes, sir. I am familiar with Caesar's work. But I've never seen one or heard of any in Isca."

"They're probably all up here." Paulinus was unable to keep the pique from his voice. "They're religious fanatics."

"Like the Judeans?"

"Exactly. And as with the Judeans, it's not so much the rebellion that's the problem, it's the religion itself. These Druids have made this a *bellum sacrum*—a holy war. They hold sway over these people, boy. These acts of torture against our men are ordered by the Druids—sacrifices for whatever gods they're bartering with to get shot of us. The harder the death, the greater the power of the sacrifice, I'm told. So one part of my mission here is to make sure that the population fears us more than they fear their holy men."

"Part of your mission, sir?"

"Yes." Paulinus rose to his feet and walked to a map of Britannia that was on a tripod at the far end of the *praetorium*: "Look here." Agricola joined him, remembering to fetch the governor's cup of wine with him, for which he received a nod of thanks. "This island," Paulinus tapped the map, "we call Mona. Gods know what they call it—you need a jug full of spit in your throat to speak their damned language—but Mona is their base. Their

Holy Island. The place where these Druids are taught. I've driven every armed man—and woman because these native women can fight—to this place. Those that we've not killed already, anyway.

"They're concentrated there—all in one place. This is another reason why I've proscribed such a war—a terrified populace will look to its gods for succor. They'll flee in the face of we 'terrible Romans' and head for Mona. And hopefully be eating these damned Druids out of house and home. For now, they think they're safe—they're on an island, after all, and everyone knows that a beachhead is a bad way to fight a battle."

"You have a plan, sir?" It was an odd sensation. Despite himself, despite all he had seen in the past days, the losses, the fighting, he could feel himself falling under the spell of Paulinus already. There was something about him, a charisma that enthralled.

Paulinus looked at him. "What would you do?"

"I . . ." Agricola floundered for a moment. "I'd have the navy patrol the strait—make sure they can't go anywhere—and starve them out."

"Sensible enough," Paulinus concurred. "Except that no one sane trusts the navy, and even if I did trust them, I need those ships protecting the trade vessels between here and Gaul. Hibernian pirates," he extrapolated. "Worse than the Cambrians, even. And then, starving them out—that'll take time. Time enough for the embers to catch again while I have my army here. Before you know it, those that haven't fled to Mona will be cutting supply lines and causing all kinds of mischief. No, Agricola. I need to make a statement here. That there is no higher authority than that of Rome—and not even their gods or their damned Druids can protect them against it. So a beach assault it shall be."

That, Agricola realized, would be costly; but, charismatic as he was, Paulinus did not strike him as a man that would care much about the cost—only that the objective was achieved. He was a pillar of the Roman establishment in that regard. "Here," he tapped a point on the map, "this looks to be the shortest route."

"It is," Paulinus agreed. "But it's deep water. Strong tides and quicksand. That," he added, "is a good thing. It'll make the Cambrians feel more secure." Agricola was inclined to disagree but held his tongue. "Here it's about a quarter of a mile of shallow water," Paulinus explained.

"How shallow?"

"Not that shallow." Paulinus' smile was thin. "If you go into the drink in your armor, you won't make it. But I suspect those type of casualties will be minor. As I have said, this part of the strait is not too choppy—in this weather, it should be straightforward enough. Now," he turned back to Agricola, "consider this a formal welcome to my staff. Your men will remain as a detachment to the Twentieth."

"Yes, sir." Agricola drew to attention and saluted. Assuming the audience was done with, he turned about and walked toward the door. Just as he was about to exit, Paulinus spoke again, making him turn.

"Agricola."

"Sir?"

"My mission is to wipe them out. To destroy this Druidic cult once and for all. It will not be pleasant, and when it is over, I *will* allow the men free rein. If you take my meaning."

Agricola looked into Paulinus' eyes, seeing only cold dispassion therein. "Yes, sir," he said. "And I feel that is regrettable."

Paulinus ignored the comment. "You were not aware of my orders before. Now that you are, I will take an extremely dim view if you countermand me again. I hope we understand each other."

Agricola met his gaze, even and unflinching, even though every part of him screamed to break the stare. "We do, sir," he said after a moment.

Paulinus' lips turned up in a ghost of a smile. "Good," he said. "You may go."

The next days were taken up in a frenzy of activity for Agricola. Being on Paulinus' staff was not—by any stretch of the imagination—an easy duty. Though in his sixties, the governor seemed tireless, waking early, retiring late, and allowing no detail to slip his gaze. He pushed those under his command equally hard—the army marched, camped, marched, and camped again. The Cambrians fled in the face of the relentless Roman war machine—any unfortunate enough not to outpace them were slaughtered without mercy. It turned Agricola's stomach, but Paulinus had been explicit—this was the strategy, and it would be carried out. Agricola wished it would be otherwise but knew it could not.

He mentioned this to both Magnusanus and Naso over a cup of wine at a hastily erected—but always present—*popina*. The little stalls sprang up all over the marching camp, a haven where off-duty men could buy drink and food. The newly made centurion and Batavian cavalryman had struck up an unlikely friendship; Agricola assumed it was because the Tenth, being from the Second Augusta, and Magnusanus' cavalry would be looked down upon by the men of the Twentieth.

"Perhaps the revenge for your men is what you should think on," Magnusanus offered. "The Cambrians, they are savages. I know this, as do you. Even him, as stupid as he looks." He grinned at Naso.

"That's fucking rich coming from you, you Batavian cunt," Naso replied; the fact that he could use such obscenity with no aggressive inflection was a true talent, Agricola reflected. "You can't even speak Latin properly."

"I speak the Latin better than you speak the Batavian," Magnusanus said, leaving Naso with no answer.

"He's right, though, Boss," Naso said, and the epithet warmed

Agricola because it was something akin to respect from the man. "There's no sense dwelling on it. This is how we deal with the locals. What's done is done—and that's the way it's going to stay."

The words of Agathon once again rang in Agricola's mind. "Even a god cannot change the past," he quoted.

"That's the truth there." Magnusanus raised his cup. "Look, you Romans like your . . . how you say . . ." he looked skywards, trying to find the words, "men of rock."

"What?" Naso frowned.

"The men and the women made of the white rock."

"Sculpture," Agricola supplied.

"Yes! Sculpture!" Magnusanus' grin was wide, and Agricola could see he was consigning the piece of vocabulary to his memory. "Well, to make the sculpture, it starts out as nothing. In fact, it is ugly. A piece of lump. But when the right man comes along with the right tools, he makes the lump something beautiful and wonderful. So it is here in Cambria. Paulinus is the man, Cambria the rock. To make it a beautiful thing, as in the rest of Britannia, he must first break the rock. Much of the rock will be wasted. Much of the rock will be dust. But when the job is done . . . it will be good."

"Basically, you can't make a sculpture without breaking a few rocks." Naso nodded, impressed. "I like that."

"I liked his version better," Agricola said.

"Permission to speak freely, sir?"

"Granted."

"That's because as long as I've known you, you like using three words where one will do."

Agricola was forced to take that one on the chin. "At least we are drawing toward the end game now. We're getting close to the sea."

"Aye," Naso agreed. "Not far to go."

Agricola placed his cup down on the *popina's* bar. "I'm going to check on the lads, Naso. Make sure all is in order."

"Very good, sir," Naso said, his face writ with the hope that he would not be called upon to accompany his commander.

Agricola eyed him for a moment. "Enjoy your wine," he said and turned away, heading toward the small part of the encampment that had been allocated to the Tenth. He was pleased to see that Naso had taken the initiative and organized a guard rota—something he had not thought of, but when he saw the duty men, he thought it was for the best. No doubt there had been some internecine punch-ups between his men and those of the Twentieth already. The presence of armed guards would dissuade any belligerent drunks who wanted to pick a fight with the men of another—and therefore rival—legion.

The men of the Augusta's Tenth were sorted into their *contubernia*, tents arranged in neat rows, fires burning outside some of them as men cooked, cleaned their armor, and threw banter around. He made his way through them, asking a question here and there: if anything was needed, how some of the men had come by their black eyes. The story was always that they had fallen, tripped, or taken the butt-end of a foolish companion's *pilum* in the face—never that they had received them in a brawl with the men of the Twentieth. That was an unwritten rule.

"Felix." He saw the boy polishing his *segmentata*. "How goes the war?"

"Oh!" Felix looked up at his senior officer, taken by surprise. He put his armor to one side and rose to his feet, saluting as he did so. "Good, sir. I mean, you know. It ain't nice, is it? What we've seen. But I can handle it," he suffixed with haste.

"I'm sure you can," Agricola said. "Just remember, Felix. What they did isn't soldiering. They went too far."

"Everyone says they were just following orders," Felix said. "If that's what you have to do when you're told, then that's what you have to do. A shame about those children, though—that was rough."

Agricola regarded him for a moment, wondering what kind of man he would become, what, if his birth had allowed, paths life would have offered outside of soldiering. The truth of it was that an army career was one of the few options for the poor to elevate their status. "I didn't get a chance to thank you properly for saving my life," he said.

Felix grinned. "Ah, well, sir. That *is* soldiering, ain't it? We'd be fuc . . . in trouble in enemy lands without a commanding officer, wouldn't we?"

"I'll recommend you for a commendation," Agricola promised. "Ought to make your mates jealous when you strut around with a decoration. And your people at home, no doubt."

"Yes, sir. Thank you, sir." Felix flushed. "My mum'd be made up."

Agricola nodded. "Carry on, Felix."

"I understand that disagreements will arise," Paulinus said. He was dressed in his war gear, and he looked every inch the patrician commander. Agricola, Flacca, and the primus were all drawn up to attention in his *praetorium*. "That is the nature of men," he added. "Something for our philosopher here to ponder, no doubt." He glanced at Agricola. "In your time of leisure. But that time is not now. We are at war, gentlemen. I cannot—and will not—tolerate petty rivalry between you. I've heard what the tribune has to say, and I've heard the primus' report. I'm disappointed, gentlemen. Flacca," he addressed the centurion, who began to sweat again. "You were out of line. I ordered termination, yes. You took it upon yourself to . . . extend . . . that order to rape and crucifixion. This, I did not order."

"Orders were to strike terror, sir," Flacca blinked sweat out of his eyes and spoke through gritted teeth. "I thought that was the best way."

"Crucifixion, perhaps. Rapine behavior, no. It's bad for discipline, Flacca. This is an army, not a mob, and I won't tolerate it at this time and certainly not without my express permission—even if these creatures we're fighting are subhuman."

"Sir, the men . . ." Flacca began but stopped short. Paulinus didn't even have to speak—he just fixed the man with his serpent stare and waited for him to wilt. Which, Agricola noted, he did rather quickly. "Yes, sir."

"Are you all right, Flacca?" Paulinus asked. "You're sweating."

"Fit for duty, sir," Flacca said. "The local food is giving me the . . . a . . . bad stomach."

"I see." Paulinus turned his attention to the primus. "As for you, I expect better. Your 'report' wasn't worth the wax it was scratched on. Having the backs of the men you command is one thing. Character assassination is quite something else. I don't care what you think of this tribune personally. He *is* a tribune, and he is now under my command. If he gives an order, the men will obey it. Even if," his gaze finally fell on Agricola, "he was unaware he was countermanding me." Paulinus let the lie hang—everyone in the room knew it for a lie, and Paulinus was daring the primus and centurion both to bring it up. They didn't, and Paulinus allowed him a slight smile that indicated that whilst they might have the real truth of it, *his* version of the truth was all that counted. "That misunderstanding has now been rectified, and I'm satisfied that Tribune Gnaeus Julius Agricola is fully appraised of my orders and my wider strategy. Are we in accord, gentlemen?"

They all responded with a militarily neutral, "Yes, sir."

"Good," Paulinus nodded. "Then the matter is settled. To cement our new pact of inter-legionary cooperation, your Second

Century, Flacca, and the men of the Second Augusta's Tenth will carry out a patrol today. You will work in cooperation; you will follow Agricola's orders—which, Tribune, will reflect my own. I will be seriously displeased if it comes to my attention that there are any . . . issues . . . on this patrol."

"Sir," Agricola spoke up. "The Tenth is under-strength after the recent action."

"I've got men coming back into duty from injury," the primus said. "I can spare a few from our Tenth as well. We'll get your lot back up to a full eighty, Tribune."

Paulinus let them stand for some time in silence before speaking again. "You may go," he said and turned back to his desk as if they no longer existed.

They exited in silence, but as soon as they were outside, Agricola determined that the governor had the rights of it. "A moment, Flacca," he said. The primus hung around, too, and Agricola met his eye. "Primus. I would like a word with the centurion if you please. Unless you are coming on the patrol, there's nothing for you to hear."

The veteran nodded and saluted; clearly, he was getting into the swing of it, too. "Very good, sir," he said. "I'll round up the spares for you." He made off, leaving the two men alone.

"At ease, Flacca," Agricola said. "Look. You don't like me. I don't like you. But—you heard the governor. We have to work together. I'll hold up my end, you hold up yours, all right? We can't afford to be back-sniping each other out there. I'm counting on you and your men. My boys don't have the same experience as yours. If the shit flies—which I hope it won't—they'll be looking to you and yours."

Flacca nodded, his lips pressed into a thin line. "Very good, sir," he said.

"That said," Agricola added, "Paulinus is right. You look like hammered shit. You sure it's just a case of bad guts? You want to see the *medicus*? Send your optio out with us? I mean you no disrespect—genuinely, Centurion. Sick is sick."

"I'm fine, sir." Flacca was admirably stoic.

"Very well." Agricola wasn't about to wet-nurse the man—he wouldn't be thanked for it. "Go and get Magnusanus and his *turma* ready to ride," he ordered. "I'll see you at the gates."

IT was hot—springtime in Britannia was all too short, and they were already getting a hint of the summer to come. Agricola rode at the front of the column, frequently glancing over his shoulder at the men slogging through the rolling grasslands. Discipline was good—the Tenth and Flacca's Second chatted as they walked—something he was prepared to allow in the spirit of Paulinus' orders. Magnusanus and his cavalry were thrown out in a screen on both flanks. He looked to the east to see the Batavian canter up a hillock, surveying the ground beneath. He dragged his horse's reins about swiftly, signaling his men to do likewise, and kicked the beast's flanks, pounding toward the column.

"What is it?" Agricola raised his arm to halt the men, who fell silent as the Batavians pulled up by him.

"There's a war band down there," Magnusanus reported. "About one hundred and fifty armed men, I reckon. Didn't stop to count in case they saw us," he added. "But they're heading toward the sea."

"Then we'll have to stop them," Agricola said, his mind made up. "Dog their progress, Magnusanus. I'll have the centuries go at the double and give them a greeting. Keep me apprised of the Cambrians' movements. Once we're in position, ride around the back and attack on the oblique."

"On the oblique?" Magnusanus raised his eyebrows.

"Yes. Flacca," Agricola looked to the centurion, "I'm going to attack head-on with the Tenth. We're eighty men; they're almost twice that—they'll think we're easy pickings. I want your boys up the rise and hidden. Once we're engaged, get yourselves down the hill and hit them in the flank. That," he looked to Magnusanus, "will force them east—as you come in on the oblique."

Magnusanus looked impressed. "Good plan," he said and rode off to gather his men.

"Flacca . . ."

"We won't let you down, Tribune," the scar-faced veteran said.

"Then let's move. At the double. And keep the noise down."

"FORM a fucking straight line, you cunts!" Naso screamed at the Tenth. "A *straight* line!"

Agricola swallowed as the war band drew to a halt some hundred yards away from them. A figure dressed in black robes was capering about in front of their massed ranks, screaming and raising his hands skyward, doubtless imploring the gods to bring death to the Romans.

He'd ordered his men to form up in two ranks of forty—presenting a thin and inviting target for the Cambrians to attack. For a moment, he doubted the wisdom of his plan—there seemed to be a lot more than Magnusanus' hurried estimate. He'd guess the number at nearer two hundred than a hundred and fifty. But the die was cast, and he'd have to go through with it now. For his part, he rode at the rear as a tribune should, ready to give orders and not get involved with the fight—unless he had to. Naso glanced back at him, ready for instruction now that the men were in line, and he felt a flush of shame. He couldn't let them go into battle and just hang back, shouting encouragement. He threw his leg over the head of his horse and slipped to the ground, drawing his sword.

"You don't have a shield, sir," Naso said. "Best you give the orders; we'll do the fighting."

"Don't worry, Naso," he said, his voice loud so it carried. "I won't get in the way. Boys! Let's close with them and give 'em two flights of *pila* on Naso's command. Put iron to the bastards, and let's see if we can finish them off before Flacca and his arse-bandits from the Twentieth can get down the hill!"

"Tenth will advance at the double!" Naso's high-pitched and nasal parade voice rent the air. "Advance!"

They took off at a trot, deaf to everything but the crunch of booted feet on the ground and the rhythmic clanking and jingling of kits as they closed the ground between them and the enemy. Agricola did not put himself in the front rank; as Naso had pointed out, he had no shield, and he'd be a hindrance there. With the centurion holding the right of the forward line, he found himself at the lowest of the low—rear rank on the left, running next to Felix. The boy looked resolute and only a little afraid—this was not, of course, his first battle. Nor was it his own, Agricola realized, but the truth of it was, his first engagement had hardly been covered in glory.

The Cambrians were evidently surprised at the aggressive stance taken by the Roman commander. The usual legion rule was to receive the famous frontal all-or-nothing charge the tribesmen were so fond of and then see who gave way first. However, under the leadership of their black-robed commander, the Cambrians swiftly recovered and, with a roar, began running toward their enemy, shrieking and howling as they came.

"First *pila*!" Naso shouted. "Loose!"

Without breaking stride, the men hurled their javelins, the black shafts arcing skyward and falling into the ranks of the Cambrians, sending many sprawling to the ground, slowing the advance as men tripped over the dead and dying. "Second *pila*! Loose!" Naso cried scant moments after the first—they were closing still, and fast.

The second flight of javelins caused far more damage than the first, the shafts killing some and embedding themselves in the shields of those that carried them. The iron shanks of the weapons bent as they sank into the shields, rendering them too cumbersome to be used. Cursing barbarians cast the things aside—causing yet more chaos in the ranks.

"Swords!" An edge of panic sounded in Naso's voice as they closed in. No man—not even a veteran—was unafraid before contact. "Shields up—get 'em, lads!"

Whatever he said next was lost to Agricola as the Cambrians smashed into the Roman line, and the cacophony of battle swept around them like a deluge. Men screamed in pain and fury, weapons clashed and thudded into shields as both sides' advance juddered to a halt and disintegrated into a frantic scrum. In the second rank, soldiers waited—hoping that they would not have to step forward because it would mean, firstly, that a man they knew had gone down and, second, because it would now be them in harm's way.

Agricola shouted encouragement to the men in front of him. Over their helmeted heads, he could see the seething mass of Cambrians, wild-haired and wild-eyed, their swords raised as they hacked and cut at the thin Roman line. Dirty fingers gripped the edges of shields, trying to rip them from the men's grasps. He saw one man succeed and receive a gladius in his throat for his pains—the dark iron went in deep, sending blood jetting all over the soldier. Shieldless, the man rolled to the left, and Felix stepped into the breach. He did as all the soldiers were trained to do—punch with the shield, head low, thrust with the sword, repeat. It was brutal, close, and effective, the Roman gladius designed precisely for this type of fight.

Agricola had to step back as the Tenth's line was forced to give way by the press of battle and, panicked, he looked to the hills to see Flacca and his men rushing down—admirably silent as they came. "Hold them, lads!" he screamed, his voice shrill with nerves. "Hold them!"

The Cambrians roared, encouraged by the slack in front of them, and the brawl intensified. Agricola saw a war axe descend and split a soldier's head in two, helmet and all. As the blade was dragged up, another legionary rammed his gladius into the axman's guts, sending him to the ground, but in doing so, he exposed himself and left his right side open to an attack. A spear lanced into his side, buckling his *segmentata*. Agricola leapt to the fore and swung hard with his *spatha*—a longer weapon than an infantryman's—taking the spearman in soft flesh between his neck and shoulder.

Huge gouts of blood erupted from the gaping wound, showering friend and foe alike, and the tribesman went down shrieking in pain, his blood soaking the already sodden grass at their feet.

Then Flacca's men crashed into the flank of the attacking Cambrians, hard enough to send the entire line lurching to the left. Agricola's Tenth leapt forward as a single iron-clad beast, swords and shields working in unison, punishing their enemy, who was now in confusion—a confusion that turned to fear and panic as they were being scythed down without mercy.

A few moments later, they were on the run, fleeing the carnage, leaving the ground littered with their dead and dying.

"Get them!" he heard Flacca shout. "Kill them! Kill them all!"

The Second Century rushed after the fleeing Cambrians, but Agricola held his tongue. His own men had done the brunt of the fighting and were spent for now, gasping for breath and cursing as they discovered wounds that they had not felt in the rush of battle.

The Cambrians were outdistancing the Second—a man in *segmentata* holding a shield could not catch a lightly armored enemy. But a horseman could.

The Batavians swirled into view—on the oblique as he had ordered. The angle of attack confused the Cambrians, who had men at their backs and now coming down on their shield sides. "Tenth Century!" Agricola shouted. "On me, at the double!" Rest time was over as he rushed to cut off their sword sides just as Magnusanus' horses smashed into the wavering Cambrians, swords cutting a bloody swath through the desperate men, the charge rending the mob in two. The Cambrians whirled in panic as the Second closed in, the legionaries running as hard as they could, blood up now and eager to get stuck into an enemy that was already beaten.

The Batavians wheeled about for another charge, Magnusanus as the tip of their wedge, shouting in his own language as the *turma* thundered back through the shattered warriors, leaving dead bodies in their wake. Utterly demoralized, they threw down their weapons, some falling to their knees as the Second drew to a halt. Agricola led his own men forward, knowing what had to be done.

"We surrender!" the black-robed man shouted at Flacca in Latin, seeing the red cross-crest on his helmet and recognizing him as a senior man.

Flacca looked over to Agricola as he trotted up with the gasping men of the Tenth. "Do your duty, Centurion," Agricola ordered.

Flacca nodded and raised his sword, but the black-clad man raised his arm, stopping the veteran in his tracks. "If you strike me, you will die!" the man screamed. "I am the representative of the gods. I am sacrosanct—you will die!"

"Everybody dies," Flacca informed him and rammed his gladius into the man's abdomen. The man—a Druid, Agricola guessed—wailed in agony as the cold metal pierced his vitals. But he had courage, and he spat a gob of blood into Flacca's face as he fell away.

"The gods will have their vengeance," he gasped. "They will . . ."

Flacca bent over and stabbed him in the neck, silencing him. "Finish them," he ordered. The men of the Second and Tenth needed no urging. They rushed in, swarming over the defenseless Cambrians and butchering them to a man. It was, Agricola thought, sickening, watching desperate men beg for their lives, hands clawing and pleading, begging for mercy where none was to be found.

It didn't take long. Agricola felt unclean afterward, the sight of the dying littered across the field, the flies already feasting on still-warm corpses. But this was not his first fight, and he did not vomit this time like a green boy.

"Look, sir!" Agricola dragged his eyes away from the body of a fallen man to see Felix holding a bloody gladius in his fist. "One of them had this. And there," he pointed with the dripping weapon. "That one has *lorica* on."

"Must be some of the ones that hit your marching camp," Flacca said, still gasping from his pursuit. "Must be . . ." He stumbled forward, and Agricola caught his arm, holding the man up. Flacca scrabbled at his armor. "My chest . . ." He coughed. "Can't breathe . . ."

Agricola was unable to hold his weight, and the centurion crashed to the ground, trying to clutch at his chest. "Get his armor off!" he shouted. "Do it now!"

But it was too late. Flacca had ceased to move, and his dead eyes stared at the sky.

"The Druid cursed him!" one of the Second shouted. "I heard it!"

"Shut your mouth," Agricola cut the man off. "He had a weak heart is all."

"Aye, and now it's been burst by magic!"

The men turned in an instant from rampant victory to fearful superstition, all and sundry making signs to ward off evil. Agricola cursed under his breath. "Shut up. All of you. Get the dead together and sort your wounded. Naso, have a tent party search these corpses, see if there's anything in the way of intelligence. Who's the optio of the Second?"

"I am, sir." A short man stepped forward. He had an indestructible look about him, and Agricola saw he had calves like a Herculean statue.

"Get your men sorted. And put any man on a charge who mentions the word 'Druid' or 'curse.' Am I clear?"

"Aye, sir." The optio didn't look convinced, his blue eyes flicking to the corpse of his centurion.

"Get them sorted," Agricola said again. He made his way over to Naso, who was detailing Felix and his mates to search the corpses.

"You think the Druid cursed him, sir?" he heard Felix ask the centurion.

Naso had no answer to that—or at least he didn't seem to want to give one. "Get on with your work, lad." He drew up as Agricola approached. "Yes, sir."

"I don't want this getting out of hand," Agricola said. "I've told the Second and now I'm telling you. No talking about cursing or Druids. Our gods are stronger than theirs," he hedged; soldiers were, by and large, uneducated and superstitious, believing in omens, good-luck charms and all kinds of nonsense. By invoking the gods of Rome, he hoped to curtail any fear of the Druids from getting out of hand. But he could see by the looks on the men's faces that it was too late. Far too late.

THE gossip spread faster than a plague, as Agricola knew it must. News of Flacca's untimely demise was all over the marching camp in a few hours, the men suddenly finding religion as small sacrifices to the gods were burning all over the camp.

Paulinus was less than pleased by the turn of events, but there was little to nothing he could do about it. Soldiers talked and the rumor mill would not be stopped, and, as it was, the governor chose to ignore it. He did, however, get the legion on the move, striking camp the day after Agricola's return, heading toward the coast. Patrols were flung out in wider and wider arcs, seeking any signs of Cambrian resistance to the flanks and rear of the army, but the men of the Twentieth had been efficient enough—the path they had trod was left a graveyard. Before them, what few villages and homesteads remained were abandoned, their livestock gone—taken to the island of Mona for supplies, Agricola guessed.

They marched hard, Paulinus clearly eager to keep the men at it and their minds off Druid magic, and they ate up the ground between their temporary base and the coast in a scant three days.

The narrow strait glittered in the sun, and there—seemingly close enough to touch—was their objective.

Mona.

The army advanced in good order, the golden sand of the beach disappearing under a sea of gray-armored bodies as the men filed onto it, each soldier knowing his place—a tool, as Magnusanus would have it, in the kit that Paulinus would use to sculpt this land in Rome's image. Agricola nudged his horse to higher ground so he could see the deployment.

From his vantage point, the entire legion was revealed to him. It looked like some mythical, iron-scaled beast that undulated over the enemy territory, impregnable and unstoppable. What a thing was the Roman army, he thought. When roused, it was a truly awesome sight—a machine designed with the express purpose of annihilating its enemies. Barbarian fury might be terrifying, their warriors may be huge and, in their own rights, expert fighters—and brave to a fault. But for all their pride and skill, they must know that they could not stand against this. Yes, Romans would die—he himself could be killed—but Rome was a Hydra.

Across the water, he could see the enemy massing on the beach. Their roars of defiance drifted across the water to the invaders, but Agricola wondered how much of it was heartfelt now that the moment of battle was almost upon them. Now that they could see the fist of the emperor raised and ready to strike them down for their impudent recklessness.

What had their Druid leaders told them? That they were safe because the sea and the gods protected them? That Rome would not dare to cross the strait to the Holy Island? That they would win? Of course that they would win. But now they would know the truth. Now they would know that to rise against Rome was death, and that it would not be an honorable one. They would be ground into the sanctified earth of their most holy place and left as food for the gulls. That was the reality.

"You thinking the deep thoughts, my friend?" Magnusanus cantered up to him, patting the neck of his mount as he eased to a halt.

Agricola smiled, but it was wan. "Yes," he admitted. "I was wondering what they were thinking. The Cambrians."

Magnusanus laughed and took a green apple from his saddlebag. "That they've made a big fucking mistake," he said. "I came to find you," he added, taking a huge bite and wincing at the bitter taste. "The governor is looking for the commanders."

THEY were all there: centurions, tribunes, the primus, and of course, the governor himself. Paulinus wore armor—not the plain stuff of a soldier, but an ornate muscled cuirass that must have cost far more money than an enlisted man would make in his entire life.

Benches had been laid out for them, and at a gesture from the great man, they sat.

"Gentlemen," Paulinus began, his voice resonant, calm and far reaching—the product of extensive oratory tutelage. "We are at the beginning of the end, as I am sure you are all pleased to hear. Across the strait is our objective. The island of Mona is the last and the greatest stronghold of the Druidic pestilence that has infected these lands for so long. Their last stand has begun. It will not, unfortunately, make the annals of history. This has been a dirty war and an inglorious one. All that remains is for us to carry out our duty in the name of Rome and the emperor. Once the Druids have fallen, all of Britannia will be at peace.

"Tactics," he said. "Tomorrow, when the light permits, onagers and ballistae will bombard the beach. The infantry will row across, seize, and hold the beach. The Batavians will ride west—to calmer waters—and swim their mounts across. Once on dry land, the onus on the cavalry is to get into good order with all expedience. They will execute a flanking attack while the legionaries fix the enemy in place.

"As soon as the enemy breaks, infantry and cavalry both will pursue and terminate. There are to be no survivors. I'll see to it that every man is paid a bonus for the action as there will be nothing in the way of slaves. And," he added, "I'll crucify any man caught stealing booty whilst a Cambrian still draws breath. I want them dead. All of them. I want their sacred places destroyed. Wiped out. Scrubbed from history. This is Roman land now." At this, the men thumped their feet on the ground in approval, causing Paulinus to smile slightly. "Questions."

"There are women there," a centurion raised his hand. "And children—"

"I'm aware of that," Paulinus cut him off. "But women will

nest hate, and children will grow to men who will remember what the Druids taught. The women—and the children—must be put to the sword."

The pronouncement saddened Agricola. Too much blood had been spilled already, too many cruelties inflicted by both sides for anyone to be magnanimous in victory. It was real war—and real war was fueled by hatred and cruelty. The histories spoke of hard-fought victories, great battles, and valor. It was easy, he thought, to write "and there was great slaughter." Not so easy to see it up close, to have a man begging for mercy as you put him to the sword. But then, that same man would have been desperately trying to kill you as well. That, Agricola thought, was the reality of it. For a while, it would be kill or be killed. Then the butchery would begin in earnest.

There were more questions, but these faded to a buzz at the periphery of Agricola's consciousness as he contemplated the coming fight. He realized, all of a sudden, that he was quite afraid.

THE boats were broad and flat bottomed, the carpenters assuring nervy men that they were sturdy enough to get everyone across. If Agricola had been afraid the night before, it was as nothing now. This was a different proposition to what he had faced before. Across the strait, the Cambrians had gathered, thousands upon thousands of them, clotting the beach with their blue-painted bodies. They screamed and taunted, loud enough for the insults to be heard across the water. In their ranks, hundreds of black-clad Druids exhorted their gods, and naked women danced amongst them, frenzied and wild-haired. They had Roman prisoners arrayed before them, thrust into the sand on their knees, and Agricola knew that these men would be slaughtered like animals to curry favor with the Druidic gods when the assault began. The first blood on the sands of Mona would be Roman.

"I'll row with you, sir," Naso offered.

Agricola smiled, all too aware that it must have looked rather sickly. "No," he said. "Better that we split up, Centurion. If our boat goes over, we'll both go down—and the lads will need leading when they get across."

Naso waved that away. "Don't worry, sir. We'll all get there in one piece. This'll be over before the sun is halfway across the sky."

"Of course." Agricola swallowed his fear in what he hoped was a decent display of bravado. "I was talking about you." Naso laughed and went away, looking for a boat to hoist himself into.

As he did so, Paulinus cantered into view, resplendent on a white stallion, his red war cloak billowing behind him. The surf sprayed under his horse's hooves, and he made him rear up, holding his sword aloft—clearly not above a bit of theater. Agricola recalled himself doing the same thing, the eyes of Lavinia Postumia on him, how impressed she'd been as he cantered around the paddock. Postumus' paddock . . . Postumus' wife . . .

The man he had once been sickened Agricola now.

"Men of the Twentieth will advance!" Paulinus shouted, snapping him from his reverie. The lines of soldiers undulated forward and shuddered to a halt. "Advance!" Paulinus shouted again, this time a timbre of annoyance in his voice. Across the water, Agricola could hear laughter and hoots of derision from the Cambrians.

No one moved. Then: "It's cursed!" a man shouted from the ranks. "They cursed Flacca, and he died!" Then another: "They have the magic!"

"What do you reckon, sir?" Felix whispered to Agricola. The boy was trying to control his shaking, but his *segmentata* was letting him down, clattering in accord with his fear.

"Don't be daft," Agricola chided, grateful to have someone more afraid than himself to mentor. "We'll get in that boat, row across, and—like Naso said—this'll be over before long. Don't worry, Felix. We'll be fine."

"The Twentieth will advance!" Paulinus was genuinely riled now—but still the men refused.. The governor shook his head. "By the gods, for shame! Men of Rome, frightened by a mob of blue-skinned barbarians. You men are the pride of the legions—or were. What now will you tell your women and your children? What advantages will you heap on your deeds this day? Lie that you were brave and carried the fight? Fail here, Twentieth, and we lose this war. Fail here, and we lose Britannia. And all men will know the shame of the Twentieth Valeria Victrix! *Victrix*," he spat. "After this, you are not worthy of the name."

"We can't fight magic!" someone shouted out and was greeted by a chorus of approval from the ranks. Centurions screamed for order, optios laid in with the stick, but the men began to back away from the water.

Agricola tried to still his shaking hands, coming to a decision. The gods could not change the past—but he could make good on his promise to Roscius. He could be a better man. A braver one. He swallowed and looked over at Naso, who nodded. "Tenth Century!" Agricola shouted, struggling to make himself heard in the noise. "Pick 'em up! Let's show them, lads! Come on now! Let's go!" In a rush before he could change his mind, he grasped the side of his boat and was grateful that Felix and the rest of the tent party did the same, staggering under its weight and that of their shields. "Come on, boys, let's go!"

It was hardly a glorious charge—more a disorganized, lurching stagger, but the men of the Tenth hauled their boats into the sea and pushed them out, shields thunking on the wood as they hurled first weapons and then themselves into the vessels.

Naso was the last, Agricola saw as he looked over his shoulder; the centurion was making obscene gestures at the men of the

Twentieth and calling them all gutless whoresons before he too gave the order to wade out.

"Will they take the beach alone?" Agricola heard Paulinus scream. "Will the Twentieth live with unpurgeable shame? By the gods, men! You can't let them die alone!"

The Twentieth at last responded, shamed by the actions of the Second Augusta, and they, too, ran forward, thousands of feet whitening the sea as they cast off. The artillery opened up, onagers hurling rocks at the massed ranks of the Cambrians on the shore, smashing their bodies to pulp as they tore through. Ballistae spat shanks as long as a man's forearm, piecing bodies and stealing lives.

Agricola looked to the shore in time to see the black-clad Druids butchering their captives. His heart lurched in his chest when he saw Roscius screaming defiance at the enemy—on his knees but fearless in the face of two Druid priests.

The Druid's sword fell and Roscius' corpse slumped forward, head rolling free and gushing blood. Despair Agricola thought he had blunted welled up inside him—to be so close and not be able to save his friend reopened the wound of guilt within him. He tore his eyes away from his friend's body, limp and discarded in the bloody sand like so much meat. "Row!" he shouted, his voice cracked and raw. "Row!"

Around him, the sea was full of men and boats, screaming in fear and praying to the gods for deliverance. A vessel overbalanced and capsized, tipping its cargo of men into the blue water. They pleaded for succor, desperate to live, kicking and swimming for their lives before the weight of their armor and weapons dragged them down, silencing them forever. Some clutched at other boats, trying to hold on, and tipped those over in turn. Soon, their own comrades were battering their brothers away with their oars or cutting away clawing hands that clutched at the wooden sanctuaries.

Something careened off the prow of Agricola's own boat, taking with it a chunk of wood. Then, the man to the fore screamed in agony and lurched to the side, causing the boat to tip precariously, and Felix reached out and hauled him to the middle, steadying them. The man's head had been smashed to bloody ruin by slingshot. "Felix, get a shield up!" Agricola shrieked, terror lacing his voice.

Black-shafted arrows arched from the shoreline, seeming to hang in the air for an impossibly long time before raining down on the helpless Romans as they rowed across the strait. Slingshot hammered on Felix's shield as he struggled to hold it in place. A boat—too close to them—upended and sent its occupants screaming into the foaming water. More arrows fell, one embedding itself in the side of their boat. Then another. Agricola hunched down, eyes all but shut, teeth gritted as he tried not to wail with dread. The fear was all consuming, and he knew that if he could, he would have fled. But he could not: to live, he must fight. "Row!" he shouted needlessly. "Row!"

Above them, their own artillery shot came so close they could hear it whistling and spitting in the air, and now the sound of Cambrian voices began to drown out the shouts of the Romans.

Their boat tipped to one side, and Agricola fell into the water.

For a moment, blind panic gripped him, and he thrashed about in terror before realizing he was sitting in the surf.

"Come on, sir!" Felix staggered to his feet and hauled him up.

Agricola reached into the boat and grabbed a shield as the Cambrians charged them, a screaming mass of iron and flesh, painted in woad, their eyes wide and full of hate and fury.

"Form up!" he shouted. But it was too late—the barbarians were on them. Agricola punched out with the *scutum*, catching a warrior in the face and sending him into the shallows. All around him, men were pouring onto the beach, and the foam turned bloody-pink as hundreds died in the first contact.

Agricola tore his sword from his belt and ran forward, attaching himself to a knot of soldiers, his own men lost to him in the chaos. The beach was now a seething mass of soldiers and warriors, hacking at each other with no semblance of discipline. This was battle the barbarian way, not the Roman. No order at all, just savagery.

He rammed his blade into the side of a Cambrian who had just cut down a legionary, the iron merciless as it slid in. He pulled the weapon free, ignoring the hot, stinking lifeblood that sprayed all over him. Agricola pulled close to the man next to him, shouting incoherently in fear as they began to form some semblance of a shield wall. It was a fragile thing, and they pushed fruitlessly at the mass of Cambrians against them.

Agricola stabbed out with his sword and felt the blade sink into flesh—the scream was that of a woman, and the stench of her shit sickened him as his iron opened her belly. He pushed forward, trampling on her body as men from behind gained the beach and forced him on. He could hear her choking and dying as she was ground to so much meat by the iron-shod boots of the Twentieth legion.

A war axe careened off the lip of his *scutum*, its wielder dark-haired, his beard matted with red ichor, his teeth stained pink with his—or someone else's—blood. The blow forced the shield down, and the axe rose again, but Agricola lashed out, the tip of his *spatha* entering just under the warrior's armpit. He fell, taking the weapon with him, and Agricola was forced to stoop and grab the fallen man's axe. He gripped the unfamiliar haft and hacked down with it, feeling it impact another warrior as the Cambrians surged at them like the tide from which the Romans had just advanced.

Slowly, inexorably, they pushed on, and Agricola felt his senses being overwhelmed with each step. The sound—an endless rolling cacophony that had no beginning and no end. The stench—of blood and feces mingled with that of the salt sea. The blood—so much blood. He was covered in it, drenched in it; it was in his eyes, in his ears, and he could taste it in his mouth. The sand at his feet was a sodden mass, thick with it. His arm was weary, but he was aware that killing was now easy. The axe rose and fell—it was impossible to miss, impossible not to inflict agony and death on the people before him.

Then the Cambrians fell away, screaming in panic as the cavalry crashed into them, horses adding their own shrill whinnying to the chaos; riders, huge and terrifying with their armor and swords, adding their own unique style of killing to the carnage. The resistance in front of him gone, Agricola fell forward, and it was only the action of the man next to him, dropping his sword and grabbing his shoulder, that saved him from being trampled by the legionaries now rushing at the backs of the fleeing Cambrians.

Gasping for breath, he staggered on, tearing the helmet from his head and casting it aside. The world tipped crazily as he walked on through the bloody mosaic of battle, the scene so horrific his mind could barely comprehend it. The beach was more than littered with dead and wounded; it was *blanketed* with them. Here a Cambrian tried to hold in the pink snakes of his guts as they kept pouring out through his fingers; there a Roman soldier crawled blindly, his face all but sheared away by some blow.

"There you are, sir!" Naso, coated in blood, pounded up to him with what was left of the Tenth in tow. "We thought we lost you!" He grinned, his teeth a white slash in the bloody filth of his visage. The centurion looked around, stood on a dead soldier's arm, and tore the gladius from his fingers. "Here," he said, thrusting the weapon into Agricola's hand.

Agricola blinked in shock.

"Look at 'em run!" Naso laughed, gesturing at the fleeing Cambrians.

There was no mercy in the pursuit, no quarter given. The men of the Twentieth did as they were ordered and cut down their foes with something more than efficiency; it looked to Agricola a lot like glee. He felt it, too, though it shamed him—somewhere close by, Roscius had died at the hands of these people. They deserved it, and he wanted to kill them all, cut them down . . . Agricola breathed out sharply, air hissing through his teeth as he quelled the black rage that welled up inside him. Roscius was dead. Rome had had her vengeance on these people. And orders had to be carried out. "We should go," Agricola heard himself say. Steeling himself, he led the men of the Tenth into the wake of the Twentieth Valeria Victrix, and the slaughter continued.

The Cambrians were fleeing to the woods that hedged beyond the beach, and Agricola led his men into the cool darkness of their canopy. The sounds of butchery and death were at odds with this place, and somewhere, he wondered if Jupiter and his kin were laughing at these barbarian gods that had dared to challenge his scions.

Gods that could no longer protect their people. Druids and their kin ran for succor to their sacred trees, as though these gnarled and ancient things could protect them. They could not, and Druid along with warrior and woman alike were put to the sword without compunction. Someone started a fire, and soon the trees were ablaze, the soldiers forcing their victims into the flames, laughing at them as they blazed.

Those were the screams that would haunt Agricola till his dying day. They were worse—far worse—than anything that had assailed him on the beach: piteous, agonized wailing that had no end.

He could stand it no more. He ordered Naso to continue, citing a pulled hamstring, and turned away from the butchery, the death, and the horror.

And Agricola wept. Wept for what he had seen, wept that he was still alive, wept that his friend was dead because of what he had done. He walked aimlessly in the scarred woods, trying and failing to blot out the sounds of the battle, wishing that he could be anyplace but here.

There was movement at his side, and he turned fast, his sword raised. Something tried to rush past him in a flurry of black wool, and Agricola kicked out.

He sent a man—no, a boy—sprawling to the ground and rushed him, placing the tip of his gladius to his throat. He looked no more than sixteen or seventeen—around the same age as Felix, his dark hair matted with gore, his green eyes wide and afraid. His robes were black, and Agricola realized that this was a Druid—one of their young ones, thin and sickly looking, but a Druid nevertheless. Agricola looked away from the boy's frightened eyes. Not a boy—a Druid. The enemy. The enemy they were ordered to destroy. Agricola's fingers tightened on the unyielding wood of the sword's handle, and he steeled his nerves, willing himself to push the iron home and carry out Paulinus' command.

The boy pleaded for his life in his strange guttural language—Agricola couldn't understand a word, but it was clear he was begging to live. Agricola looked at him again and saw tears streaming down his cheeks, his eyes bloodshot and wide with panic.

Beyond, Agricola could hear the screams of the burning, the cries of the women being taken, the shrieks of children begging for succor as they were cast into the unmerciful flames, the cries interspersed with the harsh laughter and cursing of the soldiers.

He stepped away, holding up his left hand and letting his right fall to his side. "Go," he said.

The boy looked left and right, wondering if this were some

trick or if his gods had actually delivered him. The irony of it was that though Rome had come to destroy this holy place, its dying gods had still reached out and stayed Agricola's hand from killing one of its priests. Or maybe the old gods were dead, and he simply lacked the stomach for any more killing. "Go," Agricola said again.

The boy fled into the dark green of the foliage, and Agricola sat on a dead tree stump, praying to his ancestors. For what, he did not know. But if even the gods could not change the past, at least he could change one boy's future.

PAULINUS had ordered wine boated across from the main encampment.

After the slaughter was done with, the men descended into drunkenness save those unlucky enough to draw the duty lots on both sides of the strait. Agricola found Naso, but the man was almost insensible, able only to hand him a list of the roll. The Tenth had lost forty men in the battle—the honor won by being first on the beach. Felix's name was scored out on the roll call. Agricola stared at the tablet for a long time, unwilling to accept that the boy had not survived. He spent long hours walking the beach, a jug of wine in his hand, looking for the bodies of Roscius and Felix so that he might save them from the carrion birds. He found a corpse that he knew had once been Roscius, but he couldn't find his head. He had dragged what was left of his friend to a funeral detail tasked with disposing of the Roman bodies. Of Felix, there was no sign: he'd probably already been put on a fire. A part of him hoped that because he had spared the Druid boy, the gods would see fit to save Felix. But it was clear that the gods had abandoned this place to the savagery of men.

Magnusanus found him drunk and melancholy with the

corpses. "You perhaps are lost?" he said. The man's voice was slurred—he, too, had been drinking heavily.

"I was looking for Felix," Agricola said

"The boy will have been put on a pyre, Tribune." Magnusanus glanced around at what corpses still remained. "Come. You are the hero of the day—next to me, of course, as I led the charge that saved you all. But you did well enough. Let us leave this place."

He led him through the bodies to where Paulinus was leading a grand celebration. The governor rose as they approached, embracing Agricola as though he were his own son, kissing his bloody cheeks. "I will see you honored for this," he said. "Your bravery does you, your family, and your ancestors credit. Your blood may not be Roman, but by the gods, you showed Roman courage today, boy! And you," he hugged Magnusanus, "history will remember your charge, Batavian."

"It's just the duty, sir, our honor." Magnusanus was clearly embarrassed by the praise.

"Join us!" Paulinus gestured expansively. He grabbed the wine jug from Agricola's hand and sniffed it; he wrinkled his nose and tipped the contents into the sand as though it were an offering. "And get this man something decent to drink!" The officers laughed, and Paulinus made off, basking in the glory of victory. He sat in his chair, master of all he surveyed.

Agricola wanted no part of it. He just wanted to drink until he passed out so the memories of what he had seen and done would leave him be for a while. He went to go, but Magnusanus held his wrist and made him sit.

They did not speak, but drank in silence, tipping back expensive wine as though it were Subura shop piss. Soon, the world became dim and distant as Agricola continued to throw it back, his eyes on the governor. He should, but could not, hate the man. Paulinus was a Roman to the core. He had done his duty and had done it well. That was Rome—and the *Peace of Rome* had to be maintained. To countenance otherwise was to invite the end of the empire, and with that would come darkness that would last a thousand years. Rome was the light of the world, even if its fire was sometimes fueled by blood. History would not recall the blood, he knew. It would mention it in passing and laud the deeds of men like Paulinus and Caesar before him. Perhaps, he thought, he himself would be recalled as the hero who led the assault on Mona.

The *hero* who caused his friend to die. The *hero* who caused an innocent woman and her . . . no . . . *his* unborn child to die. Agricola looked to the men, laughing, celebrating, and back-slapping. Victory was theirs—they had done their duty and done it well. It was a victory that tasted like ashes in his mouth.

He tried to wash it away with the last of the wine and felt himself falling. Lying in the sand, he felt like being sick, and then darkness took him.

"SIR!"

Slowly, painfully, Agricola opened his eyes. His head pounded, his guts churned, and for a moment he thought he would vomit. Naso's face loomed over him: the man looked as fresh as a daisy, reeking of stale booze, but otherwise seemingly untouched by his extended bout with the wine jug. "What is it?" Agricola croaked.

"We have to move."

There was an urgency in the centurion's tone that forced Agricola into full wakefulness. "What? Why?" he asked, struggling to a sitting position.

"It's Camulodunum, sir."

"Camulodunum?" Agricola tried to shake the fog from his brain. "In the southeast?"

"Aye, sir." Naso nodded, his face grim. "It's been destroyed. The people there massacred. A messenger came in the night. While we've been up here, the Britons have risen in full revolt. They say they have a queen. A warrior queen, and the woad-skins are flocking to her sword. The Ninth Hispana has been *wiped out*."

Agricola's mind whirled, unable to countenance the enormity of what he was hearing. In a few short months, the province had gone from peace to full-scale rebellion. It made no sense. He heard Flacca's voice: *Everybody knows the south is quieter than a houseful of Vestal Virgins.*

"A queen?" Agricola said. "Who is she—what tribe?"

"Boudica, sir," Naso replied. "Boudica of the Iceni."

"The one with the voice." Agricola remembered her from the funeral. "And the hair. Shit. Where's Paulinus?"

"Already gone, sir." Naso offered him his arm and hauled him to his feet. "Left as soon as he heard the news."

Agricola took a deep breath. "I'd better report to the senior tribune," he said.

"You're senior tribune, sir," Naso told him. "Two of the Twentieth's tribunes fell in yesterday's assault, and the governor took the others with him. Here." He passed Agricola a wax tablet.

Agricola read it, recognizing the hurried hand of Paulinus. He gaped first at the orders, then at Naso. "*I'm* in command?"

Naso nodded. "For now, anyway. We're to double-time it back southeast, I'm guessing."

Agricola nodded and looked around, something inside him falling over. He wasn't prepared for this, wasn't ready for this, and realized in that moment that he didn't want this. But what could he do? Responsibility was now his—he felt the full weight of it at once, bearing down on him as though he were Atlas and the Twentieth Legion the stone of the world. He could not let them down.

"Round up the centurions," he told Naso. "Bring them here.

To me. At once." As he spoke, a raven alighted on a nearby rock, its black eyes staring, unperturbed by their close proximity; Agricola guessed it was probably replete with the flesh of Romans and tribesmen both.

Naso seemed to measure him for a moment, then snapped to attention and saluted. "As you say, sir."

He turned and hurried off as Agricola surveyed the mass of hungover soldiery that had suddenly become his charges. He thought of Lavinia Postumia and Roscius. He thought of Felix and Calvus and all the men that had died in his charge. And knew that there was nothing he could do to change it. "Even a god cannot change the past," he murmured, glancing at the wax tablet.

This was the future—his future. Paulinus had ordered it, so it must be done.

PART FOUR

THE DRUID

Victoria Alvear

The gods favor a righteous vengeance.
—Tacitus

YORATH OF MONA

I prayed to awaken from what could only be a nightmare. My home, our priests and priestesses, everyone I knew and loved, gone. Killed. Set aflame.

Impossible. Yet it was no dream. All through the night, I watched across the lapping water as crackling fires tore through our sacred groves, as the cries of the dying faded to whimpers and then disappeared into terrible silence—only to be replaced by the evil, unholy laughter of drunk Romans celebrating their slaughter.

Dawn rose, and still I sat, hunched in my stolen boat pulled up on the mainland's rocky shore, weeping. The isle of Mona was a smoking ruin in the beautiful spring dawn—the sacred isle where Druids trained and prophecies came from the realm of the gods, where the people came from every tribe in this land for divine aid. Where all the Druids had joyfully gathered for spiritual replenishment after the celebrations of Beltane.

The isle of Mona, my refuge, home to everyone I loved. Destroyed.

And as I watched and wept over its ruin, three questions stabbed at my heart:

Why was I spared?

Why had the gods abandoned us?

And most important: *What do I do now?*

THE elders of Mona had known the Romans were coming, of course. We all did. But it hadn't been clear that they were coming for *us*. They'd been chasing small war bands of rebels—many of them from local Deceangli villages—and had trapped them against the coastline. And even though some of the exhausted, starved rebels had crossed the strait to take shelter with us, no one imagined that the legions would actually attack. Their presence was a show of intimidation, we thought. After all, we were defenseless, an isle filled with priests, priestesses, women, children, and anyone seeking sanctuary.

When I first caught sight of the vast army, the enormity of it had taken my breath away. I had not known that many people existed in the world. When their general did not seek counsel with our high priest, we grew concerned. It began to dawn on us then—they'd come for us. So our elder priests and priestesses had begun chanting spells of protection to keep them from crossing the strait.

"They pause!" one of the elders had cried. "Our magic is working!"

We had chanted with even greater ferocity then. A strange exultation filled me, and I remembered thinking, *I'll chant so loudly my lovely Gara will hear me all the way back in the compound. She'll be so proud of the strength of our combined magic.* I imagined describing every detail to her.

But suddenly the Romans roared in outrage. The entire army seemed to swell with a black hatred, like a giant bird of prey ruffling its feathers and spreading its wings wide enough to blot the sun.

I hadn't understood what had happened, what had changed. Then I saw bodies falling: some of the warriors who had sought sanctuary with us, men we'd *protected*, had dragged their prisoners—Roman soldiers they'd taken in a recent night attack—to the edge of the shore and had begun taking their heads.

The elder priests cried out in alarm. The warriors' impulsive actions had disrupted the magic. When the warrior closest to us drew back his sword to behead the last Roman, my elder had roared at him to stop. "You have angered the gods," he cried out as Roman horns commanded attack. "We must get the magic back! We must earn the gods' favor again!"

To my shock, he dragged *me* up to the last Roman prisoner, a bulky, red-haired man. "Boy, you must sacrifice this Roman in the Old Ways. Quickly, the gods will not help us otherwise! Recite the sacred prayers and cut his throat!"

I was sure I had not heard right. My elder must have gone mad! For a Druid to sacrifice a man was old and terrible magic. It was never to be called forth on a whim. To ignore the ancient rituals and prayers was nothing less than murder. And for me, it was forbidden. I was a Vates priest in training, prohibited from killing any living creature unless in the service of a council-sanctioned sacrifice to the gods. And this was no such thing! The priest had grabbed my sacrificial dagger from my belt and thrust it into my hands. I wouldn't take it.

"Do it!" he'd raged, his eyes wild. "Say the prayer and then *slash his throat.* It's the only way to revive the magic that will stop them crossing the strait!"

I'd refused. He himself had made me take a vow upon my life to make sure I never performed such a sacrifice!

Was that the moment the gods abandoned us? Was it all my fault?

"You idiot coward!" my elder had bellowed. I had never seen my always-calm elder so hysterical. I'd backed away, tripping and falling on my backside. The red-haired Roman must have known what was about to happen to him, for he yelled insults at us, ending with what sounded like his name. *Roscius.*

Then my elder had done the unspeakable. He grabbed a warrior's long-sword, roared the forbidden secret words, and beheaded the Roman against all the rules of our sacred training.

The man's head had rolled to a stop at my feet, eyes and mouth still working. Everything afterward came in fractured images:

The enemy's boats surging up onto our beach. The screams. A helmeted Roman slitting the throat of our High Priest of All the Tribes, the holy one's long white beard soaking up blood like a threadbare rag. Another cut down three barefoot children as easily as if flicking away flies.

In the chaos, I'd run toward the compound, praying I could make it to Gara and keep her safe from the monsters.

But Roman boots followed. They were everywhere. I hid in the shrubs. Screaming, screaming echoed everywhere. The air filled with the metallic tang of blood, the revolting stench of emptied bowels.

I was running again. Something moved, kicked out, and I went flying. One of the invaders had come out of nowhere, gleaming like a demon of death, and stood over me, his gore-covered sword at my neck.

Without thinking, I begged for him to let me go find my girl. I could tell he didn't understand a word. He only stared down at me with such chilling coldness a new fear caught in my throat. I looked young for my age, like a boy, not a man of nineteen. The Romans defiled boys with as much cold indifference as they did girls and women. Was this one about to attack me?

But to my surprise, he lifted the blade from my neck and turned away. I sprinted off, gasping for air through the smoke. The stench of burning flesh and hair scoured my lungs with spikes of hot iron. Were those Gara's screams? No, it was laughter. Roman laughter. Gods, it was too late. I was too late. Too late for Gara. Too late for everyone.

Flames from our compound's thatched roofs crackled high into the air. The sacred groves burned, too.

Why were the gods allowing such desecration?

Where was Belenos our Protector? Where was Aeron the Vengeful Slaughterer? Or Andraste the Goddess of War? Why had they abandoned us?

I didn't know how long I stood there, stupefied with horror.

My Gara. The children. Even the old women. Had they killed them all?

Someone came stumbling through the undergrowth yelling in Latin. I hid once again. Then the Latin turned to Gaulish, which I understood. "My eyes. My eyes," the man screamed. A Roman-Gaul. So many of our ancestral brothers had surrendered themselves to the Roman demons generations ago. And there he was—an unhelmeted legionary with shorn white-blond hair, almost pink from blood pouring off a cut on his scalp.

He continued bellowing, calling, I presumed, for help from his comrades. I had to stop him. He would lead them right to me.

I burst out of the thicket and ran low and fast at the soldier, crashing into his side. He fell down hard, the air escaping from his chest with a loud *hoooofffff.* He kicked out and swung, but he was weaponless, thank Briga.

Quickly, I put my forearm over his neck, pressing all my weight down. He struggled, but I had him pinned, skinny as I was. But what was I to do with him? I was forbidden from killing anything but animals during sanctified sacrifices. I could not kill a man.

And that's what had brought all this down upon us, wasn't it?

I could hardly catch my breath as my pulse pounded in my ears. Screams were still coming from the woods. I couldn't stay there. Not knowing what else to do, I dragged the Roman through the thick woods with me, holding his own dagger—when had I taken it?—to his throat to keep him quiet. Stumbling and gasping, we crashed blindly through a deer run, away from the all the fire and death. We burst onto a pebbled shore, where I found a small fishing boat. I pushed my captive headfirst into it and realized he'd stilled. *Gods! After everything, had I accidentally killed him?*

No, he was still breathing. I didn't remember paddling away, nor how long we were at sea, only that we ended up beached on a remote, rocky shore. There I stayed throughout the night, watching the unwatchable, the destruction of everything I had known and loved, until dawn.

I might have sat on the remote beach forever in a stupor of grief, but the Roman began to stir and gasp, calling out in Latin and Gaulish.

Wiping at my burning eyes in the light of dawn, I took my first close look at my hostage. He was still swollen-eyed and blinded from dried blood, a giant goose egg emerging on the back of his head. His knobby knees told me he was young, and the blisters on his feet confirmed that he was a fledgling, not a seasoned warrior. He reeked of acrid fear, sweat, and blood, mixed with a foreign oiliness—a trader had once told me that the invaders slathered themselves with the oil of a bitter green berry. The same oil they *cooked with and ate.* I shuddered with revulsion. Disgusting, murderous beasts. Maybe they basted themselves before they ate each other's flesh.

"Who has me?" My captive's voice was shrill. "What are you going to do with me?"

Because he'd spoken in Gaulish, I understood. "Quiet," I snapped in the same tongue and pulled him onto the rocky beach. His balance was gone, and I struggled to hold him up, cursing my "delicate" frame—the very reason why I'd been bound to a lifetime of memory binding and ritual rather than following in my father's footsteps as a great warrior. With my black robe heavy and sodden and my bound captive muttering incoherently, we staggered along until finally—finally—we encountered a knot of scrubby old fishermen staring at us in disbelief as we emerged from the smoky mist. "Find us sanctuary," I commanded. "Now."

THE old healer woman's house was atop of one of the high crags overlooking the sea. She treated the knot on the side of my head—I did not remember being hit—and the countless cuts and scrapes on my arms and hands with a foul-smelling balm. Her face was a leathery mass of tiny crinkles that folded into a toothless scowl of impressive dignity as she worked.

My captive crouched near the center fire over which an old iron cauldron bubbled, emitting a hot scent of fish oil and fat. Slowly, I began to notice odd shapes dangling from the beams—the skull of a bird, the empty claws of a giant crab, the spine of a small animal, interspersed with bunches of drying leaves and branches. The old woman puttered to a small table, the top of her head brushing the hanging bones, creating an eerie, clattering tune. She poured something into a cup and handed it to me. Her silence was unnerving.

I sipped the warm mead, then found myself chugging it in great swallows. "Thank you," I said, returning the cup.

The old woman bade me sit and then folded herself down in one creaky movement onto a warped, faded bench. "What have the foreign demons done?" she asked in a pained whisper.

"They attacked us," I said, still bewildered by the immensity of the desecration. "They burned everything. Have any others made it out like me?"

She shook her head. "We have found no others."

"I faced death at the hands of a Roman, but the gods stayed his hand," I said after a while, as if I had to explain why I was alive when so many had been killed.

She nodded toward the solider, awake now and holding his head in his hands. "That one?"

"No. Him I found—the gods delivered him to me—when the other one melted away."

The old woman's dark eyes glittered in the firelight. "You did not kill him," she observed.

"I am forbidden from killing anything outside the bounds of sacrifice."

"Ah. You are Vates Druid, then."

"Yes." I didn't add that I still had nearly ten more years of training to go. But it was pointless to state the obvious aloud. "It was a massacre. And they set fire to the sacred grove." The full import of the sacrilege laid me so low I almost retched. Gods, my sweet Gara!

As if giving voice to my pain and to the loss of all those innocents, the old woman began to keen, setting off the villagers who had gathered outside her roundhouse to hear news they hoped would contradict what they saw with their own eyes—that the isle of Mona was no more.

The remote village had offered up its young and able-bodied sons and daughters as servants to Mona, as did many villages in these parts, and now they were gone, too. Together we howled over our losses—over the needless deaths of countless innocents, of our most learned priests, and of our very gods.

I must have fallen asleep, for I found myself curled into a ball and covered with a scratchy wool blanket. The healer woman was talking softly to a young child, giving instructions on chopping some kind of astringent, bitter herb. It was that sharp smell that woke me, for Gara had been training with the magic of healing herbs and had often carried the lingering scents of greens or flowers of one sort or another on her skin. Sitting up, all of the events of the day before flooded into awareness, and I dropped my head into my hands and groaned.

Gara. The island. The elders. The priests. Destroyed.

The Roman gabbled senselessly in Latin.

"Speak in the Gaul tongue if you wish to speak to me," I ordered.

So he did. "What is happening? Where am I?" He sounded even younger than he looked. The old woman had cleaned him up, though his limbs were tied anew in fishermen knots. The boy's white-blond hair was no longer pink with blood. He had bruising from the top of his forehead down to both eyes, making him look like an oversized, skeletal badger.

"You are my prisoner," I said.

His head turned in my direction, and he blinked. What had once been the whites of his eyes were now shot through with red, giving him a demonic look. I shuddered. "Can you see me?" I asked.

"I am beginning to see shapes now. What magic did you use to blind me? Can you undo the spell?"

I opened my mouth to tell him I used no magic, but perhaps one of the other Druids had. And since he was beginning to see shapes, it was clear the magic was beginning to wear off—not surprising given that the priest who performed the spell was dead.

My silence clearly disturbed him. He shifted and blinked again in my direction. "Wh-Who holds me prisoner?"

"I am Yorath, son of Torkill of the Venicones, Vates priest of the Druids." I did not say Vates "in-training" priest of the Druids, for who would train me now? But surely at least one of the elders survived, too. I couldn't be the only one!

Even though I didn't ask who he was, the boy offered anyway: "My name is Sallustius Secundus Felix, legionary of the Tenth Century, Tenth Cohort, Second Augusta."

Then he began to chuckle in a despairing way.

"What is funny?"

"My name. Felix means 'lucky,'" he said. "But this isn't very lucky for me now, is it?"

When I said nothing, he asked, "What will you do with me? Am I to be traded for one of your priests?"

"I don't know whether there are other survivors," I said without thinking. "The island has been overrun and burned."

"We are victorious, then?" he said with a tight little smile.

I wanted to punch him in one of his bruised eyes, but instead I forced myself to breathe until the feeling passed. The need for dignity—to reassure the others at the very least—was critical. "If you call the outright slaughter of old men, women, children, and babies a 'victory,' then yes."

He frowned. "Your isle was the seat of the rebellion. You Druids called for the *bellum sacrum* against us. So it's your own fault."

He blamed us for *their* massacre? "I don't understand," I sputtered. "What are you—what is *bellum sacrum*?"

"A holy war," the young Roman said. "You Druids demanded the tribes fight us. We had to stop you, or the fighting would never end."

I shook my head as if I hadn't heard right. "We never 'told' the tribes to do anything, nor did we call for a holy war," I snapped, irritated at his uneducated beliefs about us. "We don't have that kind of power! Do you not know how the tribal councils work?" How dare he assume we priests fomented rebellion! We communicated with the gods and maintained the sacred knowledge that kept the balance with the unseen world. We upheld ancient laws. We were not war generals! Whatever fighting took place was not our doing, but decisions made by individual tribes and warriors. Certainly, the High Druid of All the Tribes could call for a truce between warring tribes, but he could not declare any kind of war. "Our isle had no standing army—just starved fighters you harried onto the island. You annihilated the innocent. Even your own gods are ashamed for you."

The soldier turned his face to the fire.

"The people want council with you, Yorath of the Venicones," the old woman said, watching me shrug into an old tunic after I washed with bracing-cold water.

Before I could stop myself, I blurted, "Council? With me?

Why?" and felt heat surge up my neck. So much for the dignity of a Druid.

"They need guidance and reassurance to face their losses. And they believe you have been blessed, for you are the only one to make it out. Search parties have shown no other survivors."

My heart dropped to my stomach. "There must be others! I cannot be the only survivor."

The old woman shook her head.

"I don't understand," I said. "How do you know this? The Romans allowed searches on the isle? Are they not occupying it? Perhaps they are holding prisoners!"

"The Romans left this morning," she announced. "The Iceni in the south, under Queen Boudica, launched a rebellion, and the legions are marching to stop it. Meanwhile, Mona still burns, consuming the bodies left behind. It is so utterly destroyed they did not even bother to leave guards."

The old woman swallowed, and I could see her pain. To leave our dead unattended, their souls left to wander without the ancient rites! I ached for Gara and the others. The depth of the sacrilege was beyond comprehension.

"You are the last Druid," the old woman continued in a raspy voice. "All the priests and priestesses—young and old—are dead but you. The gods let you live for a reason. You must discover what the gods want of you in order to regain their protection."

I swallowed. But what if it had been a mistake that I was still alive? What if I was an insult to their majesty?

"You must also discover what the gods want you to do with your prisoner," she said. "For I sense he is important. And so I have been preparing the sacred woad plant for you to journey into your Long Night with the gods. You must bring back guidance for your people. You must heal our rift with the gods. But first, you must help us pray for the soul's journey of all the dead."

I nodded, knowing that was the least I could do. The grief-racked villagers—those who had waved good-bye to their sons and daughters for the last time just yesterday morning—needed some signal from the gods that their grief would end. That their deaths were not for nothing.

I didn't have the heart to tell them the truth: that after staring into the insatiable maw of the murderous Roman legion, it was clear our suffering was nowhere near ending.

FELIX THE ROMAN

PLUTO'S prick, how my head pounded. Even though I could only see the haze of the hearth fire and the occasional moving body, I could tell that I'd been bathed and dressed in strange clothing. Rope chafed against my wrists and ankles, and I stank of dead fish. An old woman cackled around me, and I knew, heart sinking, that I was being held by both a Druid *and* a witch.

I prayed to Asclepius for the return of my full vision and to Mars for the means and balls to get out of here.

My last coherent memory was of watching those bastards take the heads off our captured boys. An image of Tribune Roscius' head flying from his body flashed before me. Then of Tribune Agricola shaming the other legions by splashing across the strait first.

Gods, the excitement! I had wanted to fight right next to our shining tribune! I wanted to save him again and prove my valor to him over and over. The witches and priests had certainly given the whole legion pause, though. It was as if all the demons of the underworld had shone through their maddened eyes as they screamed their strange curses and spells at us.

I would never admit it out loud, but I had been terrified. Especially after seeing what happened to Centurion Flacca after that Druid cursed him. He'd died on the spot! Their magic was frightening.

Reflexively, my fingers made the sign for protection against evil.

Once past the raving line of Druids on the beach, though, we had only found young ones. And the women. My gut twisted as the memory came back to me. A girl of about twelve had begged for her life. She reminded me of my little sister, and I'd hesitated. It was during that moment of weakness that someone brought me down. I hoped with all my might that Tribune Agricola hadn't seen me get knocked to the ground like some stupid, inexperienced boy. I was better than that!

The rest was a blur . . . of the world turning red, of confused crawling along the scrubby ground, of my desperate scrabble for my gladius, which I could not find. Again, shame racked my insides. How could I have let that happen?

The one who took me seemed young, but he was obviously a Druid given the tone the others used to talk to him. We were supposed to eliminate them. Being taken by a warrior was one thing, but a kid priestling? Gods damn it all!

I shifted on the dirt floor of the smelly hovel. Beyond the vague shapes that were all I could detect with my spell-cursed eyes, there was smoky darkness that seemed unnecessarily miserable. Ever hear of oil lamps, you stupid bastards?

Plus it reeked of the oily musk of some strange sea creature. These people lived like animals. They *were* animals.

It occurred to me that I might not be the only hostage, so I called out in Latin, but the Druidling yelled at me to shut it. That's when I realized I was probably the only Roman these savages managed to snag.

The disgrace of it was hard to take. Why had this happened

when I was destined for so much more? I'd *saved* Tribune Agricola
during that night raid when the savages attacked, hadn't I? After
such a strong start, I'd been sure that I would impress him again
with one heroic deed after another, that I would climb up the
ranks faster than anyone else. Maybe even be selected by the man
himself to serve as a junior officer. It could happen!

That would shut Optio Naso's fat mouth about the uselessness
of my skinny arse, wouldn't it?

All was not lost, I reminded myself. I could escape, burn the
village down, report that I'd removed one rogue Druidling, and
be the hero again.

Slowly, my vision began to improve. Once, when someone
walked me outside to relieve myself, I'd thought about running
away, but how could I when I didn't know where I was and my
eyesight was still half-fucked? That Druid blinding spell was
proof of their powerful magic—I'd do well to be cautious around
the boy.

Even so, Druid magic was no match for Roman might. A surge
of pride puffed up my chest. I would go back to the lads and continue the campaign under Tribune Agricola, just as soon as my
sight returned and I could get my bearings.

I was dozing by the hearth when rough hands dragged me
up. Fishermen by the smell of them. They barked commands at
me in their barbaric tongue as if I could understand them. They
sounded like seals arguing over a sunny spot on the rocks.

Still, I noticed I could see more. The blinding magic was fading. The faces were still a bit blurry, though.

They dragged me outside the small roundhouse and marched
me up to a gusty bluff, singing strange songs that sounded half-
dirge, half-supplication. The air at least was bracing, smelling of
the sea. We appeared to be on a cliff as the sound of surf crashing
against rocks drifted up from far below.

Gods, were they going to throw me off the cliff? I started fighting then, and more men took rough hold of me. Someone grabbed my head—that hurt, you fucking bastard!—tipped it back, and tried to pour something into my mouth. I shook my head free, cursing and kicking, and spat out the foul-tasting swill. Mars' cock, were they going to poison me first and *then* throw me off the cliff? Not without a fight, they weren't.

Several men gripped me in bear hugs up and down my body. When I stopped struggling to catch my breath, strong fingers pulled my hair back and again poured the strange brew into my mouth, but this time someone pinched my nose at the same time, and I swallowed reflexively. Three times they did this, and a strange yeasty warmth settled into my middle. When they moved me again, I fought as before, but I seemed to move slower, more sluggishly.

They sat me down on a rock with the surf at my back. Torches lit the bluff, and it was only then I realized it was nighttime. The flickering torches created blurry halos around them, and it felt as if I were staring at the flames and the people around me through fine gauze. The bodies were moving. Dancing. They whirled around me in a circle as people wailed in spine-chilling tones.

Another surge of fear: Were they going to burn me alive in a wicker cage like the great Caesar had described? Maybe I should throw myself off the cliff first! But when I tried to stand and turn to the surf, callused hands once again held me in place.

I was panting now as dizziness and frustration surged through me. I'd only been a legionary for less than a year. War was about valor and heroism and becoming a man, and I had only just begun that journey. It couldn't be ending now! But I was a Roman soldier, and I would not cry out or beg. I imagined Agricola standing before me, and I straightened my shoulders.

They led me to a seat on a rock. Someone sat beside me, and

new hands held my shoulders down. An old woman by the sound of her, but not the one who had tended me in the hovel house.

"I speak Latin. You will hear the names," she announced in a creaky voice. "The Druid demands it."

The names? The names of what? Was this some sort of spell-casting?

The singing grew louder, and some people were sobbing. Bodies swayed in some sort of dancing. Then a man stepped into the center, and the voices dropped away. In a heavy baritone, the man sang alone. The woman translated:

"I sing of my son, Llud, he of the raven hair and radiant smile, into the passing to the Other Side."

Moans and weeping rose with every word. "He was ten years old," the woman kept translating as the man sang on. "The proudest day of his life was when he was chosen to be the water carrier for the high priest of the Deceangli. The monsters stabbed him in the back as he ran . . ."

Why did I have to listen to this? *I* hadn't killed his boy! But then I wondered if maybe I had. I refused the momentary shame that fell over me like an invisible skin and shook it off. This was the reality of war, wasn't it?

I was a Roman soldier. Roman soldiers did not back away from the ugliness of war.

The man sang of the boy's charm and of his bravery, of the sweet way he had held his brother before the gods took the newborn. I'd never given any thought to the pain of the savages, and I didn't like doing so now. I hardened myself against the man's grief. They had brought it on themselves, hadn't they? Their priests called for a holy war against us, the governor had said.

So it was *their* fault.

Another grief-racked voice, this time sounding like a young woman. *"I sing to the ancients for the soul safekeeping of the elder priestess Galena, who sang of the healing plants of the medicines from our ancestors . . ."*

"Despite her bowed back," came the whisper overlaying the foreign words, "her extraordinary memory preserved the healing remedies handed down by the ancestors. Those precious and sacred memories are all gone now, for her apprentices both old and young were also thrown into the fire."

"I sing the song for my sister . . .

My mother . . .

My father . . .

The Bard of All Songs . . . He who spent forty years learning the songs of all the tribes. No one person knows them all now. Our ancestors weep at the loss of their stories."

"For my daughter, who stitched the sacred robes . . .

For my son, who proudly ferried visitors to the sacred isle every day . . .

For my brother-in-law, who was trapped on the island as he delivered the fish he'd caught to feed the Holy Ones . . .

For my daughter and her unborn babe, whose birth was only three moons away . . .

Of the Druid who knew the names of all the ancient gods, the ones before time, and all of their stories, never to be told again . . .

Of the Lawgiver, who could recite the laws of the people and of the gods, both from the past and the present . . ."

On and on the singing went. Whenever I drifted, the old woman shook me, demanding I pay attention and hear the names of those who'd been "slaughtered"—her word—on Mona.

A familiar voice then. The young Druid who'd taken me. With a broken tone, he sang, too.

"A girl named Gara, betrothed to the Druid apprentice Yorath," hissed the translator, as if this particular death made her angry and not just saddened. "Betrothed . . . beloved . . . singer of songs . . . devoted to Bel, the goddess of animals who healed not just beasts but men as well with a mere touch of the hand . . .”

Whether it was the potion they gave me or the heartbreak with which the villagers and Druid boy sang, I couldn't tell, but soon images began to swim before me—ghostly shadows of the dead lining up to stare at me, their shades growing brighter with the telling of their names, tribes, accomplishments, and stories.

The shade of a handsome older woman in a black robe appeared, her mouth moving with words I could not hear. “Midwife priestess . . . knew the spells and practices of safekeeping for those sent by the gods. Her secrets of healing midwifery died with her . . .”

An impish little boy with shining eyes danced a little jig up to me, and I groaned. He looked so much like my nephew—the same little grin, the same small, fat feet. “Son of Ban . . . four years old . . .”

A blind old priest. A young priest not much older than myself. A laundress. An herb grower. A bent Druid with a flowing white beard and unseeing, filmed eyes. They all appeared and stared at me, then disappeared to make room for more and more as the singers continued. “You did this,” the woman hissed in Latin. Bile inched up to the back of my mouth.

“No,” I moaned. “I was just following orders.”

“Wife, whose beauty outshone the sun . . .” The shade of a beautiful woman appeared. Her hair shone copper, and her breasts were full. She smiled at me, and I thought fuzzily, “No, not you. You are too beautiful.” To my amazement, she stepped out of her robe and stood before me shining with moonlight, more breathtaking than any statue of Venus I'd ever seen.

Suddenly, the unearthly beauty of the woman changed. Her eyes became bruised and swollen, her nose began to bleed. Teeth flew out. She screamed and fought an invisible assailant as she was battered down. "Nooooooo," I moaned, shutting my eyes and rocking, but the images did not disappear. They danced inside my head, forcing me to see the once-beautiful woman's broken, twisted body being thrown into the fire. "You did this," the translator whispered.

"No, not me!" I tried to scream, but as if in a bad dream sent by Pluto's black bats, I could not move a muscle.

This was Druid magic of the most revolting kind. I *had* to harden myself against it. I was a Roman soldier. Again, I thought of Agricola and tried to straighten.

Eventually, the images of the shades of those killed on Mona began to disappear, and the songs came to a close just as the light of dawn washed the sky with purple clouds.

I looked around at the villagers who'd stayed up all night to sing of their losses and grieve as one. Some of the women still rocked, holding their stomachs as if breathing was hard, others had cried themselves to sleep where they lay.

Blinking hard, I realized I was actually seeing things more clearly. The craggy coast. The disappearing stars. The ravaged faces of those around me. The Druid boy must have lifted the spell.

Even as the images of the shades danced in memory, I reminded myself of a simple truth: Roman soldiers do not weep for their enemies.

YORATH

AFTER the ceremony of the Songs of Passing, I set out. The sun was just beginning to peek over the hills, lighting the carpet of dewy green that glimmered, seemingly, with all of the tears shed throughout the ceremony.

Never in all the stories and songs had I heard of one ceremony going as long as this one had, but then never in anyone's memory had so many innocents been killed all at once in one place. The shock of it would reverberate through the land and my people for a long, long time.

Villagers surrounded the main roundhouse, waiting for me to pass. As I came close, I felt the weight of everyone's pain and sadness crash over me like a rogue wave. *Maintain your dignity,* my old master seemed to whisper in my ear as I caught my breath. *Let it wash over you; you must be the rock that emerges from the churning foam, slick but unmoved.*

I may not have completed all the years of teaching, but some of it stuck. I gave thanks to the spirits of the murdered priests for allowing their essence to speak to me and give their loved ones ease. As if acknowledging my gratitude, a cat suddenly darted in front of me, charging to my right side after a tiny vole. An excellent sign! Had the animal crossed to the left, it would have been terrible. The small blessing gave me the strength to square my shoulders and lift my chin.

The villagers all touched the back and top of my head—the seat of the soul and connection to the gods—in blessing as I passed. Despite my fatigue, I was glad I made it out of sight without faltering or tripping.

I walked in a daze, seeking the path toward the *nemeton,* the sacred grove of the locals, where a cluster of oaks stood among a smattering of hawthorns and ancient poplars.

The old woman had told me to follow the flying rowans.

Twisted and pushed down by the strong gusting winds from the headland, the rowan trees pointed to the sacred oaks like gnarled fingers of the gods themselves. The sight of them made my heart ache, for while they were majestic to the extreme, they still came nowhere close to the size and age of the destroyed oak grove on Mona. Our gods had been born in those mist-shrouded woods. There they'd held the heart of our faith and our people. There they'd protected the knowledge that pulsed through the earth and into our elders. And now they were gone. As were all the people who honored and served them.

How could I possibly be the only one left to carry their memories? *How?*

Once inside the grove, I prayed beside an ancient stone altar near a small spring. And then I found the biggest, oldest tree in the grove and crawled up its gnarled, bulbous roots and sides until I found a bowl-like crossing of limbs that spoke to me as being right. Like a babe crawling back into the womb, I curled into a ball, waiting for the spirit of the gods to pulse through the arms of the tree and give me guidance.

I slept without dreaming, though my face was wet when I woke. Perhaps the gods themselves were too racked with grief to hear the pleas of one such as me. Were they disappointed that I was the only one to survive? Was that why they hadn't spoken?

Still, the old woman's words echoed in my mind: You must discover what the gods want of you in order to regain their protection. You must heal our rift with the gods . . .

Once fully awake, I crawled out of the tree and prepared the woad from the dried plant. I stripped and spread the paste over my entire body, and I knew the magic was beginning to work because my skin warmed and tingled despite the wet coolness of the wood. I drank the herbal tincture the old woman had prepared for me, settled myself near the roots of the biggest tree, and waited.

Owls hooted. Small animals scurried through the underbrush. A slow-moving insect crawled over my knee. Still, I waited. The limbs of the great oak under me began to sway with the wind as if dancing underwater.

Images began to appear and disappear before me, and I was flooded with gratitude that finally, *finally*, the gods were speaking to me. Time seemed to stretch and condense as a tall woman of great power emerged from a dream mist. Her hair gleamed like dark blood, and a quiet strength emanated from her. When she appeared, the haze swirled away in tiny eddies as if a great sword had rent the air to allow her to pass. A warrior with iron-gray hair stepped out of the darkness to stand beside her. "Duro, champion to the Queen Boudica of the Iceni," the man said, bowing his head to the high priest. Beside him, Boudica made a bow of her own, tall as any goddess.

So the gods had sent me a memory. A memory of the queen who had, from what the villagers claimed, launched the rebellion that had sent the legions scurrying away from Mona. When had Boudica come to the sacred isle—last winter? The one before? Tribal chieftains often came to the sacred isle to consult with the Druid of All the Tribes. It had been my turn to serve in the elder priest's house when the Iceni delegation arrived. The queen and her gray-haired warrior had stood before the blind priest, and I had served them sacred mead. The queen's voice rang clear and strong in my memory dream as she spoke to the high priest: *There are signs . . . portents . . . we must fight and defeat Rome . . .*

Something about what she was saying agitated the great white-bearded priest. He pounded his staff on the earthen floor and made a strange growling sound. I hadn't been the only one to jump. The queen and her warrior paled.

"You dare claim to interpret the language of the gods," he thundered. "Tell me, Queen, how many hundreds of moons have *you* spent studying the sacred arts?"

"I am a priestess of Andraste," Boudica countered. "Surely that—"

"Means only that you have been sworn to serve her and know

some of her rites," he snapped, standing up. His filmy eyes seemed to glow with outrage. "That doesn't mean she speaks to you directly!"

"The gods speak to those not of Mona, too."

"There is great danger in thinking so," the old Druid continued. "The unworthy and the uninitiated cannot separate the 'signs' they think they see from their deepest desires or their greatest fears."

The queen did not flinch. "But the gods gave us the means to observe the signs. Doesn't that mean they want us to use those faculties?"

I had to admit to being impressed with the queen. Few had the spine to argue with the head Druid of All the Tribes, but she had done so without quaking, let alone skipping a beat, despite the anguished warning looks from her gray-haired champion.

"But not," the blind priest insisted, "if what they 'see' tells them only what they wish to hear."

The queen and her warrior exchanged a look. The priest cocked his head as if listening to a whispered message. "Assistant!" he suddenly bellowed, and I scrambled to his side. "Take us to the *triskelion*."

I took his elbow and led him out of his roundhouse and deep into the eastern side of the holiest section of the sacred grove, with the queen and her warrior following. At the worn rock bearing the ancient weathered image of three interlocked spirals of the oldest of our ancestors, I stopped and removed my arm from the elder's elbow to let him know we'd arrived. He took a deep breath and closed his eyes, and I shivered, as I always did, at the power of this place. Gooseflesh rippled up and down the queen's lean-muscled arms. Good. She was feeling the power of the wood also.

Finally, the priest spoke. "Tell me what you notice," he ordered.

"I see trees," the queen whispered. "Oak and alders and some pine over there." Her eyes scanned the ground and then moved upward. "There is a red squirrel staring at us through the branches of the oak right next to you. I see signs of badger setts and fox dens nearby."

"Excellent," the elder said. "You see through the eyes of a hunter. Now do you see that the configuration of the trees around us also makes the sacred shape of the fivefold knot of the elements?"

She turned in a circle, trying to see it. When she turned to face us again, her lips were pale. "No, I don't."

"Or how this configuration echoes the alignment matching the sign of the Dreamer in the night sky?"

Again, she looked around and murmured, "No."

"Or that the red squirrel is a female and that she watches us because we stand near the tree where she has buried the most food?"

Boudica gave a long exhale, looking at her feet and shaking her head.

"Our training in awareness of the invisible connections, alignments, and configurations of the trees and the stars gives us access to the true language of the gods, not one marred by the reflections of our own fears or wants. Do you understand?"

She nodded, but her gray-haired warrior touched her elbow to remind her to speak aloud to the blind priest. "Yes," she said. "I do."

"Your deepest want, your most intense desire, is to protect your people and remove the scourge of the Romans, yes?"

"It is."

"So of course, every 'sign' you see confirms this desire to fight them."

She sighed, exchanging another look with her craggy-faced warrior. Something caught my eye, and I noticed a murder of crows circling over the clearing behind us. They came down like a black ribbon unfurling, one by one, to the ground. My heart leapt at both the beauty and strangeness of it.

The priest seemed to sense the arrival of the birds, for he suddenly smiled at his visitors. "Now," he added, "I must tell you that I also see the signs. There will come a time soon when we must cleanse the land of the invaders."

The queen looked up with wonder, blinking into the old man's unseeing face. Her eyes filled with what seemed a strange mixture of relief, hope, and awe. She gave her warrior a smile of sudden radiance. He nodded in return.

I hadn't expected the queen's sudden welling of emotion, and I sensed it was an uncommon thing for such a strong, firm spirit. My heart softened toward her.

"When will that time arrive?" she asked, as I knew she must.

The priest smiled enigmatically. "You will know when. Your children will tell you." Then he stuck out his elbow, a signal that it was time to guide him back to the center of the compound. We set off as the elder muttered to me, "And you will bring your gift." But I wasn't paying attention. I was trying to listen to what the Iceni pair whispered behind us.

"'My children will tell me,'" Boudica repeated to her ageing warrior. "Does he mean Sorcha and Keena? Or my people?"

I didn't hear his answer because the memory-vision abruptly vanished and my eyes snapped open.

Dismay filled my chest as I looked around me. I was supposed to learn what the gods wanted me to *do* to make things right with them! But all that had emerged was a memory of a conversation between the high priest and the Iceni queen. Had he been warning me or the queen about something? What did it mean? Was my inability to understand the meaning more proof of my inadequacy to serve?

Stiffly, I stood up and stretched. Perhaps the message was that I was I supposed to *go* to the Iceni queen and her army.

What else could it be? The only clear instruction I'd received was to bring my "gift." The only thing I had in my possession was the Roman. Was that what he'd meant? I could not know for sure, so to be safe, that's what I would do. Together we would head south to the rebellion.

FELIX

THEY took all my clothing and burned it in front of me. But first, they ripped out the metal studs from my shoes and armor and then took all the leather from my bindings and cut them into pieces and shared the strips with anyone who wanted them.

Fucking savages! It had taken every coin I had as a new recruit to outfit myself. As soon as I was back with the lads, I'd have to get another kit from the quartermaster. Yeah, they'd take it out of my pay, but at least I'd have the last laugh when I helped nail the stupid Druid boy to a cross and watched him beg for mercy. I'd seen troublemaking rebels crucified before, and I'd thought it a harsh punishment, but now I'd be happy to wield the mallet.

Days passed with arse-aching slowness. They continued to bind my legs and my arms. Some of the people who visited the healer's hut—for that's what this smoky roundhouse was, a stupid fucking hut compared to proper quarters we Romans built out of wood and stone and marble—spit in my face whenever they came near. When I kicked out at one of them, the healer woman poured another foul-tasting concoction down my throat.

I slept fitfully on and off for what seemed like days. I dreamed I was a boy again in the foothills of my father's farm, running amidst the ripening vineyards while just barely managing not to trip over the dragging hems of the woolen pants I'd inherited from my older brother. He got the farm, so what was left for me?

Adventure and heroism, that's what. Not to mention the plunder I'd imagined taking as soon as I got out here. I'd mapped everything out—I'd serve my time in the legions and then get my own land, as promised to all veterans. Being captured by savages was never a part of the plan.

The lads would never let me live it down. How did I manage to get captured in a battle we'd fucking *won*?

I shifted on my left cheek when the ghostly images from that strange night of mourning flashed into memory. Sure, I hated that women and children and the weaponless died, but that was war, wasn't it? Plus, these savages needed to think of all the people we *saved* for the future by cutting off the source of all their ridiculous rebellions! Why couldn't they see that?

Governor Paulinus had been right—we *had* to destroy Mona, the place where seeds of rebellion grew. The witches and priests on Mona had too much power. Without them, we could rule peacefully. Long-term, this was the best for everyone. They would realize this eventually. Sometimes, the bad needs to be cleared out to make room for the good.

Still, the shame and frustration of being captured was a constant irritant. As was the embarrassing way I'd responded to the shades of the children and women who'd died on the isle. I blamed their potions. Governor Paulinus would've laughed in their faces! So would Tribune Agricola.

To toughen up and ward against turning soft, I determined to replace any vision of shades that popped into my mind with the memory of the night of the raid when I saved Agricola. The flash of respect the tribune had given me—*me*— the only one quick enough to have saved his wealthy, shiny, patrician arse, was worth more than any one of their stupid little lives. How I wanted to see that spark of respect again! It wasn't enough to escape. I needed to *do* something heroic on my return to regain my dignity, but what?

Staring outside through the tacked-up door-skin, I saw the Druid boy reappear from wherever he'd disappeared to—probably looking for some fucking mistletoe or something. I didn't even know what that was except that Caesar claimed it was their holiest of plants.

The entire village surrounded him, touching him and murmuring in their strange barbarian language. In a flash, I saw how I could earn everyone's respect back. Respect that I'd get not just from my optio or centurion—but from Agricola, too. Maybe even from Paulinus!

Paulinus had wanted all the Druids dead. Yet one still lived. *I* would be the one to bring to the general and Agricola the head of the last Druid. *I* would be the one to impress them with my survival and escape and my gift of the head of the last remaining hope these stupid people had.

Suddenly, it seemed so clear why I'd been taken. It was for *this!* So that I would be remembered and rise through the ranks faster than anyone else.

Now it was a matter of waiting for the right moment, listening for clues as to my location. I was smarter than these stupid savages. I was a Roman citizen! I'd show them—personally—how wrong they were in even daring to think themselves better than us.

I would cooperate and be passive until I could spring into action and take them all down.

YORATH

AFTER deliberations led by the village elders, it was decided. The man who regularly brought dried fish to the markets of the interior would escort me south to join the Iceni queen. This was no easy task, of course.

We'd have to travel parallel with the legions. And we'd have to avoid roving bands of Romans sent to slay any locals suspected of sneaking away to join the rebellion.

But they didn't know this land like we did.

We left in the morning. I dressed like an apprentice and rode beside the trader on his cart. We put the Roman in the back of the cart with the fish.

In farmer's clothing, the prisoner looked more like one of us than any kind of Roman foot soldier. The short hair was potentially problematic, but the trader and I had come up with a story to account for it. He was a thief, and when he was caught, the elders cut his braids off to shame him. As for the hard callous under his chin from his helmet strap, you'd have to look pretty carefully to find it under the golden fuzz coming in. And in addition to binding his legs and arms, we gagged the soldier so that he could not call out for help in the Roman tongue.

As we trundled away from the craggy coast on a creaky old cart pulled by a shaggy mare, I prayed for protection and guidance. We played it safe, avoiding Roman outposts and traveling on back roads near villages known for their hatred of the invaders.

It was slow going. It didn't take long before we were all sick to death of both the smell and taste of the "delivery" fish. It was a treat when we came near a village, for when the people heard about our journey, they came out weeping with joy that one Druid still lived, gladly sharing their meager meals in the big roundhouse of their elders.

Spring was fast turning to summer, and the first of the season's storms came with it. Fast, furious showers sometimes forced us to wait for days in one village or another as mud made our paths impassable. Often, I had to place charms of protection on our prisoner for his own sake. At more than one stop, we had to physically restrain drunken villagers from lunging at my Roman with a knife or club, bent on avenging the personal losses at Mona. Every village in the region, it seemed, had sent one or more young people to either train or serve on the sacred isle.

But until I knew what the gods wanted me to do with him beyond bringing him south, I would protect him.

At night, I dreamed of Gara. Sometimes I dreamed that I'd found her in the chaos and that she was with me on the little boat and not the Roman. But then I'd wake up, weeping.

Roman scouts were the biggest danger. They scoured the countryside making sure the marching legions were well protected from roaming bands of rebels. I was drowsing next to the trader one afternoon when he let out a string of oaths under his breath. He wheeled his horse and cart under a tree and jumped out.

"What's happening?" the prisoner asked in Gaulish. We'd forgotten to gag him after the morning meal. Before he had the chance to ask anything again, my escort shoved a piece of linen in his mouth and tied a woolen band over it. That's when I saw them, helmets and mail glimmering in the light as they raced toward us, kicking giant clods of dirt and stones behind them.

My heart pounded in my ears. The prisoner must have realized what was happening. He began to buck and scream, kicking hay up all around his legs. The cords in his neck jutted out, but the trader had tied the gag so tight his noises were unintelligible.

The Romans were there in a blink, drawing up their horses on each side of us. The beasts shuddered and huffed from the sudden sprint.

The biggest Roman began screaming at us in Latin.

We stared blankly at him.

The other one interrupted, speaking in an imperfect tongue of the tribes, but at least we could understand him. "Why did you pull off the road?" he repeated.

"This thief tried to bite my friend, so I had to stop and gag him," my companion said nonchalantly.

That Roman dismounted and walked around the cart. My mouth grew so dry it felt as if I'd glued it to the roof of my mouth. I prayed to Briga to keep us safe from detection while making myself look as small and stupid as possible. Glancing up at the mounted soldier, I saw him staring at me, and my skin prickled. What would they do to us if they knew we carried one of their own?

Our prisoner bucked and screamed, drawing the man's attention back to himself. Our captive looked insane. Good. His light hair also worked in our favor. Although we were nearing the territory of the Silures, who were dark, there were still plenty of locals with the light hair and light eyes of this Romanized Gaul.

"Why is he tied up?"

"Because he is a thief!" the trader replied. "He was caught, so the elders chopped his braids, and now he will be punished by his own village."

"Where are you taking him?"

"To the elder council of the Catuvellauni, as that's where his people are from."

"Take the gag off of him," the still-mounted Roman ordered.

"He is mad I tell you," the trader said calmly, going to the side of the cart as if he were going to obey.

Felix, whose countenance was so red by now it looked as if the chords in his neck might rupture, drew their attention. Out of the corner of my eye, I saw the trader slip something—a knife?—into the arm of his tunic as the Romans watched Felix.

"Also," he said. "We think he has the disease of the water-fear."

That stopped them both cold.

"You stupid savages," the Roman next to the cart cried, backing away with alacrity. "Don't you know you must put him down? What if he bites you? You will go mad and die, too!"

My guide took on a bewildered, foolish look—I'd learned that acting stupid around Romans was an important survival tool—and said, "But he *already* bit me!"

The Roman on the ground spoke rapidly in Latin to his mounted companion, moving toward his horse. I knew somehow, even though I couldn't understand their words, that they were discussing killing us right then and there. Native lives were of no consequence to them, especially if we posed a risk to their men.

But before I could even call upon the gods for help, my driver had plunged a knife into the standing Roman's neck. The man's surprised bellow made the other Roman's horse rear, and his effort to control the animal kept him from drawing his sword. Felix kicked at the cart's sides crazily at the melee, disturbing the horse even more.

It happened so fast it was hard to countenance. My companion grabbed the fallen soldier's sword and slashed at the horse's hamstrings. It fell screaming with a sickening crunch onto the mounted soldier's leg. But before the Roman could even respond, my guide had slit his throat. Then he calmly dispatched the injured, still-screaming horse.

Calmly, he walked back to the cart, dripping sword still in hand, climbed onto his seat, clucked at our horse, and resumed clattering away. Even Felix was silent by this point.

The trader looked at my wide-eyed expression and just shrugged. "They would've killed us," he said. "We're vermin to them."

"But . . . but will this cause more of them to come after us?"

Again, he shrugged. "When they finally find these two, they'll think that a bunch of warriors heading to the rebellion took 'em down. Just to be safe, though, I'll go the pathways the Romans don't know about."

And we continued on our way.

FELIX

I'D kicked and banged my head on the wooden planks of the cart so strongly I almost cracked it by the time the barbarian driving the cart killed my rescuers. It happened so fast it was beyond understanding.

I would not look at that trader quite so dismissively now, that was for fucking sure. These barbarians were insane!

Getting away from them was going to be a bit more challenging than I'd thought. My almost-rescuers had underestimated these little barbarians. I would have to be careful not to make that same mistake when the time came.

My rage and head-banging only made me feel ill as the hours wore on. They kept the gag on me, and despite my thirst and despair, I fell into a miserable, sweaty sleep after a while.

I awoke to darkness in the woods near a small campfire. They finally—*finally*—removed the gag, and I worked my jaw in relief. I signaled for water, and the trader poured some into my mouth from his bladder. I would have to watch myself around this one.

Staring miserably into a crackling, hissing fire, I asked the Druid boy again what he was going to do to me, where he was taking me.

He didn't answer. I still worried that he was planning to string me up in one of their spooky groves, but he would've done that by now if he'd intended to, right? And if they'd wanted me dead, they would've cut my throat just like they had the scouts. So what was he doing?

We were moving south, that much I could figure out. What was in the south besides our forts and strongholds? My stomach contracted. "Wait," I said. "Are you taking me to the slave markets?" I hadn't meant my voice to crack, damn it.

The Druid boy's eyebrows met over his thin nose, and I could tell I'd guessed right. And it made sense. There could be no other explanation as to why they hadn't killed me yet. The little greedy savages wanted to make coin off me!

"I imagine I could make a pretty pot of gold off you," the little priestling said, staring out over the land.

Well, at least I knew. But their stupidity astounded me. They really couldn't figure out that as soon as I spoke to a Roman trader, they'd both be arrested? The lads had always claimed the locals were dumber than dirt. Well, that just proved it.

Good with knives, though. I'd have to keep that in mind.

The stink of dried fish was a constant irritation. When the heat made it especially pungent, I killed time by imagining slathering myself with oil at the baths and scraping all the dirt and stink of old fish off me before plunging into the *tepidarium*. Never, never, would I complain again about the mildewy stink of any of the forts' baths. No matter how rickety. It was heaven compared to how these animals lived.

And I certainly didn't allow myself to fantasize too much about the gleaming new marble baths Agricola had recently built in Isca Dumnoniorum. There was only so much torture I could take, wasn't there?

One night, as we camped in yet some other strange, gods-forsaken wood, I kept trying to guess the Druid boy's age. I started at fifteen. I knew this was too young, but it was funny to see how this insulted him. Idiot. Trying to grow that stupid fuzz on his stupid face.

"I am nineteen!" he finally barked at me.

As someone who'd always looked younger than my age—it took my father swearing before a magistrate that I was old enough to join the legions before they would accept me—I felt a little bad for him. He was smaller and skinnier than most of the hardy barbarian specimens I'd seen.

But whenever I caught myself starting to feel sympathy for him, or thought of any of the magic-induced shades of their dead from Mona, I reminded myself of the truth: I was a Roman soldier. A Roman soldier did his duty. There was no way I was going to go soft now. I thought about Agricola often—imagining all the ways I'd impress him in battle once I got back.

Still, whenever I thought of how close I'd come to being rescued, a new anger uncoiled in my gut. A new hatred that drove me to find some way to torture my captor.

"Who is Gara?" I asked, and the way he jumped, you would have thought I'd rammed a poker up his arse.

"What?"

"You call out her name in the night. She your little girlfriend, then?"

He leaped up in one movement, his face darkening and contorting into a devil's mask of rage so fast I actually recoiled.

He thrust his face into mine. "Gara is dead thanks to you. She was a healer and the sweetest, kindest, most . . . most . . ."

His throat worked convulsively, and he suddenly straightened and stomped off into the trees with impressive speed.

Once again, I reminded myself that those "sweet" little children on the isle would've grown up to kill us despite the Druid's ongoing protestation of innocence. Agricola knew what he was doing. I was a fucking hostage because I'd *hesitated*. Trust me, it wouldn't happen again.

The trader watched the Druid boy go and turned to stare at me accusingly.

"Fuck you and your fucking fish smell," I said. He didn't understand Gaulish, but I could tell he understood the sentiment. Good enough for me.

I curled up and pretended to sleep. But you can bet your arse I kept one eye open for any sign of a knife.

YORATH

HOW *dare* that fool even say her name? The sound of it—coming out wrong and harsh, trampling the music of it as if he'd stomped on her very heart with his ridiculous sharpened boots. Gods, I wanted to slit his throat!

I leaned against an old pine, and Gara's dream-self came to me, glowing as if lit by the moon from the inside. Everything in me gathered tight in my throat as I fought back the sobs.

I should've protected her, but I hadn't. I'd had to hide, and then it was too late, and I'd had to run.

There was nothing you could've done, she whispered in my mind. The gods saved you for a reason. All of us on this side of life are helping you.

A smile pulled at my lips even as I tasted the salt of my tears. Gara always found a way to soothe and inspire. I had loved her from the first moment we met when we both sang and danced the ritual of newcomers. We were only eight years old. She'd come from the Dumnonii in the southwest on the coast close to the "Tin Islands" that the Romans controlled through the Veneti in Gaul. She was studying to be a healer. Her father's family had worked the tin mines for generations, but her mother was also gifted in the healing arts.

On that first day, she'd smiled shyly at me and had taken my hand. She had been just as scared as I'd been. Over the nearly twelve years of training since, her straw-gold hair darkened into the soft brown of elm bark in fall, but the warmth in her blue eyes only deepened. The elders were right in training her for medicine—Nodons, the God of Healing, moved within her with every breath.

We'd been lovers for years. She would've completed her twelve-year cycle of training in two moons. I had another eight years to go. During the harvest moon, before the festival of the dead, she was to return to her village in the south as a full healer.

"We are a circle together," she'd murmured one warm summer night, as we slept naked under the stars.

I'd laughed. "Yes, I do the sacrificing, and you do the saving."

She'd playfully slapped my chest near where she rested her head over my heart. "Do not joke about such things," she'd said with that ever-present smile in her voice. "The sacrifices you make sometimes do more than any healing herbs or prayers I manage. Sometimes, I kill and *you* save them on the other side."

"You never *kill*," I'd said. "Sometimes the Gods call a soul back despite what healers and priests do on this side. That is not the same as killing."

She'd nodded sleepily, and I'd kissed her hair, which always carried the scent of juniper.

I'd been dreading her departure, sure that I would lose her to some strapping warrior or miner the moment she returned to her village. Still, I'd been petitioning to accompany her on her journey home and to be sent to her people when I finished my training cycle.

The elders had always smiled and nodded, murmuring that they would seek guidance from the gods on the matter. I could tell from their expressions they were only humoring me. But really, once I finished my training and was accepted by the gods in the final rituals, they could not dismiss my requests so easily. Out of all the scenarios I could imagine—that my father would command my return to the north to serve the Venicones, that Gara would marry a local boy before I was free from the sacred isle—it had never occurred to me that she, along with everyone I knew and had come to love, would be hunted down and massacred like animals in a pen by the dead-eyed Romans.

The physical ache of her loss left me wanting to throw my head back and howl like a wolf. The only thing that seemed to calm me was envisioning tearing my arrogant Roman prisoner apart, organ by organ, limb my limb. I wanted him to know a glimmer of the suffering he and his friends had caused.

But I could do nothing until the gods told me clearly what they wanted me—the only survivor of Mona—to do to set things right. Night after night, I sought the sacred configuration of trees to commune with the gods and the ancestors, asking for help in understanding what I must do to heal our rift with the divine realm. Our gods had left us to die in Mona. What did we need to do to earn back their protection?

On the first full moon of our trip, I again sought answers in a sacred wood. And this time, finally, the gods spoke to me.

Beams of moonlight extended slim fingers between swaying branches as images flooded my awareness. I saw brilliant yellow mold blighting our wheat and barley fields in vast tracks of farmland. I saw rust spreading on an ancient sword of the giants until it disintegrated. I saw ants swarming over a dead bug until all that was left was a carcass shell. What were the gods trying to tell me?

Slowly, the images changed. Began to move faster. Pulsed with a raging energy as if the drummers of the isle had materialized and called forth the Song of War. Farmers cut the blighted grasses and set them aflame. An iron-smith burned the rust away in a river of liquid red. A foot stomped the ants until they disappeared in the dirt.

I waited. Then, as if I hadn't seen it a thousand times in my mind, the day of the attack appeared before me yet again. Of the maddened priest thrusting his face into mine, ordering me to sacrifice the large, red-haired Roman. My refusal. Of the panicked way the Druid—who taught me the spells but was never supposed to utter them himself—yelled them out of order. Of his wild slashing with the long-sword. Of the head rolling. The truncated body weaving before collapsing with a thud.

The wild screams. The press of the invaders. My panicked flight. Then it all began again. The Romans across the channel. The maddened priest. The slashing. The head flying off the Roman's thick body as the sacred prayers my elder *wasn't supposed to utter* roared in my ears. The head rolling, the blood spurting, the eyes still blinking, the mouth working. The head . . . the head . . . the head.

Why were the gods sending me these visions again and again? I sang the Song of Openness and Guidance and swayed with the wind that gusted around me, rattling the leaves.

A raven burst through a thicket with a terrible cry at the same moment—in my vision—that the maddened elder yelled at me to kill the Roman during that awful morning of the invasion. And then I understood.

My priest had enraged the gods by ignoring the ancient rules of the most sacred sacrifice of all. The gods demanded the *proper* ceremony and ritual, performed in the ways of the ancients, passed down from time immemorial. They wanted it done correctly, with respect. My elder had *done it wrong.* He'd been in a panic. And he wasn't a Vates.

Finally, *finally,* I understood what they wanted, why they were angry.

The gods had demanded a blood sacrifice, but we had not realized it in time. My elder priest understood too late and attempted the rite at the wrong time in the wrong way, without a willing sacrifice, and without following the rules the gods themselves had set for such powerful magic.

The ultimate blood sacrifice—not of enemy warriors, but of a sacrifice of the gods' choosing—had to follow the ancient rules, or the magic worked against us. The gods had saved me, one who was sanctified to perform such a sacrifice. And they had handed the very man they wanted sacrificed *unto me.*

My Roman was the gift, the sacrifice the gods required to set things right. That's why the elder priest had told me to bring him.

The shame I'd felt over running and surviving was lifted. As long as I performed the holiest of sacrifices correctly, I could be the one to save us all from the terrors of Rome.

I would not be the Druid who ran, but the survivor who brought about our people's reconciliation with the divine.

A great peace settled over me. As if in response, a mist rose from the earth and swirled around me in a languid dance of approval. My heart slowed to match its movement, and it felt as if I breathed in time with the spirit of the earth itself.

FELIX

THE Druidling was acting even weirder than ever. Beyond looking smug and staring up at stars all night, he'd stopped calling me by my name and referred to me as the "Gaul of the People of the Elders before Rome."

What in the bloody hell?

He did it again one drizzly morning, and if my wrists hadn't been bound, I swear I would have twisted that knobby head off his skinny neck in one go.

"My name is *Felix*," I growled. "I've never been a savage like you people. I am Roman through and through!"

He pointed to my light hair and smiled as he stuffed a heel of hard bread into my hands—still tied at the wrist—to break the morning fast.

Just because I have light hair and my ancestors once spread bear grease on themselves meant nothing. My people had been Roman for almost two hundred years! I'd always been more Roman than any short, dark, curly-headed sod from inner Italia.

"By Castor's cock, are you blind? Don't you understand? Rome already *owns* all these lands. It is inevitable. You will never be rid of us because our gods are stronger. Haven't we proven that enough times?"

"The gods of these lands prefer people of honor," he said. "No tribesman worth his spear would have done what you did—attack a sacred place filled with old men, women, and children. I think even your Roman gods must be disgusted."

"If your gods are so honorable, why are they not outraged when you burn men alive in wicker cages or . . . or kill them to foretell the future by reading their blood splatter!"

That stopped him. The chunk of bread on the way to his mouth hung in midair. "What are you talking about?" he cried. "We do neither of those things!"

"That's not true. The great Caesar himself wrote of it!"

"Lies!" the little Druid cried. "You make us look like savages to excuse your own savagery."

"So what do you do with your prisoners of war if you don't burn them?"

He shook his head. "We haven't burned you, have we? Different tribes deal with their enemies in different ways, but burning them alive is not one of them, unlike you monsters. More to the point, *our* warriors would not murder every living thing on a peaceful isle for sport, as your people did."

"It wasn't for sport," I cried. "We had to stop future rebellions! We were saving you from *yourselves*!"

The Druidling just stared at me without blinking.

"Also, your people take heads and hang them as trophies!" I added when I could see I wasn't getting through.

He nodded. "The seat of the soul is in the head. Only warriors do this. They would never take the heads of innocents."

"Even so, you don't think that's a bit *savage*? I've heard some of your chiefs even drink from skulls."

"According to the rules of honorable warfare," he said, nodding. When I rolled my eyes, he added, "Your people take vanquished warriors and force them to fight in a ring until they die, *just* for the entertainment of the masses. Is that not so?"

"Yes, but it's a way for them to earn honor, too."

"There is nothing honorable about killing for entertainment. That is murder and pure savagery."

Oh, now we were in a pissing contest? "Well your people wouldn't have been so easy to defeat if you hadn't spent eternity fighting each other over every little thing like the backwoods barbarians that you are."

As if he hadn't even heard me, he said, "But you and your people traded dignity and independence to be Rome's whore."

"We are not—"

"What do you get from being their whore besides having to turn your greatest wealth over to them?"

I ignored the jibe, reminding myself that barbarians would never understand. That's what made them barbarians. His stare, though, was piercing. So I finally said, "We get citizenship."

"Which means?"

"Which means . . . well, that I have rights."

He cocked his head as if he didn't understand.

"If I own land, I can vote. If I have enough money, I can run for office eventually. Or I can rise through the ranks of the legions and lead the greatest army the world ever saw. I can . . ."

Again, that stupid smile. I took a swig of mead that tasted like old piss. Why did his air of superiority get under my skin so? "The Romans brought us baths and gorgeous temples for their powerful gods and . . . and roads and . . ."

"Baths? I've heard about your baths. We clean ourselves in the living waters of streams and rivers. You sit in the dirty, piss-filled, stagnant waters of countless others." He shuddered with disgust.

"And our temples," he continued, sweeping his arm out to encompass the valley of wild woods and green hills, "are the living places where the gods breathe, not the dead marble of an empty room.

"And your roads stab through the earth without respect for its sacredness—all so it can transport more soldiers for even more killing and raping."

I sighed. Really, there was no point to any of this. He would never understand the greatness that is Rome.

"Are you married?" he asked after we finished eating.

I laughed. "I'm only eighteen. And I'm not allowed to marry while serving in the legions."

"How long do you serve?"

"Twenty-five years."

His mouth fell open. "You cannot marry for twenty-five years? By the gods of all that matter, they have stolen your mind, body, *and* soul to serve their endless appetite for blood."

I shrugged. "Most of the blokes have a local girl. Or they just use the brothels. When you've done your time, you can marry and adopt the little bastards if you want."

He shook his head disbelievingly. His ridiculous sense of superiority rankled. So I aimed where I knew it would hurt the most. "You married to that Gara girl?" I asked.

In a blink, his face took on that tight, rageful veneer but then resumed its normal appearance almost as quickly before he stood and walked away. Huh. He seemed to be getting better at mastering himself, I observed. I didn't know why, but it sent a chill down my spine.

YORATH

"SOMEONE is coming," my escort announced, abruptly pulling the horse to a stop.

I snapped awake from the half dreaming induced by the cart's rhythm. And a deep chasm of dread opened under my chest. Please, not more Romans!

"Soldiers?" I asked.

"I don't think so."

I squinted and could see what he meant. Three riders rode the natural way, not the stiff-backed way of the Romans. Colorful and checked cloaks billowed behind them, tribal cloaks, and I released a long breath of relief. Still, I could not take any risks with my prisoner now that I knew what the gods wanted me to do with him. I glanced back to make sure the gag hadn't loosened. He was fast asleep.

A woman rode in the center, blood-red hair streaming behind her. The Iceni queen? Not possible. I blinked several times to clear my vision. She was weirdly the queen and yet *not* the queen at the same time. It was only when she drew up that I understood. This had to be one of her daughters—thinner, younger, and exuding an even more feral fierceness than her mother. I hadn't known that was possible.

"I am Sorcha, daughter of Boudica, Queen of the Iceni," she called. "We come from our victory at Camulodunum to beseech my mother's sister's people to join us in our rebellion. Do you have knowledge to share about what happened in Mona? We have heard terrible rumors."

"I am Yorath, son of Torkill, Druid Vates in training."

Her blue eyes grew wide, and she grinned. "So the rumors aren't true, then! Some of the sacred ones have survived!" She looked wildly around with hope lighting her eyes, as if some of the long-bearded elder priests and stoop-shouldered elder priestesses might step out from behind the trees to greet her. "How many? Where are they? How are they protected? I can send bands of warriors to guard them—"

I held up my palm to silence her. "I am the only survivor."

She blinked several times, her forehead scrunched. "No, that cannot be," she finally breathed.

"It is so."

The queen's daughter clutched her stomach and closed her eyes. By the state of her horse and her clothing—blood-spattered and shredded—I could tell that she had set off right from the battlefield. The exhaustion on the faces of her fellow riders confirmed this. Our tribes liked to celebrate victories as much as they liked the fight itself, but I sensed that this young warrior had no patience for such trivialities. That must be why she had set off when she did. Sorcha of the Iceni seemed to burn from within with a rage that would only be sated by Roman blood, not by drunken victory celebrations.

Then I remembered the violence against her and her sister that sparked the rebellion in the first place, and I understood.

The queen's eldest daughter dismounted and circled the cart. "Who is this?" she asked. But before I could answer, she had pulled out her dirk and growled, "Roman!"

"Wait!" I called as her thin but muscular arm arced over my sacrifice's sleeping chest. "Do not hurt him. I need him!"

She stared at me as I rushed to her side, fury pulsating from every muscle in her hard-angled body.

"Explain!" she said through clenched teeth.

"Come with me," I signaled. "Leave your men here, and I will tell you all."

Her soldiers were only too glad to dismount and stretch. It was clear she'd been driving them hard.

She followed me into a small glen. I turned to her. "How did you know he was Roman so quickly?" I asked, curious.

"The blisters and sores on his feet are in the pattern of Roman boots," she said with a shudder. I must have looked confused, for she added, "The sight of Roman feet is etched into my memory in a way that will not be purged until they are all exterminated."

I looked away as I understood she was referring to her attack. An image of Gara's smiling face appeared in my mind, and I prayed she'd had an easy death. A death not compounded by the suffering this girl had faced.

"Where did you get him?" Sorcha asked.

"I took him from Mona."

"And they are not hunting for him?"

"They do not appear to know that he's been taken," I said. "I assume they believe he died in the fires. I believe it is the gods' way of protecting us."

"I don't understand."

"The gods saved me and gave me this man so I could fulfill the ritual that will ensure the success of our people against the invaders," I explained. "They have directed me to perform this most holy ritual in a sacred grove near your mother's army. That is why we travel in this direction."

Did she understand what ritual I meant? She must have, for

her eyes widened with hope. She nodded. "How can I help you, Priest?"

The lightening of her expression touched me, for it gave a brief glimpse of the bright-eyed young girl that still lived under the armor of prickly rage she'd wrapped around herself like a heavy cloak.

"We travel alone, for every able-bodied man who can wield a weapon has been streaming to join your forces," I said. "And although my guide is strong, a warrior for protection would be most welcome."

"You shall have it!" she said.

"The man you leave with me must be able to go into local villages and secure some of the sacred implements I will need for the holy rite," I pointed out.

"Of course!" she said, signaling to a young man with a blood-spattered beard. "Vanus is both Dobunni and Durotriges and will be welcomed and trusted by all as you move farther and farther south."

Perfect! I'd been worrying about how I would obtain what I would need for the rite—a rope unused, a blessed dagger, mead boiled with mugwort in a sheep's bladder, and, most important of all, a white robe. And here was a warrior princess promising help. The gods were indeed smiling down upon me! "You said you were on your way to your mother's sister's people?"

She nodded. "The Cornovii. She is on the southern edge of her territories right now. The more tribes we can convince to fight with us, the faster our victory."

"I will beseech the gods on your behalf," I said after cautioning her about the marching legions. She would likely have to take a circuitous route to avoid them and their scouts.

A swift suddenly poked its head out of a hole in a tree to my right and, with a little high-pitched call, soared into the sky in a soot-brown blur. But unlike most of the swifts that only bore a small bit of smudged-white at its throat, this one's chest and belly were as pale as a martin's. "A blessing," I breathed. The princess followed my gaze, her eyes suddenly sad.

"My people say *my* birth was a blessing—they called me 'the lucky princess.'" Her voice was so bleak. "But I don't think I bring luck to anyone now."

"You've brought it to me today," I said gently. "You *are* blessed, Princess. So am I because the gods saved me. So is he—" I pointed at Felix. "His name means lucky in his ugly language, and the gods gave him to me for sacrifice. We lucky three will bring your mother victory."

I smiled. And just as her mother had done years before in the sacred wood with the living elder, the princess' eyes filled with water. This beautiful, tall, hurting girl gave me a shaky smile of such innocent hope it nearly cleaved my chest in two.

FELIX

THE sun indicated we were moving westward as well as south-ward. Were there slave markets on the western edges of these bloody lands? That made me sit up in the cart. The western coasts of this land of horrors were not as securely Roman as the eastern. What if he was taking me to a slave market controlled by the mysterious ones that were rumored to sail off the edge of the world in black ships? My stomach coiled into knots. I'd grown lazy, thinking that as soon as we got near the Roman ports, I would speak Latin, and then they'd be done for. But if these ports were held by even stranger savages . . . I needed to get serious about breaking out.

Also, I didn't like the new guy that had mysteriously joined us. I'd awoken one afternoon to find some bear-fat-stinking sod staring daggers at me. Apparently, I'd missed the excitement when some native girl had dropped him off. A fucking girl! I could've used one of them, even if she was a barbarian savage. But no, I had to sleep through it all.

I took to baiting the idiot who, lucky for me, also spoke Gaulish. He rode his mount beside the cart when I began. "First, they will whip you," I said, explaining what would happen when I finally escaped and hunted him down. "But not hard enough to kill you—just enough to make it agony when they throw you down on the long beam."

He pretended not to hear me as we clopped along, but I could see his neck reddening. "Then they will spread your arms on the crossbeam and drive iron nails into your forearms below the wrists, right where the bones separate. Seriously, the sound is amazing. If you can hear it over the screams."

Nothing.

"We do the same thing at the ankle bones, but that takes a bit more work as you need one of the heavier mallets—you know, the ones with the iron heads. Then, when your guy is nice and bolted onto the beams, you plow the whole structure into the ground so their naked indignity can be seen by all."

There. A twitch. I was getting to him.

"It can take *days* for a bloke to die, which is part of the show. Sometimes our lads give them wine or water when their throats swell so that they can continue screaming. They take bets on when the idiot will die. Occasionally, crows will pluck out their eyes or pull at their noses, waking them up. Now that's a sight! But the show ends when the prisoner finally suffocates to death because he can no longer keep his head up."

Still nothing. Balls of bronze this guy has.

"I thought you should know exactly how you're going to die," I continued. "Consider it a courtesy."

Faster than I could blink, he vaulted off his horse and had a dagger at my neck. "You will shut your fat mouth now, or I will cut off your lips to hear *you* scream."

I grinned into his big red sweaty face.

The little Druid called him off me, as I knew he would.

The savage spit and stomped off. I could do nothing about the slimy glob rolling down my cheek except to think that getting him to lose control had been completely worth it.

Not long after, we stopped and made camp in a mysterious wood that I was sure was filled with either strong magic or malevolent spirits. The Druidling seemed to glow from the inside with a weird serenity that couldn't be budged, even when I baited him over his lost girl.

The more questions I asked, the quieter he got. And although I couldn't say why, the calmer he got, the more uneasy it made me. He kept watching the sky as if it were talking to him. And maybe it was—those Druids were powerful magicians. The great Caesar had said so. And I'd witnessed Centurion Flacca's death-by-cursing. Not to mention the blinding spell one of them had cast on me. I shivered in disgust.

Groups of locals began to camp around us. They kept me near the fires at night. Children gathered to stare at me. A couple of young women came over and talked softly to each other about me. When their eyes roamed over my body, everything tingled. And I mean everything. This only made them smile and giggle appreciatively. It was all so strange that I didn't know what to make of it.

The Druid boy started disappearing into the woods for long periods. When I asked him what he did there, he only gave me that stupid, sly smile again. What a knob.

At least it was clear we were staying here for a while, which meant we weren't headed to unknown western ports, after all. Certainly, with all the new people around us and all the distractions, it was just a matter of time before someone forgot to tighten the ropes on my ankles. ·

That's when I would run.

YORATH

SORCHA'S warrior-guard had performed his duties well and had obtained everything I needed for the ritual. Still, as we sat by the campfire, I could tell he was troubled.

"Walk with me," I said, leaving the young gawkers around my prisoner. When I was sure we would not be overheard, I asked him what weighed so heavily on his heart.

"I need not bother you, Priest," he said, not meeting my eyes.

"But something haunts you," I said. "You must clear yourself of it if you are to serve me. I need you whole for this rite."

He looked at me, hazel eyes wide with fear. He swallowed. "What the Romans did at Mona . . . it is beyond loathsome. And yet . . ." He stopped and rubbed his face.

"And yet what?"

It all came flooding out. "And yet the armies of our own people also killed civilians and innocents in Camulodunum. It was outright slaughter. We were no better, don't you see? Honorable battle I understand, but this slaughter of women, children, and old people is beneath us. I keep seeing the bodies and hearing the screams of children and women."

"As do I," I said. "This means we have not lost our sense of honor as people of the gods of this land. The Romans brought with them a savagery and cycle of violence so ugly and deep it is not surprising that we have adopted some of their ways in order to defeat them."

The young warrior continued to frown.

"When we have purged the Romans from our lands, and the Old Ways of our gods have returned, we will cleanse all of our people of the stain of the Romans," I promised. "The gods themselves will absolve you."

He nodded, thanked me, and returned to the camp. I watched him go, and my inner eye saw that while on the outside he seemed soothed by my words, on the inside he continued to be torn in two. I doubted he was the only warrior in Boudica's war band troubled by the violence he must commit to defeat Rome. Such was the cost of dealing with the Romans: even when one fought against them, the stain of their violence licked and crackled at the soul like a fire about to engulf an entire forest.

I fasted and bathed in moving waters as the night of the full moon approached. The nights were warm now—the last days of spring had passed into summer, and the year stood at its height. Here it was pleasantly warm. In the south, where Boudica's war band carried death to the Romans, I imagined it was already as hot as a forge.

My body seemed to thrum with mingled fear and awe the closer we came to performing the most sacred ritual of all. One night, I dreamed that I was back again on Mona with the elder priest and the Iceni queen. His white beard shook as he thundered, "The unworthy think to read the signs of the gods but see only the reflections of their deepest desires or their greatest fears."

When Boudica opened her mouth to argue, he roared, "And how many hundreds of moons have you spent on Mona studying the sacred ways?"

When I awoke, I wondered why the gods sent this particular

part of the memory-dream again. A cold doubt writhed in my belly. Had the elder been warning *me* and not Boudica? What if *I* was the one misreading the signs?

But I was the only one of Mona left! True, I had not trained for as long as the elder Druid had, but he was no longer here. The reality was that the gods saved me and not him. Which meant they trusted me.

No, it had to be a message for the queen.

FELIX

THEY took me to a mist-filled glen filled with so many rich shades of vibrant green it was clearly a place favored by their strange gods. I felt expansive and smiled stupidly as I looked around. Had they put something in my mead before we set off? I should have been angry about that, but I wasn't. Maybe it wasn't mead—maybe the magic of this place was powerful all on its own. It somehow filled my head with air so that it gently separated from my body and floated amidst the clouds.

Two girls came and took me by the arms—the same girls who regularly came to the fire to smile sweetly at me. Gods, they were lovely. These girls weren't savages. They smelled of sage and sunshine. Was I dead? Was this Elysium?

No, this had to be a place of magic in these strange lands. The kind of place the lads whispered about in the dark. But it wasn't a place of terror. It was a place of peace and beauty. The Druid brought me here. Why had we wanted them all dead when they knew the secrets of a place like this? I couldn't remember.

I tried to muster Agricola's face to stay strong, but it drifted away.

The girls were speaking to me, and I noticed we were naked.

When did that happen?

Gods, they were pretty. One was raven-haired and the other was copper-haired, like the Queen of Iceni was rumored to be. I glanced down and saw that all of her was that color and complimented her on her beauty. She smiled and shook her head, reminding me that she couldn't understand me. I leaned toward her for a kiss, but she pulled away, though she was still smiling.

The next thing I knew, we were all three walking into a deep, clear spring. By Numa's cock, the water was freezing! The three of us squealed and laughed. We took turns dunking each other.

The raven-haired one dove down for some time, and I could've sworn she'd turned into a fish, but then she surfaced, wet hair gleaming blue-black in the shimmering light, her hands filled with tiny shells and rocks and debris that she used to scrub me. Still, it seemed that the half of her still in the water flashed with silver-green scales beneath the sparkling water. The other one dove down, too, and they took turns washing me. I wanted to wash them, too, but they wouldn't let me.

Strangely, a flash of memory came and went like a darting swallow: my mother and sisters washing a piglet until it glowed pink on the day they would sacrifice it before the spring planting. The dark-haired girl spent a lot of time cleaning my fingernails. Time seemed to expand and shrink.

Had I fallen asleep? I was in the sunlight now, covered in blankets. When the sun touched the tip of the tallest pine, the copper-haired girl came to me. By the way she touched me— lovingly, slowly, with a sweet smile of desire—I knew that she wanted me, and for some reason, that realization made me want to cry.

I'd only ever paid for sex, and I could only afford the ones who didn't even bother to pretend to want me or to enjoy themselves. This girl *chose* me, and the certainty of this made every sensation of pleasure pulse more deeply than I could've ever imagined possible. I came with so much force and pleasure it was as if I was actually being turned inside out with it. The girl did not stop moving when I was done. Instead, she took my hand and pressed herself against it, rocking until she gasped and shuddered, too. That this girl had wanted me and actually *enjoyed* herself with me was a revelation. I wanted to stay there with her, in her, in the sunshine, naked like animals, forever.

The hours swirled together, just as our bodies joined over and over.

I must have fallen asleep again because the sun was gone. I was dressed in a tunic and trousers of fine quality. The only rope on me was a twisted decorative belt around my waist. Laughing, I realized that now that I was dressed and untied, I could escape but did not want to—I had entered a magical wood where I would happily spend the rest of my days with this girl who had hair the color of the setting sun.

Maybe the Druid was right. Maybe I was a tribesman at heart, like my ancestors in Gaul. Vaguely, I had a sense of wrongness. No, I was Roman. A soldier. But I was in a magic wood with this beautiful girl who wanted me.

I began to laugh, and she laughed too. "My name means lucky!" I said. "And this is the first bit of luck I've ever had."

She just laughed again.

"What is your name?" I asked. "Please tell me."

The girl spoke, but I could not understand. It didn't matter, though, because I could tell she still liked me by the way she stroked my cheek. She hand-fed me a type of burnt griddle bread covered in honey, the taste exploding in my mouth in a burst of strange textures and thick sweetness. She held a cup of mead to my mouth, and I drank deeply of the strange-tasting brew.

Suddenly, there were lots of people around us, and I smiled

expansively at all of them. Torches flickered in a circle, and I was moved by the sheer beauty and wholeness of it.

The Druid boy appeared, and I wanted to thank him for the gift of these woods and this day, for the miracle of the girl who wanted me. Because I knew that somehow he'd done this.

He held out his arms, and all of the people began to chant and sway in rhythm. He glowed in a moon-white robe. Arcing his hands in strange curves, he made pronouncements that sounded like gibberish to me. What did I care as long as the girl was by my side?

Suddenly, I realized he was speaking to me in Gaulish. "Felix of Gaul, of the People of the Elders before the Time of Rome, do you come to the arms of the woods willingly?"

I grinned widely and threw my arms out. "Yes, yes! A million times, yes!"

My answer sent a ripple of awe and excitement around the circle of torch holders. I looked at the girl, and she smiled widely at me.

"As long as she stays with me in these woods!" I added, but nobody seemed to hear me as the chanting grew louder and louder.

So I repeated it again and again. I would stay with this magical girl in this magical place until the end of time if they let me.

YORATH

THE girls who volunteered to take the prisoner for the ritual cleaning and rites understood how he was to be prepared. They set off with him in the morning after giving him the purified mead and sacred plants in the lamb's bladder that I'd prepared for us both.

After a long fast, I climbed the hill where I'd found the white-berried mistletoe so pleasing to the dods. Mistletoe berries usually didn't ripen until the fall. That it had blossomed so unusually early was yet another blessing, was yet more proof that the gods were pleased with my work.

I waited until the white berries glowed like tiny moons in the silvered light and then collected them. Afterward, I climbed down and sought the trees that aligned with the stars of the running Huntress, put a wad of woad into my cheek, and sipped the holy mead. It didn't take long for the veil separating me from the other side to disappear.

So many of the dead on Mona showed themselves to me, but not Gara. I began to cry. My elder Druid was suddenly before me. "Gain control of your emotions," he admonished. "Use your training. You are the elder now."

The idea of me—*me*— being the most learned of our priests once again gutted me into hollowness.

But the elder laughed as if he, too, was struck by the oddity of it, and strangely, that made me feel better. "All is prepared?" he asked. "The sacrifice is willing?"

My stomach clenched. How would I know until the very moment of the asking? All I could do was give him the very best of the "Honored's Day"—to have him bathed in pleasure and peace—and hope that was enough. "I believe he will be," I answered.

"He must be," my elder said, and I bowed my head, praying for Felix's willing heart.

"Where is Gara?" I asked after some time, ashamed of my weakness. I should've been focusing on the great ritual to come and not on my lost love.

The elder swayed in time with the leaves of the branches before me. "She has entered the Wheel of Souls, her life recast," he said.

It was as if he'd pierced me with a spear dripping with molten metal—it burned a hole clean through my heart. I'd never expected that! I'd thought she would be with me, giving me the strength to complete the ritual upon which the future of all our people relied!

"You do not need her," the elder said. "Just as we are reborn into new lives alone, you must walk through this ritual on your own."

I hung my head, trying to breathe through the hole in my chest. Would she be reborn into a soul I would recognize? *Will she know me somehow when she sees me? Will I know her?*

I wanted to pray for it to be so, but I knew the only prayers that mattered right then were prayers for the success of the ritual, for the strengthening of our gods to repel and destroy the Romans, the invaders who ate up our souls and futures like the yellow mold that destroyed entire valleys of wheat and barley.

"Complete the ritual correctly," my elder Druid priest sang, "and repair the rift with the gods. It is up to you."

I submitted myself completely to both the honor and responsibility of the task. The priest closed his eyes and began chanting the prayers of life and death, and I sang them with him. The deep tones of his singing vibrated within the marrow of my bones, and I harmonized with him for hours. All was going exactly as it should.

Light-headed from the mead and the fasting, I entered the circle of chanting torchbearers just as the full moon reached its highest point. Everyone hushed as I placed the offering of mistletoe at the feet of the great oak and turned to my prisoner.

The Gaul's cheeks were flushed, and his normally light eyes looked black in the flickering torch light. He grinned at me, and I breathed out in relief. He was joyous!

"Felix of Gaul, of the People of the Elders before the Time of Rome, do you come to the arms of the woods willingly?" I thundered, first in the language of the land and then in Gaulish so he could understand.

The people moaned with excitement when he grinned and threw his arms out as if in ecstasy. And when I translated his answer—"Yes, yes! A million times, yes!"—some of the chanters began to weep with relief. He was willing. It was the best omen of all.

The singing and dancing began in earnest as I called upon the gods of all our people and the souls of all who had not yet been recast to accept this sacrifice. To accept it as the ultimate gift of hope and victory over our enemies.

Felix was saying something to the girl who'd stood beside him. I signaled to her. She walked away from him, smiling with tears in her eyes. How much she loved him! How much he loved her! It could not have been more perfect!

I approached Felix and felt a momentary pang at the sight of his wide eyes and how very young he looked. But I reminded myself that his own ancient people of Gaul would welcome him on the other side as the true tribesman he was. He could earn no greater honor for one who had turned his back on his ancestors and pretended to be Roman.

His soul would thank me for this someday. He gave me a beatific smile, as if thanking me here and now—another sign of acceptance from the gods.

With a quick lunging move, while chanting the sacred words, I wrapped the rope around his neck and twisted. In almost the same moment, I swung the butt of my sacrificial knife hard on the spot that I used on recalcitrant bulls. Finally, to seal the magic, I slit his throat in one fast, hard move. He fell to the ground and did not move.

In that moment, an owl silently swooped over the man's head, wheeled into an open clearing silvered in moonlight, and snatched a rodent before taking off again. Everyone gasped and murmured at the sight, then looked at me.

Yes, I thought. I am your last Druid. I alone can tell you what it means.

When the sacrifice's lifeblood stopped pouring out, I held out my bloodied arms, threw my head back, and bellowed with joy.

"The gods have accepted our sacrifice!" I announced in a deeper, stronger voice than I could've ever produced, as if the gods themselves spoke in unison through me. "And they have given us a clear sign of the path of our victory! Just as the owl destroyed its victim in an open clearing, we will demolish the rodents of Rome in open battle. We will defeat the destroyers of Mona! The gods have spoken!"

When I finished, the chanters began again, and some of the people began to weep and dance in a frenzy of relief and hope. I held my arms out to the moon and filled my soul with its light and the promise of victory.

But there was a pull. One among us, I could feel, did not lose himself in the joy. One who was still afraid. I turned to find him. Sorcha's warrior. "Do not doubt the gods," I thundered, and he jumped in surprise.

"You are a warrior," I continued. "And need a warrior's sign."

He nodded. "Take his head," I commanded.

When he mounted it on a spear, I made everyone look. "The sacrifice still smiles!" I crowed with joy. "Don't you see? He was a *willing* sacrifice, pleased to be with his ancestral gods once more. His own rejection of Rome is our victory!"

The people roared again and began celebrating with even more abandon.

The gods had spoken. I had listened. I'd been redeemed and would now be the redeemer of our people.

Remembering that the ritual was not complete until I joined the Iceni queen, I turned to Sorcha's warrior. "We must go to Londinium, where Boudica's forces gather to attack," I said.

We set off right then, carrying the head of a Roman boy returned to his ancestral gods, complete with a promise from the Gods of all Wood and Water and Creatures of Our Land that victory over the Romans was ours.

As we walked in the moonlight toward the queen of the Iceni, I remembered the three questions I had asked myself as I watched the sacred isle burn in the night. I knew the answers now.

Why was I spared? To save our people.

Why had the gods abandoned us? We'd displeased them. But I'd set things right.

And most important: *What do I do now?*

Bring victory to Boudica's rebellion, and all our people.

Never had I been more certain of anything in my life.

PART FIVE

THE SON

S.J.A. Turney

The enemy was intent upon butchery: fire, hanging, crucifixion.
—Tacitus

Londinium
Two Weeks Earlier

THE summer sun beat mercilessly down upon the land, a conflagration searing the fields and towns, browning the lush greens of late spring, parching the world. The farmers, so exultant at first that a good growing summer was upon them, now lamented the general lack of water as they watched their winter stores desiccate before their eyes.

Andecarus could smell and taste Londinium, acrid and sour at the back of his throat, before he crested the last rise and laid eyes upon its northernmost edge. Dust filled the streets, and the movements of people, carts, and animals kicked up clouds of gray and brown that hung like a smudge in the air above the roofs, only slightly masking the odor of the docks and the fishing wharves that baked in the golden heat. It was a heady, nearly overpowering aroma, and none too pleasant, yet for Andecarus of the Iceni, son of Duro—and of Rome, after a fashion—even this smell was a welcome one against the pungent stink of charred timber and charred flesh, the iron-tang of blood, and the stink of opened bowels.

"Smells better than Camulodunum," murmured the lad at his side, as if reading his thoughts.

Andecarus gave an involuntary shudder as his mind relentlessly furnished him with the latest in a long line of horrifying memories of wanton bloodshed—a Roman unfortunate enough to have been taken alive by two of the more battle-maddened warriors; they'd busily dissected him in the street as he screamed for mercy—or for death, which amounted to the same thing.

He glanced sidelong at Luci on his fat little pony, an almost comical sight. The boy—an unwanted cooking-house slave with no real place in the queen's war band—had been foisted upon him as a traveling companion and had done little other than question Andecarus over almost everything they passed.

"I thought the Romans had stone houses?" Luci asked, frowning at the timber, wattle, and daubed-mud structures at the periphery of this, the new great trade hub of Roman lands.

Sighing, Andecarus gestured ahead. "The ordinary people live in ordinary houses, but beyond a few streets of these are buildings of brick and stone with delicate carving. There's a bathhouse with a furnace that never stops burning."

Burning.

How long would it be before Londinium, too, lay smoldering and littered with the dead?

"And a forum?" Luci asked, yet again dragging his attention back to the present. "I never got to go into Camulodunum before it was burned, and I've never seen a forum."

"It's just a glorified square with a few higher-class buildings," Andecarus rumbled, peering between the houses ahead. He could just make out the small forum with its tall, colonnaded basilica and there, far beyond, the wide, muddy River Tamesis with its forest of jetties and masts, thronged with boats of all sizes, from the sleek, speedy Roman *liburna* to the wide, heavy vessels of the northern Gaulish tribes to the small fishing boats of the Cantiaci, who plundered the river of its silver-scaled treasures to sell at an inflated price in the markets of Londinium. So many boats at those jetties . . . many more than usual.

"There are still plenty of people in the streets," the boy noted. "Where are we going?"

"To the offices near the basilica."

"Is that where you used to live?"

Andecarus fought the urge to gee up his horse and ride ahead of the constant barrage of questions. He forced himself to smile instead. "No. My foster father's house was a gaudily painted place by one of the smaller rivers. Not *too* far from the forum, though, I suppose."

"It must be strange to have lived here for so long?"

Home? What was home? In some ways this place *was* more home to him than his true father's holding—the roundhouse belonging to Duro of the Iceni. Following that pointless and costly rising against Ostorius Scapula a dozen years earlier, the fourteen-year-old Andecarus had been given over to the Romans as a political hostage. For the next three years, he had lived in the household of a then rather sedate tribune named Catus Decianus, treated, if not as family, then at least as a respected foster child. As the settlement had grown and expanded around them at an astounding rate, he had learned his Latin and read the humorless prose the Romans laughingly called comedy. As the jetties along the riverbank doubled in number and then doubled again all within a year, he had studied the commentaries of Julius Caesar and his wars—*that* was an eye-opener in respect of some of the local tribes, for certain. As Governor Scapula settled comfortably into Camulodunum, Andecarus had listened to the family's tutor relating the heart-stopping tale of Arminius of Germania and his revolt, which had destroyed three legions yet had brought such violent retribution from Rome it had almost obliterated the tribes—a most pertinent tale, as he now realized.

"Strange, yes," he managed.

Londinium *was* familiar, and in a way that his true family's home was not. Returning finally to the Iceni from a decade of exile among the Romans—three years in Decianus' household, another seven with the auxiliary—he had been initially uncertain what to do with himself. The tribe was as alien to him as the Romans had been when he was first taken, and his estranged father lavished attentions instead upon a fostered brute who Andecarus had been expected to call "brother." And what could be read from that fact? That the belligerent Romans had raised an Iceni hostage and produced Andecarus while, in his place, fostered by the best of the Iceni, a selfish, savage killer had been forged?

"What was it like to be taught by a Roman?" Luci probed brightly.

Rolling his eyes, Andecarus heeled his horse's flank, wincing at the pain in his knee as he did so and pulling out ahead of questions he was unprepared to answer. While he'd argued against bringing Luci along, and the boy had spun an incessant web of disquieting chatter along the way, he was trying his hardest to be patient. The Iceni slave boy had lost his father at Camulodunum and his place working in the cooking-house shortly after—no one had even bothered seeing that he had a new post until the queen's eldest daughter, Sorcha, had suggested he be given to Andecarus. As a man who'd suffered his own difficult childhood, he could hardly bring himself to contribute further to Luci's troubles, but sometimes the questions touched on raw subjects, and he was forced to draw a veil of silence over the conversation.

His steed picked up the pace on this, the final stretch of his journey, descending the gentle slope in the shadow of the old fort, used as animal pens for nearly a decade since the legions left, yet now languishing in silence—no squealing or lowing of penned animals today. His mount plodded on, weary but resolute in the lee of that reminder of Londinium's helplessness and his own last-ditch mission.

In a world of chaotic, whirling change and uncertainty—over his future, his family, even his very identity—his horse was one thing upon which he could rely. The stocky chestnut mare, Selene, was strong and swift, slightly larger than the usual Roman mounts and blessedly unconcerned over her master's lineage or upbringing. He and the beast had, in their earliest days together, formed that bond that only a cavalryman and his steed can. For after three years of learning in the quiet peace of Decianus' house, the man had finished his term as a tribune and had been recalled to Rome, as a last act sending Andecarus off to serve the rest of his hostageship in a cavalry *ala*— a detachment of five hundred Gaulish auxiliaries attached to the Ninth Legion. There he and Selene had spent the next seven summers gutting and terrorizing the enemies of Rome alongside the heavy infantry of the legion. He'd had his first true taste of the battlefield there, first against the rising of the rebel Caratacus and later against the Brigantes to preserve the sovereignty of their Roman-favoring Queen Cartimandua. By the time he left the cavalry, Andecarus had risen to the rank of decurion, commanding a *turma* of thirty bloodthirsty Romano-Gaulish riders, and by his estimation, he had killed two dozen warriors with his own hand.

The Ninth.

He remembered so vividly standing on that hill at the edge of Camulodunum—could it only have been a few days ago?— gazing out to the northwest as he absorbed the news that the Iceni had routed Cerialis' army, including that selfsame *turma* of the First Gallorum in which he'd served for seven summers until his appointed hostageship had reached its end. In response to the threat of the Iceni at Camulodunum, the new commander of the Ninth had force-marched his men—a gleaming steel centipede pounding through the dusty brown—to the defense of the *colonia*. He'd never reached it. Caught unaware by the Iceni almost within sight of their goal, they had been massacred without mercy—an echo of Arminius in Germania, Andecarus thought with grim clarity. Men with whom he had shared bread and wine and the terror of battle, gone to the gods on the tips of Iceni spears. Friends of seven years, killed by his own tribe.

Boudica's army had then turned its attention back to Camulodunum while the impetuous Cerialis and a few of his cavalry escaped to languish, brooding and humiliated, at Durobrivae once more. Just three years ago, that would have been Andecarus, wheeling his mount desperately in the press, his Roman helmet tight down over his braided hair, his spear lancing out, his heart torn in two as he fought for his adoptive people against his own. He could only thank the gods that had not come to pass. Fighting Ordovices or Brigantes was one thing—they were not his tribe—but *this* war . . . Even now he could not say in his heart of hearts for which side he would draw his blade when he was finally called upon. What was a child of two worlds to do? Throw in his lot with the estranged people of his birth and put to the sword the men who had educated him and made him who he now was? Or follow the eagle of Rome and bring terrible vengeance against his own father and cousins? How could dread Andraste, who kept a watchful eye over the Iceni, allow such things to happen? In the days before the Druids had retreated to Mona, such a thing would have been explained by the tribe's own priests, but now, directionless and lost, the people were forced to look to their own signs and try to determine their meaning. His knee twinged again, and he shook his leg out with a hissed intake of air between clenched teeth.

"Is it still painful?"

Andecarus looked around to see that Luci had sped up his own fat pony to pull alongside, his face creased into a frown of concern.

"A little," he admitted quietly, "though it's fading now." His injured knee had plagued him since spring, forcing him to walk with a stick. His father, incensed and incredulous over his "inability" to take part in the rebellion, had looked him up and down, reminded him that his old man's own bad knee had never kept him from a fight, and finally told him bluntly that he would not be missed. His foster brother, Verico, the beast in human form

that had been given over to his father's training during Andecarus' hostage years, and who, with a small cadre of mindless
heavies, had ganged up to give Andecarus that injured knee in
the first place, was apparently warrior enough to count for two.
Barely human, in Andecarus' estimation, but a monster with an
unparalleled sword arm, apparently. The truth, a canker gnawing
deep inside, was that he was in fact almost hale once more. He
experienced occasional pains and could not yet run for long dis-
tances, but he was well enough in truth to take up his sword and
ride into the fray, had he so wished.

Yet he had played on his injury and clung tight to his stick, and
through their duplicitous mercy had managed to avoid becoming
part of that gorge-rising massacre at Camulodunum. That had
drawn more than one distrustful look from the elders and the
warriors—especially from his vile "brother," Verico. Once again,
his mind threw at him an image of Verico at Camulodunum,
repeatedly smashing to a pulp the leg bones of a fallen Roman in
a frenzy of cruelty as his victim shrieked.

It had to end.

"Will the procurator see you?" Luci inquired.

A good question that would be answered soon enough.

Andecarus' desperate, precipitous plan had formed with the realization that his Iceni kin were already treading fervently in the
footsteps of Arminius, heedless of the outcome of that cautionary
tale. Queen Boudica had wiped the new capital from the face of
the land, and Rome would be incensed to say the least by what his
tribe had done. There *would* be retribution. But if it all stopped
here, perhaps Rome could still be reasoned with?

No, not Rome. *Rome* would not forgive.

But Catus Decianus knew him; *liked* him, in fact. A little over
two years ago, his Roman foster father had returned to these
shores, reoccupying that same house, this time in the lofty po-

sition of procurator rather than tribune. And Decianus was no fool, no matter that he was the root cause of this mess, nor was he a belligerent, for all the inflammatory actions of his soldiers in Iceni territory last year. If anyone could be prevailed upon to stop the coming disaster, it would be the procurator, who had both the sense to see what his deeds had wrought and the authority to do something about it. But the time he had in which to act would be short, for Boudica's army would be here soon enough. Londinium was the prime target now—Roman trade center, home and office of the procurator who had ordered their queen flogged and caused all the Iceni tribe's grievances. And after Londinium, there would be other attacks, other Roman settlements or those of the tribes who had welcomed the invader and were now seen as collaborators—*worse* than the enemy.

Odd, that, given the bonds between Rome and the Iceni that had only so recently been severed by foolishness and greed. Oh, there had been troubles in their relationship—the revolt against Scapula that had seen Andecarus hostaged in the first place, for instance—yet for the bulk of the past century, even since Julius Caesar's time, there had been ties of trade and friendship between Rome and the Iceni. It was a slim reed to cling to, but perhaps something of that could still be salvaged?

"Will there be legionaries?" Luci cut into his musings again with a nervous twang to his tone. Understandable given how his father had met his end. And yet the enthusiastic lad had managed somehow to assign his orphanhood to his father's ill luck rather than Roman violence since those legionaries had been old and trapped and fighting for their lives.

"There might be a few retired *evocati* about—the governor has a retinue—but you'll be safe enough. I need you to stay outside and watch the horses."

The disappointment in the boy's face was palpable.

"This is not a cultural expedition, Luci. This is important . . . and risky. I need you to stay with the horses and keep yourself to yourself until I'm done."

His gaze was locked on their destination now—the procurator's offices that stood beside the forum. He couldn't quite see the gleaming complex past the narrow streets of low housing, but he knew his way well enough. Had he not been coming here now for almost two years? With the old Iceni king in failing health, ties to the procurator himself, and a good command of the Roman tongue, Andecarus had been naturally tasked with lodging the royal will at the office of the governor in Camulodunum and Decianus' headquarters in Londinium. He had carved out a niche for himself there, traveling back and forth between the tribe's lands and those two Roman centers, dealing with grants of land, requests for imperial adjudication, tax problems, and legal disputes. He knew Londinium, and he knew the procurator and his staff well.

And therein lay the tribe's chance.

Boudica, he knew, would never bend her knee to the procurator who was responsible for her shocking abuse and the abominable rape of her daughters. Yet the Romans were a practical people above all else. They would certainly demand retribution for Camulodunum, but if the tribe could be stopped here—if Decianus could be persuaded to promise concessions—that might be an end to it. Peace was still just within reach, however delicate and costly it might be. And who could not seal that bargain and reconcile the warring sides if not a child born of both peoples? If the queen would not stoop to negotiation, then someone would have to take such a seemingly treacherous step themselves to save her tribe from the same unyielding fate as Arminius' people.

"I'd expected Londinium to be empty," Luci murmured.

"Lack of sense is not a trait peculiar to the Iceni," grumbled Andecarus as they maneuvered around a small crowd gathered around a doomsayer. The streets were thronged with people. Men and women of many different tribes wheeled small carts through the streets, transporting their wares. Most of the bodies he saw in the crowd were dressed in trousers and wool tunics, though here and there a Roman was visible with their bare legs and carefully cut linen *tunica*. And the folk in the steaming, choking streets were moving almost uniformly south, toward the river and its waiting boats.

As he passed into the heart of the new Roman trade center, his way became more difficult, and he found himself having to force his mount through the press, shouting for people to move in both languages he commanded. While Selene was tired from the long ride, and he had allowed her to slow and rest a little on this last stretch, time was still of the essence, and to be snarled up among a throng of townsfolk would aid no one. Finally, with some relief, they emerged into the wide, paved forum, his gaze still on the procurator's offices.

The procurator was the second most powerful man in the land after the governor, receiving both instruction and authority directly from the emperor. Such Romans were often arrogant and rarely lowered themselves to granting an audience to a native. Yet for all his faults, Catus Decianus was afflicted with no such conceit. In the three years Andecarus had lived in the procurator's house, he had come to know Decianus as a thoughtful, world-weary man more attuned to sitting in a garden with his abacus than imposing imperial will upon an oft-reluctant population. Oh, there was no denying that the procurator's treatment of the Iceni king's family had started this whole mess, but that was not the man Andecarus knew. That had to have been imperial writ. Decianus might see him, and he might recognize the feeble strand of peace winding through this nightmare and grasp it. *That* was why Andecarus had taken it upon himself to ride to Londinium ahead of the tribes. That was why he still clung to a hope that Decianus could be persuaded to make things right.

Reining in at the side of the forum, Andecarus swung down from Selene rather faster than he'd intended and staggered for a moment on his weak knee.

"Do you need help?" asked the boy.

"No," he snapped, rather more forcefully than he'd intended, and regretted his tone instantly at the look of hurt concern on the boy's face. Pausing and breathing steadily, he straightened and tied his reins to one of the hitching posts near the main doorway. "Tether your steed here and wait for me. Try not to wander off and break anything."

Turning to the door, Andecarus' interest was piqued by the lack of a guard beside the entrance. The procurator may not have the command of legions in the manner of the governor, but as he'd predicted, a small force of *evocati*—former legionaries who had re-enlisted as veterans with light duties—protected Decianus and his residence and supplied the meager force upon which Londinium could call in times of need. For all the good that would do them if Andecarus failed . . .

Of course, the procurator had sent two hundred men to take part in the doomed defense of Camulodunum, which had stripped Londinium of all but his own personal guard. Doubtless those left would have plenty of work right now that took precedence over standing by doorways and looking bored.

Chaos reigned supreme in the procurator's complex. The guard room beside the door stood empty, and one of the old soldiers in just his tunic and belt scurried across in front of the weary Andecarus carrying an armful of something neatly folded, his gait suggesting panic and desperation. Looking this way and that, fascinated to see the office in such upheaval, Andecarus stepped into the courtyard that separated these small administrative offices and chambers from the official's main building. At the center of the colonnaded square, next to the decorative pond with its leaping bronze dolphin, stood a huge stack of parchments, vellum scrolls, and wooden writing tablets, the delicate documents barely trembling in the stifling stillness. Even as he watched, another of the procurator's guard thrust a burning brand into the base of the heap and blew gently until it took, tendrils of smoke curling out from the mound and rising into the perfect blue.

Another legionary almost knocked him down, running past with a pile of thin wooden cases. Spinning from the collision, Andecarus righted himself and made for the main offices, still surprised at the lack of a challenge.

The inside was no different, and as he blinked, adjusting his vision to the dimmer interior, Andecarus could see men hurrying everywhere with piles of goods, clearing out the offices. The burning of documents was standard practice—he had watched his own commander doing the same when his cavalry unit had quit a two-year posting—as if the marauding, vengeful Iceni would care about requisition records and staffing costs.

He heard Decianus before he saw the man—that oh-so-familiar tired, faintly jaded tone. And he could identify the voice of Valeria, the procurator's wife: sharper, harder, far more imperious in its nature—another voice he had listened to for three years, ruling her house like an empress. Again, astoundingly, as he passed through the corridor and across the threshold into Decianus' own office, none of the struggling soldiers paused to question his presence. Pushing the door slightly wider, he stepped inside.

Decianus was busy stuffing all manner of small yet crucial items into a leather case while he shook his head despairingly. Valeria stood with her back to Andecarus, but he could picture her face—imperious, angry, demanding.

"What can I hope to do, Valeria? The Iceni have their swords and shields and chariots. Paulinus has his *pila* and bolt throwers and ranks of steel. I have *this*!" In exhausted ire, he lifted the seal of the procurator and brandished it at his wife, making his point bluntly.

"So you run like a frightened cur back to your villa in Gaul? And what . . . you abandon Britannia? Do you really want to be remembered as the man that cost the emperor a whole province?"

Decianus thrust his seal into the case and grasped a small stack of writing tablets, waving them at her.

"There are documents in my office of a very sensitive nature. They cannot be allowed to fall into the hands of ravaging Britons. Not all records can be burned—some are too important. And what of the new coin molds? Do we leave them to the Iceni to mint their own money in the name of divine Nero? No, Valeria. It is time to quit the place and cross the sea. And we shall *not* lose the province, for Paulinus will deal with the Iceni witch in due course. But what good will that do us if by then we are skewered up the posterior with a native spear?"

Valeria slapped both palms down on the table, drowning out Andecarus' polite clearing of his throat. "Save your barrack room language for your officers, Decianus. I am no *caupona* serving girl to be spoken to thus." She took a deep breath, as though preparing to explain mathematics to a troublesome child. "Suetonius Paulinus is still in the west, stamping out rebels. His authority is missing in the southeast at this moment, and that makes you the highest de facto authority in the land. Right now you are the voice of Rome to the natives. What message do you send if you tuck your tail between your legs and run for your Gaulish orchards and your old wine cellar and leave the land in enemy hands? Would Caesar have done such a thing? Or Pompey? Or Germanicus?"

Despite his apparent weariness and determination, Decianus rounded on his wife as he threw the tablets into the case.

"Caesar and Pompey and Germanicus, too, had more to hand than half a dozen arthritic old men, a town full of terrified civilians, and an imperial seal. I'm a glorified accountant at the end of the emperor's leash. What do you expect me to hold the Iceni back with? Curses and requisition slips? Now I tell you for the last time, our goods are already packed, but if you want any of your personal effects on board, gather them now."

Andecarus cleared his throat, attempting to draw attention, but the general hum of desperate activity and the crackling anger between husband and wife rendered it pointless. He felt a strange pang of nostalgia, remembering how many times he had stood in the doorway of their *triclinium* waiting for some edged discussion to end so he could speak and be noticed.

"You do not have to take battle to the Iceni," snarled the man's wife with a haughtiness that was usually only found in royalty in Andecarus' experience. "You just have to hold Londinium until help arrives. Cerialis is supposed to have cavalry with him less than a day's hard ride from here. Send for him, and with his men and the *evocati*, you could garrison the old Londinium fort. At least you would be seen to be doing *something* when reports reach the emperor. And Governor Paulinus will know about the Iceni by now—he will be racing this way with the might of Rome at his back. Jove, with the way those natives are busy wasting time stamping on the wreckage of Camulodunum, the legions might even get here first!"

"And if they don't?" Decianus prompted, fastening the leather case.

"Then you take your cue from a hundred generations of noble Romans. You fall on your sword and depart with honor."

Decianus stopped and glanced up at his wife. "*That's* your solution?"

"Better than departing with your tail between your legs and the stink of fear-sweat upon you," she snapped. Perhaps aware that she had gone too far, she stepped back from the table, and a leaden silence fell. Decianus straightened his back and glared at his wife.

"I should have known better than a match with you when I heard your mother haranguing your poor father. The divine Caesar claims Venus in his ancestry. Could there be a harpy in yours?"

Andecarus was suddenly grateful he couldn't see Valeria's face, though he could picture it in his mind's eye from the way she was vibrating faintly. "A better man would not need to resort to name-calling. But then you are *not* a better man, are you? *I* will not abandon this post, even if you will. If you want me on your ship, you will have to act as a husband and force me onto the gangplank."

"I've never forced you into anything, and I won't start now. You know where I'll be."

"Go, then. I will *divorce* you rather than leave here."

In the tense, expectant silence that followed, Andecarus opened his mouth once more, but a voice from behind overrode him.

"*Domine*, the cart is . . . Who is this?"

Andecarus turned to find himself face-to-face with an officer he didn't know. A tall, muscular man, the Roman loomed over him with an air of casual menace. The procurator and his wife turned in surprise at the exchange, finally noticing the wiry, well-dressed Iceni by the door. Decianus' frown quickly turned into a tired smile of recognition, and he waved a hand at the officer dismissively.

"Andecarus? He's an Iceni clerk—not dangerous."

Andecarus' spirits sank at the expression of angry disbelief that crossed the officer's face, and before he could even step back, the soldier ripped his sword from the decorative sheath at his side, bringing the point up sharply to dance beneath Andecarus' chin.

"*Iceni?*"

Opening his mouth to attempt to calm the situation, Andecarus felt the tip of the gladius prick his throat. "I . . ."

With surprising speed, the officer's hand came up and delivered a painful crack to his forehead that sent his skull back against the wall with a heavy thump. Blackness enfolded Andecarus as his consciousness sank into oblivion amid prophetic images of the procurator's offices burning and collapsing.

ANDECARUS awoke with a head like a four-day hangover. His eyes took some prying open, and for a frightening moment he wondered whether he was blind before realizing that he was just in a dim room. The sounds of nervous breaths slowly insisted themselves upon him, and he turned—gods but *that* made his head swim and his neck throb.

If only Ria were here with her ministrations . . .

Behind him, a dozen other people lurked in the near-darkness of the fetid room. Tiny slivers of light pierced the gloom from cracks in the timber walls and helped illuminate the sad group. Mostly men, though with two women and three children among them. They were all wearing native dress, and from the colors and designs, he would place most of them as Iceni or Trinovantes. He tried to recall what had happened but couldn't form a coherent thought amid the throbbing.

"Where are we?"

A man with a rough, saw-edged voice took a step forward. "Granary in the abandoned fort."

The fort? Surely . . . had the Romans won? Boudica's army couldn't have fallen here? Surely not enough time had passed for *that*.

"The Iceni . . ."

"Coming," the man replied. "And soon."

Ah. So the prisoners had been taken in the peaceful city and impounded by the few *evocati*. They had probably rounded up any Iceni or suspected sympathizer they could find. It was probably thanks to Decianus that they were merely locked out of the way and not simply hanged as many of the soldiers would have recommended. Of course, if Decianus had fled Londinium, taking hope of protection with him, who knew what the future held? A cold knot of fear formed in Andecarus' belly.

And it was not just protection that had gone with the procurator, but also any hope of a peaceful solution. A moment later, the pain in his head still pounding, he was at the barred door of the moldering old building, hammering on the timber and shouting.

"Listen . . . I am no rebel. I was the foster son of the procurator himself! If you'll just—"

The hilt of a gladius slammed into the wooden wall where his desperate fingers were clawing through the gaps, and he pulled them back quickly.

"Shut up, shit-bag," grunted what sounded like an old veteran soldier in Gaulish-accented Latin. *Evocati.* The governor had left some of his few men to hold Londinium, then. He had to admire their bravery and devotion to duty, if not their sense of self-preservation. A *legion* could hardly hold Londinium even if it had walls and ditches. A score or so old men with a derelict fort? Madness.

"You need to evacuate," Andecarus shouted through the gaps in the wood. "The Iceni will kill all of you and every living thing in Londinium. I saw it happen at Camulodunum. Are there still civilians in the town?"

But the guard had gone. Andecarus put his eye to the gap. Two old men were busy repairing the parapet of the fort wall. Insanity!

"You speak their language," the saw-voiced man rumbled from behind him.

"Are you a merchant?"

Andecarus sighed and pulled back from the wall. "Not quite. I'm a noble of the Iceni." He shuffled back across the room. "Where are the latrines?"

The man pointed to an old wooden bucket in the corner, which was already leaking into a puddle around it and surrounded by flies.

"I won't ask about the food," he grunted.

TWO days had passed by Andecarus' reckoning. It was impossible to tell from the meals, which were sporadic and basic and shoved through the door with barbaric roughness, but he had seen two sundowns, which gave him his time marker. He had searched among the prisoners and learned who they were but had found no sign of Luci, and hoped for the boy's sake that he'd mounted up and ridden away at the first sign of trouble.

While his wits had continued to recover from the painful blow to the head, he had watched proceedings through the narrow cracks in the granary's timber walls. He could count no more than thirty Romans, the senior of whom was seemingly only their commander by reason of his length of service. They were well armed and tough, for sure, though what they hoped to achieve when the Iceni finished their death dance at Camulodunum and swarmed over Londinium, he could not possibly imagine.

That first day he had tried numerous times to engage in conversation one or other of the old soldiers who were attempting to make the near-derelict fort defensible. Every attempt had been unsuccessful, and he had eventually sat back and resigned himself to the fact that he had failed. The procurator was gone, the legions were on the way, as was Boudica's army, and nothing stood between the queen's wrath and Londinium but a few tired old men and a small palisade. At least he and the other prisoners would be safe for now. If the *evocati* who kept them locked up had had violent designs on them, they'd have manifested early on during their incarceration. And when the Iceni arrived, the soldiers would have other things on their mind than the execution of prisoners. So all they could do was sit quietly and wait for the arrival of Boudica's rampaging war band.

His bowel strained, and he tried not to look at the overflowing bucket in the corner.

"What's this?" murmured one of the Trinovantes, peering intently between the slats. Andecarus struggled upright, noting how the last few twinges in his leg seemed to have faded with his enforced inactivity. There would be no denying it now: he was healed. He might smell like a goat-turd after sharing the bucket with the other occupants for four days, but physically he was as fit as could ever be expected. Scurrying across the granary's wooden floor, he found another crack close to the one currently in use and peeked through it, his eyes rolling back and forth until they caught sight of what had attracted his fellow prisoner's attention.

Horsemen!

His heart thudded, his pulse quickening. Perhaps Decianus *had* sent for Cerialis before fleeing, as well as apparently assigning most of his remaining guard to the fort? After all, Cerialis' remaining cavalry from the Ninth would be the only local force. Would they be enough to present an obstacle to the Iceni?

He remembered the sheer battle lust and unbending hauteur of both his father and their ferocious queen—and the slavering hunger of his foster "brother," too—and knew in that moment that no amount of horsemen would be enough. Unless the legions made it south in record time, Londinium was doomed.

"Paulinus," muttered the Trinovante prisoner next to him. Andecarus frowned, looking over the riders pulling into the fort. They were legionary cavalry, and he could see a *vexillum*—a flag—of the Twentieth Legion, with no small number of senior officers among them, and everyone was clearly exhausted and weary from a long, hard ride. Sure enough, in the midst of the crowd, one man's armor marked him out as a senior officer, the knotted red ribbon of a general around his midriff, his plume strikingly white and pure, if bedraggled and limp from the long sweaty journey. It was strangely jarring to see the man who had been a perfect, relaxed Roman nobleman on the rare occasions Andecarus had spotted him in his Camulodunum visits now garbed as a military man among hardened soldiers. It was like seeing a familiar, elegant hound baring its teeth for the first time.

As the cavalry moved off to one of the more deserted corners of the fort, the governor and two of his senior officers dismounted, and Paulinus clasped hands with the garrison's ageing commander on the low earth rampart. The two men began to speak, but the sound of cavalry moving in force nearby drowned out the details for Andecarus, who concentrated, trying to read anything he could from their manner. Paulinus was tall, thin, and no longer a young man, though he stood straight-backed—stiff and formal, even—while the *evocati* officer of a similar age looked round-shouldered and weary, if determined. Finally, the two began to stroll around the defenses and then, at the gate, descended and made their way back along the central street. The horses now having been corralled, Andecarus strained to hear as the two men closed on the granary.

"Several days yet at the very least," the governor was saying in leaden tones. "Longer, in fact. I gave strict instructions to move at a sensible pace. What use is my army turning up to face the Iceni bitch if they are exhausted and cannot lift a shield between them?"

Paulinus paused, looking at the hastily strengthened parapet and shaking his head. "To attempt the defense of Londinium would be idiotic. Intelligence has the Iceni and their allies less than a day away. It seems they have finally tired of desecrating my *colonia* and are on the move. You are clearly enough of a veteran to recognize that this is a lost cause—my legions cannot arrive in time to save it, nor you. In fact, my adjutant is convinced that once Londinium is a burning husk, the enemy will move on and roll over either Verulamium or Calleva, both of which have a long history of supporting Rome. Unless the enemy is ridiculously slow or careless, they will manage either or both of those before the legions arrive."

"Sir, Londinium is the chief port of the region now, bigger than Rutupiae, with the procurator's palace and the offices of a dozen great Gaulish trading concerns. There are storehouses with a king's ransom of goods. It may not yet have the prestige of Camulodunum, but it is the new heart of Roman trade—a *hub*. The procurator gave us strict instructions to preserve it."

"I don't particularly care what your orders from the procurator were, Stator, the military of the province fall directly under my command, especially when Decianus left word that he has fled to safer climes. Legions are poorly employed on the walls of forts, and their full talents are best displayed against an enemy in open field. We cannot garrison an indefensible place such as this, regardless of its commercial value. We must tempt them out into open ground and defeat them there."

"But, sir . . ."

"No." Paulinus began to stroll on once again, his hands clasped behind his back. "Londinium is lost, as is anywhere within two days' march if the Iceni wish it. The city will be abandoned. I want you and your men to kit up and march out with us, awaiting the arrival of the Twentieth and the Fourteenth to put these savages down. I will not waste veterans on the pyre of a lost hope."

"What of the civilians, sir?"

Paulinus snorted. "Those with a modicum of sense will already have fled out of the reach of the Iceni. Those who remain deserve anything they get. Put out the word that all defense is pulling out, and we advise the population to do the same. If Boudica and her war dogs decide to push their army, they could be here in mere hours, and I intend for you and my cavalry to be long gone when that happens."

The old soldier saluted, the two men now moving away from the granary so that Andecarus had to shift and strain to see them.

"And the prisoners, Governor?"

"Prisoners?" Paulinus stopped walking again.

"We've a dozen or so known or suspected Iceni and Trinovantes locked in the granary. Should we execute them or bring them along?"

As Andecarus' heart caught in his throat at the words, the governor turned to regard the granary, and for the first time, the young Iceni got a good look into the man's dark eyes. What he saw was intelligence, nobility, and plenty of determination. This was no Cerialis—throwing away good men on a foolish attack. This was a shrewd strategist who would not stop until he had beaten Boudica or had died in the attempt. Andecarus' hopes for any kind of peaceful solution evaporated under that resolute gaze.

"Leave them," the governor announced calmly, turning his back.

"Sir? They're the enemy."

"If they are the enemy, then what are they doing unarmed in Londinium rather than running around in the ruins of my palace waving swords and the heads of my household slaves? More likely they are ordinary hapless natives, but whatever the case, they are none of our concern. Prepare to move out, Stator—you have your orders."

The soldier's reply was lost to Andecarus' straining ear as the two men moved on away from the granary. He turned to see the other prisoners looking expectantly at him.

"My queen and the Iceni and Trinovantes are just hours from

here. The governor has given the order to abandon Londinium, as the legions are many days away yet. We are to be left here to rot."

"Can we escape?" one of the women asked nervously. "When the Romans go, I mean?"

"The Iceni will free us soon enough."

The woman shook her head. "You, maybe. You say you're important. We'll be seen as collaborators." She was shaking. As Andecarus looked at the three-year-old boy by her side, he realized her peril. The boy shared neither her blond hair nor her pale skin, his own olive complexion clearly betraying the origins of his father. He shivered as he pictured what his foster brother might do to a woman who had lain with a Roman, to say nothing of her half-Roman child.

"When they come, stay at the back and let me do any talking."

"Can we not escape?" asked the man who'd been at the cracks in the wall next to him.

"How? The wall might be cracked, but it's still good, heavy timber, treated against the weather and with no rot. The roof might be tiled, but beneath that it is solid timber slats. The floor is heavy beams above stone. The door's sealed with an oak bar. And we have nothing but fingernails. We wait for my people."

My people.

How odd that still felt. He'd been almost wistful at the sight and sound of the Roman cavalry harnesses and armor, the smell of oiled leather and horse sweat. Just how Iceni was he, really? Would he have been more comfortable riding out with Paulinus than waiting here for his father? Listening to the distant, muted sound of the cavalry, Andecarus found himself wondering what had happened to his horse, Selene, who he'd left tied to a post in the forum. Hopefully, Luci had led her away to safety. Or perhaps Decianus' staff had taken her in with the household animals and shipped her to Gaul?

At least confined here he could not be expected to rampage through the helpless town with the Iceni warriors. If no peaceful solution could now be found, sooner or later he would have to draw his sword and decide whose son he truly was. Unless he could find another way, without the procurator, to halt this nightmare and reconcile the two sides before he was torn apart by divided loyalties.

For just a moment, he considered that if the Druids were still among the people, they might have wrought some sense and order from this whole disaster. But no. After all, their rabid hatred of—and resistance to—Rome was what had taken the Druids to Mona in the first place. Gods only knew how they were faring now, but it was just as well they were not here. For all their closeness to the gods, the Druids would just have poured pitch onto this particular inferno.

With a sigh, he moved to the corner closest the door and sank to the floor, wrapping his arms around his knees and leaning back against the wall, waiting for his father to come.

HE'D dozed off at some point, and the first he knew of the tribe's arrival was when the Trinovante shook him roughly by the shoulder. Starting awake rudely with a snort, Andecarus shot to his feet. The sounds of the Iceni were clear and unmistakable. The cries and the clatter of weapon on shield, the thunder of hooves, and the creaking and rattling of the chariots bearing the nobles. It was not a battle. It was not even an attack. It was simply the Iceni and their allies arriving to find Londinium undefended.

His eye to one of the bigger cracks in the wall, Andecarus tutted with annoyance as he realized that the structures and rampart of the camp obscured his view of the approaching horde. He listened hard. The faster warriors among the tribes were already passing the fort and moving into the streets at the northern edge of the town, finding no defenses and no soldiers waiting for them. For long moments, Andecarus wondered whether the city was deserted and the entire population had taken the governor's advice and fled. Then the screaming started and the vengeful howl that accompanied it.

Andecarus closed his eyes and fought rising bile. What he'd seen done by his own people at Camulodunum would stay in his nightmares as long as he lived, and the sounds issuing from across the fort's walls told an almost identical tale. What had been done by Decianus' soldiers after the death of the Iceni king in the first place had been incendiary and dangerous, and the punishment and dishonoring of Prasutagus' family had been appalling for a self-proclaimed civilized people. It was inexcusable even if, as Andecarus suspected, the order for the recalling of debts and the seizing of estates on the tenuous text of the will had come down from the emperor and not from the procurator himself. That would not have been the Decianus he had known. Yes, the behavior of Rome was dreadful, but was the response of his queen in line with her grievances? Was this a reaction to those terrible acts or a simple declaration of war? Where would it stop?

He knew the answer to that, of course. He knew Rome's attitude to retribution. Thousands crucified along a great road were all that remained of Spartacus' slave army. Fifty thousand Carthaginians enslaved while their glorious city was razed to the foundations. Whole tribes in Germania so ruthlessly cut down in response to Arminius' revolt that it would be generations before the crops were worked fully again. Was this the future for his own tribe?

His ponderings were cast aside as activity outside drew his attention. Half a dozen warriors had finally swarmed over the pathetic ramparts of the small deserted fort, and others had burst through the gate. While a few of the hungrier ones rampaged around the fort's interior looking for something to dismember, a few others, carrying burning torches, began to cast them through the windows of the old, dry barrack blocks, firing the fortified reminder of Roman supremacy. He watched in surprise as one of them threw his burning torch into the ventilation channels beneath the granary, where the flames immediately caught on a decade of detritus and what might—from the smell of it—be a long-deceased dog. Even as the first waft of smoke came up through the floor, Andecarus grabbed the clearly half-Roman boy and his mother and pushed them safely back into the darkness before joining the chorus of voices at the door, bellowing for release.

Outside the granary, two warriors' voices cut through the general din, closer to the makeshift prison than the rest of the marauding Iceni.

"Don't waste time firing that."

"Burn every fucking building. Catch every fucking Roman and pull out his eyeballs," snarled the other. "That's what you said when Princess Sorcha brought back the news about Mona. A thousand charred Roman skulls for every Druid butchered, you said. Retribution for Andraste."

Mona? Andecarus felt his blood surge at the shocking words, the sheer power of those tidings stopping him in his tracks as he'd been making for the door to shout out his father's name by way of identification. The Druids' last sacred sanctuary had fallen?

The warriors' voices became all the clearer as they climbed the steps outside. "The bastard governor left none alive on Mona, so why should we here? Fuck 'em."

Andecarus was still trying to wrap his thoughts around the concept of a world without the learned priests of the tribes as the door was ripped open and the two Iceni warriors peered in from the loading platform. One bore a gleaming blade and was stripped to the waist, his long, wild blond hair and beard stiffened with pale mud, the other a darker one with a plaited beard and a mail shirt, still brandishing his torch in the face of the prisoners.

"Fucking collaborators, look," the bare-chested warrior snorted, smashing out with his sword hilt and knocking down the Trinovante prisoner with a possibly broken jaw.

His mail-clad friend grabbed his wrist as he made to bring his sword around blade-first. "Locked up by the Romans? Don't be stupid. Besides, look: that's Duro's son—the little one."

The two warriors peered into the gloom, and Andecarus pulled himself up straight, his face sour, ignoring the jibe. "Andecarus, son of Duro. These people are all ours."

The two warriors had already lost interest and dropped back down from the loading block, disappearing into the fort, looking for something to kill. Carefully, adjusting to the bright summer sunlight after days of dim shade, Andecarus stepped out onto the stone steps and took stock of the situation. The fort was more or less empty again. The few warriors who had bothered with it were now moving on, looking for anything of interest in the farther reaches of the place. Gingerly, he stepped down to the ground and gestured for the others to follow.

"You're on your own, now. Good luck." As the woman and her swarthy son exited, he grabbed the boy by the shoulder and pointed to the north gate, which now stood open and untended. "The Iceni are in the town now, and only the baggage and the womenfolk will remain out to the north. Leave by that route. As soon as you reach the palisade, wait until the coast is clear, bear left toward the sun, and then run for your life. Keep going until you reach a small river, then follow its banks north until you're far enough from Londinium that you can't hear the screams."

Waiting for the mother's nervous nod and watching the rest disperse as though they had hit the dusty ground from a great height, Andecarus took a deep breath. There were options, he knew. He could so easily find himself a weapon and join the fray. No one would stop him doing so. His father would even approve, if such a thing were imaginable. But no, he knew he could not do that. Even with what Paulinus had done on Mona, he could take no part in the ruination of Londinium, his home for three memorable years. Not to mention the fact that these people were innocent in this whole affair. So what? Leave Londinium to its destruction? Perhaps, though it did not take a great leap of imagination to see what the tribal elders would say about that when they found out he had walked away. There had already been suspicion that his absence at the sack of Camulodunum was as much a personal choice as it was down to his injuries. No, he had to stay.

Because there were two things he needed to do. Somewhere in the procurator's building there might still be an answer. Even with Decianus fled, the man had thought to send the last few men he had to hold the fort for as long as possible, and if he had thought that far, perhaps he had left someone in authority in his place? A quaestor, perhaps, who could be persuaded to sign and seal something granting the queen her rights in perpetuity? It was amazing what a man might be persuaded to do with thousands of howling enemies at his door. A sealed document of Iceni rights might—*might*—be enough to appease the incendiary queen whose army rampaged through the streets.

And maybe, just maybe, Selene was still here with Luci and his fat pony, sheltered in some empty building nearby, hungry but safe.

A rare gust of wind carried the reek of burning timbers to his nostrils, but once the breeze died again, he became painfully aware of the revolting stink issuing from his own person. Trying not to gag at the suddenly prevalent stench, he strode over to the large stone trough where horses had been watered in the old days. With no care for his body or apparel, Andecarus tipped himself into the trough, rubbing his limbs roughly, removing as much ordure and muck as he could. Relieved, he rose, brushing back his hair, much of which had now escaped the flattened braid in which he commonly wore it. His usually neat, clipped mustaches—a carryover, like the braid, from the days when they had oft been covered by a Roman helmet—had become ragged and drooping. His cheeks, chin, and neck itched with the budding beard that covered them.

The fort was now empty of the invaders, though every structure within it was ablaze, the roiling black smoke rising in a dozen columns to combine into an ever-thickening fug above the roofs, almost blotting out the azure sky. Having found the installation empty, the place had held no interest for the newly arrived Iceni, who had torched it and moved on south into the town in search of anything to kill, burn, tear down, or abuse. Coughing in the growing cloud, Andecarus ran out into the street that proceeded from the south gate and made for the forum halfway between here and the river.

As he emerged from the old fort, his heart caught in his throat. The sights he'd witnessed at Camulodunum had been few and in passing, for all their horror. He had tried to stay on the periphery as much as possible—an attempt aided most helpfully by the slave girl Ria and her tender ministrations. Briefly, his thoughts flashed back to her, and even in the midst of this horror, he almost smiled at the memory. She was pretty and kind—a combination he'd found oddly lacking in his people since his return and, while his father would spit teeth if he thought his son might dally with a slave-born girl for anything more than base lust, the idea of courting her and annoying old Duro had been remarkably tempting.

A scream drew him back to the present. There was no friendly maid to administer unction now, and there was no chance of loitering on the edge of things. If there was any hope of stopping this headlong charge into the underworld, it lay at the heart of the town, at the very epicenter of destruction. Palls of smoke hung over areas of Londinium already, and more plumes rose with every passing heartbeat. The firing of buildings had reached the forum, and he could see the new temple rising above the surrounding buildings, choking black rising from its roof.

Please, Minerva . . . Andraste . . . don't let the procurator's building have burned.

He ran. The ground, so long parched and dusty, was dry no longer. Blood and shit, entrails and organs formed the new paving, and more than once Andecarus felt himself slip on something that did not bear too close examination. Though many folk had left Londinium on the governor's recommendation, clearly many more had stayed—both Roman and native. He could picture their reasoning. The Romans simply could not believe it would happen. Even abandoned by their governor and the procurator, they still clung to the hope that the legions would come and save them or that Cerialis would reappear. No help had come. The others—those of the Cantiaci or the Atrebates, the Catuvellauni or the Regini, even a few of the Trinovantes and Iceni who had long since moved to the new port town—simply saw the approaching army as their own people and couldn't imagine they'd be taken for enemies.

How short-sighted *that* had been.

Bodies lay where they had been cut down and beaten, but the ones who had been gutted in the hurried search for loot or women were the lucky ones. Even the poor bastard whose gut-rope was now coiled around Andecarus' ankle was lucky. Because he hadn't been . . .

That one. The lad of maybe ten summers who had been nailed upside down to a door, his genitals roughly hacked off and cast into the gutter below whence his lifeblood had long since flowed to join it.

That one. An old man whose limbs had been severed at elbow and knee so that he was forced to flee the conflagration of his own house in unbearable agony on four severed stumps.

That one. The mother cut time and again so that she was almost bled dry, watching, hollow, from a pasty white face as the remains of her twins charred and crisped in the blackened pile of kindling and body parts.

That one.

And that one.

And that one.

And so few of them actual Romans, too.

Andecarus paused to vomit by the roadside where a severed hand grasped at something unseen. He might have cried. A sensible human should. Andecarus had fought in pitched battles and sieges against rebels and kings, but those had been *battles*, where the enemy brandished their own weapons and fought back valiantly. That had been war, which was horrifying yet oddly acceptable. This was *not* war. This was retribution for Mona on a scale that even the queen might not be able to control. This was joyful slaughter on a scale that would have the gods frowning in disapproval. Roman gods were civilized, he knew, and powerful. But even his own gods and goddesses—even dread Andraste of the Iceni with her love of battle—could not surely countenance such willful execution of their own. His fears seemed borne out as he straightened and wiped the puke from his chin in time to see a cat scurry from a blazing building and race across the road, leaving small paw prints in the dark red, sticky street. It had run to the left. Never a good omen. He remembered his youth before the Romans took him, his father who would not leave the house for a day if an animal crossed his path right to left.

Was this an omen for Andecarus, or for all of them? He was no Druid, trained to read such signs and the will of the gods, but the fading paw prints in the blood seemed too vast an omen for him alone.

He ran.

A blood-curdling scream issued from a building to his left. Despite repeated vows not to involve himself, he paused and peered inside. A torn, bloodied, and clearly dying woman in a Roman *stola* hung from a wall, roped by the wrists, while two Iceni warriors practiced their throwing with jugs, plates, knives, and anything else that came to hand, bellowing their hatred of the invader and exhorting Andraste to take Roman sacrifices in remembrance of Mona. A red-glazed bowl smashed painfully into her face and fell away surprisingly intact as a triumphant shout came from a third man who rose from a corner with a purse of money, bronze coins spilling out on the floor nearby.

Honestly, what had *that* woman done to the Iceni to deserve this? She had hardly rammed a gladius into the heart of a Druid.

Andecarus stifled a snarl of anger and turned away with difficulty, running on down the street. The forum, at last. Some sort of ritual killing was being performed there, the burning temples and houses and shops ringing a scene of horror the likes of which was rapidly becoming gruesomely familiar. Six old women struggled on a makeshift gibbet, their life choking out past swollen purple tongues as their feet danced merry jigs in the air. As one woman started to slip into blessed unconsciousness, a Trinovante warrior took her weight while another threw a bucket of water at her face. Instantly revived into the terror of her situation, they let the rope take the strain again so that she began her death jig anew.

His earlier fears were realized as his gaze picked out tendrils of smoke rising from the roof of the procurator's complex. It was afire, but thankfully the conflagration had not yet taken full hold. Perhaps there would be something of use still inside. His heart sank at the sight of the empty tethering posts by the door—not that he'd expected Selene to still be there, but it had been one small hope. Running, he burst through the door, past the small guard room, almost falling face-first over a sorry little mound at the threshold. Luci had not made it to safety, it seemed.

A hollowness opening inside, he crouched and turned the body over. Had the boy been caught by the raiders? The innocent, enthusiastic little gray-white face was strangely peaceful, but the single gruesome wound betrayed the nationality of Luci's killer. A lone, wide stab wound above the collarbone, straight down into the heart. An execution, carried out Roman military-style. Damn those *evocati*! Yes, he had been Iceni, but he was just a boy. What harm could he have been?

His mood blackening by the moment, Andecarus rose and strode on into the courtyard. The bonfire of documents was now little more than a sad gray heap of ash, and the body of a young man was half buried in it, just his legs and lower back visible, along with the hands bound behind him. A Roman boy from his sandals, and killed by the rampaging Iceni. In revenge for Luci in the doorway, perhaps?

Andecarus turned, and his mouth ran dry as dust, for materializing from the door to the procurator's offices was a most unexpected, and most unwelcome, sight.

Duro, elder of the Iceni, right-hand man of the queen and father of a sickened and angry son, stepped out into the light, blinking, his heavy sword in one hand and a rope in the other. The old man either did not see or did not recognize his son, striding out toward the exit with his expression oddly unreadable. Behind Duro, at the other end of the rope, came the matron Valeria, wife of Decianus. Andecarus gaped. Had her sense of honor so overcome her sense of self-preservation that she had opted to stay and face her doom? Valeria's footsteps were fast and purposeful, and despite the fact that she had never truly warmed to Andecarus during his time with her family—she had been too absorbed in her dignity as mistress of the house to truly befriend a tribesman—he found himself approving of her manner. Rather than submit to the indignity of being dragged unwilling from the building by her captor, she walked fast and proud, head held high, the very picture of a stoic Roman matron. It was an almost laughable sight as Duro reached the exit to the forum, but his new slave's accelerated pace allowed her to push imperiously past him and out to the open as though it were her leading him. At least with Duro, Andecarus reflected, Valeria would be safe from the clawing hands and vicious wiles of a thousand vengeful warriors. No one would take what the powerful elder had claimed for his own. He sighed and paid no further heed to his father, instead making for the door whence the old man had come.

He didn't see the other figure emerging until it was too late, the interior too dim after the soot-laden sunlight outside. He found himself stepping back from the threshold in order to avoid being knocked flat by the big warrior. It was only as he staggered and recovered that his eyes narrowed and his lip twisted in practiced hatred.

Verico.

The bear of a warrior who had usurped Andecarus' place as a son to Duro while he himself had been a hostage, paying the price for a failed revolt. The one responsible for Andecarus' injured knee. A monster of a man, almost as tall as the queen herself and twice as wide at the shoulder. Verico's straw-colored hair and beard were braided roughly by his own hand in a manner that Andecarus thought slovenly, though the women of the tribe in their swooning dozens seemed to find it windswept and attractive, especially in conjunction with those dead, pale blue eyes. He failed to recognize Andecarus, which was hardly a surprise given his current state. Andecarus was about to launch into a tirade of invective when his eyes widened in shock.

Like their father, Verico had apparently taken a slave, though how *this* girl came to be here was beyond Andecarus. Draped over his shoulder like a half-filled sack of grain, clearly unconscious, she was at once horribly familiar and dreadfully out of place.

"Ria!"

"Move," grunted Verico, unable to wave at Andecarus but glaring at him. Then, slowly, recognition dawned in the beast's eyes. "You!"

As Verico turned to face him, several other figures emerged from the dark interior, fanning out behind. Still locking his malice-filled gaze on Andecarus, Verico slid the unconscious form of Ria from his shoulder and heaped her onto one of the unburdened warriors behind him.

"What are you doing?" Andecarus snarled.

"Taking my spoils. Get out of my way."

Andecarus took half a step forward, his face contorted in anger, but even that belligerent half step had those animals accompanying Verico brandishing swords and axes threateningly. Though he didn't know these others, Andecarus recognized the timeless combination of bully and acolytes and knew that he was powerless. Even were he armed, there would be little he could do. One punch at that ugly lantern jaw would see him beaten within a sparrow's breath of his life—he'd be food for the ravens that even now circled in the clearer areas of sky, looking for tasty titbits in the charnel-house streets of the settlement. He was unarmed . . . Verico and his bullies were not.

"What are you doing with Ria?"

Verico leered unpleasantly. "Shagpiece? She bolted from my tent as soon as my back was turned. My boys found her and gave her a knock on the head to bring her home."

Andecarus found himself wondering whether he could take one of the smaller warriors quickly and snatch his sword fast enough to gut the brute at the center. It was a stupid idea that could only have one outcome, and yet he considered it in earnest.

"Ria is not your property. She serves the queen's house."

"Not anymore." Verico snorted and spat a wad of phlegm onto Andecarus' already blood-soaked boot. "You should spend more time with your people and less swanning off with your Roman friends, then you'd be better informed. Some of us actually fought at Camulodunum instead of skulking like a collaborator," he sneered unpleasantly, "and those of us who fought in the front were gifted whatever reward we wanted. *This* is what I wanted." He reached out with his free hand and slapped the unconscious girl, now draped over one of his cronies, on the rump. "Didn't I, Shagpiece?"

Andecarus could feel himself breaking. He prided himself on his self-control, his patience. But somehow the sight of Ria so treated incensed him beyond reason. Ria, who had so gently and patiently ministered to his injuries, now slung over a shoulder, a plaything for an animal, to be used and discarded. Ria, who had been privy to his true level of fitness for battle and yet had held her tongue. It was intolerable. It was odd to realize in the midst of all this appalling horror, that she apparently meant a great deal more to him than he had thought.

"Let her go."

"Fuck off, traitor."

Andecarus bristled. "I'll say it only once more. Let her go, or you'll swear the hand of Andraste herself squeezed the life from you."

"Ah, piss off." Verico lashed out with his free hand and shoved Andecarus by the shoulder, pushing him away so that he spun and almost fell. Righting himself quickly, he lunged for his foster brother, but the bastard's acolytes were there, blades out and poised, ready to cut him and kill him if necessary to save their master. Trembling with anger, Andecarus glared at them, wishing there was something he could do. But he was all too aware that he had suffered their beatings once before and had no particular desire to repeat the experience. Verico laughed harshly and retrieved the limp form of Ria before striding from the complex unconcerned. His cronies followed on behind, two of them playing rear guard with brandished weapons.

"Don't go getting clever and trying to follow us, *Decurion*," he sneered.

Blood surging through his veins in impotent fury, Andecarus watched their forms disappear through the doorway and out into the crowded forum. The sight of the raging mob of Iceni warriors there made Andecarus turn his face upward to the roiling sky.

"Forgive us, Andraste. They think they avenge Mona—that they do your will—but how could *this* be your will? You would exhort them to kill Romans, I am sure, not to plow and kill our own people and the other tribes. Grant the queen your wisdom, Andraste. Don't let it go on like this. This will *end* us."

His thoughts tripped once more to the tale of Arminius. The Iceni had done it now—defied Rome with not one, but two symbols of the invader destroyed in a sea of horror and blood-letting, and the retribution that had befallen Arminius' people would now come to Britannia.

His raised gaze picked out the forms of the circling ravens—beloved symbols of his people and messengers of the gods' intent. The birds were departing. It would be easy to say that the difficulty of flying in a sky so increasingly filled with boiling, sooty smoke was the reason for their departure.

But Andecarus, watching the enigmatic birds deserting the Iceni in great flurries, knew otherwise.

NEMETON

THE following days with the victorious army passed for Andecarus in strained seclusion. As Londinium lay smoldering, inhabited only by spirits and carrion eaters, the Iceni were again hungry for victory in blood. There had been arguments, he had heard, about where next to strike. Governor Paulinus had been sharp in his perception, apparently, for the two most readily spoken names were indeed Verulamium and Calleva. Many of the nobles had favored moving against the latter, for the Atrebates, to whom Calleva was a center of population and governance, were as close to Rome as any, *and* Calleva had the benefit of being farther away from any remaining Roman military threat. But the Trinovantes were a vocal group within the army, and the hatred that existed between their tribe and the Catuvellauni of Verulamium was the stuff of legend. The Catuvellauni, who were now citizens of Rome, sheltering under the eagle's wing since the capture of Caratacus.

And so it had been decided. Despite the fact that Verulamium was a twenty-mile step *toward* the legions of Governor Paulinus, the loudest, most insistent voices won the day. The army finished its looting and the grisly displaying of the corpses of Londinium on gibbets and spikes, and then slowly, inexorably, began to move northwest

Though Andecarus had acquired clean clothes and a sword, returning to the fold of his people, he had lost much in Londinium: Selene. Luci. Ria. Hope.

He'd had to fight down his own impetuousness again and again since then. To launch into something without adequate thought and consideration was unlike him, but the fact that Ria languished in Verico's tent under guard, abused and helpless, drove him to distraction.

That tent was too well guarded to consider either frontal assault or stealthy entrance by slitting the rear wall. And he could hardly appeal to the queen, all but unreachable behind her council of elders and absent much of the time anyway, scouting the territory around Londinium. After violence, theft, and royal pardon were all rejected, the worst option of all was the only one left: speaking with his father. The ageing warrior, still one of the most respected in the tribe, was in his tent with several of the other nobles, according to the warriors with whom he had spoken. Andecarus had pondered whether to leave it again until he might catch his father alone, but the chances of that were minute. Duro's opinion and companionship were sought by young and old, warrior and maid, and he was rarely alone.

One of the young warriors who owed fealty to Duro stood outside the old man's tent like a Praetorian outside a Roman legionary commander's headquarters, and Andecarus couldn't help likening his father to a legion's commander. The faint similarity between Governor Paulinus and Duro was hard to escape. Shave and trim his father's mane and put him in a bronze cuirass, and he might be the Roman's brother—almost of an age and with the same iron-gray hair, the same insightful gaze, the same determined set of jaw, the same effortless capability of a veteran of many wars.

Taking a deep breath, Andecarus strode straight through the tent's door fast enough that the surprised guard only managed to bark out a challenge before he'd ducked past. Inside, Duro sat on a shaped log draped with a bear skin, his famous red-enameled sword between his knees, point to the floor, twirling it idly by the pommel as he talked. To the left sat an old man close enough to death to display a cadaverous appearance, parchment skin stretched over sharp bones. Look closer at that living corpse, though, and the marks of a hundred battles were etched into his flesh. Arm rings and a heavy torc weighed down upon him every

bit as much as the years of his long life. The old man's beard was
straggly and pulled to a point with a heavy amber bead, and his
hair was neatly braided back away from his face. Here was wisdom and experience, Andecarus realized. Beyond the ancient sat a
warrior perhaps three or four years Andecarus' senior, yet adorned
with the arm rings and torc of a man of means and reputation—
some noble warrior who had been too aloof and battle obsessed
to show his face in council until war had risen its blood-soaked
visage. Here was strength and fortitude. Then, to the other side,
with their back to him, sat a man with the dream-caster's feather-
and-bone-tagged staff—a seer who Andecarus had seen in the
royal enclosure more than once. Here then, was piety and direction, in the absence of the Druids who had since time immemorial guided the people.

And beyond him, a young woman Andecarus recognized readily
enough even from the rear. Sorcha, eldest daughter of the queen.
Resolution and defiance. Only sixteen summers old and already
blooded and poisoned with the hate and fiery need that are the
children of vengeance and war. Her hair, red like her mother's,
gleamed in the firelight, and even in the warmth of the tent, her
shoulders were covered with an expensive pelt. Sorcha. A girl he
had once thought he perhaps loved—who might have made him
consort when she became queen—but who had turned her back on
him following her dreadful ordeal at Roman hands, as though he
were no longer of interest to her now that she had her war. Sorcha
did not turn at the new arrival. Nor did the old man. Only Duro
looked up, waving dismissively at the warrior behind Andecarus.

"I wish to speak with you, Father."

"This is not a good time."

"It never will be. I want to talk to you about Verico."

"I have no time to discuss your endless petty arguments with
your brother."

The younger warrior on the floor turned, waving him away. "The weak, the cowardly, and the disinterested have no place in this tent."

Andecarus was about to launch into an angry tirade when his father unexpectedly raised a warning hand to the counselor. "Hold, man. The boy might not be to your liking, but he could have insight for our discussion. He has served with the enemy, after all."

"Some believe he serves them still," hissed Sorcha without turning. Still that animosity burning deep inside, then. Romans had violated her; Andecarus had served with Romans . . .

"What say you Andecarus, son of Duro?" the old advisor inquired. "What will the Romans do? Will Paulinus move directly against us? Will he take up a defensive position somewhere important? Will he push for our own heartland while we are far away?" The ancient warrior studied him with a disconcertingly penetrative gaze, and Andecarus cleared his throat, trying not to catch his father's eye.

"The queen is a new Arminius," Andecarus began. "I think she knows this. I think you all do. What happened in Germania is common knowledge, but the tellers of tales and singers of songs only tell half the tale and sing half the song. They talk of the glorious defeat of three legions, the capture of eagles, the humiliation of Rome, and the death of a governor. They fail to speak of the retribution of Rome. The massacres of the tribes in those forests. The retrieving of the eagles and the destruction of the land. It is a poor strategist who looks at the glorious victory and forgets to think beyond it."

"We have an army sizeable enough to *bury* Paulinus' legions," spat the young warrior, his fingers drumming angrily on his knees.

"Yes. It is a huge army," Andecarus spat back with equal vehemence. "And Paulinus has just four depleted legions to call upon:

the Ninth at Durobrivae, the Twentieth and Fourteenth in the northwest, and the Second in the southwest They are seriously undermanned, for your army slaughtered the Ninth, and the Twentieth will have lost men in Mona . . ."

There was an ominous, tense silence at his mention of that name, and the dream-caster gripped his staff, twirling it as he warded them against ill luck. The loss of the shepherds of the people in that misty haven would have far-reaching effects on the world, even if Boudica reigned triumphant for a thousand years. Finally, Andecarus broke the silence again, his voice flat.

"Do you have any idea what a beast Rome is? You can think in terms of Paulinus' four legions, yet it is but a few hours' sail across the water to Gaul and Germania, and have you any idea how many legions there are there? *Many* more is the answer. Enough to bury this island in steel. And Rome has an endless supply of men—more legions could be raised in just months. Do not think for one moment that you are fighting Paulinus and his four legions. You have chosen to fight *Rome*, which has countless of them. But I do not think they will be needed anyway."

"Oh?" Duro cocked a spiky gray eyebrow. "How so?"

"Because Paulinus is not Cerialis. He is no impetuous glory-hunter willing to throw men at a perceived simple victory. He is clever. I have looked into his eyes and seen what lies there. I heard his plans when I was held captive in Londinium. He was calculating enough to abandon the place to us with his eye on final victory rather than defensive engagements. He will play the game of strategy until he gets us where he needs us, sacrificing whatever he has to, and then, when his time and the situation are just right, he will pounce, and that day we will all know true war. I have seen the legions ascendant."

Another heavy silence filled the tent, his ominous prediction sitting heavy for some time until the ancient warrior spoke again.

"Then pretend you are in our circle, young Andecarus. What is your counsel?"

"He's more *Roman* now than Iceni," spat Sorcha angrily, but Duro held up a hand that seemed to prevent her words emerging against her will. "Go on," he said.

Andecarus sighed. "We have forfeited our moral ground now. After Camulodunum and Londinium, we can no longer claim a righteous war—a *bellum sacrum*, as the Romans put it, for we have outdone Rome's atrocities with our own. And the massacre of the Ninth Legion set us against their military irrevocably. We will be punished now whatever happens. But Paulinus is no fool. Perhaps he will be able to see the value of a peaceful solution over one that threatens the rest of his legions and the stability of his province. He has more authority independent of Rome than the procurator did, so his word alone might be enough." With a bleak smile, he remembered Valeria's words to her husband before Londinium burned. "And no Roman governor would want to be the man who lost the emperor a province. There might still be terms to be sought if we do so now, while we are not threatened."

"Terms?" snorted Sorcha. "With the men who . . . with those *animals*?"

Duro cut in with a low, purposeful tone. "The price we would pay for peace would be impossible to meet, even if the queen was willing to consider it, which she will not." He noted his son shaking his head and leaned back. "What, then, do you think Rome's price for peace might be?"

Andecarus took a preparatory breath. "The governor . . ." His words caught in his throat. What *would* Paulinus consider acceptable? At worst, the Iceni and their allies extinct, their lands farmed by his settled veterans, their children sold in the markets of Rome. At best, the queen surrendered to drag in chains around the great city's streets. Andecarus might not agree with the el-

ders, but this was the *sine qua non*—the minimal requirement
of peace—his queen's head bowed, stretched, severed, and that
was unacceptable even to him. Try as he might, no further words
would come, and Duro nodded.

"You forget, boy, that we are unopposed at the moment, and
our record of victory grows. The Roman capital, gone. Their new
great port, gone. Soon, their staunchest allies will taste our iron.
And the more we defeat Rome, the more we take back from them,
the more peoples will join us. This *is* a sacred war, boy, and we are
winning it."

Andecarus sighed again. "To *you* it might be sacred. To the
queen, I'm sure. And while the vengeance of the Iceni might be a
great and righteous cause, we have surpassed Roman barbarism to
such an extent that the Romans will not see it that way. Even the
more reasonable ones, let alone the legates and tribunes who lead
the legions, which, have I mentioned, are almost endless?"

"Rome may have a vast supply of men," Duro countered, "but
we potentially have every tribe on this island, if we can only draw
them in. Rome must be desperate to risk what they have by re-
neging on their promises and calling in gifts as debts. And if they
need money, they're in trouble. You must have taken enough coin
with their cavalry to know how much pay a legion needs. Rome
cannot hold its province against the entire population without the
money to pay its troops. Even if you're right and we cannot win
in the end, the more we make Rome hurt, the stronger we are by
comparison. Terms are better sought from a strong position, boy."

Andecarus frowned. Had his father just cut through the tangled problem with a thread of true, decent sense? What if . . .
what if it *could* be done?

Perhaps more importantly, what *else* could be done? There was
no going back: his father had made that clear. There was nothing
now but either sit and wait for Rome to exact a terrible vengeance

or do the unthinkable—to push and drive the rebellion and hope that it was possible to beat Rome once and for all.

"When the wavering tribes see what we have done to Rome and what we are willing to do to their collaborators," snapped Sorcha, "they will flock to our banners."

There was no point in continuing his line of argument. Andecarus straightened. "About Verico, Father . . ."

"I have *not the time*!" bellowed the old man irritably. "Your rivalries and jealousies do neither of you any credit."

"This is not about him, Father. It is about Ria, who he keeps against her will."

At last, Sorcha turned, her permanently angry expression now tinged with curiosity at the mention of her former slave. "Ria was given to Verico after Verulamium, when his bravery earned him a reward and he requested her as a companion. I was riding to Mona, and Mother was occupied by other duties, so the council granted his request. He said he would consider marrying her if she ever gave him a son—it is a great honor for a former slave girl."

"She does not consider it an honor," Andecarus bit out, and Sorcha's eyes flared. The tiniest tinge of . . . jealousy? Surely not. Regret, perhaps?

Sorcha's lip curled. "She is in the best place. Verico is a warrior valuable to our cause while Ria was a washer of clothes who will now be a mother of more warriors. Leave her alone, son of Duro. There was a time when I thought better of you than this."

Again . . . was that jealousy or just a shifting of the princess' spite from him to Ria? Responding angrily to the queen's eldest daughter would hardly advance his case, so Andecarus gave her a simple nod before addressing his father again. "I could buy Ria from you, if you would only take her from Verico. As his foster father, you have that right."

Duro's expression hardened as he leaned forward, his sword

no longer spinning, knuckles white. "Forget the girl, boy. Verico stands in the forefront of our army when we face the enemy. None will argue with him while he defends the honor of the Iceni thus. Look instead to your own reputation. There are those who say you are the worst collaborator in this tribe. You conveniently managed to avoid fighting the Ninth, with whom you once served. Your *injury* kept you from the glorious sacking of Camulodunum and Londinium. Your knee is no longer fooling anyone, boy. Look how firmly you stand upon it now. You will be expected to fight with your tribe at Verulamium, to revel in our next victory. The eyes of the queen and all the elders will be upon you in the coming days, so see that you do not disappoint."

Andecarus felt a jolt of fear. Verico had the backing of the elders and of Sorcha—and therefore of the queen—and it seemed that Ria mattered little. Those with authority clearly would not be turned from their path, determined as they were to seek oblivion in the vengeful maw of Rome. And now the time was fast approaching when he would have to bite down on his resolve and either draw a blade against the Romans or flee the Iceni and know forever that he had failed his people. With a curt nod of farewell, he left the tent of his father, lost and bitter.

The gods of two peoples were not being kind to the child of both of them. With another deep breath, he decided that if he could not influence his father and the others, and if he could not free Ria, then it was time to place his fate in the hands of dread Andraste.

The *nemeton* lay silent in a small grove close to the river, where one of its tributary streams bubbled from the ground clean and new—a gift from the gods and the reason for the veneration of the place. It was old, too. Around the spring, in a circle, the ancient trees had grown into one another, forming a solid hedge of branches and intertwined limbs. Years back, it would have been neat, the foliage trimmed with loving work, the grass kept short by goats, the stonework, now barely visible through the undergrowth, polished clean. The Druid of this place had been long gone, though the small signs and markers remaining around the area spoke of its existence even to strangers such as Andecarus. He had seen the low stone with the telltale markings when the army had encamped this evening. He'd not thought to visit it, of course. Who did, in these new and Druidless days?

Crossing the circle, he crouched near the stone-lined spring and began to tear at the long, untended grass. A hundred heartbeats passed with furious defoliation before the offering pit came into view. A deep, stone slab-lined hole. Was it still occasionally used? Certainly, the elders of the army should be seeking the support of the gods when so close to such a place. It was all well and good for the queen to invoke great Andraste in her harangues of the army, but perhaps the tribe's patron goddess might be more inclined to aid them if some of their nobles were to make regular offerings. In this, he couldn't help but feel that the Romans had the edge. Their gods seemed so much more powerful, but then the Romans spoke to their gods daily. More, even: every time they crossed a threshold. Every time they faced a decision. And they gave their gods wine and silver and expensive frankincense imported from beyond the ends of the world. No wonder the Roman gods were powerful and looked after their people. Invoking Andraste as you hack off a head and hurl it into a ditch might seem appropriate, but what god would prefer a moldering head in a ditch to a feast of exotic proportions on a dedicated altar?

Drawing his purse from his belt, Andecarus opened it and withdrew a collection of coins. Some silver, some bronze—no copper. Better not to demean a god. Roman coins sat in his palm alongside those minted by the tribes, and even one from a Gaulish nation that must have come in through the merchants in Londinium. Holding his breath, he cast the coins into the narrow pit and was rewarded with the clink and clatter as they landed atop previous offerings from years gone by.

"Great Andraste and spirits of this place, I ask a twofold boon. Let this war end well, and quickly, and let Ria be delivered to me from the clutches of the animal who holds her. In exchange, I give you coin of silver and bronze and my devotion and praise." Unsure what else to say in this oddly deserted place with no attendant, he rose once more and turned.

His heart skipped and then thundered silently as he saw the rodent move. A squirrel—a small one for its type—but no russet red or lackluster brown. *This* squirrel was white as snow, white as the cold marble Romans that had been torn from the temple roof in Camulodunum and smashed, white as that striking plume on Paulinus' helmet. Andecarus shuddered. White was *good* for the Romans. Their priests wore white; the legions had their white tunics for parade dress. For the tribes of this island, though, white was rather more sensibly tied with death—with ash, with the bloodless body, with the spirits of the restless dead. It was a clear omen granted him at this sacred place, even in the absence of the Druids. It presaged dark times for the Iceni and possibly ascendancy for Rome. And when paired with the logic of his own all-too-human predictions, it told a horrible tale of the days to come. And yet, despite the foretelling of doom that seemed to apply to his tribe and the whole revolt in general, he couldn't help but worry more whether the white of death might apply to Ria, for she was part of his prayer, too.

The squirrel sniffed, apparently in disdain, and, as though finding him somehow wanting, scuttled off into the undergrowth, taking with it Andecarus' hope and spirit. Shivering and already defeated, the child of Iceni, child of Rome, walked out of the grove and into the abyss.

VERULAMIUM

"LET the die be cast."

"What?" murmured the weird, wall-eyed one.

"Oh, nothing." Andecarus' gaze drifted to left and right, playing across the warriors striding purposefully along to either side. Most of them bore swords, though a few—particularly those oddballs who he had picked out this last hour and primed for the attack—also carried spears with wicked tips, as did Andecarus himself.

Although this particular force consisted in the main of Trinovantes, it also contained a healthy—*unhealthy?*—number of the Iceni's undesirables. Queen Boudica and her advisors had been careful to place those whom they had reason to mistrust—and the idiots—far from the rest of the Iceni, keeping potential trouble out of the fight as far as that was possible. That Duro had not stood up for him might have driven an ever-greater wedge between them but for the fact that Andecarus knew he was being tested. His loyalty had been questioned time and again, and his father could not be seen to be coddling him until he had proved himself.

And so he found himself among the Trinovante warriors who lusted after the destruction of their age-long enemy—the Catuvellauni. Back across the river, the Iceni moved against the town, which nestled on a long gentle slope against the south bank of a river, in a tightening arc. The majority of the population lived much as they had before the arrival of Rome, gathered in extended farmsteads on the southern and western hills, but the place was changing rapidly. By the river had once stood a sacred site, the investiture place of their kings, until the legions came and built a fort of timber and turf there. And now, a decade since the army had moved on, that enclosure formed the center of a growing Roman-style settlement. Indeed, the hillside farmsteads had gradually extended down to the new heartland, melding with the expanding Roman center so that the whole valley had become one sprawling settlement with native structures around the periphery and a new Roman town at its core.

The Iceni war bands were even now approaching from the south, well positioned to butcher their way across the outlying farmsteads and settlements, carrying fire and death through them and down the hill, converging finally on the new Romanized heart of Verulamium as they tightened the cordon. Below them, the settlement went on in peace, seemingly unaware of their approaching doom, for the intent to sack Verulamium had been kept as secret as was possible with a force of this size, and for the last day, the wagons and noncombatants had been left to follow on while the war bands forged ahead in order to take advantage of surprise.

The gleeful Trinovantes and their Iceni hangers-on had been given the northern approach down the gentle slope, taking the small suburb on the north bank and driving across the bridge, straight at the enclosure that had been a Roman fort and now marked the center of Verulamium. The Trinovante warriors were full of eager talk of what they would do to the inhabitants of the north bank, though Andecarus knew that the bridge was the key, not the settlement. Unless they arrived quickly and unexpectedly, they could easily become bottled up on the bridge, fighting a few men at a time and unable to effectively take part in the main fight. They would have to concentrate on the bridge if they wished to be part of the main assault. Meanwhile, the Iceni bands would have their pick of plunder and slaves from the easy targets to the south and would most likely have the glory of taking the heart, too, while the Trinovantes struggled to cross the river.

Unless someone rushed in and took the bridge before the local warriors managed to plug it.

Not for the first time, he considered simply walking away. The Iceni were his tribe, but the vast majority treated him with mistrust, some also with derision. It had been almost a month since the sack of Londinium, and Andecarus had spent that time all but alone, spurned by his fellow tribesmen as the war band inched its way toward Verulamium. Only his heritage and a deep connection that he couldn't even try to describe kept him with them in the face of his adoptive people. He could have fled to the embrace of Rome. They would welcome an Iceni warrior with knowledge of his tribe and their goals and tactics, he was sure— one who could speak Latin and had served in the cavalry. But to do so would be to place himself firmly against the tribe, and he could no more comfortably do that than fight the Romans for the Iceni. There were places he could go, of course, which were neither Iceni nor Roman. The Brigantes, perhaps? After all, had he not shed blood with the legions to save their queen from her devious husband?

But finally faced with that inevitable choice, he had pushed down the uncertainty, grateful that this time the target was a town of the Catuvellauni with few actual Romans present. He could almost pretend it was an old-fashioned tribal war—in a way, for the Trinovantes at least, it was.

He had cast his spear into the ground with the rest. When the queen and her advisors drew the rough plan of Verulamium in the dust last night, plotting where the attacks would take place, he had nodded acceptance of his role. *Let the die*, as Caesar had once so eloquently said, *be cast*. All that remained was to see how lucky the throw had been.

Shaking off uncertainty with his reverie, he concentrated on the task at hand.

A tall grassy mound marked their point of descent to the river, and the warriors surged around the barrow—burial place of a king dead just a few years—like a fast-flowing river around a rock, and on down the long slope. The river lay below, a wide glittering ribbon in the early afternoon light, cutting through the dry landscape from east to west. The whole of Verulamium lay spread out before them like a banquet: that burgeoning Roman settlement by the waterside, replete with a few grand structures, numerous workshops, and houses in stone and timber, whitewashed plaster and red tile, spidering out in regular streets and meeting the straggle of native huts and houses that had spread down from the ancient slopes to meet the new.

The Iceni had come. Though their individual forms were thus far only fleetingly visible, like ants crawling among the most distant reaches of the place, wherever those tiny shapes flooded, columns of smoke began to plume up into the blue. Andecarus yelled to the squint-eyed Iceni lunatic and the bull-shouldered fellow with the misshapen skull—two of the misfits who had cleaved to him as a noble of their tribe. The Trinovantes around them would mostly concentrate on the riverside settlement, rampaging madly, but there was only one hope of achieving any sort of success with this prong of the attack, and that lay in making it across the bridge before the enemy clogged it.

As he pelted down the shallow slope, praying his knee continued to hold up under the pressure and trying not to fall foul of holes or roots, the two strange warriors passed on his words to the others he'd primed in the past hours. Those words—*the bridge, the spears, the phalanx*—spread through the Iceni undesirables like a summer fire through a field of barley stalks. He had prepared them as well as he could. *Some* had even listened.

They were perhaps halfway down the long slope when the world erupted into the din of battle. The Trinovantes whooped and bellowed their war cries, clanged their swords on shields or mail shirts. The occupants of the buildings on the north side of the river emerged from their doorways, some in panic, others determined, bringing with them swords and spears. Brave but pointless; their fate was already sealed—the Trinovantes outnumbered them by many hundreds to one. The alarm was now being raised across the settlement. Shouts of panic and anger rang out across the wide valley, a whistle blown somewhere echoed, a bell was clanging desperately at the old Roman enclosure. Screaming and cries of dismay began to rise in pitch and volume across the valley alongside crashes and rumbles, melding to form a blanket of sound—the death rattle of a town.

The Iceni were beginning to descend like a forest fire from the hills across the river, burning the majority of the structures, hacking, spearing, and maiming their way to the center. Now they were a *true* swarm of ants, small dark figures moving amid the golden thatch and the parched, pale grass. Small knots of activity were visible here and there where desperate, defiant groups of Catuvellauni warriors tried to hold off the tide of the enemy despite the hopelessness of the odds. Boudica's army was immense and strong, full of spirit and vigor, riding high on their earlier successes, certainly more than a match for a sleepy town caught off guard.

Ahead of the swarming Iceni, women, children, warriors, graybeards, dogs, cats, and horses flooded in panic for the settlement's core. Whether they thought to defend themselves at that small fortified heart or to flee across the bridge to safety, naught would come of it. Verulamium was doomed, and that had been clear from the start. It was just a matter of severity.

Andecarus yelled more instructions as he concentrated on his run and on not letting the spear's butt touch the grass. More than once in the descent, his knee had issued a sharp little pain—the legacy of his injuries still making their presence felt for all its relative strength—and it was by luck alone that he'd remained upright throughout. Finally, his legs trembling with the effort of maintaining so long a run over such terrain, he and perhaps a hundred of the Iceni reprobates and Trinovantes pounded across the short length of flat ground to the river and the bridge that was even now beginning to fill with locals flooding the other way.

Behind him, the bulk of the Trinovante force began to spread out among the northern settlement's buildings, burning, killing, and brutalizing, but Andecarus had his sights only on that old fort at the settlement's heart. Even above the press of people at the far side of the bridge, he could see it clear, for a high timber tower stood atop the old fort's northern gate, the location of that warning bell that had notified the population of danger far too late to save them.

The bridge was a heavy wooden affair—a recent Roman construction replacing the original crossing—wide enough to drive a cart across and more. The hundred or so Iceni and Trinovantes poured onto the seasoned timbers, swords raised ready, many bellowing their war cries. Andecarus ran on, oddly silent, out of place. The only combat he had seen in his adult life had been from horseback as part of a Roman *turma*, and try as he might, none of the ancient battle cries of his people would come to mind. Bellowing the exhortation for Mars and Minerva to guide his spear and shield his flesh seemed wholly inappropriate. At the far end of the bridge, frightened occupants of the town had begun to flee the southern assault, thinking to cross the river to safety, but as they spotted the fresh force of enemy warriors flooding down to block their flight, they held back, milling about in panic. Even as Andecarus and his companions pounded across the timbers toward them, the warriors among the fleeing locals came to the forefront, leveling blades.

Again, for the hundredth time this hour alone, Andecarus found himself wondering why he was doing this. Did he believe in the great cause? Not really. Was it a matter of paternal or regal or even peer approval? Again, hardly. So why? The answer came as it had every other time: *Because you are Iceni. Because the only Romans who know you are gone or in your father's hands. Because, perhaps, the die was cast long ago, before you ever even tried to stop it all. Because when Verulamium lies in ruins with Londinium and Camulodunum, the last chance that Paulinus might offer terms will flit away in the wind, and the governor would no more welcome you to his bosom than he would a viper. Because the time for dreams of peace is past. Because the tribe is watching. Because, in an odd way, you need to prove that you are a match for Verico.*

Because to leave would be to abandon Ria to her fate.

He grimaced as he cried out, "Spears!"

The small force of misfit Iceni closed at a run with that last bellowed command and lowered the tips of their spears as though they were a cavalry unit charging infantry. Amid the din of battle cries, Andecarus found himself instinctively invoking Mars anyway—alongside Andraste—and was once more grateful that the thin screen of warriors they charged were no more Roman than were their attackers. It did not do to anger gods, especially when it seemed they'd already taken against you.

His spear struck an unarmored Catuvellauni warrior in the chest. The shaft broke, and the shock of the collision ran up Andecarus' arm, but not before the tip had penetrated, pushing between ribs, scything through muscle, lung, and veins and lodging up against the inside of his shoulder blade. The man let out a cry and fell back, his sword dropping to the timbers below, but Andecarus had already discarded his spear and deftly swapped his own blade from left to right hand, bringing it up for the fight. Others around him were having less success. The wall-eyed one had managed to catch a fleeing girl behind the warriors in the face with his spear and had fumbled his blade, running with surprise straight onto the point of a Catuvellauni sword. The one with the mis-shapen head had missed entirely, his handling of the spear poor, the tip slicing through the air a clean foot above the enemy's head.

But there were five of them in that first spear-charge, and three had hit warriors square on, taking them out of the fight. Even as the front men raised their blades for the melee, the spears of the four men behind them, carefully—*most carefully*— leveled between the heads of the front line, struck. Again two missed the warriors, but two more hit, one spear shattering a foot below the tip, a dozen jagged shards of ash-wood scraping Andecarus' shoulder as he raised his sword.

Battle in earnest had begun.

Across the river somewhere, Verico would be murdering and raping his heroic way to the compound at the settlement's heart, desirous of being seen to be the greatest of the Iceni. But the Romanized brother who had learned the swing of the *spatha* and the thrust of the spear among the legions would be more than a match for the brute. If Andecarus could not steal or buy Ria from the bastard's clutches, he would outshine Verico and *win* the girl back somehow. The Iceni might see him as a seeker of peace, a too-Roman courier at best, but they had not been there when Andecarus the cavalryman had wielded his sword against the forces of Caratacus, nor had they seen Andecarus the un-horsed rider caked in blood, knee deep in bodies on the field of battle, helping save the Brigante queen from the forces of her rebel husband. They had seen only Andecarus the peace-monger, not Andecarus the soldier. After days—weeks, even—of indecision and uncertainty, the simplicity of wielding a blade and having an enemy trying to kill him infused Andecarus with spirit and strength, and he fought with a clear mind and an easy heart—for as long as the faces appearing before him were Catuvellauni and not Roman, at least.

His large sword, hampered a little by the press on the bridge, could not be used for wide swings, and so he thrust and chopped again and again, cleaving flesh and bone, heedless of whether it was warrior or fleeing civilian before him. The battle was too tight and fraught to distinguish. There was simply a sea of humans before him whose only hope was to get past, and *his* only path was to push on through *them* into the settlement.

Something warm and slimy slapped against his face and fell away unseen, leaving a watery pink tinge to his left eye and a trickling on his cheek. A tooth struck him in the forehead, and he spat as a splash of blood washed across his face accompanied by an exultant roar from the Iceni with the oddly shaped head as the man kicked a dying warrior away. Andecarus' own blade plunged into the neck of a gurgling warrior. He was a trained horseman, used to the spear and an edged, swiping blade, but he'd fought alongside the legions for seven years and seen them training with their short thrusting swords, had practiced the moves himself often enough.

The groin, the armpit, the neck. Thrust directly for precision of entry. Twist with a dual purpose—to cause maximum damage in the wound and to prevent the blade catching when withdrawn. Arm drawn back far enough to free sword, hand raised, elbow bent sharp. *Unus. Duo. Tres.* Of course, the maneuvers were greatly different with a longer, heavier blade, but at least for a short time he could handle the weight. He twisted his wrist and tore the blade from the man's neck, using the momentum of the withdrawal to bring it up in a tight swing—not tight enough since he almost lopped an arm from the squinty one—and then a chop down into the shoulder of an enemy warrior with an axe.

As the press at the southern edge of the bridge melted away under the ferocity of their attack, Andecarus realized that he was oddly proud of the misfits with whom he had taken the bridge.

Not hampered by the need to be seen as noble and brave like most of the Iceni warriors, they had fought more as a unit—more like the Romans, in point of fact. And their unified front and novel tactics had won them the bridgehead where most Iceni would still even now be facing off against a growing enemy press.

Other enemy warriors were now running to face this threat from the north, but Andecarus and his companions had reached open ground. As they launched from the bridge into the settlement and made for the timber walls of the former fort, they spread out, taking advantage of the space to ease out their arms and swing their limb-breaking swords the way they were meant to be swung. Despite the growing number of opponents, the freedom to swing a blade unobstructed made the fighting a great deal easier.

Still, only the hundred or so men he had prepared were involved in the push, the vast swath of the Trinovantes busying themselves with the destruction and desecration of their enemy's houses on the northern bank, the rape and murder of the occupants. Finally, a proportion of the tribe seemed to pay attention to the bridge, sated by their activity and seeking new thrills. As the flood began to amass, crossing the bridge, Andecarus exulted in his success, leading his odd force toward that wooden tower. The Trinovantes might be coming in force now, but all among them would know and would remember that it was those Iceni among them who had taken the bridge and secured their route into the fight.

Quickly, he and his companions fought their way past a half-built Roman structure, wooden scaffolding covering it to the partially formed upper floor. A desperate man atop the building was casting down roof tiles from a pile, trying to break the skulls of the invaders below. He fell back, an arrow in his throat, and disappeared—the Trinovante archers were making their presence felt now. Ignoring the terrified crying from within the building, they ran on, swords swiping and hacking each time an opponent emerged from a doorway or alley, the women, old folk, and children having now largely sought the illusory safety of the buildings. Theirs would, he predicted, be no happier an end than the red-haired roaring warrior who was even now staring at the stump of his right arm while Andecarus came around for a second swing. The blow dug so deep into his neck that Andecarus almost lost his grip on his sword when the man fell and pulled it out only with great difficulty.

Behind them, the bulk of the Trinovantes were now crossing the river, having left nothing alive on the far side, fanning out into the Roman-style settlement. Andecarus turned a corner, and the wooden gate tower came into view, the leaves of the gate shut tight and barred from within. Over the general din, it was now possible to place the victorious war cries of the other Iceni forces, also closing on the center from the far side. It was a race to claim the glory of finishing Verulamium, and while Andecarus felt no real animosity for the hapless pro-Roman Catuvellauni, he knew Verico would be grunting and maiming his way toward him, desperate to claim that victory. He would fail, if Andecarus had to gut every living thing between them.

A figure leapt at him from a doorway, and he instinctively swept out with his blade, catching the man a crippling blow to the neck. His gaze focused on the man, and he felt a mouthful of acrid bile burst up from his throat as he realized this was no warrior. He was a Roman workman—a mason or plasterer, probably, from the white dust that coated his tunic. The man had simply been unfortunate enough to flee a house directly into Andecarus' path.

He paused in his run, his companions sweeping past, intent on the fort, and gazed down at the Roman as the man shuddered and gasped, clutching at the wide rent in his neck and the spray that jetted between his desperate fingers. Andecarus stared. And stared. He watched the blood slow and the man's shaking become more sporadic. Then he was simply dead. Unmoving. Lifeless.

He, Andecarus of the house of Catus Decianus, former *Eques Alaris* in the First Gallorum attached to the Ninth Legion, had killed a Roman.

He delved into the depths of his soul. What did he feel? Not horror, oddly, which was what he'd expected. Not even remorse. In fact, nothing at all. No joy or exultation, certainly, but neither was there guilt or regret. Was this what his father felt like when he killed Romans? Or the queen? Or Verico? No. He'd seen the joy in their eyes with every wash of blood and every pulse of pierced organs. They lived for such exhilaration.

But still, he could kill Romans. The taboo was gone. Mars had not struck him down for such an act. Perhaps, on balance, the Roman gods were as deaf as the Iceni's. Maybe *no one* cared for which side Andecarus fought but he himself . . . and the watchful elders.

And then he was running again. Some invisible and unexpected barrier had been removed. A Catuvellauni warrior swung at him and caught him a glancing blow on his left arm, scoring a red line along it that burned like liquid fire. Two vicious blows put the man down. A Roman had found a hammer and ran at him with it raised above his head, invoking Minerva as he did so. Andecarus simply sidestepped and neatly sliced his sword across the man's midriff mid-charge. The hammer fell from spasming fingers as the Roman jerked and swayed, then fell, his spine the only thing that had prevented him being cleaved neatly in two.

The pause for contemplation had cost Andecarus his glorious lead, and as he arrived at the former fort, his misfit bunch were already scaling the old, barely defensible walls. Andecarus followed them, clambering to the top with no opposition, the defenders having been pushed back by Odd-head and Squinty, among others. The interior of the former fort was packed, and it now became apparent why such an old semi-derelict relic remained at the center of what was rapidly becoming an urbanized town. The small fort had been redesignated as a works compound, filled with stacks of tiles and timbers, unshaped stones and bags of tools, and the like. Now the desperate Catuvellauni who had thought to man it against the attackers were down among the piles of goods, fighting back in an ever-decreasing circle. A few other men were holding out in the timber tower against screaming Iceni, and Andecarus turned toward it.

The blow took him completely by surprise as he'd seen no enemy close by.

His wits swimming in a dark, roiling stream, someone grasped him by a shoulder and hauled him up, leaning him against the timber parapet until his spinning thoughts settled and his eyesight cleared. He reached up to the back of his head, and his hand came away sticky and red. Spinning as fast as he dared, he peered around the fort. There was no way the blow had come from the beleaguered locals down in the center. There were only a dozen or so left, and they had their own problems. The rest of Verulamium was in its death throes already. Every house seemed to be filled with screaming, and smoke was already rising from a number of the central buildings. Iceni warriors were emerging from doorways, dragging screaming girls by the hair, others were carrying so many severed heads that they were forced to juggle with their weapons. Verulamium was lost and far past fighting back. So who had struck him from behind with . . . what, a rock?

His gaze caught Verico vaulting down from the wall, drenched in blood, with two heads tied by the hair to his belt, desperately trying to involve himself in the last true fight before the enemy was finally overcome. Though the man might have been there for just moments, had not once looked over at this wall and was clearly now focused on the last-ditch fight in the compound. There was no longer any doubt in Andecarus' mind whence that painful rock had come.

Bastard.

Still, he felt some small satisfaction as he watched his foster brother rush to the fight to discover that he was too late and that the honor of ending Verulamium had fallen to better men. Verico raged and ranted, shoving men a decade older and more noble than he by far. He even threatened one of the older warriors until he was pulled back by two of his cronies and made to calm down. With a braying of horns, the gates of the fort were wrenched open, and the queen strode in with Sorcha, blood-spattered and filthy, at her shoulder. Andecarus had never seen the queen so proud and imperious, her daughter so . . . he wasn't sure what, but his eyes were drawn to that crimson-soaked figure anyway. Silence fell . . . a *respectful* silence. Boudica's army was undefeated, and many would now say undefeatable. Duro was close behind in the queen's retinue, gore-streaked sword still in hand. The gathered warriors waited, pensive, for an announcement, but Andecarus' attention had been grabbed by the sound of a *kraa* from above. His eyes quickly picked out the raven in the blue, the columns of smoke not yet having fully obscured the beautiful late-summer sky. The gleaming black bird circled the fort again and again, as though personally endorsing their victory on behalf of great Andraste.

And suddenly the raven was gone.

Black feathers whirled and tumbled, and his eyes were drawn by a screech to the eagle that even now swooped off to the north with the prize clamped in its beak. Andecarus felt an icy shiver run up and down his spine. His senses spun. No one else seemed to have noticed the aerial exchange. The queen was speaking to her tribe, her voice sonorous and proud, exultant and fierce, and all eyes were upon her even as the tattered feathers drifted down among them.

"As the wheat falls to the farmer's sickle, so does Roman power fall to our blades!"

A cheer.

As the feathers of the sacred ravens fall . . .

"We have destroyed Rome's very heart in our land. We have destroyed their vile port where all manner of evils arrive upon our shores, where Rome's soft, squalid, cowardly procurator seethed in his snake's nest. Now we have torn the deceitful and treacherous Catuvellauni from beneath the eagle's wing—may they see the error of their judgment and henceforth take up arms against the oppressor."

Another cheer.

We have destroyed our valor. Our right. Our own morals.

"The name Verulamium will live only short, dark days in our enemy's mind, for when they are driven from our shore, all things Roman shall be ripped out and made anew. The new masters of this land can raise a new town from these ashes, but it will be the Verulamion of old, and not some *Roman* corruption."

The cheer was more muted this time as the Trinovantes present contemplated the future rise of their age-old tribal enemy once more. Still, the mood had caught the hearts of all present. Of *almost* all present.

Andraste, forgive us our hubris . . .

Suddenly, the pain in his head seemed insurmountable, his strength all but sapped, and Andecarus slumped against the wall with heavy, shuddering breaths.

NEVER had a victory felt more hollow.

The queen and her entourage and council occupied a wealthy

farmstead that had been left intact and unburned on the southern hill. Around the periphery, the chariots, carts, and goods had been drawn up, and the farm's fenced-in pens and corrals had been made to serve the invaders' horses. Victorious warriors stood or sat in small groups, laughing about their victories, boasting and exchanging anecdotes even as they exchanged appropriated flasks of ale or jars of Roman wine. The muffled sound of oratory suggested that an important meeting was going on inside the largest hall.

Ignoring the warriors around the periphery, Andecarus strode purposefully toward the building. His head had stopped bleeding, his hair matted and sticky, though now a headache raged like a thunderstorm in his skull, doing little to improve his already black mood. The wound on his arm had been filled with honey and wrapped tight for now, though it had been little more than a deep scratch. His eyes were locked on the door to the building, for the time had come. Things had to stop. The gods had told them in the form of portents time and again what the future held, and the past had done much the same with the examples of Spartacus and Arminius.

And Boudica and her advisors continually chose to ignore signs from the gods and lessons from history, and to march on into oblivion, perhaps guided by the queen's own divined omens. Perhaps misguided. The queen had cast the die for the tribe, and Andecarus didn't have to look at them to guess the score. As Andecarus closed on the door, the warriors beside it readying themselves to prevent intrusion, his gaze happened to catch movement in the yard beside the building, and he recognized his father's iron-gray mane even from behind.

The old man straightened, raised his sword, and swung down heavily, striking the head from a kneeling man. Andecarus could see five more lined up ready, their faces bleak and drawn. What they had done to incur such wrath, Andecarus could not imagine. Still, their fate, even at the edge of the blade, was comparatively merciful given some of the things he had seen.

"Father?"

Duro looked up and gave a strange half smile that took him quite by surprise.

"I am told that you excelled yourself today, that you led the assault across the bridge and at the walls. After today, many voices that called for your exile will have been silenced."

If not praise, then at least acknowledgment. He'd not expected that. He cleared his throat.

"I am barraged by portents."

The old man looked at him quizzically and swept out and down with his heavy sword, almost casually taking the head from the next victim even as the man had started to unfold in an attempt to flee. "You think yourself a Druid? You can interpret the whims of gods now?"

"When they are clear, yes. And so could you. It would not take a Druid to interpret what I have seen. An eagle takes a raven from the clear sky? Never has there been a less ambiguous sign, even more so than the white squirrel I saw or the ravens that fled the fire-smoke above Londinium. This campaign is doomed."

"Campaign?" the old man spat on the floor. "You still talk like a Roman. Even now, the queen and her counselors determine our next move. I have put in my stance—that we should finish off Cerialis and his tattered legion—but the queen herself will decide in the end. Her will is strong."

"Father, we have to do something. The Romans are coming—you must know that by now. We have had scout reports that Governor Paulinus is gathering men in the northwest. You know they will not stop until the Iceni are but a distant memory, whispered bitterly on the wind by gods who have turned their backs on us."

"Such talk will poison our warriors' minds and weaken their knees. Keep your words behind the prison of your teeth, boy."

"Send away those who can be saved, Father. Only the warriors need die."

Duro shook his head. "The queen wants the tribe with us. Where is safer for the womenfolk than with their men?"

"Fucking *anywhere*!" snapped Andecarus. "In a ditch. In a tomb. In a Roman's bed. Anywhere will be safer for them than with us in the coming days."

"Watch the sharpness of your tongue, boy, and remember to whom you talk. I was fighting battles before you were curled in your mother's belly."

Andecarus bridled, stepping closer to his father. "Against the Trinovantes. Or the Catuvellauni. Or the Brigantes. That's different."

"We fought the Romans when Scapula was governor."

Andecarus snorted derisively. "So you did. And what a rousing success *that* was. A thousand Iceni run through with Roman cavalry spears. Mountains of gold and food, horses and goods sent in reparations. Half a hundred hostages given over to Rome, including your son. *Including your son!* And you have the audacity to spit at me for my Roman ways? Whose fault is *that*, Father? Who put me in a Roman household and on a Roman horse for a decade by starting a fucking war there was no chance of winning? And you think that just because you've burned a few poorly defended towns this is so different? The legions are on their way. How many Iceni will die on the altar of your pride *this* time? How many children will grow up thinking they are Roman in the aftermath of this? That is, if the Romans are generous enough to let any Iceni live."

Duro, taut and trembling, thrust out a hand, and one of the warriors took his red-enameled sword as he stepped close to Andecarus, leaning down so that the two were almost nose to nose. "So you would have us do what? You've already made your case clear. The Romans are coming for us. All we can do is fight and try to win."

"You can send away those who can be saved," Andecarus growled again. "The Brigantes might take them in. Or the Coritani, perhaps? Either way, they will be better looked down on by a fostering tribe than as bleached bones on a field somewhere with a Roman standard jammed down through their ribs."

"The queen will not have it, and nor should she. The tribe travels together, and the womenfolk and children will watch Rome crushed for good. Or, if your *portents* have the right of it, they will watch us perish, but whatever the case, the tribe belongs together, not spread across the land like refugees. And what Iceni woman would want to face the world without her man anyway?"

"The queen seems to be doing it quite admirably."

Duro's lips peeled back from his teeth angrily. "Get out of my sight."

"Gladly. I'll leave you with that hulking moron you've raised in my rightful place." Ignoring the spluttering elder, Andecarus turned his back and stormed off. Where he was going and what for he could not say, but his pride now that he had turned his back on his father would not let him falter or deviate, and so he stormed into the doorway of an old barn directly ahead. Whatever it was used for, it had to be better than the yard out there full of his father's lethal denial. Out of sight of the old man and in the cool shade of the huge barn, he stopped, put his hand out against the central post to steady himself, and let his eyes adjust to the dim interior.

He heard the whimper before he saw what was happening, and his hand went to his side. His sword was gone, somewhere back in the burning town. Had he dropped it in the fort when he'd been hit in the head? Left it with the old healer afterward? He couldn't remember. Hands balling into white-knuckled fists, a low growl emerged from deep within. Ria lay on the straw-covered floor in the corner, her pale legs thrashing around in desperation, her arms pinned as the huge, sweating, muscular shape of Verico lunged again and again, trying to suppress her.

"Struggle harder," the brute sneered. "I like a good fight. Teach you to keep running away . . ."

The first kick Andecarus delivered broke a rib or two. He heard the snaps. As Verico rolled off Ria, stunned by the unexpected attack, Andecarus staggered on his bad knee, gripping the post again. His hand touched cold iron, and his eyes were drawn to it, even as they watched Ria scrambling to safety. A farmer's tool hung on a peg—a sickle with a hooked end for pruning as well as reaping. His hand closed around the wooden handle and lifted it from the peg.

"You!" Verico snarled, rising with a wince and clutching a hand to his ribs. Andecarus took a step toward him. The big man, trousers still snagged around his ankles, ducked left, and instinctively Andecarus moved to block him—the oaf's sword stood propped against the barn wall. "Good. A consolation for a wasted day. I will tear your eyes out through your arse," grunted Verico.

"One-handed?"

As the brute frowned in incomprehension, Andecarus lashed out, quick and deadly, the sickle catching his foster brother on the left forearm and slicing so deep he felt the bounce of iron on bone even inside the wound. Verico screamed, partly in agony and partly in rage, but even so sorely wounded, the big man was strong and fast. As Andecarus recovered from the swing, Verico barged past him with a lowered shoulder, staggering with the trousers at his ankles and the pain in his side, and ripped his sword from its sheath, turning.

The big warrior leveled the long blade, still streaked with Catuvellauni blood, threatening the smaller man who wielded only a short farm tool. Three swings, accompanied by unintelligible roars, had Andecarus stepping back across the barn defensively. He became aware that faces had appeared at the door, drawn by the noise. Another wide swing would have decapitated him had he not ducked, and he doubled back, using that central pillar where he'd found the sickle to hold off another blow, and another. As the brute hacked chunks out of the post, Andecarus backed toward Ria, who, shaking and pale, was wrapping her clothes around herself once more while spitting hate-filled curses at her captor.

Verico was on him again in moments. Slash, swipe, slash. And then, suddenly, the big man was falling, toppling forward. Andecarus blinked and saw Ria's sweeping leg fold back in as the girl spat on the fallen warrior.

"When I get back to you, you'll regret that, Shagpiece," Verico snarled, rising with some difficulty, using only one hand, blood still pouring in torrents from the other arm.

"She'll never worry about you again," snapped Andecarus as he kicked the big sword away from his foster brother. With deliberate slowness of movement, he placed his foot on Verico's back, between the shoulder blades, and shoved him down to the floor. As the monster's breath exploded from thick lips, Andecarus moved around behind him and dropped to a crouch, his eyes catching the fury in Ria's as she nodded.

"Only a thief takes things that are not his," he hissed into Verico's ear. "Only a hubristic idiot attacks his brother warriors because they beat him to a shared victory. And only a coward would attack a man from behind with a rock. Yes, I know it was you."

With a simple, single movement, Andecarus slid the sickle under the prone man's neck, grasped the hook with his other hand,

and jerked the sharp blade upward. He felt the skin, the muscle, the tendons go, heard the involuntary hiss as the blade sliced through windpipe, saw the lake of dark liquid begin to form beneath his victim. He kept tugging until he could hear iron on bone and then let go, leaving the sickle embedded as he rose. Verico's left foot was twitching rhythmically, but otherwise, he was still.

Ria was up now, her clothes covering her shivering form, eyes dark. But her expression of defiance and satisfaction as she stepped across the body brought an odd warmth to Andecarus. If the world was to plunge into darkness and end on the tip of a Roman spear, at least he would take to the grave the knowledge that Verico had died first, and badly.

At the doorway, half a dozen Iceni nobles, wide-eyed and shocked, stepped out of his way, uncertain of what to do. Others were gathering now, and he caught the eye of Sorcha, the queen's eldest daughter. Though once well-disposed toward him, Sorcha had distanced herself from what she perceived as a traitorous figure, treating him with contempt and scorn throughout the Iceni's rampage across the country. Yet here, now, the girl who might once have been his gave him a short, sharp nod of respect. Her enmity seemed to have faded to tattered memory in the face of what had just happened. Sorcha's own experiences at the hands of the Romans would be all too fresh in her memory to overlook Verico's abuses here, even if Ria *had* been given to him. Centurion or beast, no man should be allowed to rape a girl of the Iceni.

His spirits sank a little at the sight of Duro storming toward him, disbelief vying with fury in his father's eyes.

"What have you *done*, boy?"

"What should have been done years ago," growled Andecarus. "Putting down a mad dog that would one day turn on its master."

"Verico!" Duro roared. "You would kill your own *brother*?"

"He is no more my brother than you are my father. Get out of the way."

Storming past the outraged old man without another word, Andecarus crossed the yard, a huddled Ria held protectively at his side. He would allow his father a night to grieve, even for a monster, and see what the morning brought, vowing a good clean sacrificial ram to dread Andraste and divine Fortuna both that what the morning brought was not a revenge killing. He doubted it. A brute like Verico might seem of high value when the battle rages, but the balance would tip now that it was over. Time tarnished all things, and soon enough Duro would remember mostly the animal's true nature, his baser side, the corruption that had cankered his heart.

Above, a raven fluttered in the tree's thick foliage.

"WHY should I not go with them?"

Three days had passed since the sack, and half a mile away, Verulamium was busy sinking back into the earth, naught but ash and bone. Three days Andecarus had spent with Ria, trying to rebuild a spirit eroded by the selfish actions of a fiend. Three days in which his father had raged and ranted and yet not once confronted Andecarus over the death. And this morning, when the few sensible women were climbing into the cart and their supplies loaded with them, the old man had finally emerged, his face drawn and bleak, striding over to them.

"You will leave?" he had asked in an odd, cracked voice. "When you've finally proved to the elders you are Iceni and not a son of Rome, you will flee?"

Andecarus had shaken his head, not in denial, more in despair. "I took your favored son from you, and although I knew him to be a beast undeserving of life, I can see that I have done you wrong. The tribe will now forever see me as the man who killed one of their strongest warriors in a time of need. To stay would be to cause division and do you and I both further harm. Besides, the carts need an escort who knows one end of a sword from the other. And since the entire tribe is about to march into a Roman grave, my blade will make little difference to the outcome."

The old man had remained silent, his very presence forming the question again. *You will leave?*

"Why should I *not* go?" he said again.

Duro looked his son in the eye, his expression an odd mix of resignation, regret . . . and pride? "You are my son, and my son could no more desert his tribe than he could have sided with the Catuvellauni. And if you can walk away from your tribe, then I was right and you are naught but a Roman in Iceni dress."

Andecarus remained still, his expression unreadable, and his father pursed his lips. "You have served with Rome's military. You alone among us have seen how they work on campaign. You know better than any of the Iceni or the Trinovantes how we can beat them, and with your knowledge, we can drive them from our shores."

"You still think we have a chance?"

"Andraste will not fail us. The queen is her chosen. And don't forget, boy, that with your foster brother's death, you owe the tribe a warrior." His voice wavered between quiet acceptance and suppressed anger. "He may have been unrefined to your Roman-fed tastes, but his sword will be missed unless you take it up in his place." The effort with which the old man was keeping control on his emotions was impressive and showed in taut tendons and the pronounced veins of his temples.

"Good reasons for you to want me. Poor reasons for me to stay." His eyes flicked up to the carts and then back to his father, sucking air through his upper teeth.

Duro narrowed his eyes, an uncharacteristically piercing gaze driving through Andecarus, into his heart. "And yet you will. I offer you the chance to redeem yourself among the Iceni. To make a difference."

And to redeem myself to a father? His gaze slid up to one face in particular atop the cart. Ria. She had assumed he would be coming with her, and it was only when she spoke of it that he had realized he was undecided. When he'd expressed his uncertainty, she had been surprised and afraid. She had pleaded with him to go, and he had looked deep into her eyes. Perhaps he could have? There was the chance of a good life there, even for exiles, moving on from all this horror. And Ria was a warm and thoughtful girl. He was not foolish enough to think she loved him, as much as she pleaded for him to join her. That, he knew somewhat painfully, was merely affection, possibly even just gratitude and fear. But if he went with her, perhaps someday there could be more . . .

Yet his gaze slipped past her to the distant figure of Sorcha, the girl he'd seen violated. The girl he hadn't been able to help. The daughter of a queen he served. And in a different life . . .

There was a long, tense pause, and finally the son sighed. "Yes. I will stay."

As his father nodded—the closest he would come to a smile— Andecarus gestured to the carts. Perhaps two dozen women and children sat atop them, including Ria near the front, her face bleak and worried. "On a condition, though," he added. "There are wounded warriors from today's fight who will be of little use in battle against Rome—men who will live but will never again charge a shield wall. Yet they might afford adequate protection from bandits by their presence alone. Send a few of them with the carts—see that they reach the north safely."

His father nodded his assent, looking up at the women. And Andecarus was surprised given how long he'd paced back and forth beneath the silver gleam of the moon, how long he'd wrestled with the question, at how little persuasion it had taken to keep him here.

He'd been dismayed at how few women and children were willing to join the evacuation that morning. The queen had avowed her intention to fight Rome and to win, and too many of her people were so swept along by her rhetoric they could see nothing in their future but glorious victory. Still, every life he saved on those carts was one less that would fall on the field against Rome. And the queen had consented that Ria and the rest could go—had even given coin to assist them.

The cart drivers, at a nod from Duro, began to urge the beasts forward, and the carts bounced and jostled on the turf and began to roll away toward the paddock where the healers were at work on the wounded, seeking an escort. As the last cart shifted, Andecarus looked up at Ria, who pinned him with her gaze.

"I will wait every day for news," she said quietly.

"I fear it will not be good," he replied sadly. "Go with the gods, Ria, and live."

As the cart with its precious cargo bounced away, he watched that pretty face recede and turned to his thoughtful father.

"You must see that we still cannot win?"

Duro slapped a veined hand down on his shoulder. "So you say. But if the queen, with men like you and I beside her, cannot beat the Romans, then no one can."

The *kraa* of the raven in the tree was loud and almost—almost—drowned out the distant screech of the eagle.

PART SIX

THE WARRIOR

Kate Quinn

*They will not sustain even the din and the shout of so
many thousands, much less our charge and our blows.*
—Tacitus

DURO

THE Roman's head rolled across the ground and stopped on my foot.

The peaceful hum of the evening ground to a halt. My queen had been hearing my report on the wagon-loads of refugees and wounded I'd sent north after the fight at Verulamium, rasping a whetstone the length of her sword. A bard had been plucking softly at his harp in the tent's corner, singing some plaintive lay of seal-queens and sea gods, and the lamps flickered with the cooling breeze of evening. But the guards murmured outside, letting someone in, and when I glanced up, the severed head was already lolling against my foot, staring up at me.

A legionary. I'd killed enough to know the look, though the head was withered and desiccated. A young man, clean-shaven, his hair a white-blond rarely seen in swarthy Romans. A Gaul, then, from a tribe defeated so long ago their men had no qualms anymore about serving in Rome's legions. I felt no pity for the dead boy. I would sink a knife under my own breastbone before I'd let them cut my hair and replace my long-sword with a short gladius—if this one hadn't minded being Romanized, he deserved death.

"The sacrifice was made," a boy's voice said as the harp trailed away. "The sacrifice is complete. Andraste assures us victory."

Boudica's head snapped up, and we traded glances as a young Druid came into the light. A *Druid*— we had lost our own Druid in the sack of the sacred isle of Mona, and I had seen no others since despite reports of survivors coming to join us. Hope leaped in my chest at the sight of this boy, wide-eyed and skinny, his robe grimy with travel dust and old blood spatters.

"I found him four miles north of the war band. Making his way here with a guide." Another voice, quiet and commanding—my son's voice. I had not even noticed him enter the tent in the Druid's wake. Andecarus looked older than his twenty-seven years, tired and dusty, as he always was after a long scouting ride. He'd been taking a great many of those lately to avoid me. He addressed the queen as he indicated the Druid boy. "He insisted on being brought to you at once."

"I am Yorath." The Druid came toward the queen on thorn-ripped feet. "The gods sent me visions of you, Queen Boudica, and I have traveled far to join you. The gods delayed my arrival, gave me many trials over many weeks. But I have brought you victory."

He rambled on, something about how he had survived Mona with the aid of the gods, had seen the queen's daughter, had delayed joining us to make a proper sacrifice—but it was the word *victory* that sharpened my queen's gaze.

"Andraste showed you a sign?" she asked.

The Druid smiled, serene as a lake. "When I made sacrifice, a beam of sunlight lit the open clearing, and an owl flew through to seize its prey. Victory is assured. We will meet the Romans in open battle, and we will crush them utterly."

Boudica's eyes flared, and I saw my son, Andecarus, shifting his feet. "Open battle?"

Yorath nodded. "Only by confronting them openly—placing our fate in one throw for the gods to dictate as they will—do we win."

I glanced at my queen, but she only looked back at her sword, letting the whetstone resume its leisurely rasp. "Druid, you are most welcome in my camp. Andecarus, see he is given food and shelter befitting his rank."

I picked up the severed head, returning it to him reverently. "Spread word through the war band of Andraste's favor."

Boudica nodded. The boy stroked his emaciated fingers over

the bloody white-blond hair of the sacrificed legionary. "Felix was his name. He died happy. Another good omen!"

I nodded. I wasn't a man to doubt omens. The queen did—she had a questioning mind that probed everything it saw for shadows, but my view was straighter and blunter. It was one reason we worked so well together, countering each other's strengths.

"I'll see you settled." Andecarus ushered the Druid out, still managing to avoid addressing me. I glowered at his lean back as he disappeared from sight.

"It's good your son was the one to find him," Boudica commented, seeing my gaze. "It will restore his reputation in the war band if he's the one to bring us a Druid."

I winced inside. I was Boudica's right-hand man, and no one doubted my loyalty . . . But my son was another matter. Andecarus had fostered with the Romans as a child, a hostage of good behavior after the *last* rebellion, and he'd returned more Roman in his ways than anyone liked to see, myself included. The fact that he'd killed his foster brother in a fight after Verulamium last month didn't aid his reputation, either. Even though that fight was justified, the queen needed her warriors alive and fighting Rome, not killing each other.

Sons. I swear to Andraste, they were only put on this earth to plague their fathers.

"Duro." My queen's voice roused me from brooding as the bard resumed his song. "What do you think the Druid's omen means?"

"Andraste favors us." I sat, feeling the ache in my bad knee. "Our goddess of war has given us three victories. Three cities, plucked like plums. Rome is reeling."

It gave me such fierce pleasure to say those words.

Boudica continued whetting her sword, her scarred and capable hands moving in long strokes. My queen looked not unlike a sword herself: lean and spare as a blade, nicked up and down with scars along her bare arms like a sword's nicked edge after a raid, nothing soft in her long, tense body or her hawk-like gaze. I'd stood among the king's warriors the day he wed her nearly twenty years ago, seeing a girl of sixteen, tall enough to look even me in the eye—a girl with straight, glowering brows and a bridal wreath clapped over her tangle of rough red hair, and I'd thought you might as well hang a flower garland on a sword.

"Open battle," she said at last, thoughtful. "It's not the way I'd choose to do it."

I had been hearing her thoughts on the subject for years, when this rebellion had consisted of Boudica and me in the forest on moonless nights, burying caches of weapons under rocks for some hoped-for future fight. "Our chiefs have no discipline," she had said often.

"We stand a better chance of destroying Rome's legions if we whittle them by attrition," she said now. "Melting from the shadows to fight and then melting back—that was Caratacus' way."

"Caratacus went to Rome in chains," I reminded her.

"Because his chiefs grew impatient and forced him into open battle."

"Because that bitch-queen Cartimandua turned him in when he fled to the Brigantes. You should have let me cut her throat at your husband's funeral."

"Perhaps I should have." But Boudica looked pensive, spinning her sword on its tip, her lean fingers flexing. "She warned me."

"Of what? She's afraid, and she should be. As long as she's been sucking Rome's cock, she knows what's coming when we kick them back to the pit they crawled out of. Once they're not here to protect her—"

Boudica waved that aside. "She's a coward, but it doesn't make her wrong. We don't win when we fight the legions openly."

"We've never faced them with a force as great as this," I pointed out. "And the Druid says the gods guarantee us victory." I liked open battle. Where was the honor in formations and maneuvers? A screaming charge to set the blood on fire, swift killing, burials for the dead and honors for the living—*that* was war. But Boudica was my queen, and I'd been her champion for years, ever since I'd seen she had the same fire Caratacus did. A certain madness was needed to take on a war like this, to spit in the eye of an emperor and all his legions. She had it, and I'd fight her war any way I was ordered.

"Having a Druid to read our omens changes everything. There will have to be a war council." Boudica grimaced. "I hate war councils. Why can I not order the chiefs to follow my commands and have done with it?"

"Because we are not Romans." It's the glory of our people—a frustrating glory, to be sure, for anyone who has ever tried to lead us. We do not answer cow-like to a single ruler: every chief has a voice; every chief has a vote. You wish to lead the Iceni, you must convince us *why* before we stir a finger toward our blades. We are free men. Free women. Not Roman dogs to submit to whips and inventories.

I rose from my stool, grimacing as the old ache settled into my bad knee. I had a Roman slave I'd taken from Londinium; she was a bitch, but her massaging fingers were a miracle on my old wound. "Quarrels to be settled tomorrow," I reminded my queen. "Disputes over the plunder from Verulamium."

Queen Boudica nodded, the gold torc about her neck winking in the lamplight, and I slipped from the tent. The war bands were at last on the move again after nearly a month's halt by Verulamium. The vast field of tents and campfires spread before me like a field of stars. I heard the distant shouts: men swearing, women singing, slaves working; the creak of harness and the whicker of chariot ponies and the chink of metal. I smelled smoke and blood and hope.

So many warriors had come to fight for my queen. More than Caratacus ever had. Enough to take even Rome by the throat.

I was Duro, champion of queens and adviser of kings; my name was known wherever tribesmen traded wine and song. I was the man who slew six Coritani warriors one by one, armed with nothing but a hand-axe. I was the man who defended a footbridge single-handed against the Trinovantes and dammed it either side with the dead. I was the man who faced a champion of the Cornovii, who boasted he would hang my old head from his door by my long gray hair. He might have given me the cut to my knee that still had me limping, but I ended that fight by hanging *his* head from *my* door. My sword was famous, decorated in fire-red enamel along the hilt, and the bards sang songs of my battles across six tribes. I had earned those songs because warriors may live brave, or they may live old—rarely both. But I had. I had seen fifty summers, and I was still a man to be feared in the rush of spears. I had defied the odds. I would continue to do so. I would see Rome fall, and that was a promise.

I touched my sword hilt, sealing the vow, and returned to my own tent, wishing I could make my own son believe it.

VALERIA

HER captor's son came to the tent while Valeria was lighting the lamps. "I've returned from the latest scouting run," Andecarus said, rehanging the last lamp for her. "Brought back a wandering Druid, but there was other news as well. Governor Paulinus has encamped his men and is sending for the Second Augusta to join his ranks—we intercepted one of the dispatches."

"How far away?" Valeria's hunger for news of her fellow Romans was bottomless. Andecarus was kind enough to feed it.

"Perhaps a month's march for a war band this large."

Already a month since the sacking of Verulamium. Everyone knew battle was coming next—the Iceni and their red-haired queen would at last face Governor Paulinus and the legions of Rome. *Die screaming, you savages,* Valeria thought, giving the lamps a vicious clang, but she couldn't withhold a nod of thanks for her captor's son. "Thank you, Andecarus. You're a good boy to bring me news."

He was hardly a boy—just a few years younger than she, really—but Valeria couldn't think of him as anything else. It had been her household where Andecarus had fostered as a young hostage, after all. He was a good boy, even if he was an Iceni barbarian. Valeria didn't hope *he* died screaming. Just his father, his queen, and all the rest.

Andecarus' eyes touched the tattoo at the base of her throat. She'd been the Roman lady who ruled his boyhood, the procurator's nobly born wife. Now she was his father's slave. The irony was not lost on Valeria, either.

He gave a nod of farewell—he always left before his father returned—and when he was gone, Valeria reached up and touched her tattoo: a crude symbol like a coiled moon, borne by all Duro's slaves. "What does it mean?" she had said when he marked it into her flesh the day he claimed her in Londinium. Terrified, but not showing it because a Roman did not show fear.

"It means nothing." His huge rough hand had drilled the needle along her skin like a line of fire. "All it means is *mine.*"

Later that day, Valeria had dragged herself to the dull bronze mirror in Duro's quarters and looked at the mark, revolted. A *tattoo.* She looked like a barbarian woman, blue-inked, her silk *stola* replaced by one of those hideous striped cloaks. "You are not a barbarian," she had informed her own reflection through clenched teeth, yanking at her wild hair until she'd tamed it into its usual tidy knot. "You are Valeria of the Sulpicii. Your name is proud, your blood is ancient—"

And your family would disown you, the thought continued in a poisonous whisper. *Because you offered your neck to a needle and your body to a barbarian rather than fall on a sword like an honorable Roman.*

Valeria had not looked at the tattoo since, but she could still feel it pulse at the base of her throat, like an evil god had marked her dishonor with a dark thumbprint.

But that mark meant she was *safe*— that was the bitter truth. Duro was the queen's right-hand man, champion of the Iceni. No one touched what was his, and that meant no one ever laid a hand on Valeria when she moved through the colorful tents carrying water or kindling. No one aimed a kick at her or told her to get on her knees and open her mouth. Not like the slave girls belonging to lesser warriors, the girls who Valeria had seen handed around as interchangeably as blankets. Not like the few other Roman women who had been taken alive and not killed outright—they had it even worse. And Valeria knew with an icy shiver that she, as the wife of the hated procurator who had ordered the Iceni queen's flogging, should have had it worst of all. Almost the moment she was captured in Londinium, she'd heard one of the warriors—Duro's hulking foster son, he was *nothing* like Andecarus—say casually, "We should stake that little bitch over a fire and feed her to the dogs."

Valeria had frozen in a sick, ice-water drench of terror, hearing those words. Maybe that was the moment Valeria of the Sulpicii, such as she was, ceased to exist. The moment family honor, wifely virtue, Roman *gravitas*—all those things she'd drunk in with her wet nurse's milk—fell away like a sloughed skin. It hadn't taken

very much, after all. Just a few words from a hulking savage, and
honor fell away to reveal a woman who would scheme, crawl, and
fight to the death as long as it meant survival.

Survival. What a thing to have to worry about. For so long,
Valeria's worries had seemed mountain-sized—worries for her
husband's flagging career, worries that she would disappoint her
illustrious family. But from the moment Londinium came under
attack this summer, the moment that found Valeria hiding in her
villa, helping the slaves barricade the door, all those mountain-
sized worries shrank to grains of sand. The only worry left was
survival—and survival was not the shrill yammer of ambition
and disappointment, but a small matter-of-fact voice that had
spoken up when the barricaded doors splintered apart. The voice
that said firmly, *Make yourself useful to one of those warriors who
just swaggered in, or you will be dead.*

"Well," Valeria said aloud now, mocking herself. "At least you
whored yourself out well." A lifetime of entering a crowded atrium
on her husband's arm and being able to tell instantly which of a
dozen droning men in togas was the most important—that skill
had not deserted her, because she'd chosen the queen's champion
without hesitation from the crowd of blood-splashed warriors.
She'd stepped out from the weeping slave women, straight and
proud, and nailed her gaze to Duro's. She was a craven, dishonored slave, but at least she'd enslaved herself to the right master.
For the small price of a tattoo and every ideal she'd ever held dear,
Valeria was safe.

Night had fallen, the camp outside awash in brawls and beer,
the night chilly now that autumn had descended. Valeria finished
lighting the lamps. The tent was spacious by barbarian standards:
a bed heaped with furs, a heavy painted war shield hung on the
wall beside a spear with a shaft thick as Valeria's wrist. No books,
of course, no scrolls or ornaments. A tribesman's idea of decorat-

ing a home was a line of skulls over the door. Valeria glowered at them, remembering her husband's farm in Gaul—that little rustic villa he was so inexplicably fond of. She'd never liked it; it was so small and cramped compared to their house in Rome. But it had an atrium; it had civilized couches for dining; it had proper baths with *heated water*. And no skulls. Valeria thought she would happily slit a throat for a chance to see that villa again. Preferably Duro's throat, but she wasn't choosy.

She had a sudden vision of her husband, Decianus, at that same villa, so clear she could almost reach out and touch him. Catus Decianus with sunlight on his thinning hair, patient hands fiddling with an abacus as he looked out over a field of sheep. Counting coins and sheep; it was the life he wanted, and Valeria sent a brief prayer that he was enjoying it. *You should have fallen on a sword*, she thought, *when you failed in your duties in Londinium and left your mess behind you. But I should have fallen on a sword, too, rather than let myself be dishonored, so I am no better than you.*

And of the two of them, at least Decianus could have a hot bath.

Valeria's captor entered then, ducking his massive height through the door flap. He was perhaps fifty, built like a craggy old oak, with a gray mane of hair like an aging lion. His weather-beaten face seemed permanently set to amusement, ferocity, or amused ferocity, and he slanted a brow to find Valeria curled up on the heap of wolf-skins. "You are the laziest slave I've ever picked up," he said and held out his hands. "Water."

"I know how to manage slaves." Valeria fetched a basin as he unpinned the gold brooch at one shoulder and shrugged out of his green cloak. "Not *be* one."

He splashed his muddy hands, giving a mirthless grin. "Slavery looks well on you, Roman."

"Romans wear everything well."

"I look forward to seeing you all in chains, then."

"It will be a long wait, barbarian."

He hit her, something he did very precisely. Always a snap under the chin, not hard enough to mark her skin, but precisely placed to snap her head back with a warning wrench. Valeria felt the sting sharply, but pleasure came with it. The smack was worth the satisfaction of proving to him that a Roman didn't show fear. That was the one ideal she'd been raised with that still held *any* use. Dishonored or not, a Roman woman did not cower.

So she didn't rub her throbbing jaw, just brought her eyes to his and smiled sweetly. "Towel?"

Duro shook his head. "What a bitch you are." His tone was grimly humorous. It was a game they played, the game where Valeria deliberately provoked her captor until he hit her. She suspected they both rather enjoyed it: he liked hitting Romans, and she liked proving Romans weren't afraid of savages. "I'm not surprised your husband ran all the way to Gaul," Duro went on. "You must have been the man in that marriage."

I should have been. Valeria had dreams where she was the one who organized the defense of Londinium, the way she'd begged Decianus before he'd fled and she'd refused to flee with him—in her dream, the Iceni were pushed back instead of swarming the city. Impossible dreams. The Iceni would have swarmed the city anyway. Decianus had seen that clearly—he'd been the clever one, leaving for Gaul while the going was good. Even if the savages could have been repulsed, only in the logic of dreams did women give orders to warriors.

Well, that red-haired harpy Boudica did. But she was unnatural.

Duro dried his face, raking damp fingers through his hair. His broad arms were stacked with arm rings, bronze and gold winking in the light. Iceni men adorned themselves like women.

Valeria brought mead in a looted Roman wine cup, and he flung himself down on the furs and stripped off his right boot. "I could use those magic fingers of yours on this knee, Roman."

He never called her anything but *Roman*. "It wouldn't pain you if you kept off it, barbarian." She never called him anything but *barbarian*. Another game they played.

"Sit by the fire like an old man, with my feet propped on cushions? Fuck that. I'll die in battle with a sword in hand."

Or I'll cut your throat in the night. Valeria's smile was twice as sweet.

Duro noted it. "Try anything, and I'll gut you. Then give you to my warriors for a good beating."

Someday he might, if he tired of the games they played. Valeria still couldn't stop her own tongue. "Shouldn't you do it the other way around?" she inquired as she pushed up the leg of his woolen trousers. "Beating first, then gutting?"

"That's a Roman for you. Always knows a better way to do everything."

"It's not an accident we rule the world, you know."

"Not this corner of it. And you're still a lot of know-it-all bores who should be put to the sword."

His knee was scarred by an old battle wound, seamed and purple. Valeria worked foul-smelling goose grease into her hands—oh, for the lotus oil from her private baths in Londinium!—and went to work.

Duro gave a hiss of pain, falling back on his elbows. "You work magic with those hands, but it's cruel magic."

Her massage skills were another reason he kept her, Valeria knew that. He could always find a prettier bed warmer, but not one who had learned from trained masseuses in Rome. Valeria had rubbed Decianus' shoulders when he was a young tribune—he wasn't a very good tribune; he was always pulling muscles, so Valeria learned to massage his aches. When had that fond habit fallen off? *Probably when your mother told you it lowered your dignity to tend your husband like a slave.*

Valeria blinked the memory away. "Talk," she told Duro, kneading his twisted muscles. "It keeps your mind off the pain."

"Don't give me orders." But after a moment's silence, he began speaking. He always did. "A Druid arrived in camp today."

"I know. Your son told me."

That earned her a slitted glance. Her captor did not take kindly to the fact that his Roman slave had had the raising of his only son. Which was why Valeria brought it up whenever possible. Another sweet smile. "Such a good boy," she murmured. "What a nice quaestor or tribune he'd have made instead of a barbarian in braids."

That got her another clip to the jaw. "The Druid brought us good omens," Duro continued. "He made sacrifice of a Roman legionary and brought the head with promise of Andraste's favor."

Heads again. That poor legionary. Had anyone put a coin in his mouth after he died for the ferry ride into Pluto's realm? Probably not; that would be too civilized for a Druid. Valeria gave an extra-vengeful jab at the back of her captor's knee.

"He's young for a Druid." Duro sipped his mead. "Maybe eighteen. But the gods spared him for a reason."

"Eighteen? That is ridiculous. It takes decades of training to read the future in a spill of ox-guts!"

"It takes skill to strangle a man with a ligature and cut his throat in the same motion, but our skinny little Druid evidently managed all right. Maybe our holy men learn faster than your priests."

"The gods of Rome do not approve of human sacrifice." That

was not *strictly* true, historically speaking, but Valeria decided not to muddy a good argument with minor details.

"Yes, you Romans don't kill men for your gods, but you're perfectly willing to kill them for your entertainment. Gladiatorial games—your gods smile on *those*."

Valeria dipped more goose grease, shifting mentally to stronger ground. She'd never been a great enthusiast for gladiatorial games; her family always took the view that they were vulgar and should be outlawed—but the plebs adored the whole crass spectacle, and frankly it wasn't a point in her favor when arguing with a barbarian about inherent Roman superiority. As if such a thing needed to be argued. "You may have your Druid," she said, massaging the scar. "We have legions."

He looked amused. "You think I fear your legions?"

If they were my *legions you would*. Decianus had said once that she could run a legion every bit as well as she ran a household. He hadn't meant it precisely as a compliment, but Valeria knew she *could* have run a legion. She used to tamp such thoughts down as unseemly, but nothing in life now was seemly. "Our legions have conquered the world," she said instead.

"And we've beaten them. We destroyed the Ninth at Camulodunum—"

"Not in open battle. Roman discipline will always carry the day in open battle." Valeria knew that as surely as she knew Jove ruled in the heavens. Hadn't she grown up hearing her father and uncles and cousins—legates, tribunes, men with illustrious campaigns to their names—expound on the wonder that was legionary discipline? "There is nothing that can face a properly ranked formation of Roman legionaries on well-chosen ground," she quoted her father.

Duro's smile was like the thin edge of a blade. "Who said anything about *facing* them?"

Valeria strangled her unease before he could see it. The natives loved headlong charges, and in headlong charges, they died—it was when patience ruled the day that things changed. Painted tribesmen falling from the shadows to slaughter Roman legionaries, then disappearing again—that was how Caratacus had held out so long. That was how eagle standards had disappeared before in Germania. Thank the gods most barbarians were too undisciplined for stealth campaigns.

Most of them. Valeria met her captor's gaze and saw an ocean of calm, savage patience. She found herself offering a prayer, not to any of the Roman gods but to the strident red-haired Boudica. *Listen to your Druid*, Valeria thought. *Listen to the ones who tell you the only honor is in a headlong charge.*

She met Duro's eyes long enough to prove she had not flinched, then returned to his knee.

"Silence from a Roman?" Duro rumbled. "That's new."

She finished, wiping down her hands. "Romans don't argue with the uninformed."

He sat forward, coming nose to nose with her. "I'm tired of your tongue. Put it to better use or get out of my tent."

She didn't flinch from his face, scant inches away. "Force me."

"Why?" He didn't touch her, just gave his edged smile again. "Plenty of willing ones out there for the queen's champion."

You just like watching me choose every night, she thought. *My husband had your queen flogged, your son is more Roman than Iceni because he lived in my house—and you punish me for both by making me choose to bed you.*

Valeria had chosen that from the moment she was captured—she made no pretenses, not to herself. When Duro returned from supervising the sack of Londinium, she'd been naked in the bed furs and grimly, ferociously prepared to get on with things. Her life as a slave would be easier the more she pleased her captor, and a pleasing bedmate would be better treated than a sullen, weeping dishrag. She'd given herself willing from the first night and gone right on doing it.

She leaned forward and nailed her mouth to his, sinking her teeth into his lip and hearing him chuckle, not mistaking his amusement for anything but hatred. The grapple of limbs inside the furs was just another fight, the only kind Duro had between battles, the only kind Valeria had at all. She hated the tribesmen, and he hated the Romans; it was bright, visceral loathing that leaped between them with a heat that left her bruised from the weight of his grip and him bleeding from the marks of her nails and teeth. As a substitute for passion, it worked very well. Roman wives were restrained in lovemaking, but her husband was gone, as were honor and restraint, and Sulpicia Valeria was a savage's whore.

She wondered what else she was going to become before all this was done.

DURO

THERE is a moment every morning when I wake, when the world becomes old.

Each dawn I open my eyes, and for a moment I have woken into the world of my youth. Woken into a land where Latin is not spoken, where Roman sandals have left no footprints, where the horses clop on soft earth and not Roman roads. Where there are no thrusting, foul-smelling Roman cities with their officious square temples and their even more officious gods, no Roman taxes and Roman clerks with their endless totting up of what we owe. Where families have no aching gaps where sons were torn away to toil in Roman mines. Where the only fighting is in border spats and raids for cattle. Where the land is ours and ours alone, and Rome is gone.

That is how it was in my youth. The young ones now, they look to their childhoods, and Rome was always there—but the old know better. I am old, even though my sword arm is still strong, and I remember. Every night I dream of how it was, the beauty of this land before Rome came, and every morning I wake and think I am still there. And then I rise from my bed, and the smell of the empire rushes foul and stinking into my nose—the smell of conquest, blood, and pomp—and I remember that my beautiful world is now a sad, ruined place.

They ruined it. But I will take it back and make it as it was. My queen and I. Whatever the price.

I was training the two princesses this morning—or rather, little Keena hung back with her sword tip drooping while Sorcha did her best to kill me. We had an area of trampled grass behind Boudica's tent between a rack of war shields and a line of chariot ponies, and our breath steamed white—a long hot summer had at last turned to autumn, the days still warm but the nights and the mornings cold. The queen liked to watch her daughters train, but she was settling a dispute between quarreling chiefs who had already knifed each other, and I was happier when she stayed away. In her mother's presence, Keena's awkwardness with a blade doubled, and so did Sorcha's recklessness.

The elder princess was coming at me now, lips skinned back from her teeth, rough red hair strapped into four plaits. I beat back her lunge, smacking the flat of my own blade along her ribs. "Left yourself wide, see?" She nodded curtly, came at me again, and blade bit blade. She whipped past my wooden shield, stabbed at my side, came around for my head. I deflected her thrust and knocked her flat on the trampled grass. "Sloppy," I snapped as she glared up at me. "Too fast, too careless, and now you're too dead to do anything about it."

"If you hadn't short-footed me—"

"I thought you were here to fight, not whine."

"This isn't *fighting*," she flared. "Drills with practice shields? I could do this at ten years old. You said I fought well in Londinium and Verulamium—"

"Against rickety old veterans and screaming Catuvellauni. You think hardened legionaries will die as easy?"

She gave a grudging jerk of her chin, scrambling up and flying at me again. I stepped right into her this time and caught her along the ear with my hilt. "Too. Sloppy," I growled. "You keep letting your temper get the better of you, girl, and the next Roman soldier you face will skewer you. Fight angry if you want, but not if it makes you careless. Fight sloppy, get dead."

She glowered, as much at herself as at me. Sorcha had always been a fireheaded, fire-natured copy of her mother, burning like a torch—the lucky princess, we all called her, because her birth had been blessed and she seemed to spread good fortune wherever she sauntered. Now she still burned like a torch but with a fierce white-hot hatred, her freckled face pale with an almost permanent fury. The Romans had done that—despoiled my beautiful land and despoiled my princess, the girl I'd known all her life, in whose tiny hand I'd put her first wooden practice sword. If I ever found that centurion who had tossed her on a storehouse floor and encouraged his men to desecrate her and her sister, I'd lead him to Sorcha on a leash of his own entrails so she could geld him, kill him, and banish her nightmares. If such nightmares can ever be banished.

"Practice the strokes," I said. "But slower. Control, girl." She nodded, blade already in motion as I turned to her sister. "Now you, Keena."

The younger princess stabbed at me halfheartedly. "Again, harder," I encouraged, but her stroke wouldn't have killed a field mouse. She took after her father, dark-haired and narrow-faced, and she'd always been small, but now she was a bony little shadow; thirteen years old and looking no more than ten. After that Roman centurion and his men were gone, Sorcha had walked back to the Great Hall on her own two feet, white-faced and shaking, striking away any offer of help—but I'd had to carry Keena, her legs bloody and her little body trembling inside my cloak. If that day had lit a great fire in Sorcha, it had extinguished the flame utterly in her younger sister. She sparred with me every morning because she didn't dare disobey her mother, but I could have told Boudica plainly, *This one will never make a warrior.*

"That's enough for today," I told Keena, passing my hand gently over her hair. She gave me her shadowy smile, sliding away toward the tents of the injured, where she could help the healers tend our wounded fighters—it was the only place she seemed to muster any contentment. But Princess Sorcha kept going, her sword moving through a complicated pass. "You should rest," I said, but she gave a fierce shake of her head.

"Get me a Roman to kill. Then I'll rest."

"You've killed quite a few Romans." She'd had blood up to the tops of her arms after Verulamium—I'd hoped it would ease her tense fury, but it just seemed to stoke her further. She'd get herself killed in the next fight if she didn't keep a cooler head, and I opened my mouth to say so, but just then I saw my son crossing toward me, and my pulse leaped.

Andecarus. My only son was shorter than I, lithe as a hunting dog, his hair in a dark plait down his back. Too hairy for a Roman, too neat for a tribesman. He seemed lost in this world, and he'd avoided me ever since our quarrel after Verulamium. Maybe now was a chance to patch things up. I scrambled for an opening line ("Back from all your advance scouting?" "Done sulking at me yet, boy?"), but when he halted, all I managed was a gruff nod, keeping my eyes on Sorcha.

Andecarus spoke without preamble. "Will the queen call a war council?"

"Why? Looking for more news to tell my Roman bitch?" It annoyed me, the courtesy he showed Valeria, as though he were still a fosterling. Rome had stolen his youth from me and given it to her—didn't that matter to him? "You don't owe her anything, boy."

His face hardened, and I wished the words unsaid. Why did I always prickle at him when I didn't mean to? It had been like that since he came back to me from his hostage years. He'd gone away a shaggy pup in green breeches; he'd come back a wiry youth in Roman cavalry armor. "Look at the little Roman," I'd blurted, laughing as I stepped forward to embrace him—but his hazel eyes went flat and wary, just the way they looked now, and I knew I'd made a mistake. I hadn't meant it in mockery, just wanted to raise a chuckle at how many changes the passing years had wrought—but I'd done it all wrong. After that, he kept trying to please me, and I still kept getting it wrong.

And now he wasn't trying anymore.

Sorcha called over brusquely, sword still whistling through cold air in its practice strokes. "Andecarus, I need a sparring partner."

It was a kind of apology—Sorcha's hatred of the Romans had soured her trust in my son, at least until she saw him fight with us against them at Verulamium. I used to hope they'd make a match of it, my son and Queen Boudica's daughter—Sorcha definitely had an eye for him when she was younger, and the queen and I had planned a betrothal. But then the Romans had come, and now the lucky princess had no eye for anything but vengeance. "Spar with her," I nudged my son anyway, hoping. "Make it a horseback bout." No one rode like Andecarus—he'd ridden with Roman cavalry; on a horse, he was a sweep of death in motion. "He can teach you anything about fighting from a saddle, Sorcha—"

"Very Roman, I know," my son said, expressionless. "The Iceni only fight from foot or chariot."

Not what I meant, I thought, but a clash of iron and curses interrupted us. I ducked through the tents, bad knee protesting, and Andecarus sped past me. "Fucking Trinovantes," he cursed, wading into the fight that had clearly broken out between an Iceni chief and a Trinovante chief. Their retainers were all half-drunk, though it was still morning, lurching and pounding at each other. Andecarus started cracking heads together, and I laid the red-enameled hilt of my sword across any rump I could find, but it was a good while before the two sides disentangled sullenly.

"His shield bearer stole six cattle from me," the Trinovante chief roared, but I clipped him over the ear like a puppy.

"Settle it among yourselves without blows. No brawling, queen's orders." I smelled the stench of sour beer on his breath. "And keep your men sober."

"May as well order the stars to stop moving in the sky," Andecarus said as the men dispersed.

"What, that they stay sober or stop fighting?"

"Both."

At the beginning of our march from Iceni lands, the queen had kept the war band in tight order, limiting beer and mead. But three sacked cities meant there was plunder and strong Roman wine for anyone who wanted it. Triumph was making the men happy, swaggering, and eager to brawl. I shrugged. "Of course they're getting a little rowdy. They have victory in their grasp."

Andecarus gave me an exasperated look, as though I was the child and he the gray-beard. I bit back a retort because we'd already had this argument after Verulamium. He'd been flapping like a doom-crow for months, croaking about how many legions Rome could bring across the sea and how the Iceni would be dust on the wind once they were done. I didn't care how many legions Rome had; an Iceni champion was worth ten legionaries any day—but his opinion clearly hadn't changed.

"The queen's war council," I said for the sake of keeping the conversation going. "You should address the chiefs."

He looked sardonic. "Won't I poison their minds and weaken their knees with my doubts?"

He was throwing my own words at me. "The Druid promises us victory in open battle, but the queen still favors less frontal tactics. Like you." A Druid's promise was good enough for me, but Boudica was a priestess of Andraste, and if she wanted to doubt the Druid's vision and find her own, that was her right.

"The chiefs won't listen to me. Andecarus the Roman sympathizer—"

"I'll *make* them listen."

He gave a short laugh. "When you agree with nothing I say?"

"Whether I agree or not, the queen will want to hear it." I smiled, willing him to smile back. "I'll make sure you're heard." I'd happily sacrifice a little pride if it would get him to stop avoiding me.

"I'll speak, then." He turned away. "For now, I've got a horse to find."

"Still missing that cavalry mare of yours?"

"Since Londinium. Some chief probably claimed her."

I wanted to say he had better things to do than look for a horse. I wanted to say he should come eat with me, share a flask of mead. I wanted to say—

But there were warriors, freedmen, and chiefs clamoring for my attention, bringing me the problems of war. I didn't have time to watch my son stride away.

* * *

"FIND him his horse," my Roman slave advised.

I blinked. "What's his horse got to do with anything?"

"A peace offering." She was mending my torn cloak, making far finer stitches than it needed. I'd have told her to just slap a patch over it, but if there was anything I'd learned in fifty summers, it was that women will do things the way *they* want them done. All women, whether slaves, wives, or queens. "I've known your son since he was a boy—he has a gentle heart for animals. Find him his horse; he might decide to like you again."

Her fine black brows arched, indicating just how slight she thought the chance that anybody might ever like me. Her eyebrows were terrifying things. No wonder her husband had run clear across the sea to get away from them.

"I know how to handle my son," I grumped.

She gave me that sweet, edged smile. "Yes, *that's* going well."

I glowered, wondering if I should hit her again. But shouts, threats, and clips on the jaw did not work with this one—if I truly wanted her to hold her tongue, I'd have to give her a good beating, and frankly I lacked the energy. With all the petitioners consuming my hours, I never got back to my own tent until the moon was descending, and by that time all I wanted was mead and quiet. *Tomorrow,* I promised my Roman bed warmer silently. *I'll beat you tomorrow.*

"As I said, I know that boy of yours well."

She had to rub that in. I glared again, and she returned it. She was an odd picture in the lamplight, half-Iceni and half-Roman: small, straight-shouldered, swathed in a striped cloak, my slave mark blotting the hollow of her soft white throat. She still kept those brows plucked in their fine imperious arches with a little set of tweezers, and her black hair was coiled atop her head like she was going to dine with the emperor. She was perhaps thirty (she looked younger—Roman women always did; they lived so soft) and the other warriors said a queen's champion deserved a younger, prettier bedmate, but at fifty summers, the girls of fifteen looked like weeping infants to me. I couldn't stand weeping women, and this one never wept. Maybe all Roman women were like that—I'd never had one for a slave before, and I confess the thought had pleased me when I claimed her. Catus Decianus was the man who had held my son hostage as a boy, ordered my queen flogged last year, and left my princesses to be defiled by legionaries—yes, I enjoyed having his wife wear my tattoo. But that hadn't turned out quite as I'd thought it would, and you'd think that with fifty summers to my name, I'd have learned that with women, it *never* does.

My Roman held up her bone needle with a frown. "Are there no good bronze or iron needles in this camp? Three cities sacked and you people grabbed all the wine and coin you could lay hands on; did not one of you think to loot a proper needle? In any case, barbarian, your son is a good lad. Not *quite* as barbaric when he left my house as when he arrived, I like to think."

"You turned him halfway Roman." That came out a growl.

"I turned him halfway civilized." She tied off her thread; shook out my mended cloak. "He turned out better than that brutish young man *you* fostered."

Why did I let the bitch talk so freely? My father would have sliced her tongue out by now. "Verico was a brute, but a useful brute. I made him a fine warrior, and the queen needs good warriors, whatever their other faults."

He is no more my brother than you are my father. Words Andecarus had spat at me in Verulamium, and just thinking of them made me flinch like a sword had gone through my gut. Like Andecarus' blade had gone through Verico's throat. "If they could've become friends . . ." My Roman snorted, and I slanted a glance at her. "It's how you raise sons, woman! Pit them against each other like pups. They fight, they hate each other, they brawl it out, and then they end friends."

The eyebrows again. She was straightening my tent now, like a Roman legion whirling through drills. "Is that how your father raised you?"

"Yes. I had four brothers—we beat each other, broke each other's noses, hated each other. Would have died for each other, too." All of them dead now but me. Two in the Scapula rebellion, one to a Roman patrol having a little fun, one swept up by slave traders and never seen again. I missed them all still. In the morning, when I woke to the world as it was, my brothers were still alive. "Brothers fight," I mumbled and realized my throat had gone thick.

"And sometimes brothers kill each other."

I should have demanded a blood price against Andecarus for what he'd done. My father would have taken my sword hand off himself, told me never to darken his door again. I couldn't do the same to my son, but I'd always known I was weak compared to my father. Did Andecarus know how my love for him had weakened me?

Weak old man. That was my father's voice, harsh as a raven's, loud and clear in my mind, though he'd been dead more than a decade. "Fathers and sons," I heard myself saying. How they haunted each other! "Is it the same for mothers and daughters?" Did Princess Sorcha feel it, looking at her whip-marked, sword-made queen of a mother?

"Yes," my Roman slave answered, surprising me. She had paused, refilling my mead. "No daughter can ever be her mother, and yet we all try."

Gods, what a horror *her* mother must have been. "My father thought I was the runt of the litter," I heard myself saying.

"My mother told me I failed my husband by not giving him sons."

We eyed each other with rather grim little smiles. "Childless, then," I mocked. "Yet you tell me how to raise *my* son?"

"I *did* raise your son."

"Enough of that," I said sharply and rolled up my trouser leg. She was a slave; she might needle me, but it was all she could do. "I could use your hands on my knee."

She fetched the goose grease, shaking her head at my purple scar. "That would have healed without a limp if you'd had a proper *medicus*. I suppose some Druid waved a magic feather over it?"

"A magic skull," I said, just a little defensive.

"Skulls again. Can't you barbarians decorate a tent with anything else?"

"What's wrong with a bit of bone?" I liked a nice line of skulls over the door. It said *home* to me. Mine all had names—enemies I'd killed, the notable ones, anyway, and I could tell you the story of how I'd brought each one down.

"Women don't like bones as decor, in general."

"Queen Boudica does. Got a line to rival mine."

"She's not a woman," my slave sniffed.

"According to you Romans!" I hooted. "Gods, why do they keep their women as useless as you? We *use* our women. They speak in council, they drive their own chariots—" I broke off in a hiss as she dug her thumbs into my knee's weak spot. The bitch loved hurting me. I let her because, gods, her fingers were turning my twisted muscles to liquid.

"Civilized women know their place," she informed me, kneading my old wound with a zeal well past cruelty and into the inhuman. "We take our pride in the achievements of our husbands and sons, as is proper."

"Well, you haven't got a husband or a son right now, so what do you take pride in?"

That hit her where it hurt, I could tell, but the face she turned on me was a stone shield, and her eyes spat murder. This one could have been a warrior if she'd been born to the Iceni. I liked women who could fight—Andecarus' mother had been a bitch and a half, but she could hold her own with a sword. It was a Coritani cattle raid that took her; a wound in the thigh that turned bad. I'd mourned her.

"If you're a Roman wife who knows her place," I said with another wince for the merciless thumbs digging at my knee, "did you strop your husband with that razor you call a tongue?"

"Never," she said virtuously. "Well—except the day Londinium was invaded, but that was under *extreme* duress. In all other ways, I was quiet and deferential, as a wife should be."

I snorted. "Don't believe it."

"It's true!"

"Then if you endured fifteen years of meekness, Roman, it's no wonder you're letting loose on me."

She let loose on me in other ways. She raked my back with her nails every night like she was trying to peel the flesh off my bones, which she probably was. I was wincing the next morning as I shrugged a tunic down over the new scratches she'd laid over the old ones when one of my warriors came to tell me the news: Governor Paulinus and his legions were on the move.

VALERIA

COUNCILS assembling for momentous decisions should not, Valeria decided, be this colorful. If you looked out at a sea of white togas, the effect was calming: you knew the men about to make a momentous decision were educated, calm, probably not armed, certainly not intoxicated. Looking out at Boudica's war council was not calming. Hundreds of chiefs had flocked to the center of camp in scarlet cloaks and yellow cloaks, striped breeches and tasseled breeches, torcs and arm rings of bronze and silver, plaited hair and matted hair and hair limed into spiky points. It looked like a rainbow mated with a riot, and *everyone* was getting drunk.

"Are you imagining a room full of white togas?" Andecarus asked at her side, reading her mind. He had offered to escort her to the war council, and his status as Duro's son secured them a place in the first circle.

"It's more colorful than I'm used to." The vast crowd had the air of a festival: children running back and forth, dogs sprawled on the crushed grass, slaves moving through with bread and meat, jugs of mead, and stolen amphorae of Roman wine, which of *course* the savages drank unwatered. "But I'm starting to wonder if *all* councils are the same—men getting up one after the other to demonstrate how much they love the sound of their own voices." That was perhaps the only thing an Iceni war council and a cluster of Roman senators had in common. The queen was not even present yet, and a chief in an orange cloak was already droning away.

Andecarus smiled. "All Iceni love to talk, Lady." Valeria nearly told him the honorific was ridiculous, but it was pleasant to get an honorific at all when she only heard "Roman" from Duro and "Roman bitch" from everyone else.

Queen Boudica made her entrance then, inciting a cascade of roars as she arrowed through the throng in long impatient strides like a man. She wore a rust-colored gown under a red cloak, and her loose red hair was crowned by a gold circlet studded with chunks of amber. She settled into the fur-draped chair at the center, shrugging back her cloak, and Valeria shuddered at the sight of the scars on her arms, not to mention the inked tattoo of a raven's wing. The queen of the Iceni was the most unwomanly thing Valeria had ever seen in her entire life. No wonder Roman men all over Britannia had run for the hills; she was *terrifying*.

Standing behind his queen, Duro raised his arm and roared for silence. Boudica rose, speaking into the hush. "The Roman governor has begun his march. He advances southeast, and slowly."

Another storm of cheers. "Coward!" chiefs and warriors cried. "The shitting coward fears to meet us!"

"He's not afraid," Andecarus muttered. "He's taking his time looking for advantageous ground."

Boudica calmed the storm with a raised fist, hair blowing around her like a cloud of flame. "Paulinus looks for a place to meet in open battle. Do we give it to him, chieftains? Or do we strike his army unawares as we took Cerialis?"

There was a good deal more in this vein, and every line in Boudica's bronze trumpet of a voice provoked cheers. At last the queen took her seat, and Duro rose before any other man could claim the council's attention.

"The gods promise victory in an open fight," he said, folding his arms across his broad chest. "But there are other tactics to consider. My son knows better than any how the Romans fight—we will hear him speak."

A few growls sounded, but Duro sent a glare around the assembly, and Andecarus rose into the silence. "Do not face the Romans openly. Harry Governor Paulinus through the winter instead, striking from the shadows, and his men will be corpses feeding the ravens by spring. And then"—Andecarus turned, young and fierce, to meet every wary eye—"when the Romans look west, they will think twice about sending more legions from Gaul to finish us! If we make this island too much an expense in lives, they will let us keep it . . ."

I should have left him a savage instead of Romanizing him, Valeria mourned. *If Queen Boudica defeats Governor Paulinus and Rome loses Britannia all because my husband and I taught that boy the value of discipline and restraint . . .*

If that happened, maybe Valeria really *would* fall on a sword.

"Avoid open conflict," Andecarus finished with a bow to the queen, "and we seal a lasting victory."

"Afraid to meet your *friends* head on?" a young warrior in the front circle mocked. Andecarus just set his jaw, but Duro erupted to his feet.

"My son stacked Roman corpses wall-high at Verulamium. I don't remember seeing *you* in the first line of shields, puppy. Make that insult again and I'll cram it down your throat with iron."

He waited, fist on hilt, but the young warrior wilted. Andecarus sank down silently, face set. "I wish he hadn't done that," he muttered as his father sent a final glare around the crowd

"What, defended you?"

"I don't need defending."

Sons, Valeria thought. Maybe it was just as well she didn't have any. "You made a good speech," she said as another speaker rose. *Unfortunately.*

The next chief to speak, thank the gods, argued for open battle. "Why all this discussion?" Valeria whispered. "Can't your queen simply command them to the course she prefers?"

"It doesn't work that way with the Iceni, Lady. Each chief has a voice and an oath—they gave their oaths to Boudica, but they have the right to take their warriors home at the campaign's end. To advance past the war season into the autumn, she must have their votes."

"No wonder you never get anything done! If this were Rome, the emperor would issue orders, and his orders would be carried out. It's the only civilized way to proceed. This voting business is so *inefficient*—"

"Inefficient," Andecarus admitted as more chiefs rose to speak. "But fair. One man's will does not dictate the future for all. There are no tyrants among us, only free men and free women."

"That's why we conquered you. Free men and free women do not agree on *anything*. They need an emperor or at least a senate to tell them what they want. You think Rome could govern the earth with rules this disorganized?"

"We aren't trying to govern the earth," Andecarus retorted. "Only our little corner of it. And for an island, it works well enough."

"So say you. *I* say this fair play business will be the death of you all."

A figure in a white robe came forward, and everyone fell silent for the Druid. "I saw omens today," he said simply. "A hare ran across my path, and it spoke to me of victory. A crow spiraled through sunlight and spoke to me of victory, too. But only if we put our trust in Andraste." He raised his staff, and Valeria recoiled at the human head on its spike, its features stretched in spectral decay. *Savages,* she thought all over again, *I am among savages*—and suddenly yearned for a Roman temple, clean and cool, where the only offering might be a dove or a pig but never a quaking, screaming human being. She thought suddenly of her husband, who hated to see even animal sacrifices, and wanted to weep. In this crowd of barbarians who put heads on spikes and hung skulls over doors, she wanted Catus Decianus with his ink-stained hands and gentle smile.

"We put our faith in the gods," the Druid was saying. There was something in his rapt, moon-like eyes she found distinctly unsettling, but the chiefs watched him fervently. "Andraste will reward us with victory only if we march on the Romans. We stake all on one battle, and the raven will feast on the eagle."

The roar that went up deafened Valeria's ears. Duro gave a savage nod. Andecarus leapt to his feet, protesting. Boudica's face was proud and immobile. Chiefs reached out to touch the Druid, who smiled radiantly as he raised the severed head to the sky. Warriors clapped each other on the shoulder, swearing victory.

But Valeria remembered the chill, immaculate figure of Suetonius Paulinus. The man she had met half a hundred times, with his cool gaze and pristine armor and wintry smile. And she thought, with cautious hope, *You have all just lost your war.*

It was near dawn when Valeria's captor finally returned to his tent. Valeria was curled up on the furs, smiling a little. She had been smiling since the war council ended. "What are you smirking at, Roman?" Duro asked, shrugging out of his cloak.

Valeria rose to light the lamp, brushing back her loose hair. "Imminent victory."

"Kind of you to congratulate us." He unstrapped his sword. She smelled mead and beer on him, but he was not staggering drunk as so many of the chiefs were by the time the war council broke up. "Can you be getting fond of barbarians, if you're cheering for our imminent victory?"

"Not your victory," she said sweetly. "Ours." There was no better commander in the west than Suetonius Paulinus. He might not have the advantage of numbers, but given his experience and the benefits of legionary discipline . . .

"Our war band numbers more than one hundred thousand warriors." Duro drew the words out. "Your Governor Paulinus has perhaps ten thousand soldiers cobbled together. How does he beat us with that?"

One hundred thousand. In the middle of the war band, the spread of children and dogs, cattle and wagons, warriors and chariots, Valeria had not seen that the spread was so vast. The number made her pulse leap in sudden doubt, but she thrust doubt and fear away. "Nothing beats our legionary discipline." Not even such staggering numbers. Surely that was true.

Carrhae, doubt whispered in her mind. *Rome lost there, discipline or no. And at Cannae . . .*

Valeria was not going to think about Cannae. Boudica was not Hannibal, and Rome was not going to lose.

"Ten to one odds, Roman," came Duro's implacable voice. "Think on that."

He wore such a complacent expression as he flung himself down that Valeria itched to slap him. "Tell me something, barbarian." He didn't have to tell her anything, but with that smug expression, he'd be dying to talk. "If you *do* win, what happens?"

"Life returns to what it was before Rome." Duro smiled. "This world becomes what it should have stayed."

"Nothing ever goes back," Valeria stated. "There's no returning to the days that were." *What would I do if I could go back to the day I wed Catus Decianus?* Married a different man, an ambitious man more in the mold of her ever-striving family? Not pushed Decianus to take the post of procurator, the sort of post he hated but her father and brothers thought appropriate?

Or she could have said *yes* when her husband told her to flee Londinium with him ahead of Boudica's horde instead of stubbornly refusing to run—now that would be an *excellent* decision to get back. Imagine, she could have heard about the Iceni rebellion and its mad red-haired queen from the safety of her atrium in Gaul and just said, "How terrible," and gone on about her day.

"You have no idea how beautiful this world was before you Romans came and wrecked it." Duro shook his head, staring at the lamp as though gazing into a dream. "Mist hovering over the hills, not smoke from your paved towns. Roads winding around the path of the earth, not cutting through it in your straight stone lines. Freshwater springs coming up wild, each with their own little god, not being dammed up for your wells . . ."

Oh, now, really, Valeria thought in exasperation. It wasn't like the tribes didn't have roads and wells and towns before Rome— the Romans just did them better. And that was *their* fault?

"You know how we lived back then, Roman?" Duro looked at her fiercely. "We lived clean and unspoiled, in a land more beautiful than anything outside the world of the gods. Battles were fought openly and honestly between warriors, not left to ambush and trickery. Our children grew up without the threat of being marched off in slave chains. We worshipped our own gods without seeing our holy men slaughtered, and we cast votes for our own futures without needing to hear what an emperor commanded from a thousand miles across the sea—"

"You sound like a Roman," Valeria cut him off.

Duro blinked, still half enthralled by his past paradise. "What?"

"A Roman," Valeria repeated, and there was a wild urge inside her to laugh. "You know how many old men in Rome I've had to listen to go on and on about the goodness and purity of the *Way Things Were*? How life was simple and beautiful when they had a Republic, and apparently everyone lived together in peace, and there was no murder or disease or flies in the summertime? Rome wasn't a paradise under the Republic, and I'm fairly certain Britannia wasn't either before the Romans."

Anger was falling over her captor's face like stone. "I lived it. I was *here*, I remember it, and I remember how you bastards ruined it."

"Yes, you Iceni were such paragons." Valeria heard her own voice rising, but she couldn't stop the words from flowing. How good it felt to stop biting her tongue. Hot rage boiled up her throat and into words, and she let it all out at her captor, even as she knew how unwise that was. Unlike Decianus, at least Duro would dish it back. What a *pleasure* there was in that. What sweet release. "How are the Romans worse than the Iceni, barbarian? We brought you buildings that didn't need to be patched with rotting straw, and you're burning them down. Brought you roads that didn't wash away with every spring storm, and you're tearing them up. Brought you gods who didn't demand the throttling of grown men for sacrifices—"

"We asked for none of that."

"You're still using it! Our tools and our wells and our wine, you're certainly not throwing *them* out the window as you're telling *us* to be gone—"

"Keep your tools and your wine." Duro vaulted up in one swift motion, advancing on her. "All we ever wished was to be left alone."

"No, you didn't!" Valeria retreated out of reach of his fists but jutted her chin to let him know she wasn't backing down. "Your pure, good world, what did you tribesmen do with it? Go to war every year over the same nine cattle and the same grazing lands, and you couldn't even do *that* right! Because you called in *Rome* to help you slaughter your own fellow tribesmen more efficiently!"

"Yes, and you're all about efficiency, aren't you? All efficiency and no soul. I'm sure your Governor Paulinus was very *efficient* when he murdered our Druids. Cutting down our holy men and their sacred trees, razing them to the last child—"

"Oh, you want to count dead children? Let's start in Londinium! Verulamium! Camulodunum! How many dead children there?" Valeria saw Duro's arm rising and ducked backward, around the bed of furs. "How many people burning inside their houses? How many women raped?"

"Like your Roman soldiers raped my queen's daughters?" Duro snarled. "Taking Sorcha on a storehouse floor because she tried to stop her mother's flogging. Three of them mounting Keena like a bitch-hound, her no more than a child—don't you dare close your eyes and shudder, Roman," he shouted, seeing Valeria's recoil as the terrible image rose stark in her mind. "It was on *your* husband's orders, so don't pretend—"

"*It was not!*" Catus Decianus, who had always longed for children of his own, would never have ordered Queen Boudica's daughters harmed. Never. "He didn't order that. If he'd been there, he would have stopped it! Which is more than I can say for you—your precious foster son raped anything that moved, girl or boy or *goat,* and you never—"

Duro swung at her with a closed fist, but Valeria saw it coming and shielded her head with her arm. The blow still stung fiercely. She lowered her arm and spat between his feet.

"Savages," she said, voice shaking with fury, and swore for the first time in her life. "You, your people, your precious queen. You are all. Fucking. *Savages.*"

Duro caught her by the throat, wrapping his huge hand about her neck and yanking her up against him. Valeria was still too angry for fear, every pulse another beat of pure hatred. She stared into his eyes, unblinking. She'd be damned if she showed even a twitch of fright.

"You're all fucking savages, too." His voice sank to a whisper. "You dress it up in marble and parchment and law, but you're as much barbarians as we are. You set your slaves to die in arenas for amusement, and you haul our people away in chains to mine your silver. You take what we have if you decide you want it, and then you're surprised when we object. You're no more civilized than I am, you Roman cow. You just have more marble and parchment and law."

"At least we leave something behind us," Valeria hissed around the iron grip of his fingers. "We leave the world laws and running water and *order*. What does your savagery give the world except burning cities and dead children?"

Duro flung her away from him. Valeria staggered and managed not to fall. They were both breathing hard, as though they'd sprinted a mile. Valeria still felt no fear, only rage.

"I could kill you and mount your head on a spike," Duro said. "You soft-handed, poison-tongued, yellow-spined bitch. But I want you alive to see my queen kill every legionary in these lands. I want you to look at the field of the dead, knowing that you're going to live the rest of your life a slave in my hut."

"And how will *you* live in that perfect new world you think you can create out of an ocean of blood?" Valeria spat back. "You'd still end your life dribbling and pissing in your furs, alone in your mud hovel, because your son hates you and you'll have outlived every other purpose you ever had."

That hit him hard—she could see it. She pressed forward with soft venom, going for the kill. "But that won't happen, Duro of the Iceni. I'm going to see *your* body on the battlefield when the *Romans* win—and the sight will give me nothing but pleasure."

He reached out and took her face between his huge hands, and Valeria wondered if he was going to twist her head clean off. *Die brave*, she thought with the first shiver of terror spiking her fury. *Die brave*. But he leaned down, putting his eyes level with hers, and he smiled. "What happens to *you*, if Rome wins?" he whispered. "Your people will despise you as a leg-spreading cunt. For the rest of your life, you'll be known as the woman who flopped on her back and played whore for a barbarian rather than fall on a blade."

That stabbed Valeria in her gut, but she didn't let him see it. She just stared into his eyes, so close to hers.

His smile deepened. "Played the whore with great enthusiasm, I might add."

She tore free from his hands. Duro picked up his sword and stormed out of the tent.

DURO

IT was another turn of the moon before we drew close to Governor Paulinus and his legions—the war band moved slowly, and the Roman advance down the stone road was not quick, either. I was reining my chariot behind my queen's, watching the flutter of her red hair on the wind that had turned cold with the coming of winter, when the scouts came racing up. "Legions," the man said, his grin wolfish. "Just two days ahead—" and the cheers went up.

My son, riding out on a borrowed pony, made the best analysis of the ground when the queen ordered more scouts to report on the field where Paulinus had dug in. "A valley," he said. "A broad plain on approach, slanting to a narrower defile into the gorge."

I grinned. Nothing better than a wide plain for a charge, and gods, I loved a good charge! The howl of the carnyx blast, the surge of the chariot below, the pump of blood through the veins— there was nothing like it in this world or the next. I glanced at Boudica—her face wore the shield-like impassivity she donned when surrounded by chiefs. "The flanking ground?" she asked.

"Thick woods to the rear," Andecarus said. "We can't flank the Romans—the legions are already dug in, facing the defile. The ground isn't to our advantage."

My son looked exhausted, dark circles under his hazel eyes. I wanted to scold him to find a girl, take a drink, get some sleep, but you can't be soft with sons. My father beat that into me early, so I growled, "Don't be such a damned doom-crier. We've got ten times the men; that makes up for a narrow defile."

"Not if we can't spread out," Andecarus flared back, but the queen's dream-caster spoke, waving his feather-and-bone staff, and then the rest of the chiefs weighed in. Boudica listened, her lean, callused fingers drumming on the arm of her chair, then silenced us all. She had to glare at the old bag of bones with the amber bead in his beard who tried to keep droning from his place beside the dream-caster.

"We've no time to wait Paulinus out if he's dug in," she said, and I knew she was thinking of our narrowing stores. We had taken much plunder, but a vast war band took a huge amount of food—and the Iceni had planted few crops this year, so we would need most of that plundered food to get us through winter. "We march on the Romans in two days."

Two days. In two sunsets, the last Roman army of worthy size on this island would all be dead or fleeing. I felt the wings of hope brush the inside of my throat at the thought. A quick, brutal slaughter; back to our own lands to fortify for the winter and plan our spring defenses; reinforcements called to defend the shores if the faraway emperor decided to send more legions . . .

The next day was a storm of preparation—I walked through the war band, pulling quarreling warriors apart and giving orders. Getting back to my own tent, I was surprised to see a fight had broken out, with Valeria's neat black head in the middle of it. She had my war spear in her hands, jabbing alternately between the two men circling her.

"Put the Roman bitch on her knees," a warrior with a blond plait was calling out to his stocky friend in the red cloak. "I've got something she can suck on—"

"Anything you put between my teeth is something you're going to lose." She fetched Red Cloak a *thwack* with the butt of my spear, her hair coming down and her cheeks scarlet with rage.

I was half tempted to stand back and see just how much damage she could inflict on those two numbskulls, but I didn't take kindly when young puppies infringed on what was mine. I grabbed the first warrior by his blond plait and slung him to the ground. "Why don't you and your friend scamper home to your mothers?"

"You should share her out," Red Cloak muttered with another look at the spear in Valeria's hands. "Let us all have a poke—"

I put a boot to his hip and sent him stumbling after Blond Plait, who had staggered up from the ground with mud on his fine tunic. "Go poke a sow, pup. Maybe she'll be impressed enough to give you a squeal."

The two fled, Valeria helping Blond Plait along with one last spear jab to his calf. "Bastards," she spat, and I couldn't help a sour grin. That night she'd called me a fucking savage had apparently opened her gates as far as swearing was concerned. The procurator's prim wife now cursed like Princess Sorcha.

"If they come around again, use this." I offered a bone-handled dagger from my belt. "Easier than a spear. Just put it straight through a man's throat."

"I will do no such thing," she sniffed.

"Yes, you will. You're a savage bitch, no matter how much you pluck your brows and turn your nose up at the smell of mead." I slapped the carved hilt into her hand. "Thrust hard into the throat, then twist to free the blade against the suction of the wound."

"You're giving *me* a weapon?" She eyed me coolly. "Aren't you afraid I'll use it on you?"

"Not really." A resourceful slave could always find a blade in a camp this big—if she'd wanted to stab me, she'd have found a weapon before now. No, she was still laying her bets on the Romans winning and coming to her rescue; much less dangerous than trying to kill the queen's right-hand man. I nodded at the dagger, demonstrating the move again. "So—thrust, then twist."

Valeria handled the dagger as though it were a dead rat, but she still tucked it into her belt.

"Good," I approved. "Walk with me." My knee was paining me, and I felt too restless to settle for the night—a woman was better than a crutch. A crutch said *weakness,* and I wasn't having anyone whispering that the queen's champion was weak, not two days before battle.

Valeria's nostrils flared, but she came to my side and let me lay an arm about her small shoulders. "Where are we going?"

"Looking for a horse."

She was silent as we moved through the throng of tents and dogs, slaves and warriors. We'd maintained a fierce, hostile silence since the quarrel a month ago when she called my queen a savage. She couldn't maintain her silence now for more than a moment, though. "So you took my advice."

"About finding my son's mare for him? Yes." Didn't think I'd find the beast, though. Looking for one mare in a camp of well over a hundred thousand people was like searching for a drop of conscience in a Roman soul.

"Don't you have weapons to sharpen?" Valeria steadied my gait, her arm firm at my waist. "You'll be fighting in two days, I heard."

"We'll be winning in two days, you mean."

"Well, one of us will be winning."

I smiled down at her in the twilight, and I showed every tooth in my head. "Don't."

She arched those eyebrows but let it lie as we walked on through the tents. It was cold now—autumn in our lands was short, sometimes just a matter of weeks before fading into winter. Soon there would be snow. "Why bother teaching me how to stab a man?" she asked at last.

"It's a skill every woman should know," I grunted. My knee hurt, and I still hadn't caught sight of that damned red mare.

"I can make conversation with anyone from a potter to an emperor and run a house full of slaves as smoothly as any legate runs a legion. *Those* are skills worth knowing, not knife skills. Thank you," she added, as though the words had been wrenched out between her teeth, "for running off those two bastards."

"Are you getting soft, Roman?"

"Oh, get back to your tent, you thick-headed barbarian, and let me at that knee before you walk it to pieces."

I grinned. She had the old hostile glint in her eye, the glint that said she still might decide to stab me with the dagger I'd given her, and I liked it better than stony silence. I still didn't like her, and she didn't like me, but we had prickly peace again. And I still didn't know why I put up with this from a gods-damned *slave*.

ONE day. One more day, and the world would be new.

I always hated the night before battle. A hundred things to do, yet there is never enough to fill the night. The sword has been sharpened; the shield's hides have been oiled; the chariot's wheels have been checked and checked again; the harness is ready and the ponies are fed—when all that is done, what do you do?

Many of the chiefs tonight would drink. I did when I was young, but I'd lost my taste for launching a screaming charge with a skull-pounding hangover. Many chiefs would lose themselves in women, and I tried that, tumbling Valeria between the furs until we were both exhausted and sweat-drenched. As she drifted into sleep afterward, I stared up into the darkness of my tent. Tomorrow we would put an end to the Roman scourge—there would be no sleep with such thoughts churning through my head. I rose, pulling a tunic over my head, and padded into the darkness to find my queen.

"I knew you wouldn't be sleeping, old man." Boudica smiled as the guards let me into her tent. She sat in the glow of the lamps, alone for once, sharpening her sword. She was already dressed for the next day's battle in a green tunic that left her back bare, showing her whip scars. A reminder to her warriors tomorrow of what she had borne for our sake.

"Who are you calling old?" I sat beside her, reaching for a whetstone. My sword's edge needed no attention, but every warrior sharpens compulsively the night before battle. "You're no fresh-eyed maiden yourself, my queen."

"Thank Andraste for that! My poor Sorcha has been stalking back and forth all evening like a twitchy cat, driving me mad. I finally told her to busy herself somewhere else if she couldn't sleep."

"She should find a boy to kiss for a few hours." I hoped she found my son, who was as gentle with girls as with horses. Sorcha deserved to learn that not all men were leg-spreading brutes.

"I doubt she'll spend the night kissing. Brooding on vengeance, more likely." Boudica looked at me, somber. "Is this war worth it, Duro—what was done to my daughters?"

I paused, looking at her. Since we were alone, I nudged the mass of red hair off her back and traced her scars with a fingertip. I felt the knotted edges made by the lash, and rage curdled my stomach as I heard the whip crack again in my mind. "Is it worth the wounds done to you?" I'd known she meant to bait the procurator into some show of disrespect that day—she had prepared me, telling me I must stand by and let the insults to her pass without drawing my sword. Neither of us had dreamed insults would mount to flogging, not when the procurator was known as such a mild man, but Boudica's eyes had found me as they stripped her for the lash and told me silently to continue standing down. That had not made it any less hard, standing by as the centurions striped her white back scarlet. I'd wept like a child, watching my queen sag against the whipping post.

Boudica shrugged brusquely. "Of course it was worth the wounds done to *me*. I am queen—Cartimandua once told me that she was the bride of the Brigantes, and she was right in that, even if she does suck the Roman teat for peace. I am the bride of the Iceni, and this body belongs to my tribe. I'd take every lash twice over, and every Roman who thrust himself into Sorcha and Keena. But that was *my* bargain, Duro—not theirs. And I never thought . . ." She shook her head, unable to say the rest.

"Done is done." I let my hand fall away from her scarred back. "We can only go forward."

Boudica resumed her stroke with the whetstone. "Let's marry Sorcha to your son once the war is over. She loved him once; she can again. I want grandchildren. Can you see me bouncing babies on my knee?"

"Like I bounced Sorcha and Keena on mine?" I smiled a little. "I used to pretend they were my daughters."

A little silence at that. Boudica gave me a slanted smile.

I tilted a shoulder. "I always wanted girls."

That was only part of it, and my queen knew it. Since I saw her in her bridal wreath marrying my king, I'd loved her—how could I not? The red-haired girl with the flower wreath crammed over her springing hair, and this steady-eyed woman with her proud whip-marks—I loved them both, over all other women. I always would. It did not trouble me or her.

"Duro," she mused. "What if we lose tomorrow?"

I wasn't disquieted by her words. Any good leader speaks of defeat in the dark hours of the night before victory. It is wise to do so—those who brazen victory and declare defeat impossible tempt the gods. Boudica spoke of defeat for the purpose of rendering it null, so I drew my whetstone calmly down my blade.

"Even if we lose, what of it? We have made a song of freedom that will ring for a thousand years. No one will forget the Iceni or their red-haired queen."

"Will they not?" She smiled.

I caught her eyes. "Win or lose, we are already victorious. We made Rome tremble. We shook an empire to its core. Even if we were massacred to a man tomorrow, I would not trade this year of rebellion for all the peace in the world under Rome's boot." And that was truth.

My queen gave me a sudden grin like a flash of torchlight. "It has been glorious, hasn't it?"

"That it has. Besides," I added, "we are not going to lose."

"So let us be merry, old man." Boudica called for her bard, and he strung his harp and sang the song he'd woven years ago for the duel I'd fought against six Coritani warriors, and then I called for a newer tune and he drew magic from his strings, telling of a flame-haired queen so tall her head brushed the clouds, whose spear haft was a full-grown oak and whose sword was a streak of lightning. We sang and we listened, my queen and I, as the moon fell down the sky. Tomorrow's coming triumph surged giddy in our blood, and in all my life, I had never been so happy.

VALERIA

IF there was anything that annoyed Valeria, it was how her own body betrayed her while she was asleep. She always began the night curled under the furs as far from her captor as possible . . . but the nights in Britannia were so *cold,* and at some point she invariably turned over in her sleep toward the nearest source of warmth. Never mind that it was a bloody-handed, foul-mouthed illiterate whose most fervently held beliefs involved dead Romans and bone decor, he was *warm*. Valeria's mornings invariably began with a scowl as she realized that yet again, she was cuddling with a barbarian who smelled of wood smoke, sheep fat, and sword oil. Keeping moral standards high was clearly impossible in cold climates. It was no coincidence that the empire that had civilized the world sprang from the *south*.

But dawn that morning found Duro already risen for once, plucking at a platter of stale bread and dried meat. His gaze found Valeria as she pulled her tunic over her head. "Arm me," he said, rising. "It's time."

Valeria finished tying up her hair, coming to the stack of clothes and armor he had laid out the previous evening as painstakingly as a bride laying out her wedding veil the night before her vows. "It's a pity you weren't born Roman," she couldn't help saying.

"In the name of all the gods, why?" Duro pulled his old tunic over his head, and she saw the white lines of old battle scars along his ribs and chest.

"Because you're passably disciplined for a savage." Valeria shook out his battle tunic—heavy red wool, thick enough to cushion the weight of the mail that would come over it. "You'd have done well in our legions."

"You see me with a breastplate and a gladius, setting fire to huts and drinking that sour piss you Romans call beer?" Duro shrugged the red tunic down over his head, and Valeria tugged the hem straight. "I should cut your tongue out for that."

"You haven't done it yet, and after this morning, I doubt you'll have another chance."

He gave a wintry smile as he reached for his mail coat. "We're going to win, Roman."

Valeria gave the smile right back. "You're going to lose, barbarian."

"One of us is wrong." He slid his arms into the coat. "Today we'll find out which."

Fear pulsed in Valeria's stomach despite herself. *One hundred thousand Iceni warriors,* she thought and swallowed. No matter how she scoffed at barbarians and their screaming charges, she'd spent months watching Duro and the other warriors spar: stripped to the waist, teeth bared, slashing with brutal strength. They were no mean fighters.

Legionary discipline will win the day, she told herself and sent a prayer to Fortuna for Governor Paulinus and his ten thousand men, entrenched in their valley just a scant few miles away, doubtless making their own desperate appeals to the goddess of luck.

She finished arming her captor in silence. The mail coat, rare and expensive in these savage lands, burnished to a silvery gleam. The red tunic and blue breeches. The long-sword in its enameled red scabbard. The war helm with a crest of scarlet feathers . . . Valeria could not help a smile.

"What's that smirk?" Duro caught the twitch of her lips.

"This looks like a legionary commander's helm. Governor Paulinus wears one very similar."

"I'll look for it on the field, then, so I can kill him."

Valeria stood back, gazing at her captor critically. Duro looked not unlike Paulinus: both tall men, weathered and hard-muscled, with the same smiles of calm ferocity. Cut Duro's graying lion mane short and trade the mail coat for a cuirass, and the man in front of her could have been Rome's champion instead of Boudica's; a man who could effortlessly command legions and order provinces. *The kind of man you pushed Decianus to be.* The irony was not lost on her in the slightest.

Duro rummaged in a chest under the line of skulls and tossed a bundle of cloth at Valeria. *Silk,* cool, smooth silk—with a jolt she recognized the green *stola* she had been wearing the day she was captured.

"Put that on," Duro ordered, busying himself with a pot of something foul smelling and blue that looked like woad. "You know what Roman legionaries do to our women. If the day goes ill for my queen, you don't want to be mistaken by a lot of rampaging centurions for a native woman."

He sounded sublimely unconcerned that the day could ever go ill for his queen. But he had admitted the possibility, something Valeria had not heard him do in all the months she shared this tent. Hope flared a little more strongly. She sent another prayer to Fortuna as she slid her roughened hands over the silk, remembering the woman who had worn it last. What a *bitch* that woman had been. *Perhaps I still am. But a bitch who knows something more about the world than the one taken captive in Londinium.*

She looked at Duro, who was daubing his face in blue patterns. "What does it matter to you if I'm mistaken for a native and killed by centurions? Presumably if that happens, you'll already be dead."

He turned to face her, looming in his barbaric war splendor, his face a brutal mask of blue paint. "I hate you Romans," he said. "I'd put every one of you to the sword if it gave back my world the way it was. Even you. But given a choice, I'd rather see you live, Roman bitch. In another life, you could have been a warrior, scars up and down those arms instead of pearls. Well," he amended, "if you'd drunk proper nourishing beer rather than watery Roman wine while you were growing up, and got tall enough to swing a sword."

Valeria glared at that.

Duro grinned, nodding at her armful of *stola*. "Either way, you're wasted in silk."

"And you're wasted in woad," Valeria shot back. "In another life, you could have been a legionary commander. A good one."

He laughed. "Gods, what a thought."

"What a thought," Valeria agreed, thinking of herself with a blade. The idea!

Silence stretched, and a horn sounded somewhere outside. Duro picked up his helm.

"I hope you lose this battle," Valeria said with brutal honesty. "But I also rather hope you don't die."

The words startled her. She felt no liking for him. No understanding, no friendship. But she would be sorry, at least a little, to see him dead.

Duro gripped her hand in his huge one, pressing until her bones bent, watching with his narrow wolf's gaze to see if she flinched. Valeria smiled sweetly and squeezed back, digging her nails into the back of his hand. Neither flinched.

He laughed a little. So did Valeria. He clipped her jaw one last time, in a kind of rough respect rather than anger, and then he was gone.

DURO

WE sang as we rode to war. I took the rear, urging the most hung over chiefs and their warriors into motion, haranguing the cattle drivers steering the massive wagons piled high with the treasure of three sacked cities. Many of our women and children would clamber atop those wagons to watch the battle—the treasure was safer accompanying the war band than being left back at the camp, which now held only the slaves, the sick, and the timid. I'd told Valeria to keep safe to my tent, even in such lackluster company. I smiled a little, wondering if I might be able to plant a child in her this winter once the victory was done. Nothing else to do in the snowbound months but stay inside and make your women pregnant, and anything that came out of *that* woman's womb was sure to be a warrior.

The day was brilliant, the sun shining, the air full of biting chill. Frost rimed the dry grass underfoot, and dead leaves fluttered from the oaks. It was almost winter, the year dying, but for the Iceni, I saw not death but life.

We sang, happy as children—but these children had vengeance in their hearts, and I had no doubt we made the Romans quake on our approach. We poured toward the broad plain, the greatest army ever seen in these lands, and what a roar came from our throats as we saw the gleaming blocks of the legions against the dark-forested hills below. My heart thumped in my chest as I sent my chariot rattling ahead, chivvying the chiefs into their battle lines. The Trinovantes on the left flank, our lesser chiefs of the Iceni to the right—the center belonged to the warriors like me and my son. He had fought with the Trinovantes at Verulamium, but today he'd be at my side where he belonged. I looked for him, but he was nowhere to be seen.

I halted my sturdy chariot ponies, hearing the sudden swell of cheering ripple down the line. My throat grew thick as a chariot thundered along the front rank of spears, a chariot picked out with silver so it caught the sun's every beam, and my queen pulled up before us in a whirl of mane and wheels like Andraste herself descending from the clouds. Boudica's bright hair was strapped into three flying plaits like red serpents, her face painted in swirling blue lines, her shield boss bearing a Roman skull. Her scarred back was bare and her face proud. My throat stung, and I realized I was roaring to the skies.

My queen.

She thrust her spear toward the clouds, and I half expected to see lightning crack down at her summons. "Today," she called in her voice like a bronze horn, "Rome dies."

Another roar tore at the air. I was hoarse from shouting.

"I come to you now not as a woman of royal blood." Her eyes raked her army like a hawk's, finding me, finding the old man at my left with the amber bead in his beard, finding the woman at my right with the lime-washed hair. Boudica's gaze touched us all as though addressing every one of her warriors alone and in their souls. "I come to you as one of the Iceni. I come avenging our lost freedom. I come avenging my scourged body—"

A growling roar rose from the war band as she displayed her white back with its reddened scars. Her voice dropped to a savage hiss.

"And I come avenging my daughters."

My princesses flanked their mother in her chariot. Sorcha handled the reins as her mother's charioteer, and she lifted her chin as the shouts surged up in rage for her violation. Her red hair was crammed under a bright-polished helm, her face painted not in woad but in blood. My lucky princess, lovely and lethal. Keena clutched the side of the chariot, her face ghostly pale behind the woad daubs, but she, too, kept her head high.

Boudica's voice echoed over us like a roll of thunder. "Roman lust has gone so far that not even age or virginity is left unpolluted! What can be worse than the treatment we have suffered since these men came to our lands?" We screamed back, too incensed for words. "But the gods are on the side of righteous vengeance. A legion which dared to face us has perished"—howls of derision—"and the rest are hiding in their camp or thinking of flight!" Boudica's spear pointed back toward the immobile mass of legionaries, so small against the darkness of the trees. "They will break under the din and shouts of our thousands, *much less the blows of our swords!*"

I began thumping my spear haft against the metal rim of my shield, a brutal incantatory beat. The men to my left and right picked it up, and the beat spread back through our ranks: thousands upon thousands of spears sounding the glory of our queen.

"We have come to it," Boudica said to the heart's drum of her army. "To this moment. I speak with a woman's resolve: *conquer—or die.*"

Sorcha raised her blood-painted face to the clouds and keened a savage cry like a hunting hawk. We all howled after her, screaming to split the heavens, and I realized tears were streaming down my face. I let them come, weeping bone-deep joy as the lines around me steadied to charge, and my queen pulled a heavy tunic and a mail coat over her scarred back. I felt the usual mix of terror and exhilaration that comes before a charge; the urge to sprint into the enemy's arms before the carnyx even sounds, and the countering urge to take a piss at the rear. I let it all wash over me—I had fifty summers to my name, and battle jitters were nothing new, just notes plucking at my bones like nervous fingers on a harp. Boudica was taking her shield from her shield bearer and summoning her usual charioteer; Sorcha had descended to a chariot of her own and sent Keena back to where the women and children watched. The young Druid Yorath was stalking up and down the battle line as naked as a new infant, a wreath of mistletoe around his brow, shaking the Roman head on its spike as he called prayers. I bent forward for his blessing, then called my charioteer to take the reins as I loosened my sword in its scabbard. The blade was hungry, singing for Roman blood, and I kissed her hilt and crooned that I would feed her soon.

Then I saw a familiar dark plait down a man's lean back. "Andecarus!"

My son kneed his mount toward me through the throng: a pony, too small for him. He wore Iceni mail and a Roman cavalry helm, and I wanted to chastise him for the latter, but for once, I let it go. It was a well-made helm. I called for my shield bearer, who had been hanging back all morning while I held my own shield. The man came forward with a clop of hooves. "For you," I told Andecarus gruffly and waved at the big red mare with her mane falling like flame along her arched neck.

The look on his face was worth the hours I'd tramped around the war band on my aching knee. Worth the haggling I'd done against the chief who'd claimed the mare in Londinium. Worth the price I'd paid for a Roman cavalry saddle like my son was used to riding, and a bridle and harness all mounted in silver. That mare was decked for glory, but she wasn't all I had to give him. As my son jumped off his pony and went to stroke the mare's nose with a disbelieving hand, I pulled off the heaviest of my gold arm rings. All warriors collect arm rings, one for every battle, but my son's years with the Romans meant he had none.

"This is for you, too." I held out the ring. "Well-earned at Verulamium. You fought bravely."

"I killed my foster brother after Verulamium." Andecarus' smile disappeared. "I know you cannot forgive me for that."

"He was a brute with a sword—I valued the sword, not the brute. *You* are my son." I took Andecarus' hand roughly, sliding the ring up around his forearm. "No man could have a braver or a better."

He stared at me. I cleared my throat, wanting to say something more—but I didn't know what. I just commented inanely, "Glad you don't lime-wash your hair into spikes like some of these young bloods. Too damned hard to fit a helm over it—"

Andecarus vaulted up into his Roman mare's saddle, maneuvering the beast alongside my chariot. He reached out a gold-decked arm and touched my shoulder, and his radiant grin speared my soul. I could see the boy he'd been, the one I'd told gruffly to be brave as he went off to serve as hostage to the Romans. Why had I ever let him go?

Never again. I would not be parted from Andecarus now for any reason on this earth.

I smiled back, near to tears again, and my son reined his mare into line beside my chariot as the spears went up, as the howl of carnyx horns sounded down the battle line, as the distant bugling of the Roman trumpets echoed across the broad plain ahead. As my breath caught and my spear leveled, and the world of my youth was just a breath away.

As we charged.

VALERIA

VALERIA looked at herself in the polished bronze mirror and felt a thrum of shock. The woman reflected there wore a green silk *stola;* her hair was coiled; her chin modestly lowered—but she was not Valeria of the Sulpicii, demure wife of Catus Decianus. This woman was hard as flint, gripping a bone-handled dagger as though she knew how to use it.

The whisper came harsh in her mind. Duro's words, from the most venomous of their quarrels, but spoken in her mother's voice. *What happens to you if Rome wins? For the rest of your life, you'll be known as the woman who flopped on her back and played whore for a barbarian rather than fall on a blade.*

Valeria eyed the dagger, pulse beating loud in her own ears. The camp outside with its few remaining slaves and old folk seemed eerily quiet. Her mother's voice came again. *Honor demands death, Valeria.*

"Honor—is—shit." She enunciated the profanity precisely. It was a bad habit, the swearing, but she really did not think she would be able to give it up. "I am still Valeria of the Sulpicii, honor or no, and I am not falling on a fucking blade."

Not now that she was starting to suspect she was perhaps seven months away from bearing a half-Iceni, half-Roman child.

Her own harsh laugh surprised her, bursting out of her throat like a sob. Her husband had always wanted a child. Her mother had always told her she had failed in her duty to give him one. Well, she'd done her duty at last. *Meet your grandchild, Mother. He plays with skulls and was weaned on the blood of his enemies.*

As to what Decianus would think . . . well, who knew?

Valeria heard a distant roar and shivered. She clutched the bone-handled dagger tighter. *Thrust hard into the throat, then twist to free the blade against the suction of the wound*, Duro's voice came to her. *Thrust—then twist.*

She waited to see what the day's end would bring—if she would be a slave forever or a Roman woman covered in shame. Either way, Valeria intended to live.

DURO

MY low-slung open chariot lurched as the charioteer whipped up the ponies, and I rocked with the wheels, leveling my spear. Andecarus galloped on his red mare, cavalry sword aloft. My queen's lips were sealed in a savage line, her long body taut and swaying as her chariot hurtled over the broad expanse of grass. I felt victory race through my blood like a dram of divine nectar—for the gods rode with us on that charge; I could feel them all around me. Taranis the sky god, thunder coming in his footsteps, and dread Andraste herself with her lightning sword and her savage smile like my queen's.

From the dawn of the gods to the end of days, there would never be such a charge.

The field narrowed as we passed into the valley, and the crush pressed thicker around me. I shouted at my charioteer to drive ahead, faster. I was queen's champion; I would be first against that line of Roman shields. They were a solid wall before me, unmoving—frozen by terror? Would they turn tail and flee into the woods behind them? *Die, you bastards. Die screaming.*

Somehow over the roar of the charge, I heard shrill piping from the enemy line. Movement, crisp and fast behind the shields, and then a mass of shadows winged toward us through the clear sky like falling ravens.

A javelin clanged off my shield boss, spinning away like a bent twig. All around me Roman spears were falling, I heard screams, the gurgling of blood, but the crush was too massive, and the warriors behind kept pressing forward. I saw Boudica raise her shield, fending off a spear, and my heart skittered in my chest, but she rode on unhurt. The souls of our first dead heroes soared into the clouds to cheer us on in their fight, and the charge swept on, slower but still invincible.

This time I heard the shrill cry in Latin to accompany the piping. *"Release pila!"*

A second wave of javelins soared into our ranks at a twenty-yard range. My charioteer fell with a javelin spitting his ribs, tumbling from the chariot under the trampling hooves behind. I arced my own spear into the line of Roman shields and fumbled for the reins, whipping the ponies faster. The crush was immense now, our flanks folding inward as the defile narrowed; our front line faltering under that rain of wicked little spears, bodies falling, tripping those who came behind.

But we were so close, and the Romans were advancing in their neat squares, small units with shields locked, eyes glittering under their helmets. I picked my man, a swarthy legionary with a short beard, and I brought him death. I dropped the reins, raced down the axle shaft between the ponies, and vaulted from my chariot just as the raging line of Boudica's warriors met the marching Roman edge of legionaries. I was still leaping down through the air as I brought my sword down over the edge of the swarthy legionary's shield, cleaving down through his neck.

He dropped, scream disappearing into the great cacophony of iron and agony that is battle. I landed heavy on my bad knee but felt no pain. I was reborn, made young again by joy and blood, and I came up with a roar, hefting my shield. The Romans had already re-formed around the legionary I'd killed, overlapped shields advancing. The press behind shoved me forward, but I needed no shoving, just leaped at the tidy line and hammered the nearest shield down, driving the man behind it until a gap opened and my thirsty blade found it. My sword drove along the line of his breastplate, found the armhole, and slid through. I was forcing my way into the unit, using my blade like a hammer to beat those immaculate shields down—these swarthy Romans were so much shorter than me, I was swatting them from overhead like a god killing flies. My helmet clanged as a gladius glanced off it, and I laughed as I chopped the man down.

The unit was dissolving, falling back even as more units advanced on either side, and the crush was so tight I could barely turn my head, but I still saw Andecarus killing with terrible speed, his new arm ring flashing in the sun, his mare surging obediently beneath him. I saw a blood-splashed Sorcha stalking an *optio* who'd been separated from his unit, screaming as she hacked him to pieces. In the center, where Boudica's best warriors danced the terrible dance of death, we were slaughtering the Romans like sheep.

But on the flanks, they were rolling us up like a cloak.

"Auxiliaries!" The warning shouts were barely audible over the scream of iron and wounded men. *"Auxiliaries!"*

Roman cavalry like my son had once been were sweeping out of the trees, descending on our flanks where the Trinovantes had been placed, because a Trinovante in the center of a charge was like a hinge that would fold the whole line back. They were folding now, falling back under the sweep of horses, and I saw my son crying out orders, but the weight of our own men was too heavy, and Paulinus' riders hit the flank in looping lines, sliding along the chariots rather than engaging them. A split-second later, I knew why.

The high-pitched screams of wounded horses rose; the bastards were hamstringing the ponies in their traces, bringing chariots to pitching halts, flinging warriors out over the wheels where they were being slaughtered before they could rise. "The flanks," I shouted, "reinforce the *flanks*!" I saw my queen on the right already trying to do just that, haranguing the men to advance on foot; I saw Andecarus trying to force a path through to the left, but the battlefield was too crowded, and all along the sides of the narrow defile, the Romans were killing us.

So they would make a fight of this, after all, not turn like craven sheep? I did not mind that. A great victory is all the sweeter if it comes hard-fought. I left the flanks to my son and my queen as another unit advanced on the center toward me, short blades of the gladii flickering like serpents' tongues. The man on my left went down clutching his gut; I smelled the sudden stench of opened bowels. All I could do was tread him underfoot as I advanced, swinging my blood-dappled sword. I hit the man on my right in the backswing, glancing off his helm, so I bulled forward to make room for myself, trying to force a gap in those locked shields. They hung locked against me, stubbornly, and I felt a gladius hit my armored ribs with a force that would leave the flesh bruised black. *I'll make a drinking cup of your skull and toast your writhing soul while my Roman bitch rubs that bruise down.* I beat over the legionary's shield with my heavy pommel, crushing the dome of his forehead like an egg. The ichor of youth and triumph still ran through me, and I was stacking Roman souls on my sword . . . but my queen's warriors were falling back.

"No retreat!" someone was bawling—Boudica's dream-caster, shaking an axe in one hand and his bone-and-feather staff in the other. "*No retreat!*" and then a centurion filled the dream-caster's mouth with a gladius. I turned, barely able to squeeze around in the vicious clench, and I saw the Trinovantes throwing down their shields and running. "*Bastards!*" I screamed, trying to hack closer to the flank. "*Stand and fight!*" But those yellow-spined cowards were fleeing like dogs.

The monotonous, tinny blat of the Roman horns sounded again, and the lines of legionaries advanced. They were like insects, identical and swarming, until the moment you made them bleed, and then they became men again. I was sending them to their gods as fast as I could move my sword, but there was always another stepping into his place. We had so many swords, but we were packed so close we couldn't swing them. I bashed at skulls, using my hilt like a club and trying to force myself forward into those locked ranks, but all around me warriors were in retreat.

Falling back.

"*No retreat!*" I howled, staggering as I slipped in a mess of spilled guts, but there was space around me because my fellow warriors were edging back from the Romans. I tripped again on a fallen shield, nearly losing my own, looking around me in a daze. I did not understanding what I was seeing.

My queen's war band was fleeing.

Fleeing. Packed along the narrow defile, hemmed in by those circling auxiliaries, frantically pressing back toward the open plain where we had launched our glorious charge. I suddenly felt the drench of sweat gluing my hair to my skull, the bone-deep ache in my sword arm that had been rising and falling for what felt like hours. *Not lost*, I thought. *Not lost, not yet!* If we could lure the Romans to that open field where we had room to fight, we could pull them to pieces from all sides. I filled my burning lungs, ready to call for a shield wall where the narrow gorge fed out into the wide plain—but the warriors of the Iceni were already streaming past, casting their swords aside, sprinting for the hills. I could not find Boudica. I could not find Andecarus. *Where was my son?*

And everywhere—everywhere—the Roman units were advancing, scything into my fellow tribesmen like a sickle through an upturned throat.

A strangled howl burgeoned in my throat, but I killed it before it could escape. *Not lost*, I thought in fierce, frantic hope. *Not lost!* We could retreat, melt into the woods as our people had always done. My queen could reassemble her army. Even if a third of us fell on this field, we still outnumbered Paulinus' men more than six to one. We would choose another battleground and fall on the Romans unawares—the plan my son had proposed at the war council. The chiefs would not brush that advice aside this time, nor would I. *Run today, fight tomorrow,* I thought, gut churning, and as I shifted into a run, knee screaming pain in the cold sweat that had swamped me, I saw Boudica: bloody, desperate, *alive.* Holding her own whipsawed reins because her charioteer hung limp off the rail like a gutted sheep, screaming her ponies forward, her face a mask of gore and mud, but *alive.* My queen was alive. As long as she lived, all was not lost.

But then I came out into the crest of the open field and saw, outlined against the cruel blue sky, the wagons drawn tight around the mouth of the valley. Massive wagons weighed down by the treasure of three sacked cities, further packed by eager women and children, who had piled atop the heaped loot to watch the

Romans die. Those enormous wagons and their placid teams of oxen plugged the valley like a cork, and I watched the first surge of fleeing warriors wash up against the barrier and break like a wave.

No, I thought, but the howl died unspoken. The scream was all in my mind, the scream of a child who wakes to find the dark infinite and knows the night is full of teeth. I was still running, slipping and sliding on slicks of blood and fallen swords, nests of entrails and dying men begging mercy, but there would be no mercy today for any of us. The world's teeth had snapped shut about us all.

Some of Boudica's warriors slipped between the tight-drawn wagons, crawling between wheels and lunging for the freedom beyond. Others hacked at the cattle, trying to cut them down and climb over the bellowing corpses. But too few—far too few. Wave after wave of fleeing warriors slammed blind and frantic against the barrier, clamoring, clawing, those behind pressing so frantically on those in front that they slipped into the churned grass of the wheel ruts and disappeared shrieking under so many trampling boots. The wagons rocked from side to side, too heavy to spill easily, and now the women and children inside had seen the danger and were fleeing like mice from burning thatch, but too late.

Too late. The words came in a harsh raven's caw, brushing the cavern of my hollow chest. Because the Romans now came at a sprint, shields locked, orderly units lunging over the narrow defile and into the expanse of the plain. Five units sprinted past me unstopping; what did they care for a solitary gray-haired warrior at the rear? They had their gaze fixed on the prize, and with another tinny blat of their ugly horns, they fell on the frantic churning rear of Boudica's army.

I was on my knees. When had I fallen? I was on my knees,

rocking back and forth in the mud, sword clutched loose in my hand as I watched my people die.

This was not battle. It was slaughter. Every blink of my lashes saw another fifty fall as the Roman swarm advanced into the chaos and left wet red death in its wake. I saw a small boy fall from the wagons and disappear under the trampling feet of the warriors below. I saw a scarred woman trying to beat her way free of the crush with a broken shield, going down with a sword through her spine. I saw a warrior with lime-washed hair sag, head flopping half-severed—

My vision skipped. I was still on my knees, limbs stone-heavy, mouth working soundlessly. Some warriors were trying to turn and fight—my queen's second adviser with the amber bead in his beard swam out of the chaos as crazily distinct as though he stood beside me, screaming for a new shield wall and then sliding into the muck of tangled bodies. There were so many of us, still so many, if only we could turn and fight! But panic had come on death-white wings, and panic is the death of victory. We were no longer gods of the field; we were cattle in a churn awaiting the axe, and the Romans were building a dam of our broken, blood-webbed bodies.

The gods had not ridden with us today, after all. The gods had betrayed us.

I staggered to my feet. I took two faltering steps, my sword tip trailing the blood-soaked grass, and I tripped over a limp form and crashed forward again. A shriek rose as I realized what I'd fallen over: the Druid Yorath, so newly dead blood still pulsed from him in slow ebbs. His naked body lay white and bony as a child's; the wreath of mistletoe had fallen away as he tried to stuff his own guts back into his belly. The precious severed head on its spike, the sacrifice that had promised us victory, lay flattened by Roman boots.

I screamed then, and screamed again, clenching my own hair in bloody hanks, trembling and shaking as though I'd drunk a bellyful of dream-mead. The gods had not betrayed us—the gods were dead. They had died on Mona, murdered by Rome, and now the last Druid had gone to join them, and he had not gone serene as our priests are supposed to go to the world beyond. He had died howling, godless, and pissing himself—and so would we all. Our triumphs of this past golden year were nothing but lies. Nothing but the death throes of a world that did not realize it was dead.

The world I loved was gone, and I was the last to see it. A blind old fool.

A hard fist suddenly yanked my head back. I heard a snarl of Latin, felt the edge of a gladius at my throat, and I was still blind with tears, but I moved with the instincts of fifty summers worth of battles. I flung myself back against the Roman, knocking his gladius a few precious inches from my throat, and my sword had slipped from my hand, but the spike where Yorath had so proudly carried the severed head was at my fingertips. I seized it, still sobbing my grief for a lost, mist-wrapped world, and I stabbed the Roman up under the chin, driving the spike up through his jaw, into his brain, until I felt it scrape the inside of the skull. I screamed for my dying tribe and our dead gods.

Then I seized my sword and took off across the field of death in a shambling run, looking for my queen.

VALERIA

THE screams seemed to rise from everywhere, like a chorus from Tartarus. Valeria bolted up from the stool where she'd been waiting for what seemed like hours. Women screaming, and children—and then the beautiful, distant sound of a Roman *buccina* instead of a howling Iceni carnyx.

She flew outside the tent and found the camp in chaos. Women were seizing bundled babies, grabbing baskets, trying to drag goats by rope halters—then finally just dropping everything but their children. "What's happening?" Valeria screamed into the spreading panic. *"What's happening!"*

No one paused to answer, but suddenly she could hear hoof beats thundering. The hooves of Roman cavalry horses, not shaggy mountain ponies.

Hope leaped in her throat, dizzy and desperate. *Have we won?* Had ten thousand legionaries really prevailed against ten to one odds? Her head swam. A crippled man on a staff shunted past, knocking Valeria off her feet and hobbling on with a shouted curse. Hastily, she scrambled back into the tent. The camp still had hundreds of Iceni who had been too young, too old, or too timid to join the wagon train that trundled off to watch the battle—who knew which of them might decide to kill the Roman bitch as they fled? The protection of Duro's name would not matter now. Blank, cold shock chilled Valeria then. Duro—was he dead?

The sound of hooves grew louder, louder, louder still. Then came the clash of iron and the jingling of mail, and the hateful companion to that sound—screaming voices. Women too slow to flee, paying the price the women in Londinium had paid, and Verulamium, and Camulodunum. Paying the price the unarmed always paid when battles were lost, whether the victorious swords belonged to Romans or tribesmen. Valeria pressed her hands to her ears. "Stop," she heard herself crying, "just *stop!*" She never wanted to hear the clash of swords again or the screams of desperate women and dying children. Never. Never. Never.

The tent wrenched open, and Valeria looked up to see a

centurion—square Roman face, Roman gladius, Roman helmet. She could hear his fellow soldiers dispatching the survivors outside, but she still felt a kick of violent relief at the sight of a fellow countryman. The words spilled over each other in their haste to leave her lips. "I am a Roman woman." She rose so he could see her *stola,* her coiled hair. It was over. It was *over.* Life as an Iceni slave was done. "I am the procurator's wife, Valeria of the Sulpicii, and if you will—"

"Tattooed slut," he snarled, and his gladius rose. Valeria froze in a moment's ice-cold shock, seeing the white about his eyes, the gore on his armor, the blankness of his stare. Too maddened from the battle to know a Roman woman when he saw one, or—

"*I am Valeria of the Sulpicii!*" she shouted in Latin, backing away from the gladius, but the centurion wasn't hearing her. He wasn't *seeing* her, either—or perhaps all he saw was another tattooed woman, and that to him meant Boudica and the other screaming harpies he'd fought on the battlefield. He came at her, stinking of blood and ready to gut her where she stood, and Valeria flung herself forward, past his sword, against his breastplate before she had a chance to think. Duro's bone-handled dagger snaked free from her belt, all but leaping into her scrabbling hand, and she screamed as she stabbed the centurion through the throat. "Thrust," she heard herself shriek, driving the blade with all her strength, "then *twist*—" and wrenched the dagger free. She stabbed him again, blood pattering warmly over her face, and the centurion dropped gurgling at her feet.

Valeria stood for a moment, listening to her own harsh breaths rasping in and out. The tent was a pocket of stillness in all the commotion outside. Her hand wouldn't release the dagger. She stopped trying. She sat down on the ground all at once, looking at the blood splattered down her silks. *Thrust, then twist.* Never in her pampered, well-ordered life would Valeria of the Sulpicii

have known how to tear a man's throat open. *You told me that in
another life I'd be wielding a blade, Duro . . .*

She wondered if her captor was still alive at this moment. She
wondered what her husband was doing at this moment, in his
villa in Gaul with its rows of grapes and its tiny atrium, which
wasn't so grand that a baby couldn't play naked in the center pool.
That villa hovered in the air, the most beautiful place on earth
to Valeria as she waited, bloody-handed and entirely ready to
tear open another throat if necessary, to see if she would survive.
Rome had won, and all she had to do now was survive the victory.

DURO

MY queen lived. Her tribe was dead, her gods were dead, her
dream was dead, but she was alive.

I found her near the valley's mouth, bare-armed and blood-
streaked, a sword-slash down one arm and no trappings of a queen
left. No chariot, no dream-caster, no bard. Only her daughters—
Sorcha raging and shield-less, Keena with tear-tracks erasing her
woad, and gods only knew how Boudica had managed to extri-
cate her youngest daughter from the bloody chaos of the wagons.
I could not find my son anywhere—I could only hope, agony
splintering my soul, that he had died quickly. Around my queen
and my princesses there was only a small band of surviving warriors, most of them wounded.

The slaughter had spread wide across the trampled field, the
legendary discipline of the legions fading as the easy killing at the
dam of wagons spread out. One or two of the wagons had overturned, and the Romans were rampaging past a hundred fortunes
in spilled silver and gold toward the war band's temporary camp
a mile or so distant, where the survivors of the battlefield were

trying to flee. They were being cut down as they ran like sows in a butcher yard. That should have grieved me, but I had gone entirely numb with the death of my gods. What did these final, frantic death throes of mortal men matter? We were all dead and abandoned.

But when gods are dead, men still have oaths, and I had one oath left: the oath to my queen.

"The trees," I shouted, my voice hoarse with screaming. "Get the queen to safety!"

Our exhausted little band of survivors reversed from the fruitless fight at the valley's mouth, running in a crouch to escape scouting eyes. I could barely lift my sword; my bad leg dragged; my chest heaved like a river in spring floods. Spring—I would never see another spring. The year was ending, and so was I. I had no wound yet, unlike the whimpering young warrior whom I was hauling along by an arm missing its hand. I was not wounded at all, but then, Duro of the Iceni had always been lucky.

There were far fewer Romans at this end of the field, just scattered legionaries hurrying to join the slaughter at the wagons—but one unit spotted us, coming in red blurs. I limped forward tiredly, stabbing a Roman over the shield, thrust and twist. He gurgled and died as Boudica stepped in to my left and Sorcha to my right. Their blades flashed in terrible unison, and two Roman heads rolled, but three more of our few remaining warriors died before we could chop the remaining legionaries down. And my queen, I saw in a lurch of terror, was clutching her ribs.

"She's wounded," Sorcha shouted. "We need to get her off the field—"

"I will not flee," Boudica sawed out.

A muddy stumble of hooves sounded then. *"Father!"* My heart squeezed violently at the sight of my son on his mare; under the mask of gore and filth, he seemed unwounded. "To the rear of the battlefield, there's a way up the slope into the woods. Our best chance—" He led the way, slashing down another legionary, and we followed at a stumbling run, crouching low to avoid drawing Roman eyes. Keena fell with a cry; I slung her over one shoulder and kept running. I felt her weeping silently, her arms clinging to me as though she were still a child. "We're going to die," she hiccupped. "We're going to die—"

"You're going to live," I said, weeping myself. "I swear it."

Down to the tree line Andecarus led us, the rear of the field where Paulinus had first arrayed his battle lines. Not many Romans here now—a few were dispatching the wounded, but most had advanced to join in the slaughter of the fleeing war band. My son pointed straight up a rocky slope toward the wooded hills. "Through there and up into the woods. Legionaries will never be able to pursue in force; the trees are too thick—" He saw a riderless cavalry horse and veered his mare after it, leaning to snag the reins.

"I will not flee—" Boudica was shouting, but Sorcha shouted over her.

"They'll take you to Rome in chains like Caratacus, and as for us—" For her and Keena, it would be the centurions again, taking turns between their thighs. I could see the ghastly, shuddering horror of it in Sorcha's eyes, and her sister's as she slid down from my shoulder.

"Flee," I told my queen. "For them—flee. I'll buy you time." The slope into the woods was narrow, uneven, flanked by tumbles of rocks to each side. My eye had already assessed what could be done.

Boudica looked at me, at her daughters. She nodded.

It all took only seconds. At any moment, we might be spotted by scouts or scavenging legionaries. Andecarus swung off his mare, ordering the last of our wounded fighters back to head off any scavenging Romans who might draw near. Sorcha babbled at me: "Meet us in Luguvalium, we'll go to Venutius' lands. Or if we cannot get so far north, we'll go to the Cornovii, to my mother's sister—" I would not be meeting my queen or her daughters anywhere, not in this life, but I gave my lucky princess' bloodstained cheek a final rough caress and turned to Boudica. I met her eyes, and a heartbeat became a year. I saw the flame-haired bride in her wreath of ivy and lilies; I saw the woman sagging proud and unyielding against the whipping post as her back wept scarlet; I saw the goddess riding to war with a sword in her hand and a crown on her head. I saw them all in the woman before me, wounded and bloodied but still straight as a spear.

"We made Rome tremble," she said as I helped her lift Keena into the saddle of Andecarus' spare horse. "We shook an empire to its core, Duro."

"I would not trade this year of rebellion for all the peace in the world under Rome's boot," I said and took her in my arms. I felt the quick, fierce clasp of her embrace, and I whispered into her red hair. "Sing songs of our deaths, my queen."

"Songs to live a thousand years," she whispered back. And she swung into the saddle behind Keena and was gone.

I turned, dashing my tears away, and heard Roman voices. Our brief respite was done; I saw scouts shouting as the fleeing horse was spotted disappearing into the trees.

My son had already boosted Sorcha onto his big red mare. One fast squeeze of her bloodstained hand—those two who in another life might have married instead of losing their young dreams in this bitter, godless world—then Andecarus sent the mare cantering through the narrow defile after Boudica's. And I realized what he'd done.

"Go with them," I shouted, advancing on him as he turned back to me. "Damn you, go with them!"

"You have an oath to your lady, and I have an oath to mine." He nodded after Sorcha, his hazel eyes clear as a peat spring in his bloodstained face. "We need to buy them time." The narrow place between rockfalls, where pursuit into the woods led. Narrow enough for two swords to hold, at least for a while.

"The others will aid me—" But none of the other warriors had returned, either cut down fending off scouts or falling to their wounds or simply running to save themselves. There was no one left here but me and my son.

Rome was coming now, with terrible efficiency. I could see the shields approaching at a trot.

"Run," I begged Andecarus, and heard my voice break. "Run and *live*—"

"I'm already dead," my son said. "The dream is done, Father. Let's make an end to it."

Gods knew I wanted it to end! I was so tired. I was no longer afraid or raging or despairing. I was just tired. And the Romans were coming. They would always be coming. They are a breed that will cover the earth, civilizing as they go.

"Please," my son begged. "Let us end it."

I gripped Andecarus hard, cradling the back of his head as I'd done when he was a boy, and I kissed his hair. He hugged me back, and then we turned side by side in that narrow space and drew our swords.

"We will make an end to sing of," I said. "An end to make our names ring." For if the gods were dead and the world I loved gone forever, there was only one thing left—and that was to die well.

The Romans came for us. Let them come. They would not capture my queen to parade in chains through Rome—that I vowed, my last vow, and I felt a final pulse of that savage battle joy that made me feel young and invincible. A gift blown as a kiss from a dying god, perhaps, and I was grateful. I would not die a tired old man pissing my furs.

I would die a queen's champion.

Andecarus swept low and I swept high, and we killed the first two legionaries in two whistling strokes. We took an identical half step back from the thrashing bodies so the next Romans would have to advance over the corpses, caught each other's eye, and found ourselves smiling. How good it was, standing side by side with my son! Why had we let anything come between us? I could not remember.

The next legionaries came more cautiously, shields locked, but we sent their souls screaming. We were gods, the last warriors standing on this field, screaming for the Romans to come and die, and we piled them at our feet in that narrow path into the trees. Every corpse was another galloping stride as my queen and her daughters widened the gap toward safety. I took a sword slash to the shoulder and then the hip; Andecarus lost half the fingers of his left hand to a spear, but we felt no pain. We kept fighting. We piled dead Romans like cordwood, and still they kept coming.

My son died first. A gladius stroked into his neck and out again, taking his life in an eye-blink. He never even knew he was dead, his soul flying free before his graceful body could stiffen and then finally slump to the ground.

An eye-blink, and my son is gone.

I do not weep. I do not scream or cry out vengeance. I just cut down the Roman who slew him, and tread the man underfoot. Andecarus waits for me behind the curtain. I am only a few heartbeats from joining him.

I parry another gladius, and it deflects downward into my knee, slicing deep along the line of my old scar. I smile even as the agony lances in a white spear and the blood pours down. There will be no healing my knee this time—even Valeria's magic hands could not massage it well again. I wonder if she still lives. I hope she does.

More Romans come. A sword goes into my side, but I chop it out of the legionary's hands. I am still swinging, still on my feet, spitting blood. *Boudica*. I hope she and her daughters are far enough away. I have no more time to give them. Another blade bites at my shoulder, and this one I cannot strike away.

Dimly, I see a young tribune dismounting his horse, pushing through his men. Tall, sandy-haired. He looks grim-faced. He looks like my death.

I meet him grinning.

VALERIA

THE ravens had come. Black swirls of them descending through the clouds, alighting for the feast.

The weasel-faced centurion at Valeria's side couldn't stop cursing, then blushing, then apologizing. From the moment he'd laid eyes on her in Duro's tent, he'd bawled to his men, "Stow your blades, you namby cunts, we've got a fucking lady present!" then looked abashed and begged her pardon.

"Quite all right." Valeria kept a careful eye on his men.

"No need to worry about them, Lady." The centurion saw her gaze. "Tribune Agricola may be a pretty boy, but he keeps his lads on a tight leash. They keep their fucking cocks to themselves or they know they'll lose 'em." Another blush. "Sorry, Lady—"

Agricola—Valeria knew that name, but couldn't remember where she'd heard it. She could hardly focus at all. The battle was done and the day dying; she was wilting from exhaustion and thirst, and blood had dried all down the front of her *stola*. She had killed a man—the weasel-faced centurion eyed the stiffening body rather uneasily, then looked at Valeria, who stretched her lips in a thin smile that he clearly found unsettling.

"He couldn't keep his fucking cock to himself," she explained, her voice coming out from very far away.

He blinked at her language several times, and his eyes flicked to her tattoo. Then back to the dead man. "Fuck him," the centurion said and led her to safety.

Governor Paulinus, it appeared, was already throwing up a camp to house his legions. Valeria could have wept at the sight of sturdy palisades going up with typical Roman efficiency, huts being erected and campfires lit . . . But ravens circled over everything, black wings against a bloody sunset, and she could neither laugh nor weep. She could not see the battlefield where so many Iceni had perished, either, but she could smell the corpses.

"Sulpicia Valeria." A tribune rose from his slates as she entered his tent, bowing as though they stood in a civilized atrium. "I could not believe Naso when he said he had found you—thank you, Centurion."

"She's a fuc—a lucky one," the centurion said, blushing as he exited. "Sorry, Lady."

Valeria could not stop looking around the tent. So orderly. That clean-burning lamp, so Roman. Wax tablets, because people here knew how to write. A row of small busts—the tribune's ancestors, not the skulls of his enemies. "Thank you, Tribune," she managed to say.

"You are welcome, Lady. Let me assure you that your husband's conduct in Britannia does not reflect ill upon you. Governor Paulinus will be glad to make you his guest and see you escorted back to civilization with all haste."

The tribune under his surface formality was grainy-eyed and wilting, his left arm bound in a sling—and Valeria realized with a start that she knew him. "Gnaeus Julius Agricola," she said slowly. The boy with the gleaming teeth and the gleaming muscles who had flirted with her almost a year ago before the funeral of Boudica's husband. Valeria could barely recognize that boy in this exhausted young officer.

He was looking at her, too, as though she had changed beyond all measure. She saw his eyes find the tattoo. Avoiding his gaze, her eyes fell on something that made her entire body go numb. A sword hanging from his belt, not a Roman *spatha* or gladius, but an Iceni long-sword decorated with fire-red enamel and bronze. A rare and famous blade in these parts. She had seen that blade every day when Duro ducked into the tent and unbuckled his sword belt.

She pointed at it, asking quietly, "Where did you get that, Tribune?"

"From a tribesman I killed. The man who broke my arm." Agricola touched the sword with his good hand. "It seemed too beautiful a piece to leave in the mud. Their art is striking, isn't it? All curves, like the Greeks . . . Not much like our square Roman corners."

"No." So her captor was dead, then. Valeria had expected no less. She touched her belly and did not know what she felt. Not sorry. Not glad, either. She simply did not know.

"Did you find the queen?" she asked, still numb. "Boudica?"

"She has fled with her daughters. Governor Paulinus is confident he will recover them."

Valeria was not sure how to feel about that, either.

Agricola was pouring wine, saying something about the battle. ". . . Casualty reports still being compiled, but early numbers estimate close to eighty thousand Iceni dead . . ."

Eighty thousand. *Eighty.* She took the wine gratefully. Watered, as it should be. She could cry for all the civilization lapping softly around her. Or just cry for crying's sake. "Roman casualties?"

"Perhaps half our force." Agricola sounded cynical. "Doubtless the number will be downplayed in the report to Rome."

Doubtless everything about this day would be downplayed in the report to Rome. Who wanted truth? Boudica was defeated; that was all anyone would want to know.

Agricola was saying something about the Second Augusta now, the legion that had apparently failed to march and join them in the fight. Giving Valeria time, she understood, to collect her visibly shattered thoughts. "Paulinus is already demanding Prefect Postumus' head on a spike. He'll probably end up falling on his sword."

Valeria downed her wine in one swallow. "When did *that* ever solve anything?"

Agricola blinked. "Honor demands it."

"You don't look terribly convinced," Valeria said. "May I have some more wine, please? Don't bother watering it."

Agricola filled her cup again, sandy hair shining in the lamplight. He had greenish eyes, like Duro's son. Had Andecarus died too? The boy who had joined her household as hostage. Would her husband consent to raising another child of Duro's getting?

"Lady," the tribune said gently. "Where do you wish to go?"

Valeria drew a shuddering breath. To be offered a *choice!* To not be a slave anymore; to have a decision about anything at all . . . "Gaul," she said. "My husband has a villa north of Narbo."

Agricola looked surprised. "I heard you had requested divorce from Catus Decianus. At Londinium."

She sipped more wine. "We did not part well, but there was no official divorce." If only because there was no time.

"Still, Lady—do not feel you must return to him. His mishandling began the revolt, and then to leave his wife to the tender mercies of barbarians?" Agricola's face hardened. "Throughout the empire, he is in disgrace."

"So am I, Tribune. Or I will be. The woman who became a barbarian's whore rather than die like a Roman." Valeria's hand touched her waist again, unthinkingly, and Agricola's quick glance told her he had not misunderstood the gesture. She braced herself for disdain, but he just swirled his wine cup in his hand.

"Will your husband take you back? And your . . ." he tactfully trailed off. "I knew a man who killed his wife when her belly swelled with my—with another's get," he said quietly. "Prefect Postumus of the Second Augusta, actually. The man has been a wreck ever since; no wonder he could not stir himself to join the fight."

Layers here, and more layers. Valeria poured Agricola more wine this time and did not water it, either. "Whatever his other failings, my husband is the last man in the empire to slay a woman for dishonor." That she knew in her bones. Decianus might not *want* her back; he might decide to divorce her. But that did not matter. "I go to him because I owe him. I owe him . . . so many words."

That she was sorry she had ever urged death before dishonor. That she was sorry she had not fled with him from Londinium. That she was sorry she had ever turned up her nose at his dream of a quiet life in Gaul. That she was sorry she had not borne him a child . . . but that there was another for the taking, if he wanted.

Then, it was up to him.

She drank again. "We could be small and peaceful in our mutual disgrace, I think."

"There will be no disgrace for you, Sulpicia Valeria," Agricola said. "Not in any public report or official word from me. You were a captive. The fate of captured women is well known. You carried yourself with all the honor a Roman woman could, and so I will inform your husband or anyone else who thinks otherwise."

She looked up at him: the thoughtless young flirt turned kind and capable officer. "Thank you." How he had changed. Britannia seemingly had the power to change every Roman who came to its shores.

He touched her shoulder. "This land has drunk a sea of guilt, shame, and blood, Lady. You owe it nothing more."

"I will dream of it forever," Valeria heard herself say. The land it was, and the land it might have been had Boudica's army been the one to prevail. Her child would have been a warrior in that world; a lime-washed savage smelling of wood smoke and sheep fat and sword oil. Now if he was a boy, he would be a legionary commander. Probably a very good one.

"It is a great deal to ask, Tribune." She pointed at Duro's sword. "But may I buy that blade from you?"

Agricola met her eyes and she saw the question hovering. She raised her eyebrows, commanding silence, and evidently the gesture hadn't lost its imperiousness because he took the blade from his belt and offered it at once.

"My gift to you." He surrendered the hilt to her hand. "I believe you have a warrior's soul, Lady."

"Thank you, Tribune." She felt the cold, dead weight of the iron in her fist. "You are not the first man to tell me so."

Valeria of the Sulpicii had survived the rebellion, and she might be Roman to the core, but she understood now why the Iceni took trophies. Reminders of those they had fought and those they had lost, those they had conquered and those who had conquered them. Duro's sword would hang in her villa in Gaul, that Valeria swore.

Better than a line of skulls.

PART SEVEN

THE DAUGHTERS

E. Knight

All the ruin was brought upon the Romans by a woman,
a fact which in itself caused them the greatest shame.
—Dio Cassius

KEENA

MY name means brave.

However, I was anything but, and I knew it.

"You have everything to fear of this world, Daughters," my mother said as we hunched by the river, miles from the battle-field, our lathered horses greedily drinking up the offered water. The waning light of the setting sun surrounded us, and the cold was bitter. Tall grasses stirred in the breeze, batting wearily at my shoulders while only the occasional glimmer of light broke the sullen darkness of the waters, rippling when Mother dipped her hands into the depths. She cupped her hands, pulling the icy liquid to wash the blood from her face.

I never thought victory was possible. All through the thirteen years since my birth, our people had struggled against Roman edicts. No swords. No way to protect ourselves but to rely on the Romans. Thank the gods our hunters were good with arrows and slingshots. And thank the gods as well for mother's insight, that she continued with our tribe's secret training and hoarding of weapons—had she not, we might have perished a year ago. No, I never thought victory possible. But I know our defeat for a certainty now.

Our people had been slaughtered. And Mother was injured, cut deep in a place I'd seen kill warriors slowly. A wound I'd tended on many in the last year, in the healing tents where I'd honed my skills.

"What have I to fear?" My sister, Sorcha, said, her voice haughty as it often was when she was scared. She tugged her lean-muscled shoulders back, oblivious to the muck that still marred her skin from battle, now covered in a crust of dirt and sweat from our frenzied ride away from the field. Lost now. Everything and everyone lost. The Iceni, all shadows of the past . . . except for us. "We will hide in the mists. Raise a new army. We will come back at the Romans harder than before. We will make *them* live in fear."

Mother looked at Sorcha as if wanting to believe her, but when she turned to me, her expression was guarded. "Yes. Perhaps you're right. We need to keep running."

We had been running since the battle's end yesterday, only stopping briefly to rest as night fell and continuing on as a blood-red dawn rose. Now another night was falling, and Sorcha had come up with a plan, a haphazard one. We would seek refuge and assistance in the north with Venutius, the estranged husband of Queen Cartimandua of the Brigantes. Since he didn't support the Romans, he was the most likely ally we'd be able to find at a safe distance from the battlefield. At the very least, he could keep us hidden from Rome until mother was healed.

Mother attempted to mount her borrowed horse, refusing Sorcha's help at first, though it was painfully obvious she needed the assistance.

"Mother," I said softly, touching her shoulder.

A shuddering sigh of defeat escaped her. Not another word was exchanged, but she allowed both Sorcha and myself to lift her mighty body up onto the saddle. Sorcha mounted the prized mare of one of our warriors—that warrior was likely dead now. Andecarus was his name, and I heard Sorcha whisper it to the horse.

With a deep sigh, I climbed onto the saddle behind my mother. We had but two horses, and with the both of us sharing this one while Sorcha rode the other, it made the journey slower.

My muscles were sore. My head was heavy. My sister, strong and determined, sat tall before us. As the horse walked, every sway of my body jarred the aches in my bones. It was worse for my mother, who leaned over the withers of our mount. I gripped the reins around her middle when the leather slipped from her fingers. I had insisted on riding behind Mother; told her that as a brave fighter, I would take up the rear guard—but it wasn't bravery. I was too afraid to be in the front with Sorcha. Too afraid that Sorcha would sense my fear that we had reached the end and call me a coward for thinking it.

Sorcha . . . My older sister was the most capable girl I'd ever met. Even before we'd both grown breasts, she was always the leader. Like Mother.

I'd hoped that I would become a warrior, too, since my father was one, and I looked like him. But I could barely cut a hunk of venison, let alone cut an enemy with a sword. My only skill seemed to be for the healing arts—at best, I'd make a budding priestess. Sorcha, now—she was a master with a blade.

And I'd sometimes hated her for it.

Hated Sorcha for being so bold in mind and spirit. Hated her because Father doted on her and Mother admired her. Hated her because our fiercest Iceni warrior, Duro, loved her and trained her. Hated her for being the shining beacon light of our tribe. Even before I was born, Sorcha was the favored child. The one who'd been saved by the goddess Andraste. Lifted up from the depths of death to bring good fortune to our tribe. What good fortune that was, I'd yet to find out. To me she was hotheaded, spoiled, self-centered . . .

Well, I could go on forever about the various reasons I resented my sister, but the fact was, I resented her most for being what I wanted to be. And I admired and loved her for it, too.

Sorcha . . . The strongest girl in all the tribes. When the bastard Roman soldiers tore through our bodies with their thrusting and their jeers, I had died inside. Had not wanted to move afterward. But Sorcha shoved down her tunic, ignoring the mix of blood and seed dripping down her thighs, and walked away with renewed fury.

Meanwhile, I had lain like one dead until Duro lifted me high in his strong arms—but even raised up high, my shame sank me low.

"Faster, Keena," Mother gasped, bringing me back to the present.

Even from where I perched on the back of the horse, I could see blood seeped from the bandage wrapped around her waist, staining the dirty linen a dark maroon-brown. The warmth of it soaked into the sleeves of my gown.

She was barking orders at me that I was fairly certain were meant for herself. *Hurry . . . Do not fall . . . You're making too much noise.* The fast-fading sun gave the undulating hills an eerie gray glow. The forest, filled with the thick trunks of oaks and the wild needles of the pine trees, had given us coverage as we fled the battlefield, but forest had given way to farmlands, meandering rivers, and rising knolls. There was no cover but long grass, browned and trampled in some spots and wavering knee-length in others. We were exposed.

Where we might find sanctuary, I did not know. Where we might find a place in the world to escape the Romans, I could not fathom.

Still, Sorcha rode with her sword at the ready for any lurking enemy, sweat glistening on her exposed arms, ready to slice into anyone who leapt from the grass. Mother's sword drooped along the horse's side, but she stubbornly refused to tuck it back in the scabbard at her hip. I held tight to the reins, white-fisted, my dagger tucked into my belt, certain it would do no good.

The Romans had beaten us. But they had already beaten me a year ago.

I still felt the echoes of their assault on my body. I still dreamed of the vile liquid I helped concoct, the liquid that the birthing women slipped down my throat so that I would not bear a Roman child.

The agony and despair of bleeding out a baby I did not want, nor wished to exterminate. Knowing all the while that it did not matter, for whether I bore the child or not, everyone knew what had been done to me. The Romans took away from me any value I might hold and instead filled me with shame.

So why bother to keep running from them? I was not built for this. I rarely rode. I rarely fought. My lungs burned from the exertion. Perhaps if I stopped now, just fell off the horse and laid down on the ground here, I could convince my sister to leave me to the wolves—be they animal or human. I would gladly give up. Gladly surrender to darkness.

Let the ravens pluck out my eyes so I no longer had to see the world for what it had become. The Romans had annihilated us. Our entire tribe . . . gone. We had nothing. No one. Why was I the only one who seemed to see that?

Abruptly, our horse lurched, the sound of cracking bone mingled with the animal's scream of agony. And then we were falling. I clutched my mother as we thudded to the ground hard, my entire body jarring, and a sharp sting throbbing from my toes all the way to the hair on my head. Mother's cry of pain echoed in my ears. I scrambled up, lucky to not have been pinned by the horse's weight.

But Mother was not so fortunate.

"What in the . . ." Sorcha wheeled her mount around and leapt to the ground. "Mother!"

My mother lay in a heap, her leg trapped beneath the keening animal, its own leg at an odd angle in a deep rut in the ground. The great queen bent forward, gripping her leg, her long plaited hair falling over her shoulders and touching the ground. She pressed her hands to her knee and coughed, gagged, like she was going to retch.

Sorcha approached the fallen animal, sword drawn, and quickly sliced its throat. "Help me, Keena."

I nodded. "How?"

"I'll push the dead horse," Sorcha said. "You tug mother from beneath it." Mother was more than a foot taller than me and twice my weight in muscle. But I had to try, even if I thought us all doomed.

"Go on," my mother said, panting in pain. "Go on without me. There is no time to waste. The Romans are hunting us. You must get away."

But Sorcha would not have it. "We . . . cannot . . . leave . . . you." Sorcha spoke between grunts and bursts as she heaved at the horse's body. I gaped at her strength even as I gripped Mother's elbows so tight my knuckles turned white. She gripped me back, both of us trying to match Sorcha's ferocious energy.

Little by little, the horse's body moved, and I tried to tug my mother free. She gritted her teeth with every heave. Sweat trickled over our brows, and the sun sank below the heath, but at last she slid free.

I fell backward from the force of my last tug, landing hard on my rear, the impact reverberating up my spine.

"Mother," I whispered crawling on all fours toward her, heedless of the rocks and other things piercing my knees and palms.

She glanced up at me, pain etched around her eyes, but a small smile of encouragement touched her lips. Even now, felled by a horse, she tried to give me some hope.

Seeing that our mother had been freed, Sorcha wiped blood and sweat from her brow. "Let's go. Mother, you ride the remaining horse; Keena and I will walk."

Walk? Dear Andraste, how? I'd not thought it possible for us to get far enough north on horseback, and now we would have to do so on foot?

All I wanted to do was curl up in my mother's embrace and wish away this moment and all the ones preceding it in the last year.

"Make haste," Sorcha said, still refusing to look at me. "We will be slow as it is, and the Romans are certain to chase after us the moment they are sure Mother is not amongst the dead or the captured. They'll find this dead horse and have an even better idea we are close." She searched the horse, tugging from it anything we might be able to use. The sacks tied to the saddle, the blanket, the saddle itself. "I said hurry! I told Duro we would meet him at Luguvalium. We cannot disappoint him."

"Duro is dead," I snapped, though it hurt me to say his name. Mother's right-hand man—he'd been a pillar throughout all my life. "We are *all* dead."

My sister did look at me then, her teeth bared. "Duro is a strong warrior. He could have made it."

I noticed her eyes darted to Mother when she said it. Did my sister aim to keep hope alive for Mother, that Duro might have lived? Because as we'd fled into the woods and away from the battlefield, I'd seen him going back to face the Romans all but alone, buying time for us with his sword. He could not have survived. He'd had no intention of surviving. And if our fiercest warrior had not survived, then none of the Iceni had survived. Surely Sorcha knew that.

"We will not make it to Luguvalium *or* Venutius' lands. He's too far," I said, challenging my sister. I thought it a bad plan and now somehow had the courage to say so. "We have to pass through enemy lands to get there." Where Roman forts stood tall along well-trodden Roman roads; if we were lucky to pass by unnoticed—a miracle—then we'd still have Queen Cartimandua of the Brigantes to deal with. And she was a friend of the Romans. "The risk is too great."

Sorcha visibly gritted her teeth, and I half hoped she would use the shining sword at her hip to strike me down. "What other choice do we have?"

It was on the tip of my tongue to suggest we give up, but I kept silent.

With a shake of her head, Sorcha turned to my mother. "Mother, do you want to rest or keep going?"

"We keep going." Holding her wounded side with one hand, our mother half crawled, half heaved herself up to standing, her gaze warning us both to stand back. All of the blood drained from her face. Her teeth chattered in the cold. Ignoring all protests, Sorcha rushed forward, lifting Mother's arm over her shoulder to hold her up.

We all scanned the horizon then. I wasn't sure what we could hope to spot. Duro riding a stolen, frothing horse? Father risen from the grave? The Roman Emperor Nero himself giving the Iceni a pardon? Or at least, what was left of the Iceni . . . just we three.

"If we cannot go north, then go west. To the Cornovii, to my sister. They will help us—" Mother winced in pain as she straightened.

My mouth fell open at the name. Sorcha had gone to visit the Cornovii, asking them to join in the rebellion, but a vote against rising up ended with their refusal. The saddest part was that my mother's sister begged and pleaded with her people to say yes. She wanted to join her sister in the rebellion. "Mother, surely you remember . . . her people were against joining the rebellion, and their lands are occupied by Romans."

Mother shook her head, the effort of it making her waver on her feet. "I've had word from my scouts. The Romans left to join Governor Paulinus and his legions weeks ago." Mother took the lead, hobbling toward the only horse we had left, Sorcha helping her.

For a moment, I thought to remain rooted in place. Let them go without me. For they were courageous and strong, and I was cowardly and weak. Then fear of being alone overcame my fear of everything else, and I hurried to join them.

We walked another hour or more before spotting smoke curling into the sky, perhaps a mile from where we stood. A village, maybe. "There," Mother said. "It is not my sister's home, but we'll seek shelter there."

"They will know who we are," I protested. How could they not? Mother was well known in all the land, even before the great uprising. There were not many who looked like her. A warrior queen with long, fiery-colored hair, standing a height that topped most men. Even if she tried to disguise herself, her eyes would give her away. Fierce, blue fire-filled eyes.

Sorcha closed the distance between us, so close her breath fanned my face. "What other choice do we have? Stop nay-saying unless you have a better idea! Mother needs a healer better than you. Now."

I nodded, knowing she was right. "Let us seek the solace of their fire."

Even if it meant the embrace of the gods. The satiety of Andraste come to claim us at last.

SORCHA

HEAR me, invincible war goddess, Andraste, the battle raven.

You are victory, the proud warrior woman who never falls. And yet you were not with us this day of bloody battle. Your priestess, who led your Iceni people against the Romans in your name, rides a borrowed horse, weak and wounded.

She is your priestess.

She is our queen.

She is my mother.

Boudica is her name, if you have forgotten. But I cannot let you forget her or any of us because I think I shall soon die, too, and with no one to bury me. No Druid to give me the rites that will guide me into the next life. All my people dead, unburied, rotting on a battle-field, with no one to remember them to you and the other gods.

Except for me.

I am cold. My skin covered in prickles. I am hungry. I bear the marks of this rebellion on my soul, my body. Scars on my arms, on my fingertips. I am exhausted. But sleep does not find me. We seek shelter and succor from strangers who may very well turn us out into the night. Staring up at the sparkling stars in the sky, I hope the gleam of your moon means you are listening. I hope that after accepting from me so many bloody sacrifices of the Romans I killed, you will now hear me. And remember the stories I tell you.

Ah. Your wind, fierce as your smile, waves over the ground, rustling the leaves from the oaks that line the road, creating a circle around my body. So you are with me. You will hear my stories from the black rage of my heart and remember my fallen.

I want you to remember my mother. My father. My sister. My mentor. The young man I might have loved if the ability to love had not been stolen by the Romans. And I want you to remember me . . . if not in the next life, then in this one, to those who follow.

For surely the desire for freedom will live on. There will be those who fight for it long after we Iceni have breathed our last. I would like them to know our story. So help me tell it, goddess of victory and light. Help me finish my story. And help me to give it an end.

I was not born a princess.

On the day of my birth, the sun did not shine. Snow covered

the ground, and icicles dripped from the thatched roof of our hut, creating icy divots in the snow.

My father was one of the leading chiefs of our tribe. My mother was of noble blood, priestess of Andraste, who was goddess of victory, of ravens, the patron of our tribe. With two such powerful people joined in a union, they made a captivating force.

But the forces of nature and the will of the gods do not distinguish those of noble blood from those without.

The story of my coming into this world was retold around the campfires of our tribe on the anniversary of my birth each winter. A celebration of who I was and the good fortune I was supposed to bring to my tribe.

As the story goes, my mother was woken in the early hours of predawn with pains in her belly. She woke with a start, hands wrapping around her middle as waves of pressure mounted. Something was wrong. I was coming, but I was coming too soon. They were not expecting me for thirty dawns or more. Yet, here, my mother's body was demanding to expunge me from my warm cocoon into the frigid air of our roundhouse.

"Prasutagus," she said, one hand pressed over her belly, the other reaching for him, shaking his warm, sleeping body. "Wake. I need you."

My father roused, alarmed. He leapt from bed, reaching for the sword that was no longer there and then for the wooden club he kept hidden.

"There is no enemy," mother laughed between gasps of pain.

Father lit a torch from the flaming brazier. "What's happened?" My mother gasped as another pain struck her. Doubling forward, both arms wrapped around her middle, mouth open in a silent scream. My father rushed from the hut and out into the darkness, returning quickly with the birthing-woman.

Her cold, bony fingers slithered snake-like over Mother's belly, palpating her womb. "The gods demand the baby's breath." Her words were whispered but might as well have been shouted loud enough for every man, woman, and child of Iceni blood to hear.

When Father caught the words, he hurried once more from their hut out into the darkness and awakened our Druid. The two men brought a cold swirl of snow with them upon their return, a draft of cold that mother embraced, so covered in sweat was she from the exertion of the pains.

The Druid walked with a straight back and flat face to the brazier, reached his bare hand into the embers, and wiped the soot in a semicircle on his forehead. "You must bite the afterbirth thrice, Priestess."

All those in the surrounding roundhouses woke and danced, their hands stretched out to the sky as they pleaded to the gods and waited for my mother to give birth to the first of Prasutagus' heirs. Their breaths mingled in puffs of frozen clouds despite the leaping bonfires. As their lips turned purple from the cold, my mother cried out.

I burst my way into this cold world. I was small. I was blue. I issued only a quiet whimper as I gazed out into the void of my new world with glassy eyes. The Druid thought me a bad omen, a mark of darkness upon our tribe.

Whispers loudly echoed like the wind sweeping over the heath in a storm, and my mother and father stared at each other, at me.

"This child of Andraste has a fate we cannot decide," the Druid shouted. "We must leave it to Andraste herself." I wasn't the first and only babe to be taken outside the roundhouses and left on the sacrificial mound centered in the circle of sacred oaks. If a babe was left and found alive the next morning, then the child was meant for greatness. If a babe was found dead, the gods had not accepted it—and woe to the mother of such a child, for her fate was then never certain.

Not an hour after pushing me into this world, Father wrapped Mother up in furs, and they walked together into the forest, with me curled quietly in her arms. With great wretchedness, they placed me on that sacrificial mound. I am told that I wailed at the injustice of being abandoned to the cold—the first cries I made—and my mother took off her fur cloak and wrapped it around my tiny naked body.

Mother dropped to her knees on the snow-covered ground, raised her hands up to the stars, and shouted, "Andraste, hear me! I call upon you, as a humble daughter of your virtue. I speak to you as a woman to a woman, I pray for the life of my sweet child. Do this for me and I will forever be a servant to your will." Tears streamed from her eyes, freezing on her cheeks. She begged her goddess to return her child to her, for the good fortune of our tribe.

The wind whistled, the branches of the barren trees creaked and moaned. Was it Andraste? Was she listening? Father lifted Mother into his arms, wrapping her in his own thick fur cloak, and carried her back to their hut. Father was very strong, for Mother was never a small woman.

Before the sun rose, the world turned gray. Was this when spirits walked the earth? Was this when death would come to claim those the gods had chosen? To choose me?

It was my mother who chose me.

My mother, whose beauty was unmatched and ethereal. Beyond her burnished red locks and startling blue eyes, she had an energy that spoke to one's soul. I always felt as though the silent ones floated from the ether when I was with her. Blessing us. Protecting us. As she had protected me in my first night of life.

Just before the first fingers of dawn stretched over the roundhouses, while my father still slept exhausted, my mother crept back into the forest, skin tingling with fear. The closer she came to the sacred groves, a sound grew louder in her ears. The echo of tiny wails.

I was alive, and I was angry.

She ran forward, scooped me up, thrusting my body toward the sky and shouting her thanks to the gods for blessing me.

I often wondered if she'd waited, what would have happened then?

From that moment on, I was told again and again that I was our tribe's lucky charm, the blessed one. Our harvests thrived. Father was named King of the Iceni, mother Queen. The wealth of our tribe grew in leaps and bounds. I had a lofty ideal to live up to, a great banner waving metaphorically above my head, and yet I could not see the symbol it brandished. I only knew I must not fail. And for so long, I did not.

I was rarely ill. I thrived.

I believed I was invincible.

I was the child that leapt, arms outstretched, into the river when I'd not yet learned to swim. I was the child that ran toward the edge of the cliff to see if I could fly as high as the ravens. I was the daughter of a king who wanted to train to be a warrior, to fend off an opponent's blade with nothing more than my wit and the strength of my arm. I was the daughter who sought vengeance against those who'd dared to take my virtue. I was the daughter of a great queen who rode headlong into battle and cut down my enemies.

Learning that I was not invincible, that life does expire, that the gods did not always protect me—that was perhaps the hardest lesson of any. Trying to find the meaning behind such cruel neglect from our gods seemed impossible. Because now I *had* failed. Our tribe had thrived in so many ways, but now we were crushed. Our warriors slaughtered. Our Druids dead. Our past erased.

Were the Roman gods stronger than our great battle raven, Andraste?

KEENA

WE approached the village as the moon rose. Sorcha battered at the doorpost of the largest roundhouse.

"Please, I beg you, let us in. We need a healer and shelter for the night."

A man appeared in the doorway, a lamp in one hand, a sword in the other. He held the light up to my mother, studying her, and then my sister and I. I could see the moment when he realized who we were. He blanched, eyes widening with fear.

I pressed a hand to his forearm. "Please. We will leave come light."

He pressed his lips together, but his eyes met my pleading gaze, and he mumbled, "A moment."

He retreated, and we were allowed to follow. The roundhouse was no Great Hall, but there was a fire and the smells of mead and meat. A cluster of villagers huddled together for warmth, fear in their eyes as they looked at us. They barely made eye contact as they provided me with an herbal poultice, ointments, thread, and needle. I worked quietly by a brazier to clean and stitch our mother, who nodded encouragement at me. When my hands started to shake, a healer reached forward to help, but I pushed her aside. This was my calling. Had been. If I was going to come to terms with the whole of my world changing, at least I should hang on to this: my skill as a healer, my need to help my mother.

They let us sleep upon the floor of the roundhouse. And when dawn lit the fields, they pushed us out just as quietly as they'd let us in.

They did not offer anything for us to take. Not even to fill our water skin. They just wanted us gone before the Romans, who were surely on our heels, arrived. By not uttering our names, by not giving us anything to take, there was no proof we'd ever been there. Strangers passing through the night.

Two days passed since leaving that solemn village.

By the time we reached the outskirts of the Cornovii stronghold, my aunt's domain, the scent of peat fires filled the air, and an eerie quiet blanketed the moors. High up on the hill, we spotted the wall of the hill fort, lit by torches.

Was it possible the Romans could have beaten us here? Gone past us in the night while we slept? My knees shook, and I had to wonder if Sorcha would show even the least bit of fear. Mother listed heavily to the side of her horse. Sorcha pushed her back on while I carried mother's sword.

"They will help us get north. They will help renew us." Though her voice was hoarse, there was a queen's strength of will in her words.

I was not too full of pride to admit I wanted to run the other way.

"Wait," I said, my voice shaky. I stopped walking, my feet feeling as though my boots had been filled with iron. "We should check first. *They* could have returned."

Sorcha nodded. "Watch Mother." My older sister walked our chestnut mare toward a thick bramble hedge. Mother tried to dismount from the horse, and Sorcha was there to catch her before her knees buckled. I spread a fur on the ground in front of a tree for her to rest upon.

Sorcha cleared her throat. "If I'm not back by the time the moon follows the line of that large oak, take the horse and go north."

I shook my head, gaze darting from Mother's prone body to

the hill fort. "Do not leave us here." My voice had grown shrill. At least before, I had Sorcha to protect me. Mother's once-great strength had ebbed away, and those strong arms of hers now hung limp. If left alone with her, *I* was the one who'd have to be strong. And I had no strength left in me.

Sorcha sighed, the way she had all the while we'd grown up. It was a resigned sound, one that spoke volumes of disappointment. She pressed her hands to my shoulders. "Keena," she said matter-of-factly. "Be brave. Your mother needs you. *I* need you. You must be brave for once."

My entire body trembled, and I clenched my teeth, gripped tight to the sword in my hand. She needed me. Those words I'd never heard before from Sorcha. I was a healer, not a protector. No one needed *me* to guard them, least of all Sorcha and mother. And yet . . .

"You can do this. You must do this. Somewhere inside here"— Sorcha tapped my chest, causing my heart to skip a beat—"there is strength. Call upon it."

I blew out a ragged breath, on the brink of tears or laughter at the absurdity of it. I was without a doubt close to hysteria. "I do not think I can."

Sorcha smiled, her teeth flashing in the moonlight. "That is because you cannot see the Keena I see. But I can. She shines like a beacon."

And then she was gone, leaving my arms outstretched and empty as she rushed, body hunched, crossing the moors toward the hill fort.

I wanted to sink to the ground beside Mother, but I couldn't. Sorcha was counting on me. Mother was counting on me. Dragging myself to the bushes, I stood as tall as I could, and I held the sword with two hands, prepared to swing if someone should happen upon me.

I shivered.

"Keena . . . my brave, Keena," Mother whispered.

I glanced down at her, seeing her soft smile.

"I'll protect you, Mother," I said, forcing my teeth to still their chatter.

Some creature cried overhead, and I leapt, a gasp echoing on the wind from my throat. Every noise had me twisting. Swerving. Heart pounding. Dizzy.

Sweat trickled down my spine, over my brow, despite the frigid cold. I swung at the bats that darted in a path over my head, screeching as they passed. I reeled toward the grass, cutting in an arcing pattern when it swayed with the breeze. I parried the night wind, swinging as I'd seen my mother do. Fighting like a great Iceni warrior.

I nearly cut my own foot when a rodent scurried over it.

But I stood tall until my sister returned with several tribesmen.

"Keena." She rushed toward me, arms outstretched, gripping me in an embrace we'd shared more over the past few months than we had our whole lives.

"You returned," I said, my voice carrying more uncertainty than I wanted it to.

"Of course." She gestured at the darkened shapes of men. "They are here to help."

The men grunted, one lifting Mother into his arms. She barely made a sound, her arm flopping nearly lifeless to the side. Another man led the chestnut mare. I wanted to rush forward, to grab the reins—feeling stubborn in the fact that the precious horse was our only way to freedom.

"Come. We have shelter for tonight," Sorcha said before rushing to walk beside the warrior carrying our mother.

I came behind in a daze, not letting anyone take my mother's sword from my grasp. This was mine now. I wouldn't let it go. Couldn't. It was as much a part of my mother as her heart, which I willed to keep beating. It *had* to keep beating.

You know how badly she is wounded, my thoughts whispered. But I couldn't bring myself to think the truth. That she was dying.

The stronghold was quiet. Our feet scuffled on the hard-packed dirt until we were brought into the warmth of the Great Hall. The heat hit me like a wall, the sounds inside seemed distant to the rush of blood filling my head. I had been holding my breath. I was close to collapsing.

Strong hands braced me, urging me. I looked to see a woman close to my mother's age, familiar in her height and the bone structure of her face. She led me toward a fire lit in the center of the room and furs piled on the floor. I sat, my skin thawing in painful prickles. A cup was shoved in my hands. "To help you sleep."

I drank. Mead. An essence of herbs.

I spat it back into the cup.

Soft laughter sounded. "It's not poisoned. I promise." The cup was taken, the contents drained into the mouth of the woman with the plaited dark hair—my aunt. She smacked her lips when she was done in an exaggerated move, then refilled the cup and handed it back. "Now drink. The mead will soothe, the herbs will help you sleep."

I pushed her offer away and shook my head. "My mother—"

"Is in good hands. You are safe here." Her eyes implored me to believe her. "I would never harm her. Or her daughters." My aunt stroked a calming hand over my shoulder. She pushed the cup back toward my lips, and I drank.

Contemplating the orange-and-yellow flames, I said softly, "We lost."

My mother's sister looked sad, face falling into shadow. "I see that." Behind her, I heard whispers from the other Cornovii, moans, prayers.

"My mother . . ."

"Hush now, child. You must sleep."

I jutted my chin forward. "I'm not a child."

My aunt smiled, the same curl to her lips my mother used when I threw tantrums as a child. She pushed to her feet, hands on her hips, and gazed down at me with kindness. "All right, little *woman,* go to sleep."

"I need to help my mother. I'm a healer."

"You are brave, daughter of Boudica. But let us help *you* this night."

Brave. It was not something I'd ever thought to be. But perhaps I was learning.

My aunt tugged at a fur around her shoulders and wrapped it around mine. "You shall rest here for a time."

I was too tired to argue, though I knew as soon as Mother could utter a word, we'd be on our way. She would not want to risk staying in one place until we got farther north. My eyes started to droop, and I was suddenly so heavy, so filled with exhaustion I could barely sit up straight. I set down the cup of mead, only half-drunk, and looked around the Great Hall. A crowd of people surrounded my mother, but Sorcha slipped into view, hurrying to join me at the fire.

"Keena, you should be resting." Her own voice was filled with exhaustion. She looked and sounded more like Mother moment by moment. Whatever energy she'd been able to muster on our journey here was sapped. Now that we had found safe haven for a short time, her body must have realized it, even if her mind had not.

"*You* should rest. You did more than me today," I said.

Sorcha turned her head toward Mother, fear etching her features. If Sorcha wouldn't take care of herself, shouldn't I be the one to do that? Our aunt was the younger sister of my mother, and that was what she was doing. Mayhap sometimes the younger did take care of the elder.

I picked up the half-filled cup and handed it to Sorcha. "Drink." She took the cup and downed the contents. Then the corners of her mouth turned down. "That was filled with some concoction."

I shrugged. "Herbs. It will calm you. Help you sleep."

Sorcha nodded. "Then I should drink a vat."

I smiled. "We have to be strong on the morrow for Mother. You know she will wake, and then again we will be running."

"Perhaps they will lend us a cart."

I nodded. "And a pony? We can lay Mother in the back of the cart while one of us drives and the other rides Andecarus' mare."

"Not as fashionable as when we used to travel . . ."

Sorcha trailed off, and I knew she spoke of the Roman games we once attended in Londinium, when we'd arrived in a gold-ornamented chariot behind Mother and Father's own ornately carved one. "A cart won't be as celebrated as the chariot you rode into battle, either."

Sorcha nodded, almost wistful despite of all the bloodshed that came with that chariot. I laid my head down upon the gathered furs and felt her sink beside me.

Just as I drifted off to sleep, I heard Sorcha speak, her voice far-off, as though a dream. "I am proud of you. You were brave, standing guard alone. Have courage, Keena. We may depend on you again one day."

Depend on me? Until recently, I could barely depend on myself. I'd wished to die more than once. But Sorcha's words . . . they gave me a spark, just the tiniest, dimly lit glow to heat my heart. Did my sister speak the truth? Did she know how very much I wanted to be like her? How much I'd admired her and despised her for all her strength?

Sorcha was the blessed one.

Sorcha was the strong one.

Sorcha was the warrior.

Not me. Not *me*.

I was the quiet one. I was the small one. I was the weak one. Wasn't I? I saw myself on the dark moor, holding my mother's sword. Acting as protector. A strength I'd not known existed flowing through my veins. But that night I dreamed vividly of standing upon a hill. No one was with me. A hundred ravens circled overhead, and I glanced up to follow their path of flight only to see that I held in my hand a sword that dripped with blood.

And I didn't scream or run in fear.

SORCHA

THE man who taught me how to fight was not my father—though I know he wished he had been. My father was a proud warrior before he was king, but I was taught to fight by Duro, my mother's right hand.

Duro hated the Romans with an all-encompassing fire, and I wondered if a part of him looked down on my father for honoring the Roman prohibition against our tribe carrying weapons. My father asked us to see the prosperity in what the Romans brought to us even as they took our swords and spears, for he believed we could find peace in partnering with the very men who sought our destruction.

For every injustice the Romans offered us year after year, I watched Mother's face grow darker. The smiles that used to come easily lessened. Lines etched at the corners of her eyes and be-tween her brows. She whispered in corners with her kinsmen. Father did not see it, but *I* knew she was planning something.

I was my father's heir, along with Keena. One day, I would have to take care of my sister, in addition to our kingdom. Keena was weak. I knew that she would always depend on me, that I was meant to protect her.

Three years younger than me, she was shorter, much thinner, her coloring dark like our father. I took after Mother, tall, broad of shoulder, fiery locks, and blue eyes.

I'd heard it time and again. I was a protector. When the gods had gifted me with life on that moonlit winter night, they had spoken—I was blessed. I wanted to be more than blessed. I wanted to make my parents proud.

I also wanted to make Duro proud. I'd grown as close to him as I had my own father. When I was very young, I'd followed him into the woods where I heard rumors he trained the men in secret away from prying Roman eyes. I watched for a time behind a tree, flexing my fingers, eyes trained on every precise movement they made with their wooden swords.

When the men left, covered in sweat, dirt, bruises, and smiles, Duro called out. "I know you're there."

I bit my lip, wondering if I should run. I stepped from behind the tree and said, "I want to train to be a warrior."

Duro raised his brow. "A warrior? You are a princess. Should you not concern yourself with more diplomatic affairs?"

I frowned. "But I want to learn how to fight. I want to be strong so that I can lead my tribe one day. Am I not the lucky princess?"

Duro grunted, his gray brows rising as he appraised me. "What do you think the principal duty of a warrior is?"

"To protect."

"And the second?" His fingers flexed around the wooden hilt of his sword.

I raised my chin. I knew this one. "To honor his king and queen."

"I think you have it backward." Before I could ask what he meant, I saw a glimpse behind another tree of a dark, curly head.

Ria. My half sister, the get of my father upon a slave girl. Everyone knew of her kinship to me, but no one would speak it aloud, and I never did, either. My father was fond of her, insisting that she be a part of our household. A mistake, I thought, for Ria's age alone spoke of my father's indiscretions. And no woman, much less my mother, wanted a constant reminder that for a few brief moments her husband shared his passion with someone other than her.

The sight of Ria ducking back behind her tree had distracted me, but not Duro. "You will always be expected to honor your king and queen," he said. "That oath always comes first."

I rose to my full height. "For most warriors, perhaps. But when I am queen, there will be no one above me, and so I must honor my duty to protect first."

"What about your husband?" Duro asked. "He will be your consort."

"But not my king," I snarled. "*I* would be the queen."

"Even so, your husband will likely be chosen for you, whether negotiated for you by your parents, elected by the tribe, or appointed by Rome."

I jutted my chin out in defiance. "Then I will not marry."

"Ah, but there you are wrong. You are the lucky princess. You must marry in order to carry on your legacy through the birth of your children."

I crossed my arms over my chest. "Perhaps it is Andraste's wish that I fulfill my destiny in some other way."

Duro smirked, baiting me on purpose. "Nonsense. Andraste may have already chosen a husband for you." He waved away my cry of outrage the same way he batted away a fly. "Now take this stick; we've wasted enough breath on talking. Time to show you a thing or two about fighting. Weapons instead of words."

Years passed, and by the time I was almost thirteen, my training had intensified, and I had a few scars to prove it. Duro let me lunge, sometimes awkwardly, sometimes with grace, slapping at my ribs with the flat side of his wooden sword. I was tall, growing toward my mother's height, but all that growing meant I'd not yet become accustomed to my own body.

We continued the dance every afternoon, the only sound our grunts and the loud reverberating sound of our wooden shafts slamming into one another until Ria again dipped her head from behind a tree. Always hiding. Always sneaking about.

"What is it?" I called out to her, annoyed that she should break my concentration and earn me a slap from Duro's stick.

Ria bowed her head, hands folded before her, and spoke softly to Duro. "Your son Andecarus has returned."

I glanced at Duro, watching him blanch. "Your son?"

Duro pursed his lips and nodded grimly. Andecarus had been given to the Romans as a hostage years before. Forced to fight in their auxiliary. Another reason Duro detested the Romans.

Duro cleared his throat and returned his attention to me. "Let us continue."

"Do you not want to see your son? He's been away for a very long time."

"He can wait."

I jabbed the floor of our makeshift training ground in the woods with the tip of my wooden sword. "He can. But you should not have to. I am Princess of the Iceni, blessed one of Andraste, and I *command* you to bring your son before me."

I was truly only playing with my newfound power as a young royal woman when I said it, and I fully expected Duro to punish me for my arrogance. I expected him to say no, that he'd not bring his son, gone so long with the Romans, to our secret training ground. But Duro surprised me. He turned to Ria and gave her a curt nod, then launched into a full attack, knocking my sword to the ground.

"Your tongue is sharp, your mind impulsive. Be quicker with your hands if you wish to lead the strong."

I nodded, biting my tongue and forcing myself not to react.

"Don't you trust your son?"

Duro hesitated. "I don't even know my son."

"So let us meet him."

A moment later, Andecarus strolled into view. I'd been too young to remember him leaving—somehow I'd imagined him a boy, but he was a man fully grown. He was shorter than his father and leaner. Handsome, too. Long dark hair was pulled back in a flattened braid, an unusual look for an Iceni, for our men wore their hair either limed stiff or in undisciplined chaos. He had eyes the color of the woodlands in autumn, and they met mine with a fire that matched my own. We could be friends, this young man and I. I did not want him to dismiss me as a mere *child*.

I held up my wooden practice sword, pointing the tip toward him. "You've been away with the Romans. Show me what you've learned."

A direct challenge from a woman, likely to anger any man, but Andecarus was not any man. And I was not any woman. He was Duro's son, and I was his princess.

He glanced at his father, who gave his approval with a warning that no blood be shed. The two of us agreed. I balanced on nimble feet, rocking back and forth, the weight of the wooden sword starting to strain the muscles of my forearm and shoulder.

"Give me everything you've got," I challenged.

Andecarus laughed. "Silly girl," he said.

Duro made a half-strangled sound; I couldn't tell if it was outrage or amusement. "That is no way to address your princess."

Rebellion flared in Andecarus' eyes. He remained rigid; then, with an audible sigh of annoyance and an irritated flash at his father, Andecarus begrudgingly begged my forgiveness.

"Warriors do not beg," I said. "That is a value the Iceni and the Romans both hold. Raise your sword and *fight* me."

The next moment, our blades clashed, and I thought—just what did Duro mean when he said, *Andraste may have already chosen a husband for you?*

THREE years into training together, Andecarus finally let me have it.

The sun shone, though beneath the blanket of leaves from the tallest oaks, we were shaded, and a good thing because both of us were covered in a thick layer of sweat.

We were alone, as we were most of the time. Duro didn't like it when I trained with the other warriors. They eyed me sideways now that I was a woman grown, which made Duro glare protectively. He was as fussy and protective as a hen sometimes. Andecarus' sword arced in the air, muscles beneath his tunic bunching as he brought it down toward my own wooden blade. We'd been sparring partners for more than three years, and in all that time, his height had remained the same, whereas mine had grown considerably.

I was a good hand taller than him, a fact that irked him considerably given that I had sixteen summers to his twenty-seven, and I'd finally grown used to my own height. My movements were fluid, practiced, and deadly. I ducked, sweeping my sword toward his ankles, and he leapt into the air, twisting. He brought his sword down in a sideswiping move that would have dislocated my shoulder had I not also twisted out of the way, hand glancing off the ground to balance me.

Whenever we fought this way, I imagined what it would be like next summer, when my father and his father would make an agreement that we should marry. When Mother would pray to Andraste, sacrificing a hare to bring the gods' blessings upon us. I did not know if Duro had raised the matter with his son, but Father had raised it to me. Andecarus, my husband and consort. I would walk to him next year in a wreath of summer flowers, as my mother had walked to my father, and one day we, too, would be Queen and King of the Iceni—if the tribesmen willed it and if Rome allowed it, but why shouldn't they?

Andecarus was like my father, and I like my mother. We were well matched.

The moment's dreaming was enough to make me falter in my steps, and Andecarus immediately dropped his sword, reaching forward to catch me. His arms encircled me in a warm embrace, my breath caught, heart pounded. I bent my knees a little so we were closer to eye to eye, and not at all because my legs felt wobbly.

I'd never been this close unless we were battling. But right now I was the only one holding a weapon. At least a tangible weapon. For I feared Andecarus' true strength when it came to me was his quiet, unwavering eyes. Eyes that made my heart ache and yearn when they rested on me.

Was this love? After three years, I thought it must be, for I had never felt this ache with anyone else.

His hand slid over my arm to where my fingers clutched the hilt of my practice sword, and he held tight to it.

"Do not ever let go of this, Sorcha." He had always used my

name, casually, because we were friends. It had never felt intimate before . . . well, before this moment, where something sparked and the air felt literally filled with heat.

"I will not let go," I said and gave the hilt a squeeze under his hand.

"You're better with the sword than some men." His voice had grown low and gravelly.

I leaned closer, and I told myself it wasn't because I needed his strength to stand up. My knees were *not* weak, I swear it. Me, the blessed one, the princess born for greatness—I couldn't go weak at the gentle touch of a man. But I was, and I knew it.

I cleared my throat. "Thank you."

"You do not need to thank me. I speak not to praise you, but out of truth." His throat bobbed as he swallowed. "I have seen and learned much of the world. Both here and in my time with the Romans. I could teach you a few things."

"And?"

"We live in a changing time."

"What do you see?" I felt he knew something, as though the gods had visited him in a dream and shared with him some secret that I'd yet to learn.

He shook his head. "Its not so much what I see, but what I've learned."

"Tell me."

"The Romans are not all bad. There are some bad apples in the barrel, but generally, they want good things for this land. For the people who inhabit it—both Roman and tribesmen. Growth. They are willing to work with us."

I smiled. "That is why my father agreed to be a client king."

Andecarus laughed, the sound scratchy. "Yes."

"But what of the fact that we still train with wood instead of iron?"

"Someday we will prove to them we are their allies and they have nothing to fear from us."

A rush of excitement filled me. Perhaps this would happen when Andecarus and I were officially matched. I couldn't think of it. Felt the heat rising to my cheeks.

"Shall we finish our training?" I asked, feeling flustered.

He didn't answer, only studied my face with an increasing intensity that set my blood on fire.

"I—" He abruptly cut himself off.

I cocked my head. "What?"

"I find you . . . thought provoking."

"Thought provoking?" I raised a brow. That was not exactly the praise a woman wanted from a man.

"And fierce. And beautiful." He whispered those last precious words as he pressed his forehead to mine.

Our eyes remained locked on one another. Would he kiss me? The thought had my heart leaping into my throat and my stomach dropping to my feet. My fingers trembled around the hilt of my sword; his own trembling on top of mine.

Andecarus leaned a little closer, his lips only an inch from mine. I kept my eyes open, not one to shield myself from what was happening right before me. If this was to be my first kiss, then I wanted to remember every detail from the crease in the center of his forehead to the golden-brown flecks in his eyes and the droplet of sweat that traced the length of his brow.

Warm breath fanned my face, and I gulped, couldn't swallow around the dryness in my throat. I arched my neck so that our lips might meet should he dare to press just a little closer.

"Princess."

Our moment was broken by Ria's voice.

I jerked away from Andecarus. Had she been hiding behind the tree again? Spying on us?

"What is it?" I asked tersely, letting her know just how much I did not appreciate her intrusion.

"The queen wishes to speak with you."

I nodded, willing her with my fierce glare to leave me. Ria dropped her gaze, resentful, and left us.

"Apologies, Princess," Andecarus started, but I cut him off.

"There is nothing to apologize for." And without looking back, I left him in the middle of the clearing, wishing I'd taken the leap and kissed him. Because then maybe I would have known one gentle kiss in my life instead of violence, and love in my soul instead of a black heart of hatred.

KEENA

"WE may have lost the battle, but Rome has not beaten us. We have fought them and won before. We will do so again."

It was these words from my mother that roused me from my herb-and-mead-induced stupor. The Great Hall was still mostly dark. A thin strip of light sneaked through the door, and a single torch was lit nearby. The brazier had banked at some point, but the heat had been retained inside.

I rolled over, wiping dried crust from the corners of my lips and eyes and gazed up to see Mother arguing with her sister, as I so often argued with mine.

"It's far too soon. You'll break the stitches. And you may yet come down with fever."

Mother grunted. "If the Romans come, and they will, they must not find me or my daughters here."

My aunt's hands on her hips fell to her sides. "We can hide you. You're not yet well enough to travel."

Mother struggled to sit up, managing to plant her strong feet on the ground. "It is pointless to argue with me, Sister. We are leaving today, and that's final. As we speak, the Romans could be moments away from discovering our whereabouts."

Catching me awake, Mother made a motion toward me. "Get a crust to break your fast. Wake your sister. We leave soon." Hope alighted inside me. Perhaps the rest, the work of the healers, and some food had done her good. Just days before I'd thought us beaten, thought mother's death to be imminent, but she seemed to be rallying. Perhaps Andraste was working to mend her mortal wounds.

Our aunt's tribe provided us with a cart, a mostly fit pony, five sacks full of provisions, and several skins of mead. They gave us linens and a salve to help keep Mother's wound clean and plenty of fur pelts to keep us warm. Again, hope sparked. We'd lost so much, but maybe there was something worth grasping on to.

We ambled outside, Mother's arms over Sorcha's and our aunt's shoulders. We gingerly settled her in the back of the cart, but even soft treatment couldn't take away her pride. Mother sat tall, pushed our hands aside when we tried to cover her with blankets. She was not yet too weak to cover herself, she said as she studied her sister who held out a shield to her. "We must learn to live with it or make a change. And I'm not taking your shield. Mother gave you this."

"Take it. You will need it more than I," my aunt said. And with that, she argued no more. She pressed her lips together, a hard expression on her pretty features, and watched us ride away.

Would I ever see her again? I doubted it, though I desperately wanted to.

I climbed onto Andecarus' horse, whispering and smoothing my hands over the mare's red mane, as I'd seen Sorcha do. I let my sister take the lead with the cart. As we left the hill fort, I kept turning back, watching our kin grow smaller and smaller in size until they disappeared altogether.

Despite having the cart, pony, and a horse, we seemed to travel slower than when we'd had only one mount and the two of us walking. Perhaps it was that the sound of our transport was so loud that we could not hear anything surrounding us, so we stopped often to listen, or maybe it was that when we went through particularly sopping grounds, we sought a different path as to not leave our tracks—which was nearly impossible given the icy rain fell once more in droves. We were lucky we didn't get the wheels of our cart stuck in the ground.

We were nearly always wet and always cold, and fires at night did not last because the storms seemed only to grow rather than abate. We huddled beneath our furs in the back of the cart we'd led off the road, seeking shelter beneath the trees. A swath of wool, fitted to stay in place above us, served as a roof of sorts. The nights were miserable. The days only slightly better. Were the gods weeping for all of our people lost upon the battlefield? Could they even remember us with the Druids gone?

We carried on that way for three days. Together, my sister and I tended Mother's wounds, we fed her, gave her mead to drink. We cared for each other, too, reminding each other to eat, drink, sleep.

My hard-found flash of hope faded because fever pounced on my mother despite all our efforts. Her skin burned, her wound leaked, and she faded from lucidity to muttering delirium. She woke from dreams ready to do battle with Romans that weren't there.

The hope I'd had for her healing, for her strength that had shown itself at the Cornovii hill fort, was fading. My mother was going to die. Were we to die with her?

I had thought I *wanted* to die.

I wasn't so certain anymore.

SORCHA

WHEN I was small, my father would lift me into the air and toss me about.

We played rough; we loved hard.

His strong, capable arms would encircle me, and I felt protected from everything. Just as I knew Mother would swing her sword to keep me safe, I knew Father would sever the head of any enemy who dared touch his lucky princess. Yes, he honored the Roman edicts, but he was first and foremost our protector.

I knew that one day the Iceni tribe would depend on me. But I'd not expected that day to happen in the winter of my sixteenth year.

Mother's cries wrenched the air, startling me awake. The sun rose with the piercing wail coming from her sleeping chamber at the back of the Great Hall. I clambered from bed, my heart lurching, stomach burning, and in my gut—I *knew*.

He was dead.

My father, the Iceni King, was gone. Though he'd been ill for a long time, it was still shocking. We'd hoped he was on the mend and then . . . nothing.

Why did so many die in the night? As though they wished to kiss us and deliver us with sweet dreams before taking their leave of the world. We drifted into sleep, and while we thought only to say good-bye until the morning, we were, in fact, bidding them farewell in this life.

He looked peaceful in death. The lines of concern that had creased his brow, eyes, and cheeks for as long as I could remember had smoothed. They would not let me near Father, nor Mother. I could see her clutching his body, great sobs racking her form. And then, just as suddenly, she stopped. As though someone had cut off her breath.

She stood, smoothed her skirts, and wiped at the tears on her face. She placed coins over his eyes, and then she walked out of the Great Hall, pushing past the guards, past the roundhouses, toward our sacred grove. Mother, ever the priestess of Andraste, would pray for her husband, the father of her children, the king of her people. She would offer up a sacrifice to the gods that they take him gently along their path, that they protect her people from hardship, and bargain for the future of her daughters.

I wanted to follow her, watch her speak to her goddess, watch her make the sacrifice. To study her. Because my mother fascinated me. There were moments she was everything a mother could be, washing my face and kissing my wounds. But there was another part of her, an untouchable part that made me want to stand in her shadow *and* bask in her light.

Keena pressed her waifish body beside mine and looked up with huge tears in her eyes, spilling over to stream down her cheeks. Awkwardly, I patted her hair. She let me, but I could see she wanted to rush forward, to drape herself over our father's body and check his breathing just in case someone had made a mistake.

"Go to him," I said.

Keena nodded, and as she approached, another figure darted from the darkness to kneel beside him.

Ria.

Another of father's daughters.

Keena stilled abruptly and wavered enough I feared she would fall. For one brief moment, Keena reached for Ria's hand as if she were our sister in truth before one of the slaves tugged Ria away to make room for the legitimate daughter alone. I'd never before sensed the wrong in this—that Ria, because she was a product of an indiscretion, because she was a slave, was never thought to have the same needs of her father as Keena and I.

And until now, it hadn't really mattered. But this girl, this dark-haired slave, she deserved as much as anyone to say good-bye to her father.

And yet, if I said anything . . .

I frowned, gazing about the darkened room, shadows bouncing where the light from torches and the brazier didn't reach. What did I care? Mother was not in the room to reprimand me, nor to order Ria back.

I stepped toward the girl whose shoulders trembled, though her jaw was tight. She wasn't allowing herself to sob outright. That I understood as I bit my tongue and gritted my teeth. I grabbed her hand, wanting to pull her to the other side of my father not occupied by Keena, but she resisted.

"I need you, Ria," I said. *Blame me for it. Let them think I cannot go forward without leaning on your shoulders.*

Ria's eyes connected with mine, and I nodded, grim-faced, hoping she would understand my meaning.

I don't know if she did or if she simply followed my orders, but she placed her arm around me and led me forward, an awkward sight I'm certain given I was so much bigger.

We knelt together, praying as our people lamented and off in the distance somewhere, Mother's calls to Andraste swirled on the wind.

IT is no small occasion to bury a king.

For days before the funeral, people arrived to pay their respects. Even the oft-gossiped Queen Cartimandua of the Brigantes came from the north to honor my father, though she departed before the funeral pyre was lit. Mother kindled that flame on a cold winter's morning, me at her right hand and Keena at her left. All around us, the bright cloaks and carved torcs of our people mingled with the pristine armor of Roman soldiers and the white togas of the procurator and his officials. I wished the Romans could have taken themselves away like Cartimandua. I wanted to grieve for my father, not be stared at by greedy Roman eyes. One of the centurions, a rodent-faced man named Helva, had been leering at me throughout all the ceremonies. We'd yet to speak beyond a simple introduction, and I hoped I'd never have to speak to him again. I didn't like the way he looked at me. I pushed my chin up and stared him down through the smoke of my father's pyre, willing him to show me respect, but it only made his hungry smile more pronounced.

"Do not speak to them. Do not look at them. Stay clear of the Romans, Daughters. Let me be the only one of us to speak to them," Mother had warned when the procurator and the rest of the Romans first arrived.

Dutifully, though begrudgingly, I ceased staring down the centurion, returning my eyes to my father's body.

We watched the flames engulf the great king. Bathed and dressed and presented to all as much a Roman as the Roman guests attending, the only difference a bright Iceni plaid cloak draped over his frame.

Though Mother stood tall, expressionless, I could feel her tremble every so often beside me, and I knew it was not the quiver of a woman mourning her husband, but rather rage for the injustice she saw being caused. Father had insisted on a funeral pyre because it was the Roman way. But it felt all wrong. Too Romanized. Mother worried that Father would not be accepted into the next world, and so she hoped that burying his ashes with all his worldly possessions would appease the gods.

We both had our doubts.

The great king was reduced to a pile of ashes, which were gathered in great iron cauldrons, clouds of his burned body swirling up with the wind, refusing to be tamed or constrained to a tiny vessel. Flecks of his bones landing on those who stood near.

The burial ground had been dug near our sacred grove, accompanied by a sacrifice of a lamb, which would be buried with his ashes. Mother invoked Andraste. Father's great sword was laid out beside his shield. On top of his wood-and-iron shield, my mother placed his gold crown.

When his ashes were placed beside his weaponry, she gripped my hand tight enough that I knew I was the one holding her up. She loved my father so much—I did not think she would ever love another. Her responsibilities now were to the tribe, to our people, to Keena and me. We would support her in her grief, and she would advise us.

If the Romans would only honor my father's will. I felt tension seep through her as she watched the Roman procurator leave the burial early, heading for the Great Hall. We smiled, tight-lipped, as the funeral continued, each of us wondering, what next?

Midday had passed by the time the funeral was done. Trailing back to the Great Hall from my father's grave, I saw the rush of white togas. Bright armor. Roman slaves.

The procurator had taken the opportunity to begin ransacking our home. My feet rooted in place, and I wavered. Keena rushed forward, Ria on her heels. Two swift arms held out by Duro stopped all of us from moving forward.

But no one stopped Mother.

It is now legend through all the tribes: how she argued with the procurator, how he ordered her stripped, how a stake was thrust into the ground, and she was bound to it. It was the seed of her legend, that moment—but all I saw, horrified and furious, was my mother naked and exposed.

That greedy-eyed centurion named Helva stood center, gaze riveted hungrily on my mother's body. "Harlot queen," he snickered.

Roman guards formed a half circle around her punishment, their swords drawn, blocking anyone who might try to stop them. Our people wailed and cursed.

"They will not dare flog her," I whispered frantically, praying that someone would wake me from this living nightmare. "They will not dare."

But the lash descended.

My hand flew to my mouth as the line of blood opened across my mother's white back. I stood there, helpless, motionless, stunned. The procurator strode away, and Helva wielded the whip mercilessly. Three more angry stripes marred her flesh.

I reached for Duro, gripping his arm. He, too, stood transfixed.

"Harlot queen. Iceni bitch—" Every epithet from Helva's mouth was followed by a stroke of the lash. The sound of leather slicing through the air and tearing across her beautiful, strong back jarred me from my silence.

I screamed, "Why?"

No one answered me. Everyone's tongues seemed to have been cut from their mouths. I looked for the procurator—the only Roman with authority to command this, or stop it—but he was riding away as though a creature from the depths of the earth were chasing him.

I tried to run forward to help my mother, but Duro grabbed me tight. Keena and Ria cowered behind us, clinging to each other as Duro whispered in my ear, "No! They will only punish you, too, if you go to her."

"Mother!" I shrieked. This could not be happening. They could not be humiliating her this way. She was Queen of the Iceni. And she was my mother. "Cease this at once!" I cried with all the authority of the lucky princess, the ones the gods themselves blessed at birth. "Do not lay another mark on her body!"

I broke free of Duro, and then the voices sounded as though they'd been waiting for just that moment to speak again.

"Grab her!" one of the guards shouted.

"Not my daughters!" Mother's fierce voice bellowed out above the rest. *"Not my daughters!"*

Ria grabbed Keena's hand and started to run, but I could see them being circled by Roman guards, their shrieks of fear overriding the blood pounding in my ears.

I grabbed for the dagger at the belt of one legionary, freeing it before he could stop me. As the iron hilt grazed my palm, I knew it was a bad idea to take it. But I was powerless to stop. Incapable of doing anything beyond trying to protect my mother, my queen. A warrior's first duty.

And so I rushed Helva, who was still mercilessly lashing my mother's back. The sounds of shouting, the whistling of the leather through the air, blurred together with the pounding of my own heart. I stabbed at Helva, but violent hands grabbed me from behind, wrenching me backward.

The dagger was twisted from my grasp, slicing into the soft pads of my fingertips.

I ground my teeth, lunging in the direction of the men who held me. The pure animalistic will to survive roared to life within me. Chaos had erupted everywhere I could see. Screaming women clutched their children; our warriors lunged for the Roman soldiers only to be beaten to the ground. I saw Duro and Andecarus vanish into the Great Hall, trying to drive off a centurion dragging a woman by the hair.

"Get your hands off the princesses!" Mother roared, her beautiful, hard face turned over her shoulder, fear and pain etched onto her features. "Sorcha! No!"

"Princesses?" A Roman smirked, pinching my breast painfully. "Property of the emperor now."

I bucked, head jerking backward, connecting with someone's face, only to have my arms wrenched upward, eliciting an unintended cry from me. They'd not hear me cry out again.

"You'll all be executed." Helva stopped flogging my mother, turning to glare at me. He seemed to carry more weight than the rest as he stepped closer, glowering fiercely. I hated him. Hated everything he stood for.

I spit in his face, watching the spray land on his cheek, and bared my teeth. Helva snarled and wrenched back his arm, slapping me hard, leaving the copper taste of blood on my tongue.

My vision blurred.

"I'll teach you never to insult me again," he growled, wiping at the spittle on his cheek.

He turned to his men, his arms raised to garner more attention. "We have a law against executing virgins. We'll have to remedy that barrier."

A resounding round of bloodthirsty calls answered. They chanted his name with raucous approval. "Helva! Helva! Helva!"

Pain still radiated where he'd struck me. I could feel the skin swelling and knew I'd be bruised. This man sought to humiliate me, but I did not fear him. Romans might be cruel, but they wouldn't defile a queen's daughters.

And yet they flogged a queen.

My throat tightened. Breath ceased. *No. No. No.*

They were dragging us away from the whipping post. Keena was screaming, and I saw a legionary yanking at her tunic. The cries of the men sounded like beasts gone mad. They no longer cared for anything but the taste of dominance and blood on their tongues. The procurator was gone. My father was gone. We were left to the mercy of vicious soldiers now, who claimed they were free to treat my defense of my mother as an act of war.

We were vulnerable, all of us. The Iceni. My mother. *Women.* Nothing but an example to be set.

I refused to be an example of a woman broken.

I stood taller.

I would not be beaten, no matter what they did to me. No pain, no humiliation, nothing could take from me who I was. What I was meant to be. I would survive this if only to exact my revenge.

"Filth! The lot of you!" I bellowed as their hands pawed at me. "You are not worthy of the air we breathe. And if you don't leave my family and my people in peace, the gods will strike you down and let me dance upon your graves!"

Helva's violent blow slammed against my face, almost felling me to the ground. I tasted more blood upon my tongue. My ears rang as they dragged me away. In the distance, I could hear my mother shrieking and the laughs of the men. Then, just as swiftly, all the sound was dulled as I was tossed beside Keena and Ria upon the storehouse floor. The dust from the ground rose up and into my mouth and nose. I kept my eyes open as they fell on us. Watched Ria crawl away to hide, her whimpers sounding distantly beyond the vicious cheers.

I kept my gaze steadily on Keena. Locking her in and mouthing for strength as, one by one, they tore at our clothes. Helva wrenched my thighs wide and stole my virtue as another legionary fell upon my sister. I kept my gaze on hers, seeing in the periphery Roman feet. Tight leather lacings. Red blisters, callouses, flesh bulging at their hairy ankles. They walked around us, waiting their turns upon our unwilling bodies. As tears gathered in the corners of my eyes, I gritted my teeth to not make a sound.

Keena relented, wailing, her eyes closing tight and tears spilling down her precious cheeks.

It felt like hours. I was violated by many. But there was only one that I vowed to kill, to slit his throat before the end of my days.

Helva.

Helva's feet were slow moving, as though he wanted to take in everything, to absorb what he saw before he called an end to it. He ordered the men out, leaving us huddled on the ground.

We would not be executed, then. The torment they'd unleashed on us was enough, and perhaps now, Helva, as centurion, was worried what the backlash would be.

He offered no apology when he left, only the violent, bloody memories of his presence.

I was born a fighter.

From that first moment when my parents left me to the gods and I raised a fist against the injustice of it.

I trained hard with Duro. I trained harder with Andecarus. And when my mother called for our Iceni people to fight, I did. For vengeance. For our lost honor. For the liberty we wanted for ourselves, I wielded a sword for my people.

The Romans *tried* to break me.

They failed.

Except in one thing. The day after the Romans left us, when I stood with Mother before our shocked people, Andecarus rushed to offer me assistance. But I turned away. I could not bear to see myself in his eyes now, despoiled. And I knew I could never look at him the same way again. Never look at *any* man with fondness.

If there was one thing the Romans had stolen, it was my future with Andecarus. They had stolen my love from me. Turned my heart black and filled it with hatred.

So I turned away from Andecarus as if he had some part in the shame of what happened.

That night we gathered in the silent Great Hall, the Romans gone. Their inventory complete. Mother sat stone-faced and rigid. Her wounds from the flogging had been tended, and while a weaker woman might have needed to rest for days, to sleep, to heal, she was already vowing to be out of her bed by morning. Now she sat before her people, her two abused daughters beside her.

Keena looked so frightened, like she wanted to sink inside herself. I just wanted to protect her before she disappeared completely. Did she not know the depths of the quiet strength that lived inside herself? All the confidence she'd exuded before had been stripped from her. She was a pale, frailer version of herself. The Romans had stolen my love, and they'd stolen my sister's strength.

No one spoke to the queen. No one spoke to me. Or to Keena.

And was their silence because of shame? For when the Romans raped us, they raped our tribe. They tore from us our honor, our dignity. Or at least that was what they'd hoped to do. They sought to make us afraid, but I did not smell fear in this room. The air within the Great Hall was charged, edgy. It trembled with rage.

No, I realized—there was no shame here. In the face of such tragedy, such atrocity, they were angry. They loved us. They supported us. And so they cared for us.

When the sun rose, muted by dark storm clouds, Mother stood. She went outside to invoke her goddess in the sacred grove. This time, I did sneak out to watch her. I crept along behind her, hobbling, as my body had hardly healed from the assault. Aches bruised my body in places I'd not known were possible. Mother paused once, listening to the wind, and I suspected she knew it was me behind her. Then she continued on, weaving, barely able to keep her feet. A slow rumbling of thunder shook the earth beneath my feet.

By the time mother stood at the center of the sacred oaks, a light sprinkle of rain had started. I leaned my hands against a large stone jutting from the ground, pressing as close to her as I dared, ignoring the sting in my cut fingertips. I closed my eyes, tipped my head back, face toward the sky, letting the water from the gods wash away my shame.

From somewhere, Mother produced a soft white-and-brown hare. It wriggled in her arms, unaware that when she placed it upon the sacrificial mound, it lay in the very same place I had sixteen years before.

Brandishing her dagger with the bronze hilt, she sliced the hare's neck and uttered the incantations to Andraste that sounded to me like a lullaby, a mother's sweet song whispered on the wind and the breast of love.

"Come here," she said.

I startled from my hiding place but obeyed without question. Her eyes radiated a fierce, savage pain, filling with tears as she saw how it hurt me to walk.

Mother opened her arms and brought me to her, circling me in her warm embrace. We stood like that for some time, and I felt her tears touching the top of my head. I squeezed my eyes closed as I tightened my hold on her and breathed in her familiar scent.

"I am so sorry," she said softly, her voice hitching.

My throat swelled.

"It's not your fault, Mother." *What happened to my sister and me . . . it was my fault. I should not have acted so rashly.*

"When a woman's child is harmed, she always feels blame." She stroked my hair, kissed my forehead, and then held me at arm's length. "I love you, child."

"I love you, too." I bit my lip to keep it from trembling, my heart swelling.

"I can see you take the blame on yourself. Know this: what happened was no fault of your own."

"But—" I strangled on the words. *If I'd not rushed Helva with a dagger, intent to kill him . . . if I'd not spit in his face . . . kept my mouth shut . . .*

"It wasn't, child. The Romans . . . they sought to not just take your virtue, but to tear dignity from our tribe. The fault lies entirely with me." Mother's lips went thin, agony filling her eyes. "I should have hidden you away. But for all the vileness in them, I did not think the Romans capable of what they did to my daughters. To me, yes. But to you . . ."

"We would not have remained hidden. We are Iceni. The daughters of a king and queen. We would not cower."

Mother dragged in a ragged breath and glanced from me to the hare upon the mound. The she nodded and straightened.

"Sorcha, daughter of light, gift from the goddess Andraste. The gods have spoken. They wash away the crime of the Romans, and they bless you." She dipped her fingers in the warm hare's blood and swiped them across my forehead, nose, and cheeks while she whispered urgently, "*I* bless you."

The rain caused the blood to drip into my eyes and mouth, but it didn't bother me. If anything, it lifted me up. I had the blood of the gods running through my veins. The bond I felt with my mother at that moment was stronger than our shared flesh. Light and fire and ice, all of it at once, surged inside me. I stood upon the ground, and yet I soared. I was cleansed of the stains of my violation.

Mother's eyes locked on mine, as though she were reading my very soul. "Your people need you now more than ever, Daughter. For we are about to embark on a treacherous journey. We will go to war."

I knelt before my mother, before the sacrificial altar inside that circular sacred grove, and I made a pledge. The cold, wet ground seeped into my gown, but it could not cool the fire that had ignited. "However the gods need me, however you command me, let it be so." Out of this darkness, I would be the light. The lucky charm for the Iceni. The Romans couldn't strip me of that.

"You are a daughter of Andraste. A carrier of her message—victory for her people. Victory for the Iceni."

"I will fight for my people. I will rip the hearts from the Romans." *From Helva.* "I will make them bleed as they have done to us."

When spring came and the snows melted and our wounded flesh was healed, I climbed into the war chariot with my mother and sister, no longer a girl but a woman. The chariot was freshly painted red and gold. Gleaming silver and gold chinked from the harnesses of two beautiful, shiny-coated horses. Our faces were painted—Mother's and Keena's with blue woad, mine with blood. I wore armor and a helmet forged just for me, a battle raven carved deep into the side. Men lined up behind us in the thousands, woad-painted, hair spiked with lime, weapons dripping from their limbs. They were ready to fight. Ready to show the Romans we would no longer cower to their will. I breathed in the scent of horses, banked campfires, spring sunshine, and another sharper fragrance—that of thirst, of hunger, of need for vengeance.

I glanced at Keena, pale-faced and quiet. I would protect her. She would come out of this with me. I had to help her find her strength again.

Mother handed me the reins. "Daughter, you will be our charioteer."

I puffed with pride. "Are you certain?"

Mother nodded, a small smile tugging at her lips. I gripped the leather of the reins, tightening my scarred fingers around them. Feeling the excitement and thrill of what was about to happen. We were going to charge a Roman city—Camulodunum. We were going to sack that Roman city. The first of many. Today I would take the life of a Roman soldier—and I begged the skies to let it be that of Helva.

When I raised my sword and bellowed a battle cry that carried through the men in our army, I was not just a princess wronged but a warrior born.

"I am Sorcha, Princess of the Iceni. Daughter of Queen Boudica and King Prasutagus. I am an emissary of Andraste. I *am* the blessed one. Let victory be ours this day!"

And then I whipped the horses, and our chariot jolted forward, charged with the energy of thousands of vengeful warriors.

KEENA

WE'D reached the end of the world.

The sky had gone dusky with the storm, though it was only midafternoon. Black clouds swirled over our heads, crashing into each other in thundering booms. Rain drizzled over us. My hair was plastered to my chilled face. Fingers numb. I rode Andecarus' mare, as Sorcha was better trained at driving a cart. We rode to the top of a ridge where it seemed we could see the entirety of the world beyond. There was nowhere else to go. The world dropped off into a deep and wide gorge. The only way around it was to backtrack and try to find another route. I turned the horse— Sorcha was still several paces behind—and I walked the mount back to her.

As I did, I happened to gaze down the embankment to my left and noticed that the ridge created an overhang. I reined in the mare and dismounted, wondering if perhaps that overhang could be our shelter for the night. Sorcha halted the cart and waited for me to examine the spot. I walked and half slid down the edge to find that the overhang formed the roof of a narrow cave.

Shelter. Thank the gods.

I did not hear anything from inside the deep cavern, but still, that did not mean we were alone. Wolves, outlaws, any number of things could have sought shelter there. I glanced back up the crest to where Sorcha and my mother waited. I couldn't call Sorcha down here. I had to check on my own. Taking a deep, ragged breath, I straightened my spine and tugged Mother's sword from the scabbard at my hip. Brandishing it inside the darkened space, I waited for attack. Nothing.

The breath of relief I let out was strong enough to blow the dripping water on my face away.

"Sorcha," I raised my voice to be heard over the pounding rain and pointed. "A cave."

Sorcha nodded, though I noted the lack of smile at such a good find. She'd grown more resigned over the past few days, and I could feel a subtle shift in both of us. Gone was Sorcha's burning desire for vengeance, and gone was my burning desire for death. The last year had changed us both dramatically, more than once. Neither of us were the same girls we'd been the morning our mother was flogged, and neither of us were the same from the morning of the final battle.

Was it possible we might yet meet in the middle? Become of like mind?

She went to the back of the cart, beckoning me to help. We emptied the stores, putting them into the cave, and then carried Mother, each of us putting one of her arms over our shoulders as we took the precarious trip down the embankment toward the mouth of the hollow.

We settled mother inside the cave, wrapping her in furs. Then Sorcha went to hide the animals and cart while I gave mother sips of mead.

Perhaps a half hour later, Sorcha returned, soaked to the bone and shivering. Mother had managed a few sips but was otherwise delirious.

"I'll gather wood," I offered, and Sorcha nodded. I hadn't expected her to, but she was coming to rely on me. To trust in me and my newfound strength.

The icy winter rain slowed to a sprinkle and then a mist. I looked for fallen branches beneath brambles and the blanket of leaves I hoped would have kept them dry, and I did find several.

A loud cawing above me drew my attention, and I straightened from where I'd been yanking a particularly long branch from its perch, hanging halfway off a tree.

The raven landed on the other end, cocking its head as it stared at me. A sign. Sorcha had once told me of a talk she had with the lone surviving Druid who survived the sack of Mona. He'd talked to her of signs and symbols from the gods. What could this sign mean? Ravens came when death was near. Carrion birds to peck at the flesh of the dead and dying. Was he here for my mother? I clenched my jaw. No. Not yet.

"Shoo," I said, waving my hand. "This is my branch."

The raven cawed, studying me like he could see inside me. See inside my soul. See my deepest thoughts. My fears. My desires. Did this mean I was about to die and he wanted to pluck out my eyes? No. I wasn't ready for that. Death could not yet claim me.

"Go away, Death," I said, this time with more conviction. "Leave us. No one wants you here. Not even me. Not anymore."

And it was true. With a startling clarity, I realized the words I'd spoken were genuine. I didn't want to die.

But he didn't leave me. He flew forward, perching on my shoulder and pecking at my hair. I shrieked, waving him off, and he flew back to the branch to stare into my eyes.

This raven was not here for my mother. He was here for me.

If not death, then what?

He was only a bird, but his eyes seemed familiar to me, as familiar as my own father. Had the raven inherited the spirit of my father? *Nonsense.* And yet the more he gazed on me, the more I felt I knew him.

"I *will* live," I professed to the bird. "I am *not* beaten."

Perhaps my eyes were deceiving me, or maybe it was a trick of the wind ruffling that raven's feathers, but I swore I saw him nod his agreement. Death was not mine yet. Death would not steal me away. And then he was flying away, up into the graying sky— toward a shaft of light that had broken through the clouds.

SORCHA

ON top of the rise, the sun had not yet risen. Mother and Keena slept soundly in the cave below while I kept watch on the ridge. In the distance, I could hear the clanging of Roman shields. After all our running and trudging, hiding and scheming—after all my endless worry, my ears forever straining behind us for the sound of pursuit—they had tracked us down. Judging from the clang carried on the wind, they were miles away still, but even though it was not yet dawn, they marched. We had a few hours at most before they'd find us. Because Romans never slept, never stopped to rest their weary, blistered feet. When the Romans wanted something, they harnessed the power of darkness and slogged ahead, forsaking the wants of the body and soul.

Well, maybe not *all* the wants of the body. When I closed my eyes, I could still hear Helva's laughter as he pushed his body away from me. His harsh voice as he goaded his men to mount me in turn. Their distorted Roman feet. I could still see Keena's eyes staring into mine as we were both taken. Her cries of agony.

I had thought it was my fault, even when Mother told me it wasn't. I knew now the blame was not mine. And neither was it my mother's. Those men were looking for a reason to attack us. They were looking for a reason to slake their violent lust and need for bloodshed. They'd come to our village with intent. I could have been quiet. I could have been still. The outcome might have been the same.

The sound of Roman swords and Roman feet approaching should have sent me into blind panic. But I sank to my knees, holding still, and the power of Andraste swept around me. She was in the wind. She was in the chill of the earth beneath my fingertips. She was in the light of the fading moon and the graceful stroke of clouds passing over the slowly lightening horizon.

Dawn approached, dusky pink. And I had to be prepared for what was coming.

Death, humiliation, or slavery.

We would never make it to Venutius' lands.

Something rustled, and I turned around to see a white hare creeping toward me with the rolling mist. The animal locked its eyes on mine—not the eyes of a wild thing. They were knowing eyes, filled with intelligence. Could it be? Was this my sign from our great goddess?

I reached out slowly to stroke the softness of its head between its ears, and it let me, scrunching up its tiny pink nose. Peace filled me, warmth cloaking my skin and taking away the cold of the air, the chill of the wet ground upon my knees.

"Have you come to give me a message?" I asked.

The hare did not answer, only stared at me, and warmth washed through me.

My heart warmed, swelled, overflowed with love. Not just the love of my goddess, but the love of others both on this earth and in it. I loved my mother. I loved my sister. I loved my people. Even in death, I loved Andecarus, my father, Duro, those we'd lost in battle.

I had loved them all along. Love had made me fight, not vengeance. Because we are never really willing to die to satisfy our craving for blood. We are willing to die to satisfy the injustices that have been placed upon us and our loved ones.

The Romans were coming. My mother was dying. Keena and I couldn't both make it out of this alive. Only one of us would be able to escape.

I had to save my sister.

That was the ending to my story. The end of my tale that I'd begged Andraste to help me see. This was my story: *My love returned to me. Sorcha, the protector of her sister.*

I had safeguarded her throughout our lives, and I would protect her one final time. My love had helped Keena remember her strength, for it had never really left her. If a Roman bastard had been growing inside my womb, I would have gone mad and stabbed myself to death, whereas Keena was patient, taking the potion she'd made herself and allowing the magic to take away the life thrust inside her.

The Romans were drawing closer. I could almost see them now, vague movement on the dark slope far below. I had to hurry back to our cave. I couldn't let them find me here alone or find my mother on the brink of death, with Keena at her side. I wouldn't be able to save my sister.

I locked eyes with the white hare and said, "Thank you, goddess of victory. You have not forsaken me."

The hare sniffed my palm one final time, then turned and hopped away, disappearing into the mist that now blanketed the entire ridge.

I stood and ran, toes sinking into the earth, the mist swirling around my ankles. Down the embankment I skidded until I found the mouth of the cave. The rising sun was burning off the mist; soon it would reveal our hiding place to anyone who happened by. Even if we hid our steps with rotting leaves and the branches of shrubs, there was no hiding the scent of the campfire we'd lit to stay warm during the frigid night.

Our cart would be found not far away, and our pony and Andecarus' mare.

"Sorcha," Keena said, waking up from what I hoped was a good sleep, for she would need it.

My gaze slid to Mother, who breathed shallowly, her pale face turned golden by a shaft of rising sun piercing the cave opening. Keena pushed back the furs and stood. Her eyes widened as a sound drifted up: the distant blare of a Roman bugle.

"They come," she said.

I nodded. They would find us very soon.

And I knew they'd not let us go.

"DAUGHTERS," Mother said, her voice weak but her resolve strong.

She knew the end was near. She slid up the side of the cave wall, wobbling on her feet. Face pale. With one hand braced on the wall, she drew her sword. Blood dripped in a steady stream from the bindings at her ribs, over her hip and down her legs. Even had the Romans not been coming, her wound would kill her. Our frantic flight had never given her the chance to mend.

"Every warrior's dream is to die honorably." Mother's voice was hitched with emotion, and she pressed her lips together for a moment before she spoke again. "And you must both do so, with me. I cannot let them violate you again."

I studied Mother, her face so pale against the vibrant red of her hair. The woman who must have been born with one fist in the air and another grappling for a sword. The woman who nearly brought Rome to its knees. The woman who rode into cities occupied by the enemy and burned them to the ground. My mother. The greatest warrior queen our land had ever seen. And she'd almost won this great war. I revered her all the more for it.

I glanced at Keena, who had seemed to grow taller in the last week since we'd been running. She'd barely eaten. Barely slept. And though she trembled, looking at the mouth of the cave for what was to come, she was braver now. Stronger, too.

I sucked in a breath and straightened my shoulders, recalling the hare—*Andraste*—who'd come to see me on the ridge. She had spoken to me—perhaps not in the physical sense, but I'd known all the same what I needed to do.

"Die with me, Daughters," my mother was saying. "We will join your father with Andraste. From the next world, we will see the Romans buried."

No. Keena had to live. At least one of us had to survive this.

And if that meant I had to go against Mother's wishes, then so be it. Because my duty was to make sure my sister survived. She needed to carry on. Mother wouldn't understand. Her desperation was in seeing that no more worldly harm came to her daughters. And I understood that, too. But the gods had spoken.

This would be my final gift to Keena. The gift of life.

I owed her that much as her protector, as her blood. I would bear the pain of death—or worse—if only she could survive this.

To Keena, I said, "Remember the days of old, where our world was filled with magic and innocence. Recall a time where no pain touched you. Remember our people who perished. Remember the injustices done to us by the Romans. Remember why we fought and what we believe in."

My sister cocked her head to stare at me as though I spoke another language entirely. "I remember," she finally whispered.

I opened my mouth to speak, my chin wobbling. I tightened my entire body, willing emotions to take a step back from what I needed to do. "Never forget."

She bit her lip, and I knew she must be thinking that she was about to die, and there would be no time for remembering at all.

Nearly a year had passed since the first stripe was laid on mother's back. Now the only thing left for us, for me, was to ensure that Keena lived, that we were remembered to our gods. And I couldn't do that if the Romans killed us both. There was a path down the rise where Keena could sneak away. Small in size, dark of hair, dressed in rags, she looked nothing like Mother. No one would know who she was. They'd not guess her to be Boudica's daughter.

"They will want to take us as prisoners," Mother was saying. One hand still holding on to her sword, anchored into the cave floor for support, she pulled a needle-thin dagger from within the depths of her long, thick, gathered hair. "But we will not let them." Mother's eyes closed for a brief moment, tears slipping from her eyes. I'd not seen her cry much in my life, and it left me shaken.

I wrapped my arms around her, hugging her tight. I knew what was to happen. How this was going to end, but knowing didn't make it any easier. Only harder.

Mother pressed her sword against the wall, letting it go, then cupped my face with her free hand and stared into my eyes. "We will never be prisoners."

I nodded, swallowing around the lump that had formed in my throat. The great queen would try to take matters into her own hands. I could not accept that. She thought there was no way out of this, that not even one of us could survive.

"Andraste awaits us." Mother grasped her dagger with both hands and pushed it toward Keena, then seemed to change her mind. Tears brimmed in her wide blue eyes, and she looked on my sister with a mixture of regret and hope. When she spoke, it was softly. "I will show you how it is done bravely and so that it is not so painful. No more pain for any of us." She implored us with her eyes, and we both nodded, though I would not see that silent promise through. "Keena, you will do this after me. Sorcha, you will do it last."

"Sorcha . . ." Keena drew out my name like a question.

I glanced at her, trying to impart comfort but seeing the fear slicing her features. Would her courage slip? Would the strength returned to her over the last week be stripped away once more? Would she cower, beg Mother to make the dagger thrust for her?

No. Keena grasped my hand tightly, her chest puffing, and the fear marring her features was replaced with that strength I knew she'd possessed all along.

"All will be well, Sister. Stand tall. You have my vow," I said.

"And you have mine," Keena whispered, then pressed closer to mother, kissing her softly on her cheek.

"A warrior is never full of fear when their great reward is at hand." Mother's voice was scratchy, her eyes full of love. "Soon we will lead an even greater life in the next world. Together."

The Romans were coming closer, their dogs howling, and the sound of it chilled my blood.

"Sorcha, give me the water skin," my mother said.

I pulled the skin from our pile of belongings.

"We'll drink together," she said, taking it from me, then lifting her face toward our unseen gods. "As a priestess of Andraste, I offer this last libation. And ourselves, our bodies, will be our final sacrifice to you in hopes you will guide us into the after-life."

I sipped the mead and then passed it to Keena, whose fingers remained steady as she drank. Mother whispered incantations that would open the gates into the life beyond.

"We must make haste to Andraste's arms." Mother bent closer. I embraced her as she reached out to us, suddenly afraid that she would stab us both, thinking it a final kindness. But instead, she kissed us on our foreheads. To me, she said, "You have always been my little warrior, fighting passionately with every breath. From the first raise of your tiny fist, willing the gods to bless you on that cold mound. I have always seen so much of myself in you. Little Boudica." To Keena, she said, "And you have always been my little healer, filled with quiet, strong resolve. You give me peace and calming comfort. I have seen much of myself in you—another priestess. The best parts of me reborn. I love you both. I am proud to be your mother. I will see you soon."

Then she raised the dagger and brought it up beneath her ribs. A guttural cry rushed from her throat, though she quickly cut it off with a press of her lips as the blade pierced her body and entered her heart. At the sight of our mother's mortal agony, Keena wavered on her feet. An otherworldly whimper issued from my sister's throat, eyes drawn to the blood seeping from Mother's wound.

I leapt, catching my mother's body as she fell forward. I laid her onto the bed of fur pelts. I knelt, her head in my lap. She looked up at me, eyes wide, lips moving. "Do it," she said. "Do it now."

I nodded, yanking the dagger from her chest and watching her take her last breath. All the life of a great warrior woman evaporated within the span of two heartbeats. I choked on a sob, recalling every touch of my mother's hand upon my cheek, every word she spoke, every brave deed of her glorious life. Mother reached up to touch my cheek, her fingers faltering, sliding down to drop beside her. She issued a great, shuddering sigh, her spirit melding momentarily with mine. I closed my eyes, unable to breathe. Unable to move. But only for a moment. There was no time to mourn. She was . . . gone.

And the enemy still lurked outside.

I turned my attention to Keena, frantic now. "I will sacrifice myself. Just as mother did. For you. You must run now. Run and do not look back. Live, Keena. Live and remember. Have courage. Have faith that Andraste will guide you." I swallowed, feeling my throat tighten around the words. "Go."

Standing frozen, Keena looked from me to my mother and back again. Panic filled her face. Mouth agape, eyes brimming with terror. "I cannot let you do that for me. It is not courageous for me to run away while you sacrifice yourself!"

"I said *go*. The courage is in going north on your own. For remembering us to our gods. There is no other way. Slip farther down the embankment, away from the ridge and Romans. Run. Run until you cannot breathe, and then run some more. Go now, before it's too late!"

Keena trembled violently, reaching for me. "But—"

I waved away her outstretched hands, perhaps the hardest thing I'd ever done, for I wanted to embrace her, hold her tight to me and never let go. My sister. My beloved sister. Keena, who finally had lived up to the meaning of her name—brave at last. "We all have a destiny. I have mine, and this is yours." I tugged mother's torc from around her still warm neck and gave it to Keena. "Take this. And remember."

Keena thrust the torc around her small neck with trembling fingers and teary eyes. "I love you, Sorcha. I *love* you."

"I love you, too," I whispered, wishing that I'd been able to tell her sooner. She tried to say more, but I waved her away. "Say no more. Take mother's sword. Go now, or suffer death."

Keena slipped from the cave, her shoulders squared, Mother's sword held tight in her fist. She would find her way north. She would continue on the journey we'd started, all by herself. Remembering our people. Remembering us. I pulled a fur over my mother's body and closed her lids. I kissed her brow.

And I prepared to die.

"IN here, you limp-cocked milksops," I shouted.

It felt exceedingly good to shout such vulgarities at the bastards. The sound of their marching boots crunching on the leaves and branches echoed in the trees and met my ears inside the small cave. I wanted to distract them from the dogs that might be howling after Keena.

I stood in the center, my face painted in my mother's blood, my sword and her shield in my hands.

But I nearly cowered when the first man's voice I heard was that of Helva. It must be Andraste's doing, to send him on my trail of all Rome's centurions. She did indeed want to test me, but she also wanted me to have what I had vainly sought all year, across three sacked cities—*his* blood.

He stepped into the dim light of the cave, eyes widening slightly at the sight of me. He made a *tsking* sound with his tongue, that slow, leering grin creasing his face. Dressed in gleaming armor, his hair cropped short, his weapons glistening, the man was just as repulsive as I remembered. Three legionaries followed, filling the entrance of the cave and blocking my way out—a small scouting party, probably one of many combing these lands to find my mother. As they advanced inside, Helva made a swift cutting move of his hand. With the cave so narrow, none of them would be able to move around him. I'd have to fight one at a time, which is just what I wanted.

Both of us knew I wasn't getting out of this alive.

But neither was he.

Helva glanced toward the ground where Mother lay. "I see we came too late," he drawled out.

I laughed bitterly. "You're right on time."

He laughed, too. It was that same sharp, gravelly sound I'd heard the entire time his men thrust inside me. A sound that made my blood run hot and cold at the same time. A sound that fueled my fury.

"Where is your little sister?"

"Dead," I lied.

He laughed again. "Shame, I rather liked—"

"Shall we play a game?" I cut him off and tightened my grasp on my sword.

"The only game we'll play is *call me master*." He drew his own sword. "On your knees, bitch."

I smirked. What did I have to lose but my pride? At least I would go out of this life with a smile. "You do not seem to under-stand the rules."

He bared his teeth to me, obviously irritated that I showed no fear. The man had learned nothing in the year since we last met.

"Barbarians do not make the rules," he ground out.

"So you say, but have you not been trying to beat us the last two decades? Did we not rise up against you every time?"

He dragged his feet back and forth on the ground as though he drew the lines of a makeshift arena. "You lost."

"Not every time. And not yet." My words were clipped, an intentional call to his anger.

"You *will* lose today." His face had turned red, and he spoke with bluster.

"I doubt it." I rather enjoyed mocking him. Why not go out of this life having a bit of fun with this cur?

My confidence rattled him. It rattled *me*. War had hardened my soul. I'd fought for my life and those of my people for the past year. Killed my share of Romans and maimed plenty more. I was wholly prepared for what was to come, and still, the sight of my enemy's shield swinging toward me, his sword poised to stab me in the gut, sent a shiver racing up my spine.

This was real. This was happening. And we advanced toward each other.

I breathed slow and deep, growling when I attacked and hissing when I blocked. The clang of metal against metal echoed in the small cave. Sparks ignited with each clash of the swords. *Block. Attack. Block again.* Each move was precise. Each move was calculated. Andecarus had taught me the way the Romans fought, and I could anticipate their moves.

Helva was no different.

But he did have one advantage on me. Helva was bigger. He weighed more. He was stronger. He'd not starved and been deprived of sleep. He'd not been chased and hunted like an animal. He'd not just witnessed his mother's suicide or worried over the well-being of a sister dear to him.

Block. Attack. Block again. "I'm going to gut you," Helva said. "Then I'll bathe in your blood while I bury my cock between your thighs as you die."

I laughed and lunged left, arching right. "A task you'll be hard-pressed to complete without a sword or your cock."

Helva didn't like my taunting. He was already angry that the fight was lasting as long as it was. His men were watching silently behind him, and I knew he must be imagining they thought him weak, a failure.

His started to attack me with quicker, rasher strokes. Not at all like a Roman. Romans were usually patient and methodical. But in his quest to annihilate me, he adopted the moves of my own people. I raised my sword to block, but his blow jarred my arm, sending shattering numbness into my shoulder. But still I swung, though my grip was not good enough to cause any real harm. He attacked again, and this time my sword flew from my fingers, through the air, clattering on the cave floor near my mother's body.

All the air rushed from my lungs, and my stomach plummeted. This could not be the end. This was not how it was supposed to be. I was supposed to kill him. *I* was supposed to be the one bathing in *his* blood.

The bastard's face creased into a punishing smile. "I win," he taunted and slowly stalked forward.

My sword was too far. The only weapon I had was my mother's shield save for the dagger strapped to my hip. A dagger couldn't win against a sword. But it was all I had.

I returned his smile and beckoned.

His eyes raked over my body, taking in all he was prepared to plunder yet again. I stepped back, allowing him to advance on me but also to retreat farther from his men. Last thing I needed was some over-eager foot soldier wriggling into the narrow opening to join our battle just when I had Helva in the right spot.

When I stopped walking, he stilled, considering how best to rush me, but it wasn't more than a breath or two before he flew toward me, sword arcing and slamming down. I blocked with my shield, punching my arm up, hoping to tire him. Again and again.

Sweat covered me, dripping into my eyes, over my back, against my palms. Muscles screamed with exhaustion. If I was tired, he had to be tired. Didn't he?

And then he misstepped. "Thank you, Andraste," I whispered, knowing my goddess had a hand in his faltering footwork.

I jabbed forward with my dagger, finding the side-gap in his armor, ramming the blade into his ribs. I thrust hard, bellowing as I did it. Feeling the tip of my dagger pierce every layer, feeling the pop of his organs giving way to my blade, and then I yanked it upward, the muscles in my arm burning.

My dagger sank deep, all the way to the hilt. His blood, warm and slick, spilled over my fingers. I'd delivered a deathblow.

Duro had taught me well.

A rush of relief fell over me. I would die, but he would die first. I felt peace in knowing that. Felt the love for my sister, my mother, my people. My blessed mission complete. He stared into my eyes as he stumbled forward, the sheer weight of him pushing me back. A guttural, feral noise fell from his open lips. Blood dripped from the corner of his mouth.

"*I* win," I whispered right into his face. "*You* die." I yanked out my dagger, and his blood came pouring with it, soaking the front of my chest with its warmth.

His eyes met mine, widening, for I was right. I had won, and he'd not once believed it could be.

Helva dropped to his knees with a futile gasp for air. He reached for me, and I smiled, shook my head, took a step back. Those few seconds seemed to pass by slowly, and I looked toward his men. At their startled faces.

I grabbed Helva's sword and braced myself for their onslaught.

Another one came at me, and I resolved I would take them, one at a time, until I could take no more. A blood-curdling battle cry tore from my throat, and the last thought I had was of Keena, and that I had set her free.

KEENA

I will never forget the imagined sounds of my sister's screams.

I will never forget the strength it took for her to give me life.

I will never forget *her*.

Sorcha makes me strong. Sorcha's voice guides me on this path now. I trudge along on legs that are much too tired, but strength fills me. A need to survive and carry our story to the gods.

I turn back every few feet to stare into the distance. I listen for the sound of an approaching army. But I hear nothing.

Every gentle sway of the wind is Sorcha pushing me forward.

Every low whistle of a breeze is her soft murmur telling me not to stop.

I am traveling north. I am continuing on our path because, with Sorcha's help, I found my courage. My strength returned to me from where it had been buried deep.

And she is right. The Romans are not following me.

All through the battles of this long year, Sorcha had pushed me back. Made me hide. Kept me hidden and safe. She was my protector all through my life until the last breath she gave. They would not look for me. I was nothing to them.

But I am something to my people. I am brave. I am the beacon of light that will carry on the memories of the Iceni, their rebellion, and of my mother and sister. I will remember them to the gods so they do not forget, and someday history will record the sacrifices that were made.

These are the thoughts that keep me moving.

I stop only for a moment to rest, my feet blistered and bleeding in my leather shoes. My mother's sword is heavy, as is my heart and the duty left to me. Leaning a hand on a tree, I drag in a chilled breath, watching it puff out in a cloud of vapor. It is cold. But I cannot stop. I must keep going or I will freeze to death when night falls.

A familiar caw sounds above, and a raven lands on the branch just over my head. His eyes meet mine, and I see the same intelligent animal, the one with the eyes that bore into my soul.

"Hello, raven," I say.

He caws back, then flies up in a circle before bolting north. I watch him, wishing I could fly to where I need to go. Wherever that is.

Pushing off the tree, I wander toward a stream. I kneel and wash my hands and face, sip the cool water, and stare at my reflection. I look haggard.

Can I go on? Have I failed? No. I cannot let Mother and Sorcha die in vain. I cannot let all of our people's struggles be for nothing.

Tears sting my eyes. "Sorcha," I whisper to the wind. "I am sorry."

Just then, the raven returns, sweeping down to the ground beside me. His wing brushes my chilled hand. I must be brave. I must live up to my name. I must be the woman Sorcha believed I could be. I have to survive.

The raven lifts up, flying in a circle and then landing in exactly the same spot. He cocks his head from side to side, then opens his black beak and lets out an irritating squawk.

In it, I hear my sister's voice in my head. *I am proud of you. Have courage. You cannot see the Keena I see. But I can. She shines like a beacon from within your soul . . .*

And I am renewed.

The raven soars into the sky, beckoning me, and I follow wherever he might lead.

My blood sparks to flames, and I run. But I am not fleeing from my enemies, rather rushing toward my future and the woman I am destined to become.

EPILOGUE

Stephanie Dray

CARTIMANDUA

ANOTHER prisoner is brought before me in shackles. This one a girl. Dirty and slight of build, with a nest of wild hair, she sways before me as if the chains are too heavy for her to hold up. Still, she manages to stay on her feet when my loyal armor bearer reports the reason for her arrest. "We found her huddled in a tree trunk for warmth, insect-bitten and murmuring to a black raven. We thought her half-mad, but in her delirium, she kept murmuring your husband's name."

My husband. *Venutius.* The man who covets my crown and would take my kingdom from me if he could. But what does it mean that some girl in a tree was murmuring his name? It might mean nothing, of course. She might be a kinswoman of my husband's. A servant. A bastard child. Who can guess?

In the devastating aftermath of Boudica's failed rebellion, my wayward husband still imagines himself the great prince who will finally unite the Britons and expel the Romans from our shores. It will come to nothing, and I think my people know it, yet in spite of the tragedy that has befallen the south, they stubbornly cling to a failed dream. A *deadly* dream.

Boudica buried thousands of Britons. My hands are not so bloody, and my mind is clear on the need for reconciliation, and yet, in their helpless rage about the slaughter of the tribes to the south, my Brigantes prefer my husband's incendiary talk.

Remember Boudica, he cries, and the warriors cheer.

But this girl standing before me is no warrior. She is, in fact, little more than a shivering child. And in an act that is unbearably familiar, I say, "Remove her chains. Then bring some bread, meat, and wine. The poor thing is half-starved."

I rise from the ivory *curule* chair that an emperor of Rome gave me from whence to dispense justice and find a more comfortable seat by the fire. My white snake is in a basket there, and I curl the creature in my lap, stroking it softly as I beckon the girl to me. "Come. Warm yourself. Tell me how it is that you know my husband."

The newly unfettered girl looks dazed as she drops to her knees before the fire, her dirtied face awash in its glow. But she doesn't answer me. Not even when I prompt her again. "Are you seeking my husband out for some reason?"

She gives me one, long side-glance that is filled with hostility and fear.

Still, she says nothing.

I begin to fear that she is just a feral girl who has been touched by the gods, her senses in another world, her body in this one. But when the bread and wine come, she doesn't lunge for them when offered. Even though her eyes glisten as if she were fighting the temptation to ease her hunger and thirst, she turns away from food and drink and back to the fire.

And that, I know, is not a gesture of madness . . . but of contempt.

"Girl," I snap, impatient now as I take the cup of wine and raise it toward her lips. "I am Queen Cartimandua of the Brigantes. I command you to drink and to answer me."

"I know who you are," she replies softly before taking one sip of the wine—only to spit it back into my face. "You are the *Betrayer of the Britons.*"

So then, I think, wiping the spray of wine from my cheeks. I shall not have to wait to die before Brigante children spit upon me. They're happy to do it while I'm still alive. Except that something in the way she speaks tells me that she is not Brigante.

Her inflection is Iceni. Which is no great surprise.

The few survivors of Boudica's war who have not been captured by the Romans have gone into hiding with the tribes. Some taken in by kinsmen, others reduced to servitude, and some to madness. But again, I see no madness in this girl's dark gaze. What I see in those eyes is . . .

A resemblance to a man I loved.

But no. It cannot be. King Prasutagus has been dead a year now. His lands seized. His wife flogged. His daughters raped. His royal kinsmen taken as slaves. His people slaughtered.

The Romans told us that Queen Boudica and her daughters killed themselves rather than be captured. We were told they did it to deny Governor Paulinus his prize—for the Romans love to march their prisoners in great parades, during which their people may humiliate and torture the captives.

That is what we have been told, here in the kingdom of the Brigantes.

But I remember standing by the bier of a dead king a year ago and looking down into the eyes of this very same girl. Unless the gods are playing tricks on me, I am staring into the face of Princess Keena, the last survivor of the Iceni royal family.

"You look very much like your father," I say to let her know that I recognize her. Though I half suspect she will fling the silver dish at me, I still offer her a platter of dried and salted fish. "I knew him very well. So you should eat and drink of my hospitality in his honor, even if it comes from my hands. Because your father was a very dear friend to me."

"But not my mother," the girl says, sullenly refusing the salted fish but losing her fight against thirst. She gulps down the wine so quickly it drips from the corners of her mouth.

"No, not your mother," I agree, softy. "Your mother was not my friend. But neither was she my enemy."

The girl makes a little sound of derision, as if she has trouble believing that there is any ground in between. "Rome is your friend. Which made my mother your enemy. Otherwise, you might have sent an army to help us against the Romans."

She is not a child, after all, I decide. No. Not given what she has been through. Violated by the Romans. Riding in a war chariot with her mother. Somehow surviving the slaughter and finding her way here . . . by herself. She has been through too much for me to treat her like a child. So I tell her honestly, "Yes, I am friends with Rome. Which is why I had no cause to send Brigantes against Roman legions. But even if I had ordered my soldiers to fight in your mother's cause . . . I've heard tell of how the battle was fought. If I sent an army against the Romans, my people would have been trapped between the wagons and Roman swords just as your mother's army was. It was not numbers of soldiers that your mother lacked."

The princess doesn't reply. But she does take wash water from the basin when my servant offers it. She tries to clean her face and hands, but I fear it is an effort in vain when the water runs black. She will need a long bath and a scrub and new clothing. "I will order you a tub of water and attend to your washing myself."

"Do queens play the part of wash girls here in the kingdom of the Brigantes?" she asks with no small bit of bite.

It's rumored that of the two Iceni princesses, she was the mild-tempered one. Either she's been hardened by the tragedies in her life, or it is yet another thing about Boudica's legend that people get wrong. "No. Queens do not play wash girls here, but your mother once helped sponge blood off me when an assassin attacked me under her roof. This is some small repayment. Besides, if it is true that your mother and sister killed themselves, then I fear what you might do to yourself if left to your own devices."

It is the mention of her sister that seems to rattle her most, and the princess looks away. "I wanted to die. For a long time. Now I can't. Not if there's any chance—" Keena breaks off, piercing me with a stare that reminds me so much of her mother that it stops my heart. "What will you do? I know that I am a prize that Governor Paulinus would pay handsomely to get his hands on."

She is that. I cannot deny it.

What will you do? Boudica once asked me the same question, and now, repeated by her daughter, it seems to echo from the past. If the Romans knew that I had Boudica's daughter, they would demand that I turn her over. They would likely pay me again with a chest of gold, just as they did when I gave Caratacus to them. They would take Boudica's daughter away in a cage. Then, after they marched this poor girl through the streets of Rome to be violated *again* by the jeering crowd, they would strangle her to death.

I have no doubt about that. Emperor Claudius was a genial man who could afford to be merciful. But Nero, that pompous fool? No. Emperor Nero will kill this girl, just as he's killed so many others for spectacle in Rome.

And I will not be a part of it.

The decision comes upon me at once, like a thunderclap, with resounding finality. "I will shield you," I tell her. "You're safe in my kingdom. You may live here with me, in freedom and under my protection as my ward."

She seems almost as shocked by my words as I am.

I infamously gave over to the Romans Caratacus, Hero of the Britons. But now I can make a different choice. I *will* make a different choice. I will protect this child of Prasutagus as I was not able to protect the one we once made together. It is no breach of my treaty with Rome to protect this girl, for they don't need her. As far as everyone else knows, she is already dead. The Boudican rebellion was put down. And no matter the delusions of my husband, it is over. *Over.* Rome won, decisively. Completely.

And with such devastation that an entire tribe is no more.

There has been enough killing.

Nothing can be served by giving them this girl.

I simply will not do it.

"Is there anyone left alive who might know you?" I ask.

Keena's eyes fill with tears, but she bravely holds them back. "Only . . . well. My sister."

Princess Sorcha is alive? Now that *does* surprise me and threatens to ruin all my plans. The younger princess I can take into my household without rousing suspicion. But the older one—the one who swung a sword with as much fierceness as any battle goddess, the one who bathed in the blood of Romans—she would be impossible to hide. "We were told you and your sister both committed suicide with your mother."

Princess Keena shakes her head of matted and tangled hair. "No." A knob of emotion bobs in her throat as she speaks, but her voice is, nevertheless, emphatic. "Sorcha did not kill herself; she fought! The Romans are probably ashamed because she would have killed some of them before they killed her . . . but she is dead. She gave her life for me. I didn't think I could make it this far, not on my own, but my sister believed I was strong enough to do it." Princess Keena chokes back a tiny sob. "She believed in me."

How far did this poor girl travel by herself, grieving for her lost family? For her lost people? For her lost gods? My heart fills with sorrow for her, and I want to pull her into my embrace as the child I never had. But it is too soon for that, I know. And I worry that even if Princess Keena is not mad, she is confused. "If Sorcha is dead, then what did you mean when you said your sister might recognize you?"

The princess gets hold of her emotions and warily takes a nibble of bread. Only after she swallows does she say, "I meant my other sister. My half sister. Ria. She was sent away to safety after the sack of Verulamium. She's only a freedwoman. The Romans won't be hunting her, will they?"

"No," I say, heartened by the relief I see in the girl's eyes. "I'm sure your half sister is safe. We will look for her if you want. But it would be safer if we waited some time, and only if you took a different name."

Given the way Princess Keena inches toward me, I believe she is beginning to accept the idea that I mean what I say. That she will survive, after all. That I will protect her, for her father's sake.

But that is only the half of it.

I will protect her for her mother's sake, too. With respect and gratitude. For though it is true that I did not side with Boudica in her fight with Rome, I benefited from it. Given the vengeance "a mere woman" orchestrated against them, Romans will no longer take me for granted as a client queen. And I am not the only one who will benefit for her sacrifice. The Romans will be more careful now. Warier of dismissing the people they conquered as unthinking animals.

Boudica.

You've heard her name. Of course you have. Everyone has. And when you've heard it spoken, you've heard the hushed awe of her admirers or the grudging respect of her enemies. You've heard her legend.

Because she did not fight merely for lands or even for freedom. She fought for her humanity and the dignity of her daughters. Because of that, her name will always serve as a rallying cry for those who seek justice. And for as long as there are tyrants in the world, the name of Boudica will strike fear into their hearts.

I can see to that.

So even as I bow to Rome, I will honor Boudica. I will shield her daughter and nurture the story of the warrior queen of the Iceni until it becomes a legend to last a thousand years. Boudica will be a hero, and I will be despised, but I can make my peace with that.

Watching the girl eat hungrily by my fire, I ask, "What name shall we call you now that you are to have a new life?"

Keena stops chewing, and closes her eyes with pain, as if the thought of parting with the name she's earned for herself is too high a price to pay. But then, at last, she says, "Branna."

Raven, it means.

And it's a good choice, too. For the Romans are wrong; it does not all begin and end with them. It all begins and ends with ravens. Ravens, who have seen all the great tragedies of the world unfold, and whose cry is eternal.

ACKNOWLEDGMENTS

WE would like to thank our friends, families, and beta readers, including Erin Ahlstrom, Rebecca Alexander, Brenna Ash, Hillary Brown, Robin Carter, Andy Downie, Annalori Ferrell, Audra Friend, Nikki Green, Ashleigh Inglesby, Hoff Inglesby, Maria Janecek, Robyn Lucas, Matthew Parker, Ash Parsons, Jessica Payne, Tanja Peterson, Kelly Quinn, Andrea Snider, Tabitha Smith, Ernesto Spinelli, Kristen Stappenbeck, Stephanie Thornton, Bill Wahl and Sally Whitfield. We'd like to thank our cover designer, Kim Killion, Dave Slaney for promotional images, and Simon Walpole for the iconic Raven design. Also, our copy editors, Adam Dray and Jennifer Quinlan.

For resources, we owe much to Tacitus and Cassius Dio. Also, Cartimandua: Queen of the Brigantes, by Nicki Howarth Pollard; Boudica, by Vanessa Collingridge; Boudica: The British Revolt Against Rome AD 60, by Graham Webster; The World of the Celts, by Simon James; The Towns of Roman Britain, by John Wacher; The Land of Boudica, by John Davies; The Boudican Revolt Against Rome, by Paul R Sealey; The Philosopher and the Druids, by Philip Freeman; Blood and Mistletoe: The History of the Druids in Britain, by Ronald Hutton; Who's Who in the Roman World, by John Hazel and Daily Life of the Pagan Celts, by Joan Alcock.

NOTES FROM THE AUTHORS

THE QUEEN

ALLOW me to begin by thanking my colleagues for their generosity and talent. I have learned so much from each and every one of them because this book was no small task to put together. Tricky decisions had to be made about everything from story order to which characters and plotlines would carry through the entire novel. And each author lent expertise to a specific job.

Mine was to introduce a number of characters and give context to the rebellion.

Given my focus on client kingship in the *Nile* series—featuring Juba II and Cleopatra's daughter Selene—I was probably the natural choice to write about the consequences of royalty allying with Rome.

Yet, I never intended to write about Queen Cartimandua.

My original idea was to write about the wife of the Roman procurator, who would watch Boudica's mistreatment unfold with sympathy but helplessness. Fortunately, Valeria wouldn't cooperate with me. (And as you've seen in Kate Quinn's story, she is anything but helpless.) Instead, the voice of an imperious Brigante queen came to me in the middle of the night saying, "You cannot know Boudica's story without knowing mine."

It's a rare thing when characters speak to me—even more rarely do they wake me up in the middle of the night—so I couldn't refuse the ancient queen who wanted to be my muse. Researching Cartimandua, I realized that she was right. We *can't* understand Boudica's story without comparing it to Cartimandua's.

Of the famous Britons of her day, Cartimandua alone witnessed it all and survived to tell the tale. It was only through *her* eyes that I could show that Boudica's revolt did not arise in a vacuum. The resentments and abuses of Roman imperialism had built to a boiling point. And Cartimandua was a part of that milieu, from the start. She ruled over the Brigantes as a sovereign queen *in her own right* for almost thirty years by Roman counting. She appears to have been an astute and calculating leader whose kingdom prospered, but who ultimately needed to be rescued by the Romans from an uprising led by her husband Venutius. After she was driven out of the kingdom of the Brigantes, she may have lived out her years in Rome. The rebel Caractacus was probably dead by then, but it tickles me to think that they may have run into one another at the Forum.

Now, a confession of my sins.

Truthfully, we don't know much about the religious practices and gods of the ancient Britons. (We don't even know what they called themselves, though assuredly it wasn't *Britons*.) Most of their religious beliefs are lost to history. So for the re-creation of Cartimandua's worship I relied on Neo-Druidism. (You can learn more at www.druidry.org.) That's where the snake came from and not just because I have a thing for queens associated with snakes.

As for the timeline of Cartimandua's marriage, divorce, and subsequent remarriage to an armor bearer, the historical record is actually quite conflicted due to Tacitus mentioning two similar instances, first in the *Histories*, then in the *Annals*, with different details and dates. I have adopted the scholarly "flashback" theory that Venutius led two different rebellions in the kingdom of the Brigantes. The first in the AD 50s, before Boudica's rebellion. The second in 69, after Boudica's rebellion, when Cartimandua found a new husband, possibly a Roman one. Roman or not, her new husband wasn't a popular choice amongst her people, and he cost her the crown.

As to her other suitors, we have no idea whether Caractacus or Prasutagus ever vied for Cartimandua's hand, or even if Venutius was her first husband. We don't know if Caractacus was the *youngest* son of the Catuvellauni king, but he certainly was the most famous. Though Venutius' tribal origins are not known, he is most often associated with the Carvetii, so that is reflected in my work.

There are several competing theories about how Boudica's husband came to be the King of the Iceni. The first is that King Antedios died in a failed rebellion against Quintus Ostorius Scapula, the second governor of Roman Britain. Thereafter, Prasutagus was allegedly installed in his place as a Roman puppet. There is good reason to think this is true, but there are also several problems with the theory, including the fact that the Iceni allegedly elected their kings. Another problem is that, having put down an Iceni rebellion led by a supposed Friend and Ally of the Roman People, the Romans had excellent motivation to annex the Iceni lands then and there. That they did not suggests something more complicated was going on—much more complicated than could be explored in a single story—and so, in the interest of simplification, I adopted the theory that the various tribes of the Iceni had more than one leader and that Prasutagus had been one of the chieftains to swear his friendship to Emperor Claudius from the start.

With regard to Prasutagus' funeral, again, we know little about the rites that would have been given to an Iceni king. Discovered burial chambers lead us to conclude there was a belief in another life. But how differently the Iceni may have approached death from the Romans, we haven't a clear grasp upon, so I had Prasutagus *choose* to be cremated in imitation of old Romans like Julius Caesar.

When it came our "accountant," Decianus, I played fast and loose with ancient prices by inventing figures that fell somewhere between the highest and lowest estimates I was able to find in the sources. My main goal was in making sure that the king's horse was worth more to the Romans than his daughter, the slave girl, which assuredly would have been the case. Finally, there is some dispute about Decianus' name. In *The People of Roman Britain*, Anthony Richard Birley argues that Tacitus inverted the names. Nevertheless, we called him Catus Decianus because it's most commonly used.

What is uncommon, of course, is my interpretation of the allegedly rapacious procurator. Decianus comes down to us through history as being single-handedly responsible for the entire Boudican rebellion, after which he fled into obscurity and shame.

It might have happened that way: he might've been a greedy procurator, a predictably twisty-mustachioed villain who put his boot on the throat of the Iceni tribe, ordering the enslavement of royals, the flogging of a queen, and the rape of her daughters simply because he *could*. But that's not very interesting, is it? Besides, it's a story you've all read before and Romans of the day weren't big on mustaches, twisty or otherwise.

I thought I owed it to Decianus—and to readers—to think a little more deeply about how such a crime and catastrophe might come to pass without dismissing his motives as base or simplistically evil. Because that kind of dismissal is exactly how we miss seeing crimes and catastrophes coming . . .

—Stephanie Dray

THE SLAVE

HISTORY—EVEN when we all think we know what happened—is surprisingly hard to pin down. Already I'm hesitating over "No one knows exactly where the Iceni royal family lived," because I expect there are people who are certain they do know. Besides, new evidence may turn up in the time between my typing this and anyone reading it. In the meantime, Ria (who of course knows exactly where she is) lives in an amalgam of the most likely locations.

As for the sequence of events she recounts—well, in one version Tacitus says the Iceni "flew to arms," as if the rebellion began with a spontaneous outburst of fury immediately after Boudica was flogged. His other account, along with that of Cassius Dio, suggests the uprising may have been a more deliberate process like the one that Ria tries not to see. In any case, as far as the Romans were concerned, all Iceni weapons had been confiscated. So either the tribe were very good at hiding them (which is always possible) or the Iceni smiths needed time to build up the supplies.

The Iceni were certainly good at burying treasure. Amongst the hoards that have turned up in their lands, there are several—notably the Crownthorpe Hoard, for those who care about these things—that date to the time of the rebellion. The tragic implications of this are that there was no one left who could go home to retrieve them.

The better news is that thanks to this ancient custom of burying valuables, readers who want to "meet" Boudica's people can now enjoy fantastic displays of gold torcs and ornate metalwork—along with much else—in the Castle Museum in Norwich.

But while we can admire the handiwork of the native people of Roman Britain, their voices are silent. The stories that have come down to us only give the occupiers' view of events. Even the speeches put into the mouths of British leaders are Roman inventions, so I've chosen to follow this fine tradition and invent my own. Because how can anyone rely on the words of men who failed to record the existence of Prasutagus' third daughter?

—Ruth Downie

THE TRIBUNE

TAKING on the life-story of one of Rome's great men is a huge task. Fortunately for me, I only had to take on a tiny period in that man's life, which I feel very fortunate to have been invited to do.

We know a good deal about Gnaeus Julius Agricola, Governor, General, Praetor and so on, but I was lucky enough to write the part that we don't know so much about—less about his great deeds and more about the young-man-yet-to-be-a-great-man. I decided from the beginning that the story would be a coming-of-age one. Reading about Agricola in his later life, it's hard to imagine him as a cuckolding rake—but when I was offered the chance to write his viewpoint of Boudica's uprising, the first thing that sprang to my mind was a line from Shakespeare's *Henry V*:

> *And, be assured, you'll find a difference,*
> *As we his subjects have in wonder found,*
> *Between the promise of his greener days*
> *And these he masters now*

As any man of a certain age will know: we've all been young, we've all been stupid, and we've all done things that we wish we could change. I think this was my starting point for Agricola—and the events that transpire in the story I fancied changed him profoundly. It's cool to be a young Roman officer when there's no real war going on, but the reality of war scars Agricola as I have him. But, at the same time, he's a servant of Rome and for a Roman citizen of standing, which he certainly was, his attitude was that war had to be conducted for "the greater good"—or the Glory of Rome if you prefer.

It's one of the great joys of writing historical fiction, wondering more about the characters and less about the deeds of these long past lives; and writing fiction is something that I would encourage anyone reading this book to do. All writers are readers: reading sparks something in you (for me it was Donna Gillespie's *The Light Bearer*, the works of the great David Gemmell, and Wallace Breem's *The Eagle in the Snow*—not, I hasten to add, that I'm in the same league or division of those great people!) that, once ignited, can't be put out. It's a bizarre compulsion and it's often hard, depressing, frustrating, and all of that. But ultimately, I think that this Frank Norris quote sums it up best for me: "Don't like to write, but like having written." It's a bit of a hard graft, but when you finish a piece of work, there's really no way to describe the immense satisfaction of turning it in.

We live in an age where the doors to publication have been flung open by the Internet. Writing is no longer the province of the lucky few. Today, anyone with the wherewithal to finish a project can get it out there, and I would encourage anyone who has an idea, some itchy fingers, and a blinking cursor up on their screen to just do it.

I did—all the brilliant and wonderful people I worked with on this book did—and you can, too. Of course, the real work comes when you think the work is over: editing. How we all love it when someone comes along and points out all the flaws in our magnum opus. But it's a fundamental and necessary part of the process.

I've been very fortunate with editors. On this project, the awesome task of melding together timelines, picking up inconsistencies and making this whole story from seven different points of view, was taken on by the redoubtable Kate Quinn. She'll poo-poo this, so I'm saying it here: *A Year of Ravens* could not have happened without her. She's a legend.

Thanks also to my fellow collaborators on the project: Eliza, Ruth, Simon, Stephanie and Vicky. You guys were awesome to work with (and special thanks to Ruth, who pointed out that my merry band of soldiers would have ended up in the Irish Sea if they'd have gone to Aquae Sulis instead of Glevum!) and of course Kate herself, whose story moved me to tears at the end.

I also need to thank Ed Handyside at www.borderscripts.com. Ed was my editor on the "Gladiatrix" books and is now offering his not inconsiderable expertise to beginning writers who want to get a foot up on the publishing ladder. Without Mr. Handyside, I never would have got a start in this game.

To my lovely wife Sally and my daughter Sam who put up with me wailing, gnashing my teeth, and living for days on end in my man-cave and writing about swords and sandals. You are the best things in my life and nothing means anything without you.

Finally, to those of you who are reading this book, thank you for giving it a whirl. I sincerely hope you enjoyed our perspectives on this war, Britons and Romans, Warriors and Soldiers, Slaves and Royalty. Without you guys, we can't do what we do—thank you so much.

—Russ Whitfield

THE DRUID

IMAGINE if an invading army marched into Vatican City and killed the pope, all his cardinals and bishops, and all of the worshippers who lived around them; then set fire to the faith's most sacred churches and museums in an unprovoked attack.

The outrage and pain of loss would be beyond comprehension, wouldn't it? Yet that's essentially what the Romans did to the Druids during the Boudican rebellion. They attacked the Isle of Mona (today's Anglesey) and killed Druid priests, priestesses, and worshippers in an unprovoked attack, and then set fire to all their sacred spaces.

The only account of the attack came from the Romans. They, of course, had a vested interest in making the Druids appear barbaric and threatening in order to justify the assault.

Because the Druids did not keep written records, we know very little about what they believed and how they practiced their faith. Writing from a young Druid's point of view gave me the opportunity to imagine both the spiritual aspects of the religion and the trauma of watching it all go up in flames.

Some historians believe remnants of the religion continued in Ireland and Scotland and in pockets of Britain until the advent of Christianity, but in general, most agree that Druidism was dealt a deathblow on that fateful day in 69 AD.

Julius Caesar wrote about the Druids more than one hundred years before Boudica in his famous *Gallic Wars*. There, he claimed the "common folk were treated as slaves" and implied that human sacrifice was routine. He even described the infamous wicker man—a giant cage, "woven out of twigs," stuffed with live men and set afire. However, no corroborating evidence for these accusations has ever been found.

However, these claims served as excellent propaganda for justifying extermination. Despite the fact that Caesar himself claimed that the Druids "hold aloof from war," later Romans claimed that the Druids at the Isle of Mona fomented rebellion. Again there is no corroborating evidence for this accusation. More likely, the Romans wanted to "break" the Briton spirit by cutting out the heart of their religion.

Some scholars point to "Lindow Man" as proof that the Druids did indeed perform human sacrifice (http://ow.ly/TcbDE). Killed around the time of Boudica's rebellion, Lindow Man—or the bog man—was executed in what most believe was a ritualistic fashion. He was hit on the head, garroted, and then had his throat slashed. Lindow Man was found in a peat bog in northwest England and while he inspired the sacrifice in my story, my account is entirely fictional. Though I didn't hesitate to have my young Druid kill his sacrifice in the same way.

While writing, I became fascinated with the mental gymnastics involved in excusing the mass murder of civilians and innocents (both sides were guilty of this), which I explored in conversations between the Druid Yorath and the Roman Felix. I found no answers because there are none. Only this truth: everyone suffers.

Rome generally tolerated defeated peoples' religions. Occasionally, it tried to ban certain faiths from within the city: Isis worship, some of the ecstatic rites of Dionysus, and even early Christianity. However, it only ever attempted to exterminate two religions on their own native lands: Judaism and Druidism. In each case, the Romans firmly believed that the religious elite fomented rebellion against Roman rule and that peace could only be achieved by removal of the religion. Judaism, of course, survives today and is the base from which two other major world religions were launched—Christianity and Islam.

If ancient Druidism had survived, what kind of modern religion might have morphed out of it? Sadly, we'll never know.

However, modern Druidism anchors its practices and beliefs on what we know of Celtic culture as well as a deep respect for and connection to nature. Still, even though the ancient Druids are long gone, they continue to live on in all our collective imaginations, surviving as iconic "magicians" like Merlin, Gandalf, Dumbledore, and countless other famous wise wizards in our stories, movies and games.

—Victoria Alvear

THE SON

WHEN I was approached to contribute a tale to this magnificent story, I imagined taking on one of the conflicts of the revolt from a Roman perspective (that being my forte). I found myself instead looking at a brief to cover one of the Britons during the height of the revolt's brutality and wondering how best to do it. And the more I looked at it, the more I found myself wondering how one of those Romanized natives—a Cogidubnus of sorts—would see the actions of the Iceni. Thus was born Andecarus, son of Duro.

The Roman practice of taking hostages has a long and illustrious history and helped to Romanize new lands, giving the sons of native nobility a taste of Rome and then sending them back to their people to influence the locals. Andecarus is clearly conflicted by his ability to see the horrors of the rebellion from both sides. He seemed the perfect pair of eyes through which to view the moments of the war that were both great and terrible, to give a more objective view than either side alone might achieve.

My portrayal of Londinium is based largely on the scant knowledge of pre-Boudican London, material evidence of which is on show in the Museum of London, and the extrapolation and theories of John Wacher in his *Towns of Roman Britain*, where he conjectures about the likelihood of an early fort guarding the Thames crossing and abandoned by around 50 AD. So little is known for certain that conjecture is our best hope for recreating that early settlement. It is entirely plausible that Catus Decianus was based in the growing settlement, since he fled sometime after the destruction of Camulodunum, suggesting that his office was not located there, he sent soldiers to help at that conflict (from where if not Londinium?) and the Procurator was certainly based in Londinium shortly thereafter. We know that Londinium had been partially abandoned before the revolt but that people must have stayed (judging from the layer of destruction and the records of barbaric violence given by Tacitus and Cassius Dio). We also know that Paulinus visited the city and decided it was not defensible.

Verulamium was a much different place in Boudica's time even than it became in the next century—still largely a Catuvellauni settlement with new Roman additions. The original focus of the town on the hill shifted to the riverside with the arrival of the conquering race. There is some conjecture as to whether the town had been abandoned in advance of its sacking due to the absence of coin and grain hoards. I have chosen a different angle, partially for the progression of the story, and partially because the Catuvellauni probably did not know or believe the Iceni and their allies were coming for them. Thus far the marauding warband had focused on Roman sites, not native ones. Moreover, the absence of such hoards might be explained by a fled populace, but it can also be explained by a surprise attack and subsequent thorough looting by the aggressor.

The final form of this tale owes a great deal to excellent input from the other authors of the collection, who have taken Andecarus and given him a history and . . . well, not a *future*, but you know what I mean. It grew in the telling from a simple individual story to a living thing that sent out ripples across the whole book and I am very grateful for being asked to contribute alongside such wonderful authors. *Vale*, Andecarus. *Salve*, Roman Britain.

—S.J.A. Turney

THE WARRIOR

THE exact site of Boudica's doomed final battle against Rome is unknown. Tacitus is precise in his description of the terrain the Romans chose—a position flanked by woods, approached by a narrow defile which widened into a broad plain—but landscape has a way of changing over the course of two thousand years, and today we cannot pinpoint with certainty the place where Boudica's dream of freedom died. We know that she took her vast war-band northwest from Verulamium along a Roman road known today as Watling Street, and that Governor Paulinus marched his soldiers southeast to meet her. At some point along that path, they met and fought. I have focused my own story on landscape details as described by Tacitus and not tried to solve the mystery of whether Boudica was defeated at Mancetter in Warwickshire, at Towcester, or somewhere in the Chilterns.

The size of the two armies that clashed that day is another point of contention. Boudica left posterity no records, and Tacitus states that she brought a force of 230,000 Iceni fighters (ha!) against Governor's Paulinus' 10,000 legionaries. Either the Romans inflated her numbers to make their victory look better, or Tacitus' figures take into account the huge number of wives, children, slaves, and hangers-on who would not have taken part in the battle. I took my best guess that Boudica's fighting force was somewhat less than half Tacitus' estimate, but whatever the numbers truly were, Paulinus was vastly outnumbered. He owed his victory to the discipline of his troops and the advantage given by the ground. Boudica's tribesmen were too tightly packed by the narrow defile to swing their long swords effectively, and the slaughter of the Iceni was sealed when, as I have described, their retreat was blocked by the watching ring of spectators and wagons. Tacitus lists the Iceni dead at 80,000 and the Roman dead at 400, but like his earlier numbers, this seems highly suspect (a bit like Shakespeare claiming in *Henry V* that, at Agincourt, the English lost 25 and the French 10,000). Paulinus won the day against Boudica, but I have zero doubt he lost more than 400 men. The Iceni, however, lost everything: their independence from Rome, their lives, and their queen, who fled the battlefield to an unknown death.

Boudica's pre-battle speech is written down by Tacitus, who wasn't there and moreover didn't know anyone who was (his primary source was probably his father-in-law Agricola, who as a young tribune would have been quaking in his boots on the Roman side, and far out of earshot of even Boudica's famous voice). Tacitus was less interested in historical purity than in amping up the drama of the moment, so the words he places in Boudica's mouth—particularly the ones that subtly paint her as an unnatural female bringing moral decay and male subjugation in her wake—are highly suspect. I used some of Tacitus' words in my story, but gave Boudica her own as well.

Duro and Valeria are both fictional; none of Boudica's warriors were named by history, and it is not known if Catus Decianus was married (Tacitus, disapproving as he is of the procurator's actions, never mentions an abandoned wife). My contribution to *A Day of Fire* also featured a man and woman quarreling on opposite sides of the same issue, so it seemed natural here to use a Roman woman and an Iceni warrior as my vehicles for the entire Rome vs. Britannia struggle: eternally on opposite sides, loathing everything the other stands for, disagreeing sometimes ferociously and sometimes humorously on everything from democratic policy to running water to skull decor. Duro's red-enameled sword is based on the Kirkburn Sword, a third century BC weapon found in an Iron Age grave. Decorated in red enamel and bronze, it stands as a fine example of La Tene-style scrollwork—the early Britons, for all Valeria's jibes about their mud huts and lack of advanced engineering, were superb metalworkers and artisans. The Kirkburn Sword resides in the British Museum. Duro's sword went to live in Valeria's new home in Gaul, where (I imagine) she and her procurator husband lived a quiet life much enlivened by a huge, hell-raising son.

I vowed, after writing about the Bar Kokhba Rebellion in my last book, *Lady of the Eternal City,* that I was done with massacres for a while, but *A Year of Ravens* made an oath-breaker of me. From the moment I joined the project, I knew I wanted to put on my Bernard Cornwell hat and write the final battle: the glory and the agony, the horror and the blood, the dashed hopes and the doomed last stands. I couldn't have done it without my co-authors: Simon, who thrashed out with me over many emails the father-son relationship between his hero and mine; Stephanie, who showed so marvelously the other half of Valeria's marriage; Vicky, who gave me my first scene, and Russ, who gave me my last; Ruth, who fact-checked me like a champion; and Eliza, whose brain-child this was from the beginning. If you have to write a massacre, it's a lot more fun to have a team like this one behind you.

I hope you enjoyed my story. Normally my aim is to make my readers laugh—this time around, I hope I made you cry.

—Kate Quinn

THE DAUGHTERS

FIERCE, independent, strong, cunning women are some of my favorites to read and write about—especially when these women rise up against tyranny, triumphing, even if only in some small way. Boudica's story, though tragic, is one that I have admired from the very first moment I heard about her as a child. A widow beaten, her daughters raped—she turned an entire country on its ear. Not just because she sought vengeance against those who mistreated her and her daughters, but also because she didn't want this to happen to anyone else. She wanted to defeat the enemy. To grind them to dust and make them disappear. But what about her daughters?

Who were they? What did they desire? What were their strengths and weaknesses? What did they look like? What were their names?

Nearly everything about them, other then their existence and mistreatment, has been forgotten. While Boudica was immortalized in the writings of Tacitus and Dio, her daughters receive no more than a mere mention. I think they deserved more than that. I think that in this massive rebellion undertaken by their mother, Boudica's daughters would not have faded into the background as our two historians portray. The majority of artistic depictions of Boudica show her riding her chariot with her two daughters beside her, or depict her standing tall, her daughters clutching onto her. I find it sad, though not surprising, that her daughters were brushed aside as unimportant to Tacitus and Dio—then again, perhaps they never knew their names to begin with. There is some question about whether or not Boudica is actually our warrior queen's true name.

Boudica's daughters. Not even named. Our names—they mean so much to us. They are who we are. They identify us not only to ourselves but also to the world. They mean something. When I decided to write a story about Boudica's daughters, I just couldn't wrap my head around the fact that no one knew their names. Certainly there are guesses. Beautiful speculations. But that's all they are. I couldn't use them. I had to name these girls myself, and so I chose names that meant something. For Boudica's eldest daughter, born in the likeness of her, their tribe's lucky charm, a warrior, I chose the name Sorcha, which means "bright light" or "princess." For Boudica's younger daughter, I named her Keena, which means "brave." Both of these names were chosen based on the girls' personalities and their journeys to find themselves and the meaning of their own lives.

In my story, I made Boudica a priestess of Andraste, the warrior goddess who leads her people to victory. I did this for a couple of reasons, one is that Tacitus' account talks of Boudica releasing a hare from her skirts as a sacrifice—something a priestess or Druid would do, but it is unlikely she was a Druid. Additionally, there is some speculation that a priestess of Andraste would have a better chance as a warrior, gathering enough support and troops to take on the Romans, than as a simple consort queen who'd just been widowed (even though she and her daughter were abused).

On the topic of human sacrifice, and in regards to the weak infant Sorcha, we know that human sacrifice has been part of religious cultures for thousands of years, and the Druids were not exempt from this practice. Whether infants were sacrificed, there is some speculation. In regards to the sacred grove near the Iceni village, Celtic Lore and Mythology puts Boudica there when she made sacrifices and invoked her goddess. (Not that all lore and mythology is true, I know, but I think there can be some measure of faith or trust in stories repeated generation and generation, and after all, we are writing fiction!) Now speaking of lore and druidism, I had the Druid in the beginning of my story tell Boudica to "bite the after-birth thrice." This wasn't something I simply made up, though I wish I had, because it's so peculiar and interesting. In fact, I found it in, *Survivals in Belief Among the Celts*, written in 1911 by George Henderson.

For a final thought, I'd like to take a moment to explain the ending of my story. Tacitus and Dio both differ on how Boudica died. Dio states that though she escaped the final battle, Boudica died of her wounds, and there is no mention of her daughters' deaths. Tacitus says she and her daughters poisoned themselves. I decided to take a bit of both of these accounts for Boudica and make it hers. The truth is, we have yet to find a final resting place for Boudica (though there are guesses and suspicions) and since the two accounts give different ways in which she died, and we have no proof, there is truly no way to know for certain. I did not use poison, because, on the run, where would she have gotten poison? I believed that a warrior queen would have chosen a death by her own blade. But I did not want her two daughters to die the same way. I wanted Sorcha to take the life of the man who tormented her. I wanted her to die defending not only herself, but her sister, too. I wanted her to die heroically. And Keena, sweet brave girl—I wanted Keena to live on, even if in secret, to give hope that though their people were beaten, not all was lost.

Using research and a liberal amount of creative license, I wrote a version of events that took place during the last year of Boudica and her daughters' lives, and I hope that in living through them— their pain, their happiness, their loves and friends, their personal triumphs, their losses—we can memorialize their lives and give them the peace of mind that we still remember them and the sacrifices they made.

—E. Knight

ABOUT THE AUTHORS

RUTH DOWNIE is the *New York Times* bestselling author of the Medicus crime series, set mostly in Roman Britain, and featuring Roman Army medic Ruso and his British partner, Tilla. Ruth lives in Devon, England, with a patient spouse, two cats, and an archaeological trowel, which she is happy to wield whenever the chance arises.

STEPHANIE DRAY is a *New York Times*, *Wall Street Journal*, and *USA Today* bestselling author of historical fiction. Her award-winning work has been translated into ten languages and tops lists for the most anticipated reads of the year. She lives in Maryland with her husband, cats, and history books.

BEN KANE's passion for history has taken him to almost seventy countries, and all seven continents. His novels are commonly seen in the UK *Sunday Times* top ten; published in thirteen languages, they have sold more than a million and a half copies worldwide. A former veterinarian, he lives in Somerset, England.

ELIZA KNIGHT is an award-winning, *USA Today* and internationally bestselling author. She is the creator of the popular historical blog History Undressed; cohost of the History, Books &

Wine podcast; and cohost of the true-crime podcast Crime Feast. Knight lives in Maryland with her husband, three daughters, two dogs, and a turtle.

KATE QUINN is the *New York Times* bestselling author of many historical novels, including *The Alice Network, The Rose Code,* and *The Diamond Eye.* A native of southern California, she attended Boston University where she earned her degrees in Classical Voice. Kate and her husband now live in San Diego.

VICTORIA ALVEAR is the author of multiple books about the ancient world. She writes as Vicky Alvear Shecter for children and as Victoria Alvear for adults. Her novels include *Cleopatra's Moon* and *Curses and Smoke: A Novel of Pompeii.* Her biographies include *Cleopatra Rules!* and *Warrior Queens.*

S.J.A. TURNEY is bestselling author of more than fifty Roman and medieval historical fiction, fantasy, and Roman nonfiction books. He lives with his family and in rural North Yorkshire.

RUSS WHITFIELD is the author of the Gladiatrix trilogy, a historical fiction set in Ancient Rome. He lives in South West London, UK.